Translatio
Volume 1

The Spanish Hermes and Wisdom Traditions in Medieval Iberia

Translatio

Key words, concepts, and texts all gather new force – and encounter new obstacles – as they move between languages, cultures, and societies. Translatio explores translation between languages in relation to other migrations – of peoples, objects, and practices; images, forms, and media – across the continents and islands of the medieval and early modern world. It treats translation as the basis, then and now, for a rethinking of the humanities. It welcomes research that not only relates to the translational but also calls that concept into question. It encourages submissions that in this way challenge, realign, and remake the disciplines of the humanities, and which unsettle their established geographical and historical boundaries, including the period categories – 'medieval' and 'early modern' – offered as points of departure for the series as a whole.

By publishing work in a range of formats – including monographs, long and short; new, facing-page English translations of primary texts; and multi-authored collections – the series seeks to harness both the critical and creative possibilities of the translational humanities.

We are happy to consider both conventional and Open Access models of book publishing. Further information about the series and guidance on submitting a proposal can be found on the Durham University IMEMS Press website. Other books in the series may be viewed on the Boydell & Brewer website.

The Spanish Hermes and Wisdom Traditions in Medieval Iberia

Alfonso X's *General Estoria*

Juan Udaondo Alegre

Durham University
IMEMS PRESS

First published 2024

A Durham University IMEMS Press publication
in association with
The Boydell Press
an imprint of Boydell & Brewer Ltd
PO Box 9, Woodbridge, Suffolk IP12 3DF, UK
and of Boydell & Brewer Inc.
668 Mt Hope Avenue, Rochester, NY 14620–2731, USA
website: www.boydellandbrewer.com
and with the
Institute of Medieval and Early Modern Studies
University of Durham

ISBN 978 1 91496 709 2

A CIP catalogue record for this book is available
from the British Library

To the four essential women in my family:
my mother María Consolación, my aunt María Dolores, my sister Ana,
and my daughter Natalia

Contents

Acknowledgements

My exploration of the connection between Hermes Trismegistus and the works of Alfonso the Wise in the context of medieval cultural exchange between the East and the West began with my research at the University of Michigan, and I am privileged to thank my mentors and colleagues there. They include Enrique García Santo-Tomás, who masterfully helped me navigate unfamiliar academic territory; Ryan Szpiech, who showed me that the Middle Ages contained more intellectual subtleties than I had previously suspected; George Hoffmann, Renaissance luminary, always by my side; Alexander Knysch, who ignited my passion about Arabic culture; Brian B. Schmidt, who unearthed the wealth of Hebrew heritage for me and has been a constant friend since then; and Sara Ahbel-Rappe, who allowed me to be a member of her Neoplatonic Academy, where I translated the wisdom of Hermes and the Greek philosophers for the first time. Part of my merry scholarly team were also Persephone Hernández-Vogt, Jaime Hernández, Luis Miguel dos Santos Vicente, Priscila Calatayud, Helena Skorovsky, and Lorena Bolaños Abarca. The stimulating discussions with all of them influenced my initial thoughts on this project, and Lorena in particular read (and thoughtfully critiqued) some of its very early pages.

This book came together definitively over the past few years in State College. I wish to thank my encouraging colleagues in the Department of Spanish, Italian, and Portuguese of Penn State: Giuli Dussias, Sherry Roush, Mary Barnard, Krista Brune, Matthew Carlson, Matthew Marr, Karen Miller, John Ochoa, Manuel Pulido, Rena Torres Cacoullos, Sarah Townsend, Maria Truglio, Susana García Prudencio, and Miguel Ramírez Bernal. All of them have offered invaluable feedback on my work and have made the last five years a pleasure. I want to especially express my gratitude to Judith Sierra Rivera and Marco Martínez, who quickly became close friends, like family. All my bibliographical needs have been resolved by our courageous librarian, Manuel Ostos, who is now an indispensable comrade along with Lauren Reiter. Manuel took on the essential assistance and backing that Barbara Alvarez had started for me at the University of Michigan. Gonzalo Rubio patiently read the manuscript and provided me with invaluable suggestions, drawing on his extensive knowledge of both ancient Semitic traditions and recent bibliography. Nicolás Fernández Medina believed in me and then in this project, and I am proud to acknowledge him here. Ronica Skarphol read and offered considerate feedback on two chapters of the book, which greatly improved their legibility. Stephen Wheeler checked part of the Latin contents and translations, and I greatly appreciate his *placet*. Lori Watkins has shown constant interest in the development of the project, and I greatly appreciate her care. I would also like to acknowledge the contributions of three of the students in my 2019 seminar, 'Interreligious Cultural Exchange and Hermetic Sciences in Medieval Spain': Íñigo Huércanos Esparza, Jonathan F. Correa-Reyes, and Jacqueline García Suárez. Graduate students from subsequent cohorts have also inquired about this project, and their sympathy has made my life and work happier; I want to especially mention Sara Arribas Colmenar, Ana Sofía Semo García, María José Andrade, José Miguel Fonseca Fuentes, and Ramsés Martínez Baquero.

My department, as well as the Liberal Arts College of Penn State, generously funded my research trips to libraries and archives in Spain. This project was also supported by the Humanities Institute, where I was a Faculty Scholar in Residence during the fall of 2022. A version of Chapter Three was presented as part of my residency activities; on that occasion, I received priceless feedback from my fellow scholars, and especially the Humanities Institute director, John Christman, to whom I am very grateful. I also included sections of Chapters Three and Four in a presentation at the 2021 International Congress on Medieval Studies in Kalamazoo, Michigan. My article in *eHumanista* 41 (2019): "'Et esto dixo el grant Hermes en uno de sos castigos': desvelando al Hermes árabe en la literatura sapiencial castellana," has been updated and translated into English to become part of Chapter One. Throughout this book, I have also taken advantage and sporadically mentioned the work I conducted for a paper I published in the *Journal of Medieval Iberian Studies*, vol. 14, no. 2 (2022): "'If You Want to Pray to Mercury, Wear the Garments of a Scribe:' *Kuttāb*, *Udabāʾ*, and Readers of the *Ghāyat al-Ḥakīm* in the Court of ʿAbd al-Raḥmān III."

I have been extremely lucky to find Durham University IMEMS Press and Boydell and Brewer as the editorial house for this project. I wish to thank the editorial board of the Translatio series, especially Richard Scholar for his encouragement and editorial guidance in bringing this project to completion. I would also like to thank Stephen Taylor for his expert management of the publishing process, and Elizabeth McDonald for her attentive coordination, as well as her thoughtful reading and invaluable feedback on my manuscript. The anonymous reviewers also significantly improved the quality of the project and the initial versions of the book. Rebekah Zwanzig provided crucial professional assistance in refining and enhancing all the chapters of the manuscript.

During my travels to Spain, and also through calls and messages, my older friends kindly supported me and inquired about my project. They helped me clarify my ideas and present them to a non-specialized but bright audience; among them, Enrique Pena González, Regina López, David Merlán Castro, Félix Collazo López, Jesús Blanco Bellas, Domingo Costalago Astray, Irene Liaño, Francisco Notario, Pablo Varela, Carlos Domínguez Lema, Rafael Irimia Iglesias, Nieves Abarca, Fito Vázquez Rodríguez, Adi Romero, Azul López Garrido, Carmen María Pérez Mira, Carmen Caberta, José Leis, Vicky Pérez, Ana Sánchez Bálgoma, Tania Quintás, Isabel Risco, Rebeca Vecino Bilbao, Alberto Pérez, and especially Moncho Mato Lodeiro, who is always there when I need someone to listen to me.

I have dedicated this book to the four essential women in my family: my mother, María Consolación Alegre Ortega, whom I strive to make proud every day; my aunt María Dolores Udaondo Durán, the first really educated person who had a substantial influence on my life and my readings, and still has; my sister, Ana María Udaondo Alegre, truly my first friend, who has always celebrated my achievements with a smile; and finally my daughter Natalia Udaondo Fernández. She deserves this dedication the most, because my career has deprived us of essential time together, yet she has become my biggest success and the most accomplished woman I could ever dream of.

Note on names, translations, transliterations, abbreviations, and quotations

Since this Spanish version of Hermes is predominantly the result of a translation process, as one might expect, this book includes numerous translations. If not otherwise specified, all translations are my own. Many of those translations are passages from the *General estoria*, which to date has not been translated into English. I have tried to remain as faithful as possible to the original meaning while also rendering the convoluted grammar of old Castilian into pleasant, readable English. There are also many translations from the *Picatrix*, for which I have followed Pingree's Latin edition. I have also looked at the recent (and excellent) translation by Attrell and Porreca; however, I have produced more literal translations of some Hermetic and magical terms, especially when I contrast them with their Arabic originals in the *Ghāyat al-ḥakīm*. For this last work, I have followed Ritter's Arabic edition.

When I translate texts from Castilian and Latin, I have included the originals in quotation marks in footnotes. To enhance their relevance, I have occasionally included words or short sentences in Castilian and Latin within the body of texts in italics, sometimes in parentheses. While I have not included the original Arabic texts, I have included many important Arabic words, titles, and short sentences that have been transliterated. Titles of books and concepts in sciences, philosophy, and magic are written in italics, while proper names, names of cities, etc. are written in roman. I have also transliterated some words in Hebrew and Greek, to highlight their relevance; I have kept some terms of the latter in Greek script.

I have not used many abbreviations in this book, but there are two very important ones. For evident reasons the most quoted book in this work is the *General estoria*, which I have abbreviated as the *GE*. For these quotations I have followed the only complete edition of all existing parts of the *GE*, which has been undertaken by Sánchez Prieto-Borja, assisted by a team of other scholars. The entire work consists of ten volumes. The first four parts each take up two volumes, and the final two volumes contain parts five (volume 9 and part of 10) and six (part of volume 10). When I reference the *GE*, the Arabic number refers to the part and the Roman numeral to the volume, followed by the page number(s) (e.g., *GE*1 II, 78 refers to page seventy-eight in the second volume of the first part). The second important abbreviation is for the section of Ovid's *Metamorphoses* that includes "the story of Io," which I thoroughly analyze in Chapter Three and refer to as *TSOI*. For its several quotations, I also abbreviate the *Metamorphoses* as *Met.* followed by book and verse(s) – thus, *TSOI* is in *Met.*I.567–745. For titles of books in Castilian, Arabic, and Latin that appear repeatedly in the text I have chosen to mention them using the first or most important word of the title (e.g. *Bocados de Oro* is referred to as *Bocados*, *Ghāyat al-Ḥakīm* as *Ghāya*, *Kitāb murūj al-dhahab wa-ma'ādin al-jawhar* as *Murūj*, and so on).

Finally, I would like to point out that even though I am well aware that King Alfonso did not produce the *GE* and the other books from his *scriptorium* by himself, I will follow a convention used by previous scholars and use the singular "Alfonso" when referring to the author of these works and his hypothetical aims – thus avoiding repetitive formulas such as "Alfonso and his team of translators and collaborators" etc.

Introduction

Johannes Trithemius (1462–1516), a Benedictine abbot and polymath who lived at the beginning of the German Renaissance, was greatly influenced by the cultural heritage of the Middle Ages. Trithemius was an expert in numerous fields, particularly occultism and magic. In *Antipalus maleficiorum* (*The enemy of the witches*, 1508), Trithemius displays his in-depth understanding of medieval literature related to these subjects. He thoroughly scrutinizes and denounces 103 books, of which an alarming forty-three are steeped in magical arts, while the remaining sixty arouse suspicion for harbouring such elements. We are familiar with most of these books, although a few remain unidentified, such as the twenty-first entry: *Liber secretorum Hermetis Hispani* (*The book of the secrets of the Spanish Hermes*).[1]

Trithemius does not provide a lot of information on this book – or on most works in the list – he just reproduces the *incipit*, the first words of the book: "He who desires talking to the spirits," and explains that "It is, similarly [to previous books in the list], a work [that is] vain, superstitious, and diabolical, full of characters [symbols] and conjurings of demons."[2] This makes us curious about who exactly the *Hermes Hispanus* of the title was, and what it was about his background or attributes that, in the view of the unidentified author, classified him as "Spanish." Other books listed by Trithemius provide us with interesting insights that highlight the connection between Hermes and Spain. It not only contains numerous medieval books believed to have been authored by the famed sage Hermes Trismegistus, or in whose authorship he was involved in some way, but it also features several that were translated in Spain. Some of them are translations commissioned by King Alfonso X "el sabio" (the Wise or the Learned) of Castile (1252–84). For instance, the fifth on the list is "the work of seven books called *Sepher Razielis* (*Book of Razielis*)."[3] We have a preserved manuscript of the *Liber Razielis*, which is related to Jewish astral magic tracts from the twelfth century.[4] In it, King Alfonso not only ordered a translation of the seven individual books, but he most likely compiled them together for the first time – as suggested by

[1] This book does not appear in the thorough list of preserved medieval Hermetic works by Paolo Lucentini and Vittoria Perrone Compagni in *I testi e I codici di Ermete nel Medioevo* (Firenze: Polistampa, 2001).

[2] "Item est *Liber secretorum Hermetis Hispani*, qui incipit: *Qui cum spiritibus loqui desiderat.* Opus est similiter vanum, superstitiosum et diabolicum, characteribus et daemonum conjurationibus plenum." Johannes Trithemius, *Antipalus maleficiorum*, in *Paralipomena opusculorum Petri Blesensi et Joannis Trithemii*, ed. Johannes Busaeus (Mainz: E. Balthasaris Lippi Typographeo, 1605), 297.

[3] "Item est opus 7 librorum, quod nuncupatur *Sepher Razielis*." *Antipalus maleficiorum*, 294.

[4] This manuscript of Alfonso's *Liber Razielis*, Ms. Reg. lat. 1300, is in the Vatican Library.

the translation's prologue.[5] The originals, written in Hebrew, and also probably Aramaic, from which the translations were made, are lost, but it is evident that the compilers working for Alfonso incorporated Hermetic components.[6]

Trithemius also talks about a book of magic of much greater renown that was created in Alfonso's *scriptorium*: "*Picatrix* truly composed a volume of four books, out of 224 old books – as he says – which begins in this way: 'As a wise man said: the first thing we must do [...].' The *Picatrix* was translated from Arabic into Latin in the year of the Christians 1256."[7] Indeed, Trithemius presents the *incipit* of the *Picatrix* and supplements it with his knowledge of the remainder of the book. Despite insisting that it is a translation from Arabic, the abbot did not know that the author of the book was not the unknown Picatrix – as the Latin translator mysteriously affirms – but the Iberian Muslim Maslama b. Qāsim al-Qurṭubī (906–64), who called it *Ghāyat al-ḥakīm* (*The aim of the sage* or *The goal of the wise man*). The *Picatrix*'s prologue affirms that the work was completed in "anno Domini MCCLVI." Nonetheless, as Pingree infers, the *Picatrix* must have been finished between 1256 and 1258 – at the beginning of Alfonso's reign – and the Latin translation was made using an earlier Castilian one.[8] The prologue merely mentions that "The wise philosopher, the noble and honourable Picatrix compiled this book out of more than 200 books of philosophy and gave his name as the title";[9] much later the author states that he used 224 books.[10] This exactitude demonstrates that Trithemius knew the complete work. The abbot evaluates the *Picatrix* using criteria very similar to that in his scrutiny of *The book of the secrets of the Spanish Hermes*. According to him, in the *Picatrix*

> many frivolous, superstitious, and diabolical things are at the fore and openly discussed, although a certain number of natural [philosophy] matters also seem to be intermixed [among them]. It makes prayers to the spirits of the planets, and also talismans and rings that possess numerous and diverse characteristics, all of which the Holy Mother Church condemns as illicit and superstitious.[11]

5 Alejandro García Avilés, "Alfonso X y el *Liber Razielis*: Imágenes de la magia astral judía en el *scriptorium* alfonsí," *Bulletin of Hispanic Studies* 74, no. 1 (1997): 27.

6 García Avilés, "Alfonso X y el *Liber Razielis*," 36.

7 "*Picatrix* vero magnum composuit volumen librorum quatuor, quod sic incipit: 'Ut sapiens ait: Primum quid agere debeamus;' ex ducentis et 24, sicut dicit, veterum libris anno Christianorum MCCLVI; ex arabico in latinum traductum." *Antipalus maleficiorum*, 293–4.

8 David Pingree, "Between the *Ghāya* and *Picatrix*. I: The Spanish Version," *Journal of the Warburg and Courtauld Institutes* 44 (1981): 27.

9 "Sapiens enim philosophus, nobilis et honoratus Picatrix, hunc librum ex CC libris et pluribus philosophie compilavit, quem suo proprio nomine nominavit." David Pingree (ed. and trans.), *Picatrix. The Latin Version of the Ghāyat al-ḥakīm* (London: The Warburg Institute, 1986), Prologue, 1.

10 Pingree, *Picatrix* III.v.4.

11 "[...] in quo multa continentur frivola, superstitiosa et diabolica in fronte sermonis aperti, quamvis etiam naturalia quaedam videantur intermixta. Orationes facit ad spiritus planetarum, imagines quoque et annulos cum multis et variis characteribus, quae omnia sancta mater Ecclesia condamnat ut illicita et superstitiosa." *Antipalus maleficiorum*, 294.

In the book, many of those prayers are attributed to Hermes or dedicated to his implied alter ego, the planet Mercury, with whom talismans and a ring of mercury/quicksilver are also associated.[12] Hermes Trismegistus's presence is certainly pervasive throughout the *Picatrix*. The quote from the prologue that Trithemius reproduces is incomplete, and the complete version reads: "As a wise man said: the first thing we must do in all the things of the world is give thanks to God."[13] This expression of thanks to God is part of the Hermetic tradition and a similar thanks can also be found in the Hermetic treatise *Asclepius*.[14]

Not surprisingly, Hermes also plays a central role in a significant number of the 224 books to which al-Qurṭubī refers. Various Hermetic books found their way to al-Andalus throughout the rulers of the Iberian emirate and subsequent caliphate periods, and then were translated into Latin in Christian lands. Trithemius includes several of them in his list. For example, the fifty-seventh work is "*The book of the talismans* [*praestigiorum*] by Thabit, in which, through the composition of diverse talismans, wondrous accomplishments are promised";[15] and the sixty-ninth is "the book of Thabit, *On the talismans* [*imaginibus*], in which wondrous accomplishments are promised through the influence of the stars."[16] Both titles refer to a lost Arabic work by Thābit Ibn Qurra (826–901 CE), who came to Baghdad from the legendary city of Ḥarrān, where stars were worshipped and Hermes was regarded as a prophet. Indeed, the *Picatrix* quotes this book as one of his sources.[17] It was later translated twice during the twelfth century, both times by a resident of the Iberian Peninsula – first by John of Seville, *De imaginibus*, and then by Adelard of Bath, *Liber prestigiorum Thebidis secundum Ptolomeum et Hermetem* (*The book of the talismans by Thabit, according to Ptolemy and Hermes*)[18] – this is the reason it is mentioned twice in Trithemius's list.

The *Picatrix*'s prologue also provides us with a crucial hint about the potential features of a "Spanish Hermes." According to it, Picatrix was a philosopher who composed his book using other books of philosophy. As we will see, Alfonso believed that a philosopher, above all else, specialized in the liberal arts, the *trivium* and the *quadrivium*. In several passages the *Ghāyat al-ḥakīm* insists that only he who masters all the philosophical sciences, especially mathematics, will be able to practise magic; the *Picatrix* interprets this as meaning that the magician must be learned in all the known sciences, the natural and mathematical sciences of the *quadrivium*

12 Juan Udaondo Alegre, "'If You Want to Pray to Mercury, Wear the Garments of a Scribe': *Kuttāb, Udabāʾ*, and Readers of the *Ghāyat Al-Ḥakīm* in the Court of ʿAbd Al-Raḥmān III," *Journal of Medieval Iberian Studies* 14, no. 2 (2022): 223–5.

13 "[...] in omnibus rebus mundi est Deo regraciari." Pingree, *Picatrix*, Prologue, 1.

14 *Picatrix. A Medieval Treatise on Astral Magic*, trans. David Porreca and Dan Attrell (University Park: The Pennsylvania State University Press, 2019), 285. *Asclepius*, 41.

15 "Item est Liber praestigiorum Thebit, in quo per compositionem diversarum imaginum mirabiles pollicetur effectus." *Antipalus maleficiorum*, 304.

16 "Item est liber Thebit, De imaginibus, in quo per influentias astrorum mirabilis pollicetur effectus." *Antipalus maleficiorum*, 304.

17 *Ghāya* I.5, 37; and *Picatrix* I.v.36.

18 Charles Burnett, "The Establishment of Medieval Hermeticism," in Peter Linehan and Janet L. Nelson (eds), *The Medieval World* (Abingdon: Routledge, 2001), 127.

in particular.[19] This is why Trithemius acknowledges that the *Picatrix* contains "a certain number of natural philosophy matters." In the *Picatrix,* not unsurprisingly, Hermes/Mercury is connected to the liberal arts as well as magic.

Thus, from a historical and intellectual perspective, Trithemius's list highlights that Hermes was closely linked to the Iberian Peninsula throughout the Middle Ages. Not surprisingly, at some point the idea of a "Hermes Hispanus" was formulated, and his mysteries were unveiled in a book which unfortunately is no longer available. In this project I aim to make up for that loss and search for the overlooked, yet important, Spanish embodiment of the old sage, as well as his significance. According to my research, Alfonso the Wise expended considerable effort into associating Hermetic lore with the Iberian territories, and his most fruitful representation of the "Spanish Hermes" is encapsulated in the *General estoria* (*General history*; hereafter referred to as *GE*). This historical work restates, translates, and interprets previous accounts pertaining to Hermes, the wisdom traditions he inherited on his way towards Spanish lands, and the changes he experienced there. Moreover, in the *GE* Hermes/Mercury displays attributes that can be explained only through the scientific, astrological, and magical books that the Castilian king produced. As Trithemius's notes also suggest, the knowledge bestowed upon Hermes during the Middle Ages was not solely confined to esoteric practices like astrology and magic; thus, Alfonso presents Hermetic wisdom as expansive, accommodating the entirety of every previous period's accumulated knowledge. In this way, by centering my research on Hermes and Alfonso's Castile, I also aim to present a unique interpretation of the translation of knowledge and an intellectual history of the Iberian Middle Ages.

Throughout this book we will see how Hermetic knowledge, including legends about the origins and transmission of wisdom, came to Spain in an exceptional way compared with the rest of Europe. Iberia – where Near Eastern, Classical, Arabic, Jewish, and Christian traditions merged – provides an exceptional vantage point for understanding how the legendary sage and the works associated with him underwent a process of translation and intellectual exchange over the course of 1,000 years and across a region spanning the western and eastern margins of the Mediterranean Sea. As Peter Kingsley points out, Hermes Trismegistus established "a tradition of translation, the hermeneutical tradition *par excellence*, dedicated to upholding its originator's name for continually inventing, re-assessing, and re-interpreting."[20] Hermes Trismegistus's patronage of translation could not find a better ground for enduring than medieval Spain, where an unmatched process of Eastern-Western translation took place.

The first Hermetic writings claim to be Greek translations of Egyptian works. These texts, which guided readers in the divine wisdom and sciences allegedly created by Hermes – such as magic, astrology, and alchemy – were in turn translated into Latin, Armenian, Coptic, Hebrew, Syriac, Persian, Arabic, and other Eastern languages. Previous studies on the Hermetic tradition describe how the works were translated into these languages and cultures during the Middle Ages and then

19 For instance, *Ghāya* II.1, 57; and *Picatrix* II.ii.3.

20 Peter Kingsley, "*Poimandres*: The Etymology of the Name and the Origins of the Hermetica," *Journal of the Warburg and Courtauld Institutes* 56, no. 1 (1993): 23.

how Marsilio Ficino translated them into Latin during the Renaissance. However, academic works rarely mention the first translated version in a Romance language: the Castilian Hermes.

This book presents how Hermetic knowledge was brought to the Iberian Peninsula, how Hermes became the ideal teacher and philosophical mentor for elite Iberian Christian, Jewish, and Arabic intellectuals, and how Hermes was rendered into Castilian by Alfonso the Wise. Alfonso's cultural and scientific grandeur – unparalleled in Europe – was possible due to the multicultural nature of his kingdom; he translated, organized, and disseminated the intellectual heritage of the different religious communities present in Spain. This work examines the ways in which different versions of Hermes converged in Alfonso's works in what can be understood as a new hybrid, "Hispanic" version of this figure. Hermes was redefined due to the perspectives of different religious communities interacting in the same cultural space, and thus operates as a metaphor for the Castilian and Spanish composite intellectual identity.

Previous studies analyze different embodiments of Hermes in the cultures he touched: Garth Fowden, *The Egyptian Hermes*; Claudio Moreschini, *Hermes Christianus*; Kevin van Bladel, *The Arabic Hermes*; Valeria Buffon and Claudia D'Amico, *Hermes Platonicus*; Fabrizio Lelli, "Hermes among the Jews"; and the various volumes of *Hermes Latinus*, begun by the late Professor Paolo Lucentini. My work builds on this scholarship and presents the development of a vernacular "Spanish Hermes" on Iberian soil, where the different Hermeses from the abovementioned studies converged and were rendered into Castilian during the Middle Ages. My analysis of the Iberian transformations of Hermes Trismegistus reassesses and sheds new light on the influence of Arabic texts within the intellectual history of Castile, Spain, and Europe more generally. It adds a new dimension to the ongoing dialogue concerning how ancient knowledge was filtered and reframed through a personage who was shared and assimilated by representatives of the three monotheistic religions – Judaism, Christianity, and Islam. It also presents Alfonso the Wise as an interpreter of earlier traditions, via translation, who transformed Hermetic texts according to his cultural project and brought previously inaccessible knowledge to the forefront.

Obviously, when I refer to Spain or Spanish in the Middle Ages, I am indicating all the Christian and Muslim kingdoms on the Iberian Peninsula that occupied the area of ancient Roman Hispania. In this sense, I am close to the concept Alfonso used in his other great historical work, *Estoria de España* (*History of Spain*), and most probably to the Spanish Hermes in the lost book alluded to by Trithemius. In fact, the composite monarchy of Spain – the foundation of the modern country – arose through the marriage of Isabel of Castile and Fernando of Aragon in 1479, a few decades before Trithemius's treatise. Even though this book is the first specific study of Hermes Trismegistus in medieval Spain, it does not cover all possible aspects of this rich topic or all Hermetic traces in all territories on the Iberian Peninsula. To streamline the discussion and condense the volume, I have also refrained from including an exhaustive bibliography and typically address just the most crucial or beneficial works relevant to my narrative.

Likewise, to keep the volume at a manageable size, after an introductory chapter where I summarize the origins, development, and historical acclimatization of Hermes in Iberia, I narrow my focus to Castile, Alfonso the Wise, and his *GE*. Hence, I have structured the last four chapters around a series of close readings of passages from the *GE* where Hermes/Mercury or Hermetic-related themes appear, and have analyzed how they relate to specific intellectual motifs found in medieval Europe and Castile; namely: the reception of Arabic genres intertwined with Hermetic traditions; the interpretation of Ovid through Arabic culture and Hermetic sciences; the theories on the origins of wisdom with regard to the Arabic legend of the three Hermeses; and finally, the relationship between Hermes, medieval knowledge, and liberal arts as expressed by Alfonso.

The first chapter introduces Hermes Trismegistus and recounts how he "came twice" to Spain during two waves of engagement with Hermetic ideas. His first arrival occurred thanks to the interconnected Mediterranean of late antiquity. It documents traces of Hellenistic hybridity and Hermetism in the writings of the heretic Priscillian in late Roman Hispania, while also examining the first significant references to Hermes Trismegistus – in the *Etymologies* of Isidore of Seville (d. 636 CE) – after the Visigoth takeover. The second arrival happened after the Muslim conquest. I argue that the "Arabic Hermes" – as defined by Van Bladel – reached Spain during a process of "orientalization" that took place during the ninth century when emirs from Córdoba sought to emulate the cultural splendor of Baghdad by importing books and customs from the distant reaches of the Mediterranean Sea. The culmination of this process is the *Ghāyat al-ḥakīm*. Then I examine the consequences of the breakdown of the Caliphate of Córdoba in 1031. The disappearance of a strong, centralized Muslim power made Muslim cultural treasures accessible to the Christian kingdoms of the north, and also to erudite men who gathered in Spain from far and wide and began the crucial process of translating Arabic texts. I connect the development of a Hispanic Hermes in Iberia with the three centuries of cultural exchange between Christians, Jews, and Muslims that followed the Caliphate's fall, and single out specific personalities from "the three cultures" who revered Hermes prior to Alfonso the Wise. Finally, I offer a glimpse into Castilian sapiential books, most of which were translated from Arabic; a process that started during the reign of Alfonso's father. In these works, Hermes is presented as one of the main ancient intellectual masters.

Chapter Two introduces Alfonso the Wise and his works, in particular the *GE*, his most important historical production. Then it focuses on how Hermetic Arabic knowledge filtered into the intellectual endeavours of Alfonso, not only through translations of astrology and magic books – on which previous scholarship has tended to focus – but also through the historical and geographical sources of the *GE*. The chapter contextualizes the *GE*'s main Arabic sources within Muslim intellectual production, connects them with *adab*-related geographical genres, traces their origins, and points to specific characteristics, such as intrinsic wondrous and Hermetic content. Then it examines and reassesses Arabic materials in places where the *GE* uses them extensively: in the sections on Abraham, Doluca, and Nebuchadnezzar. The chapter concludes that some *adab* genres influenced the *GE* as a whole and served as a transmission channel for Hermetic, astrological, and magical traditions.

Chapter Three examines how Alfonso reinterpreted episodes from Ovid's *Metamorphoses* and introduced them in his *GE*. A close reading of the mythological story of Io demonstrates the presence of elements unfamiliar to the Latin culture of the time that can only be explained through Alfonso's translations from Arabic into Castilian. The descriptions of illustrious men and women do not adhere to other European models: they study the liberal arts, write books on the sciences, practise astrology and magic, and excel in good customs and courtly pursuits, such as music and falconry. These components are distinct characteristics of the figure of Mercury, who is an accomplished magician, musician, and expert in the *trivium* and *quadrivium* – skills that he uses, along with his Arab-like *alfange*, to kill Argus and thus to allegorically educate the "bestialized" Io. Based on several allusions in the text, the chapter suggests that Alfonso reframed the Roman Mercury as a personification of Hermes Trismegistus.

Chapter Four explores the Castilian version of the "legend of the three Hermeses." Some ancient and medieval thinkers believed that the cognomen "Trismegistus" indicated that three Hermeses had existed throughout history. The origins of this belief are unknown, and scholars such as Charles Burnett, Kevin van Bladel, and Emily Cottrell are engaged in an ongoing debate about when and where it began. Alfonso includes a rendering of the three Hermeses' story in his *GE*. This chapter points to an unexplored Castilian source for this narrative, relates it to other still-ignored Latin precedents, and offers new material for current debates on the three Hermeses.

Chapter Five investigates how Alfonso's works show Hermes as a patron of the liberal arts, the *trivium* and *quadrivium*, in such a way that they offer a unique theory about Hermes during the Middle Ages. According to the *GE*, Hermes was granted the moniker "Trismegistus" on account of his mastery of the medieval *trivium*. Hermes's wisdom in a variety of disciplines and skills – including mathematics – led to him also being considered a forerunner of the *quadrivium*. This chapter examines Hermes's relationship with the liberal arts in different sections of the *GE*, proves that this connection is a product of both the European and Arab traditions, and establishes a dialogue between Alfonso's historical, scientific and magical books. Moreover, I argue that these works are connected through their common Semitic sources and the figure of Hermes, on whom Alfonso bestows characteristics specific to the syncretic culture of thirteenth-century Castile that make him a veritable Spanish Hermes.

The Conclusion confirms that Hermes represents a significant connection between Alfonso's scientific and historical narratives. Furthermore, it verifies that his presence in the *GE* is intended to serve as a guiding model for a knowledgeable Castilian elite. These individuals worked together on Alfonso's projects, hailed from diverse religious backgrounds, and were influenced by Hermetic doctrines.

Perhaps we may never uncover the secrets of the Hermes Hispanus that the lost book listed by Trithemius promised. Nonetheless, it is my hope that this book will help in understanding possible ways they could be formulated.

1

Hermetic Wisdom's Arrival in Spain and its Diffusion Among the "Three Cultures"

Introduction

Hermes Trismegistus was the result of a symbiotic process that occurred between Egyptian and Greek culture, and we can follow his path to medieval Iberia, the country "of the three cultures," where he became a symbol of syncretism and cultural exchange. If Hermes was already a relevant figure within the translation and interpretation process that configured culture in the early Middle Ages, his passage through the Iberian Peninsula enhanced his image. While still retaining his core essence, Hermes Trismegistus had to adapt to different cultural circumstances; not a difficult task for a god associated with movement, instability, and change; that is, a figure who was "mercurial." According to Kingsley, because of the overarching influence of the god Hermes, the Hermetic tradition was by definition a tradition "which was perpetually shifting, changing, refining itself, moving beyond itself. It was a tradition that managed to retain its essential power at one level by, at another level, staying in a state of perpetual flux."[1]

This volatile nature was once again demonstrated when Hermes "came" or "was brought" – figuratively speaking – from the eastern Mediterranean to the Iberian Peninsula during late antiquity and the beginning of the Christian Middle Ages; and he came a second time through the cultural exchange between Muslim Spain and Abbasid Baghdad, where translations of Greek, Persian, and Syriac works took place. Due to the cultural developments that took place in Córdoba, Hermes eventually made his way to the Christian kingdoms in the northern Iberian Peninsula, where learned men once again translated and interpreted the Egyptian sage and his works; thus, Hermes, the interpreter and translator of the Greek gods, underwent a continuous translation process during his sojourn in the Iberian Peninsula. Moreover, just as Abbasid Baghdad presented Hermes to the Arab world, the multinational and multireligious teams who translated Hermetic wisdom in Castile and Aragon constructed a Hermes that fitted within the cultural grandeur of the late Middle Ages. Castilian culture had reached a point of maturity that allowed Hermes to be translated into a vernacular language (i.e., Castilian) that was still young but knew

[1] Peter Kingsley, "An Introduction to the Hermetica: Approaching Ancient Esoteric Tradition," in Roelof van den Broek and Cis van Heertum (eds), *From Poimandres to Jacob Böhme: Gnosis, Hermetism and the Christian Tradition*, (Leiden: Brill, 2000), 26.

how to integrate secular traditions into their cultural productions. Let us explore what Hermes represented originally and then look at the different stages of this figure's development within the cultural and intellectual history of the Iberian Peninsula.

Origin of Hermes Trismegistus

Hermes Trismegistus represents the epitome of religious syncretism in the Hellenistic era, as the Greek god Hermes became assimilated with the Egyptian god Thoth. Because of this syncretism, he is found in many different religious traditions – transformed into an ancient theologian or remembered as the founder of disciplines such as rhetoric, magic, or writing. Shortly after Alexander's conquest of Egypt in 331 BCE, writings attributed to Hermes started to appear in the Near East, and many more circulated in different languages until the end of antiquity. The writings attributed to Hermes are referred to as *Hermetica*, which, despite some scholarly discrepancies, is still divided into two interrelated kinds: philosophical and technical.

The technical *Hermetica* was the first to appear and is associated with arts such as magic, astrology, and alchemy, all of which were characterized as inventions of Hermes. The philosophical or theoretical *Hermetica* appeared later, during the second and third centuries CE, coinciding with the so-called Middle Platonism, as well as with later developments of other two great philosophical schools, Stoicism and Aristotelianism, and served as the conceptual setting of the technical *Hermetica*. Walbridge points out that the greatest difference between the *Hermetica* and Greek philosophy is that the first is revealed, not argued.[2] However, at the time, philosophical discussion incorporated matters that now would be classified as religious, such as the search for salvation, astrological beliefs, purification of the soul, and knowledge of a transcendental reality. There was also an emphasis on the mystical and mythical side of Plato and a tendency to see him as part of an Orphic and Pythagorean tradition. An eclectic orientalism also developed, which considered Plato the interpreter of an "Oriental wisdom," a primigenial revelation coming from eastern countries.[3] The *Hermetica* offered a devotional perspective on the relationship between humans and God's creation and also included ethical encouragement for a specific way of life – the "way of Hermes" – leading to spiritual rebirth and eventually divinization through heavenly ascent.[4]

Therefore, it is not strange that the *Hermetica* uses the vocabulary of the Greek philosophical tradition – the lingua franca of the time. It also contains elements from Judaism, Christianity, and Middle Eastern, especially Egyptian, religions – whose wisdom it proclaims it is translating. In fact, Mahé has demonstrated the connection between the *Hermetica* and Egyptian wisdom literature.[5] The Egyptian background

[2] John Walbridge, *The Wisdom of the Mystic East: Suhrawardi and Platonic Orientalism* (New York: State University of New York Press, 2001), 42–3.

[3] Walbridge, *Wisdom of the Mystic East*, 8–12.

[4] Christian H. Bull, *The Tradition of Hermes Trismegistus* (Leiden: Brill, 2018), 3–4.

[5] See Jean-Pierre Mahé, *Hermès en Haute-Egypte* (Québec: Presses de l'Université Laval, 1978).

of the *Hermetica* is better understood today, but for decades it was contested and considered an Alexandrian forgery.[6] As Fowden points out, the milieu that produced and preserved the *Hermetica* "had been long, and so it seemed, irreversibly Hellenized in its language and thought-patterns; but that had not made it into a Greek milieu."[7] More recently, Bull has thoroughly studied the sociological context of the *Hermetica* and came to the conclusion that Egyptian priests familiar with Hellenistic philosophy created the *Hermetica* by acclimatizing and translating their traditions into Greek.[8] The Greek transmission channel and context of the *Hermetica* has led many scholars to focus primarily on Hermetic philosophy. In a recent and innovative contribution, Hanegraaff has suggested that to truly understand the *Hermetica* we must understand the "Hermetic spirituality," because those texts primarily "claim to reveal the true nature of reality and describe a way towards liberation from mental delusion."[9] While Greek philosophy conveys knowledge through words, the knowledge (*gnōsis*) provided by the *Hermetica* pertains to an ineffable and spiritual experience that results in salvation.[10]

Ancient *Hermetica* has come to us in different forms and languages,[11] but two prominent works are important: *Corpus hermeticum* and *Asclepius*. The *Corpus hermeticum* refers to a collection of eighteen Greek Hellenistic treatises. It is possible that they were compiled in Byzantium in the eleventh century, yet likely all or part of them had been gathered together at an earlier date. The corpus was not known in Europe until Marsilio Ficino and then other scholars translated it into Latin at the end of the fifteenth and the beginning of the sixteenth century. In contrast, the *Asclepius* is the Latin translation of a Greek treatise called *Logos teleios* ("perfect discourse" or "perfect revelation"), and it was appreciated during the European Middle Ages. This work suffers from internal tensions between pagan elements, philosophy, monotheism, Judaism, and likely Christian influences. It also contains traces of ceremonial theurgy – "godly working" practices aiming to reunite an individual with the divine. Neoplatonic philosophers such as Iamblichus and Porphyry debated about theurgy in their writings. In *City of God* Augustine quotes and praises the *Asclepius*'s monotheistic harmony with Christianity, yet he also mercilessly attacks its idolatry.

Since I am particularly interested in the narrative and literary aspects of the *Hermetica*, it is worth mentioning its dialogical setting and recurrent list of *dramatis personae*: Hermes Trismegistus, his disciple Asclepius, his son Tat, Ammon, Horus,

6 For instance, in the pioneer study by André-Jean Festugière, *La révélation d'Hermés Trismégiste*, 4 vols, 3rd edn (Paris: Gabalda, 1950).

7 Garth Fowden, *The Egyptian Hermes: A Historical Approach to the Late Pagan Mind* (Princeton: Princeton University Press, 1993), 43–4.

8 Bull, *Tradition of Hermes*, 13–15.

9 Wouter Hanegraaff, *Hermetic Spirituality and the Historical Imagination: Altered states of knowledge in late antiquity* (Cambridge: Cambridge University Press), 1.

10 Hanegraaff, *Hermetic Spirituality*, 3–5.

11 For a complete introduction to the matter, see Brian Copenhaver (trans.), *Hermetica: The Greek "Corpus Hermeticum" and the Latin "Asclepius" in a New English Translation, with Notes and Introduction* (Cambridge: Cambridge University Press, 1996), xiii–lxi.

Isis, Agathos Daimon, etc.[12] Throughout this work, I will provide many other details about the ancient *Hermetica* insofar as they reverberated throughout the centuries.[13]

Heresy and Magic: Hermes in Visigoth Hispania

The first mentions of Hermes Trismegistus in the Iberian Peninsula that I have found are in the *Etymologies* by Isidore of Seville (560–636 CE). The significance of these quotations makes it extremely possible that Hermetic doctrines arrived in Spain much earlier, either through written testimonies or accompanying some of the Hellenistic syncretic cults that spread throughout the Roman Empire. Both written sources and archaeological and epigraphical materials demonstrate the presence and flourishing of oriental mystery religions in Hispania; they possibly intermingled with autochthone societies and their sacred traditions.[14] Thus, the philosophical and religious-eclectic Hellenistic developments that gave birth to Hermes Trismegistus were soon imported to Spain. We can single out the Neo-Pythagorean Moderatus of Cádiz (first century CE), who was born in Gades (now Cádiz, in southern Spain), but wrote in Greek. Moderatus influenced Middle and Neoplatonic philosophers such as Numenius (second century CE) and Iamblichus – both connected to Hermetism.[15] We also have the testimonies of numerous Greek philosophers, geographers, and historians who visited Gades in the first centuries CE.[16] The alleged visit of Apollonius of Tyana (first century CE) is significant[17] because Arabic, and then Latin, traditions would connect him with Hermes Trismegistus, alchemy, and talismanic magic.

There is archaeological evidence that eastern Mediterranean cults existed in Spain. We have numerous inscriptions dedicated to Syrian deities, such as the *Dea Mater* or Atargatis, even more dedicated to the Egyptians Isis and Serapis.[18] The last two gods are particularly relevant because they appear in the *Hermetica*. Bull thinks that "Hermetism might have been found side by side with the cult of Isis and Osiris

[12] Fowden, *Egyptian Hermes*, 32–3.

[13] For a complete introduction to Hermes and his writings, see the work of the specialists cited in this introduction: Festugière, Mahé, Fowden, Copenhaver, Bull, Hanegraaff, etc.

[14] See the classical study of Stephen McKenna, *Paganism and Pagan Survivals in Spain Up to the Fall of the Visigothic Kingdom* (Washington: Catholic University of America, 1938), 20–4. For recent studies and bibliography, see María Paz de Hoz and Gloria Mora (eds), *El oriente griego en la Península Ibérica. Epigrafía e historia* (Madrid: Real Academia de la Historia, 2013). https://www.ccel.org/ccel/pearse/morefathers/files/eusebius_pe_00_intro.htm (last accessed September 28, 2022).

[15] Francisco García Bazán, "Los aportes neoplatónicos de Moderato de Cádiz," *Anales del Seminario de Historia de la Filosofía* 15 (1998): 16–18.

[16] See Pilar Pavón Torrejón and Inmaculada Pérez Martín, "La presencia de la cultura griega en Cádiz: la figura de Moderato de Gades," in Amado Miguel Zabala, Francisco Álvarez Solano, and Jesús San Bernardino (eds), *Arqueólogos, historiadores y filólogos: homenaje a Fernando Gascó* (Sevilla: Kolaios, 1995), 209–14.

[17] Fernando Gasco La Calle, "El viaje de Apolonio de Tiana a la Bética (Siglo d.C.)," *Revista De Estudios Andaluces* 4, no. 1 (1985): 13–22.

[18] See María Paz de Hoz, "Cultos griegos, cultos sincréticos y la inmigración griega y greco-oriental," in María Paz de Hoz and Gloria Mora (eds), *El oriente griego en la Península Ibérica. Epigrafía e historia* (Madrid: Real Academia de la Historia, 2013), 224–5.

around the Mediterranean world."[19] An epigraph from Cartagena (south-eastern Spain) supports this claim. It states that a certain T. Hermes built a sanctuary for Isis and Serapis. This epigraph was found in an area where pottery with Greek inscriptions dedicated to Serapis has also been found.[20] In Ampurias (north-eastern Spain), there is a bilingual Latin-Greek inscription about the construction of two sanctuaries for the cult of Isis and Serapis. One of them has been identified as the archaeological remains found in an area close to the sanctuary of Aesculapius (Asclepius), where the famous statue of the Aesculapius of Ampurias was found.[21] It is debated whether this statue actually represents Serapis, or even Agathos Daimon.[22] Both Asclepius and Agathos Daimon (or Agathodaimon) are Hermetic-related characters. These remnants are evidence of Hispania and Egypt's frequent commercial and cultural contact. Chadwick has pointed out that by the third/fourth centuries, trade between Alexandria and Spain "was so normal and everyday, that Palladius of Galatia attests a Greek epithet *Spanodromos* for Egyptian merchants regularly 'on the Spanish run.'"[23]

This contact has also been used to explain the most important heresy that arose on Spanish soil, Priscillianism. The first evidence of Hermetic-related doctrines can be found around the same time as this heresy. Ecclesiastical authorities accused Priscillian (*c.* 340–85 CE), bishop of Avila, of obscenity, performing magic, and Manichaeism. After years of dispute in Church councils, the case was handed over to the imperial court. In 385, in Trier (Germany), Priscillian confessed and was sentenced to death for performing magic (*maleficium*).[24] His cult continued after his death and was intensely vilified by Ithacius (or Idacius *c.* 400–69 CE). Ithacius witnessed the de facto end of Roman rule in the Iberian Peninsula and how in 418 new Germanic and "barbarian" powers took its place. The Suebi would occupy Gallaecia (Galicia, north-western Spain) – where Ithacius was bishop – while the rest of the peninsula fell into the hands of the Visigoths. The Hispano-Roman Ithacius opposed both the Suebi and the Priscillianists, whose cult had spread throughout Hispania, and even to other parts of Europe. As Chadwick notes, once the Suebi freed Priscillianists from Church pressure, they flourished in Gallaecia.[25] Centuries later, Isidore included Ithacius in his *De viris illustribus* (*On illustrious men*):

> Ithacius, bishop of the Spanish, celebrated in name and eloquence, wrote a certain book in apologetic form in which he demonstrates the abhorred dogmas of

19 Bull, *Tradition of Hermes*, 454.

20 José Beltrán Fortes, "Greco-Orientales en la Hispania Republicana e Imperial a través de las menciones epigráficas," in Paz de Hoz and Mora, *El oriente griego*, 191.

21 Beltrán Fortes, "Greco-Orientales en la Hispania," 192.

22 See Stephan Schröder, "El Asclepio de Ampurias: ¿una estatua de Agathodaimon del último cuarto del siglo II a.C.?," in Jaume Massó and Pilar Sada (eds), *Actas, II Reunión sobre escultura romana en Hispania* (Tarragona: Museu Nacional Arqueològic de Tarragona, 1996).

23 Henry Chadwick, *Priscillian of Avila: The Occult and the Charismatic in the Early Church* (Oxford: Clarendon Press, 1976), 22.

24 On Priscillian, see Chadwick, *Priscillian*; and Virginia Burrus, *The Making of a Heretic: Gender, Authority, and the Priscillianist Controversy* (Oakland: University of California Press, 1995).

25 Chadwick, *Priscillian*, 151.

> Priscillian, his arts of witchcraft, and his shameful lust, showing that a certain Mark of Memphis, most expert in the art of magic, was the student of Mani and teacher of Priscillian.[26]

Thus, Ithacius connected Priscillian to Egyptian magic, which was commonly related to Hermes Trismegistus.[27] Priscillian's alleged master, Mark of Memphis, was a disciple of Mani (*c.* 216–76 CE), the founder of the Manichaean heresy. This information was endorsed by Jerome, whom Ithacius had met while travelling to Palestine. In a series of five scattered passages (dating *c.* 400–10), Jerome scornfully refers to the Priscillian heresy as "Spanish incantations, Spanish foolishness, and Egyptian portents" – as Burrus points out, for Jerome, Priscillianism was a Hispano-Egyptian heresy.[28] Chadwick refers to Sulpicius Severus's testimony in his *Chronicon*, which maintains that Priscillian's movement began "when he fell under the influence of an aristocratic lady named Agape and an orator Elpidius, both of whom had been friendly with a gnostic teacher Mark of Memphis, who came to Spain from Egypt" – in fact, Memphis was a legendary centre of the magical art.[29]

Augustine also wrote against the Priscillianists and the Manichaeans – whom, as a former member, he knew very well. He was also friends with the Gallaecian historian Petrus Orosius (*c.* 385–418) and corresponded with Spanish bishops.[30] Orosius's *Commonitorium* or *Letter of instruction concerning the error of the Priscillianists and of the Origenists* includes a report concerning certain astrological ideas held by Priscillian and his followers.[31] According to Augustine, Priscillianists mixed dogmas from the Gnostics and the Manichaeans[32] and believed that

> human souls are of the same nature and substance as God; that on their journey to earth, the souls gradually pass through seven heavens and seven kingdoms, and they fall into [the hands of] an "evil prince" to whom they attribute the facts of this world, and through this prince they are planted into different bodies of flesh; they also say that man's fate is bound to the stars, and our body is composed according to the twelve signs [of the zodiac] – just as those called astrologers [*mathematici*] by the plebs – thus they place Aries in the head, Taurus in the neck [...], etc.[33]

26 "Itacius, Hispaniarum episcopus, cognomento et eloquio clarus, scripsit quemdam librum sub apologetici specie, in quo detestanda Priscilliani dogmata, et maleficiorum ejus artes, libidinumque ejus probra demonstrat, ostendens Marcum quemdam Memphiticum magicae artis scientissimum, discipulum fuisse Manis et Priscilliani magistrum." *De viris illustribus* XV. My translation.

27 Copenhaver, *Hermetica*, xxv–xxvi.

28 Burrus, *Making of a Heretic*, 132.

29 Chadwick, *Priscillian*, 20.

30 McKenna, *Paganism and Pagan Survivals*, 63.

31 Tim Hegedus, *Early Christianity and Ancient Astrology* (New York: Peter Lang, 2007), 339–40.

32 "Priscillianistae [...] Gnosticorum et Manichaeorum dogmata permixta sectantur." Augustine, *De haeresibus ad Quodvultdeus*, 70.

33 "Hi animas dicunt eiusdem naturae atque substantiae cuius est Deus; ad agonem quemdam spontaneum in terris exercendum, per septem caelos et per quosdam gradatim descendere principatus; et in malignum principem incurrere a quo istum mundum factum volunt atque ab hoc principe per diversa carnis corpora seminari. Astruunt etiam fatalibus

We can relate many of those features with Hermetic doctrines. The descent of the soul is strongly reminiscent of Neoplatonic philosophers who had close ties to theurgy and Hermetism, such as Iamblichus.[34] Hermetic Egyptian priests might have guided their disciples through "alienation from the world, through the rebirth and to the heavenly ascent"[35] – in this way, initiates reversed the original descent of the soul. Priscillian's "evil prince," who manages this world, has been connected to the *Archons* of Gnosticism and Manichaeism, who are servants of evil; however, as Sylvain Sánchez points out, the Neoplatonic (and "Hermetic wise") Iamblichus defines the *archons* as masters of the world (*kosmokratores*) who rule the sublunary elements (*stoichéia*).[36] Iamblichus's similarities with Priscillian can also be appreciated in the Neoplatonic doctrines of the One, the different classes of deities, daimons, or angels inhabiting the three realms – air, earth, heaven – and the three orders – beginning, middle, and end.[37]

Augustine and other Christian authors emphasize Priscillian's link to astrology, particularly in its Egyptian variety. Even though astrology was developed in Babylon in the second half of the first millennium BCE, two Egyptian figures surfaced as the presumed founders and authorities of astrology: the king Nechepso and the priest Petosiris. As Beck explains, the works of Nechepso and Petosiris are Hermetic "because of the ultimate attribution of many […] texts to a revelation of Hermes."[38] References to astrology in Priscillian are among the first of their kind on Spanish soil. For instance, Pope Leo I (440–61), who had been informed of this doctrine by Thuribius, bishop of Astorga, condemned Priscillianist astrological beliefs. In his letter to Thuribius, Pope Leo mentions that the Priscillianists taught that the soul of man was a portion of the divine substance, and as punishment for sins committed in heaven it had been sent to earth. The devil, according to them, was the principle of evil, and the human body, which he formed in the womb of the mother, was essentially bad. The Priscillianists also preached that the stars influenced man's conduct, and the harmful influence of certain stars could be obviated only by the practice of astrology.[39] The negative view of the human body – presented as a prison or grave of the soul – was related to gnostic beliefs but also appears in the *Hermetica*.[40] For instance, in the thirteenth treatise of the *Corpus hermeticum*, Tat "is exhorted to turn into himself and to cleanse himself from the twelve tormenting

stellis homines colligatos ipsumque corpus nostrum secundum duodecim signa caeli esse compositum, sicut hi qui Mathematici vulgo appellantur, constituentes in capite Arietem, Taurum in cervice […]." Augustine, *De haeresibus ad Quodvultdeus*, 70.

34 On the descent of the soul, see especially John Finamore, *Iamblichus and the Theory of the Vehicle of the Soul* (Oxford: Oxford University Press, 1985).

35 Bull, *Tradition of Hermes*, 392.

36 Sylvaine Sánchez, *Priscillien, un chrétien non conformiste* (Leiden: Beauchesne, 2009), 207.

37 Sánchez, *Priscillien*, 252 and 291.

38 Roger Beck, *A Brief History of Ancient Astrology* (Hoboken: John Wiley & Sons, 2007), 18.

39 "[…] ut per magicarum artium profana secreta et mathematicorum vana mendacia, religionis fidem morumque rationem in potestate daemonum, et in effectu siderum collocarent." *Leonis Magni Epistolae XV.*

40 *Corpus Hermeticum* I.18, IV.6, and VII.2–3, cited in Copenhaver, *Hermetica*.

spirits of the material world, which are somehow connected with the twelve signs of the Zodiac."[41]

A century and a half after Priscillian's death, Pope John III convened the council of Braga (561 CE) to wipe out the remnants of this heresy. The council's canons decreed that if anyone who believes that human souls are subject to the movement of the stars by fate should be excommunicated, as well as anyone who believes that the twelve signs are distributed in each limb of the body.[42] These prohibitions ascribe to Priscillian the belief in fate – that is, the idea of *Heimarmene*, which the Hermetic writings adapted from the Stoics. As a Christian heresy, "Priscillianists shared in the early Christian confession of the defeat of astrological fate through Christ that was appropriated through baptism."[43]

The other important astrological belief associated with Priscillian and alluded to by the council of Braga was the *melothesia*. This practice involves assigning zodiac signs to different parts of the body, enabling the comprehension of afflictions and treatments based on their celestial significance. The practice of *melothesia* emerged with the development of the twelve signs of the zodiac in Babylonian astrology, which were later incorporated into astral medicine. However, it underwent significant advancement in Egypt, where *Melothesia* became part of the Hermetic medicinal astrology known as *Iatromathematika*. Bull points to an anonymous astrologer who talked about an *iatromathematical* book of Hermes in 379. This treatise dealt with maleficent influences and passions (πάθη) sent by the decans to the body parts they rule over – the decans were an Egyptian subdivision of the zodiac signs, each divided by three. Bull also points to *The Holy Book of Hermes to Asclepius*, a ritual manual for making finger-ring amulets that was written in Greek, likely in early Roman Egypt.[44] After a brief introduction – ascribed to Hermes Trismegistus and addressed to Asclepius – the treatise explains the doctrine of the zodiacal *melothesia* and then presents thirty-six entries on decans.[45] The *melothesia* was included among Manichaean beliefs, as it appears in the *Kephalaia*, a corpus of Manichaean literature translated into Coptic in Egypt in the fifth century.[46] The *melothesia* reflects the notion of the universal sympathy of the cosmos and its correspondence with the human body – also known as the theory of the macrocosm and microcosm, which is related to the Hermetic tradition and magic. The famous Andalusi book of magic *Ghāyat al-ḥakīm* includes lists of correspondences between body parts, flavours,

41 Roelof van den Broek, "Hermetic Literature I: Antiquity," in Wouter J. Hanegraaff (ed.), *Dictionary of Gnosis and Western Esotericism* (Leiden: Brill, 2005), 491.
42 In Marcelino Menéndez y Pelayo, *Historia de los heterodoxos españoles*, 4 vols (Madrid: La Editorial Católica, 1978), I, 109.
43 Hegedus, *Early Christianity*, 344.
44 Bull, *Tradition of Hermes*, 392–3.
45 See Spyros Piperakis, "Decanal Iconography and Natural Materials in the Sacred Book of Hermes to Asclepius," *Greek, Roman and Byzantine Studies* 57, no. 1 (2017): 136–8.
46 See Hendrik Schipper, "Melothesia: A Chapter of Manichaean Astrology in the West," in Johannes van Oort, Otto Wermelinger, and Gregor Wurst (eds), *Augustine and Manichaeism in the Latin West* (Leiden: Brill, 2001), 195–204.

locations, animals, plants, minerals, stones, constellations, and planets.[47] In fact, the *Ghāya* also refers to amulet-rings – Hermes owned one that was made through the alchemical procedure of solidifying mercury.[48]

Notwithstanding these Hermetic-related beliefs, Priscillian was condemned to death because of the accusation of practising magic. In Sulpicius Severus's fifth-century portrait of Priscillian, he affirmed that the heresiarch cultivated profane arts (*profanarum rerum scientia*), had practised magic since his youth (*magicas artes ab adolescentia*), and was accused of sorcery (*maleficium*).[49] This was why, in his letter to Ctesiphon, Jerome called Priscillian a follower of Egyptian doctrines and one who was also "very devoted to Zoroaster the magi" (*Zoroastris magi studiosissimum*).[50] Based on these grave testimonies, Priscillian was summoned to Trier (Germany) to be held accountable for his crimes. There he was accused, among other things, of enchanting the earth's fruits through spells and chants.[51] During the judicial examination Priscillian confessed "to his interest in magical studies, to having held nocturnal gatherings of [loose] women, and to having prayed naked."[52] In light of the evidence, Priscillian was charged with practising sorcery and committing heresy and was thereby executed.

Although we know that the sect used numerous texts, most of them are lost because the Church systematically destroyed them. For instance, Turibius of Astorga (d. 460), talked about many "secret" and "occult" treatises used by the Priscillianists.[53] However, a late-fifth-century codex, which reproduces eleven Priscillianist texts, was discovered in the University of Würzburg in 1885. According to Hegedus, this code "supports the evidence of Orosius concerning astrological doctrine in Priscillianist thought."[54] Chadwick compares the Priscillianists' astrological focus described by Orosius with a passage of the codex that defends the use of an amulet inscribed with the divine name in Hebrew, Latin, and Greek, and bearing the legend "rex regum et dominorum dominus."[55] As we will see below, amulets and talismans were distinct components of medieval Hermetic magic. It is otherwise difficult to determine to what extent these writings reflect authentic – or complete – Priscillian doctrine because they were written to defend Priscillian from the Church's accusations. Yet as Menéndez Pelayo argued, it should not be necessary "to insist on the importance of astrology, magic, and theurgic procedures in Priscillian" because all testimonies agree on this, even preserved and exculpatory testimonies from Priscillian's time.[56]

47 See Liana Saif, "The Cows and the Bees: Arabic Sources and Parallels for Pseudo-Plato's *Liber Vaccae* (*Kitab Al-Nawamis*)," *Journal of the Warburg and Courtauld Institutes* 79, no. 1 (2016): 11.

48 *Ghāya* III.7, 221.

49 In Hegedus, *Early Christianity*, 350.

50 In Hegedus, *Early Christianity*, 345.

51 Menéndez y Pelayo, *Historia* I.VIII, 132.

52 Chadwick, *Priscillian*, 139.

53 Menéndez y Pelayo, *Historia* I.V, 114.

54 Hegedus, *Early Christianity*, 343.

55 In Hegedus, *Early Christianity*, 350. See Chadwick, *Priscillian*, 202. On possible Priscillianist talismans found in Spain, see Menéndez y Pelayo, *Historia* I.VI, 120.

56 Menéndez y Pelayo, *Historia* I.VI, 120.

Thus, these testimonies from important religious authorities connect Priscillian's beliefs with Egypt and the Near East and characterize him as a practitioner of disciplines closely associated with Hermes, such as magic and astrology. We cannot say that Priscillianism was a Hermetic doctrine, but it is likely that Priscillian's beliefs and practices paved the way for Hermes's doctrines in the following centuries.

Priscillianism was still alive and controversial when Isidore of Seville – one of the most conspicuous authorities of the Middle Ages – became the first Iberian author to mention Hermes Trismegistus. Isidore was a descendant of Hispano-Roman nobility on his father's side; his mother was probably from an important Visigoth family. Isidore cultivated himself by studying all kinds of ancient knowledge and was able to gain the patronage of the most learned Visigoth king of Hispania, Sisebut (612–21). His most significant work is the *Etymologies* (*c.* 634), an enormous encyclopedia of pagan and Christian antiquity that systematizes all branches of knowledge. Magic, astrology, and Near Eastern doctrines occupy a significant place in his works. According to Fontaine, Isidore's oeuvre is steeped with astrological ideas, which can be explained by his intellectual curiosity, the scrupulous respect he had for his authors, and the atmosphere of Baetica where he lived and where commercial and cultural relationships with Eastern peoples had long existed.[57] King Sisebut dedicated the *Carmen de luna* (*Song of the moon*), "ascribed to the Hellenistic tradition of astronomical poetry," to Isidore, who responded with *De natura rerum* (*On the nature of things*) and *Liber rotarum* (*Book of the wheels*).[58]

Isidore coined the first Latin mention of the microcosm. The macrocosmic-microcosmic connection can be found throughout Isidore's works, but its richest expression is found in *Sententiae libri tres* and the *Etymologies*. In its Greek form, the term had already appeared in the *Liber de diffinitione*, a Latin work attributed to Boethius or Marius Victorinus, which says: "*ἄνθρωπος εστί μικρόκοσμός τις, id est homo est minor mundus*" ("man is a small world").[59] But in the *Etymologies* Isidore was the first to transliterate the Greek word in a Latin context and not just give its Latin equivalent: "But just as this proportion in the universe comes from the revolution of the spheres, so too in the *microcosm* it is so powerful beyond the voice that without its perfection, man, lacking harmony, does not exist" (my emphasis).[60] Fontaine sees the influence of Roman schools of philosophy, like Stoicism and the Church Fathers, as well as oriental astrology, in Isidore's ideas about celestial phenomena. As a bishop and canonist, Isidore had to come to terms with the consequences of Priscillianism,

57 Jacques Fontaine, "Isidore de Séville et l'astrologie," *Revue des études latines* 31 (1953): 271 and 289–94.

58 See Helena de Carlos Villamarín, "Achegamento a poesía de epoca Visigoda: a poesía de Tema Científico," in Eva María Díaz Martínez and Juan Casas Rigall (eds), *Iberia cantat: estudios sobre poesía Hispánica medieval*, 9 (Santiago: Universidade de Santiago de Compostela, 2002), 12–13; and Juan Vernet and Julio Samsó, "The Development of Arabic Science in Andalucia," in Roshdi Rashed (ed.), *Encyclopedia of the History of Arabic Science* (Abingdon: Routledge, 1996), 245.

59 Fontaine, "Isidore de Séville," 283.

60 "Sed haec ratio quemadmodum in mundo est ex volubilitate circulorum, ita et in microcosmo in tantum praeter vocem valet, ut sine ipsius perfectione etiam homo symphoniis carens non constet." Isidore, *Etymologies* III.xxiii.2.

the remaining astrological beliefs among the population of Baetica, and the infiltration of astrological practices into the hierarchy of the Visigoth Church; however, he was also fascinated with astrology as part of the ancient wisdom of antiquity.[61]

Isidore's *Etymologies* also includes several references to Hermes or Mercurius Trismegistus, expressing both positive and negative views. Talking about "the originators of Laws" (*De auctoribus legum*), Isidore affirms that "Mercurius Trismegistus was the first to give laws to the Egyptians,"[62] and places him with other celebrated legislators, such as Moses, Solon, and Lycurgus. Isidore could have taken this information from the *Divinae institutiones* by Lactantius (*c.* 250–325 CE), who was "the main champion of the *Hermetica* among Christians."[63] Isidore also provides an etymology for Hermes, "named after the Greek term *ἑρμηνεία*: 'interpretation' in Greek, in Latin 'interpreter'; on account of his power and knowledge of many arts he is called Trismegistus, that is, thrice great [*termaximus*]."[64]

This etymology might come from Augustine's *The City of God*,[65] or from Lactantius.[66] Yet Isidore adds something intriguing: "They imagine him with a dog's head, they say, because among all animals the dog is considered the most intelligent and acute of any species."[67] I think Isidore refers to, or is confused by, Hermanubis, a syncretic deity with a polytheophoric name – the assimilation of Hermes and the Egyptian god Anubis – who is depicted with a dog's head. As Benaisa explains, even though Hermes was traditionally associated with Thoth, "his function as psychopompos encouraged his association with Anubis."[68] Therefore, the quote from Isidore is further evidence of how Near Eastern religious syncretism reached Spain.

These two quotations about Hermes/Mercury contrast with the noticeable inclusion of Hermes/Mercury in one of the most famous sections of the *Etymologies*, "On the Magicians."[69] In late antiquity, the magi, originally Persian priests, had evolved to include all kinds of sages, sorcerers, diviners, poisoners, astrologers, and fraudsters. In this section, Isidore classifies all magicians and names several famous ones. He starts with Zoroaster[70] – with whom Jerome associated Priscillian – and Hermes/Mercury is not far behind.

61 Fontaine, "Isidore de Séville," 294–7.

62 "Mercurius Trimegistus primus leges Aegyptiis tradidit." *Etymologies* V.i.2.

63 *Divinae institutiones* I.6.2–3, cited in Copenhaver, *Hermetica*, xxxi.

64 "Hermes autem Graece dicitur APO TES ERMENEIAS, Latine interpres; qui ob virtutem multarumque artium scientiam Trimegistus, id est ter maximus nominatus est." *Etymologies* VIII.xi.49.

65 Augustine, *Civitate Dei* VII. xiv and XVIII.viii, respectively.

66 *Divinae institutiones* I.7.2.

67 "Cur autem eum capite canino fingunt, haec ratio dicitur, quod inter omnia animalia canis sagacissimum genus et perspicax habeatur." *Etymologies* VIII.xi.49.

68 Amin Benaisa, "The Onomastic Evidence for the God Hermanubis," in T. Gagos (ed.), *Proceedings of the Twenty-Fifth International Congress of Papyrology* (Ann Arbor: University of Michigan Press, 2010), 67–8.

69 "De magi." *Etymologies* VIII.ix.

70 *Etymologies* VIII.ix.1.

According to Thorndike, Isidore identifies magic and divination in this section.[71] However, Klingshirn has responded that although Isidore places magicians and diviners under the general heading of magi and explicitly included divination among their arts (VIII.ix.2–3), he also took pains to organize the chapter in such a way as to distinguish magicians – who performed occult actions (VIII.ix.4–10) – from diviners – who provided occult knowledge (VIII.ix.14–29). According to Klingshirn, Isidore not only differentiates between magicians and diviners but also adds the category of "boundary-crossers" between them. This group includes necromancers and hydromancers, practitioners of "magical divination" (VIII.ix.11–12), enchanters (*incantatores*, VIII.ix.15), those whose incantations summon demons for divination (VIII.ix.11), and those who use amulets containing curse-charms (VIII.ix.30).[72]

Among the first class of magi – magicians per se – we can identify another three subcategories, and I consider worth noting that Mercury/Hermes is included in all of them: 1) those who perform illusions (*praestigium*), such as the pharaoh's magicians, Moses, Circe, and the Arcadians; 2) those who raise the dead, such as the Virgilian Massylian witches, the biblical witch of Endor, and Mercury/Hermes; and 3) those who do evil (*malefici*, "witches"). The most renowned representative of the first category is Mercury, because "he is said to have first invented illusion [*praestigium*]," which "is called illusion, because it dulls the acuteness of the eyes."[73] Regarding the second category, Isidore quotes from *Against Symmachus* (1.90) by the Hispano-Roman poet Prudentius (348–410 CE):

> "It is said that [Mercury] brought perished souls to the light by the power of a wand that he held, but condemned others to death," and a little later he adds, "For with a magic murmur you know how to summon faded shapes and enchant sepulchral ashes. In the same way, he knows the harmful art: how to deprive others of life."[74]

This last sentence clearly puts Mercury in the third category of magi, the evil-doers. Since the *Etymologies* became one of the most popular books of the Middle Ages, Isidore's classification of mages and kinds of magic was extremely influential. During the twelfth century, Isidore's *Etymologies* remained the renowned encyclopedic work of the medieval era.[75] Porreca suggests that the medieval identification of the god Mercury and Hermes Trismegistus could be ascribable to their proximity in the *Etymologies* and mentions several authors who were influenced by Isidore's depiction

71 Lynn Thorndike, *A History of Magic and Experimental Science: During the First Thirteen Centuries of Our Era* (New York: Columbia University Press, 1923), 1: 628–9.

72 William E. Klingshirn, "Isidore of Seville's Taxonomy of Magicians and Diviners," *Traditio* 58, (2003): 62–3.

73 "Praestigium vero Mercurius primus dicitur invenisse. Dictum autem praestigium, quod praestringat aciem oculorum." *Etymologies* VIII.ix.33.

74 "Prudentius quoque de Mercurio sic ait (1 con. Symmach. 90): 'Traditur extinctas sumpto moderamine virgae in lucem revocasse animas, ast alios damnasse neci.' Et post paululum adiecit: 'Murmure nam magico tenues excire figuras, atque sepulchrales scite incantare favillas. Vita itidem spoliare alios ars noxia novit.'" *Etymologies*. VIII.ix.8.

75 Charles Haskins, *The Renaissance of the Twelfth Century* (Cambridge: Harvard University Press, 1927), 81.

of Hermes.[76] When Latin translators were seeking a classical Latin equivalent to the Arabic *ṭilasm* (talisman), they sometimes used *prestigium*, a word Isidore relates to Mercury. Thus, in the twelfth century, Adelard of Bath translated a lost book of talismans by the famous Ṭhābit Ibn Qurra and called it *Liber prestigiorum*, which in several manuscripts adds *Mercurii* (of Mercury) or *secundum Ptolomeum et Hermetem* (according to Ptolemy and Hermes) to the title; likewise, in his translation of the pseudo-Ptolemian *Centiloquium*, Hugo de Santalla rendered talisman as *prestigium*.[77] Santalla was particularly interested in finding categories of divination that used the four elements described by Isidore in the *Etymologies*: "aeromantia," "piromantia," "idromantia," and "geomantia" – which he identified with Arabic sand-divination.[78]

Development of Hermetic Knowledge in al-Andalus

When Muslim conquerors defeated the Visigoth kingdom in 711 CE, the new society they created was, in its initial stages, far removed from the cultural brilliance that al-Andalus would reach centuries later. Since few learned men arrived with the Muslim troops, the persistence of Latin culture extended until at least the rule of ʿAbd al-Raḥmān II (822–52), when Andalusi culture began to blossom, and some Visigoth scientific productions and practices survived until the eleventh century, in particular Visigoth medicine – often practised by Christians.[79] This surviving Latin science was embodied by Isidore's *Etymologies* and *De natura rerum*.[80] Astrology was also among these sciences, rooted in Visigoth traditions, that the Muslim conquerors inherited. The known history of astrology in al-Andalus starts when Amīr Hishām I (788–96) summoned the astrologer al-Ḍabbī from Algeciras to Córdoba to predict the length of his rule. Algeciras, located at the southern end of the Iberian Peninsula, had contact with cultures along the other Mediterranean shores for centuries and was considered a centre of astrology. Al-Ḍabbī used a basic astrological procedure embedded in a Latin tradition: *ṭarīqat aḥkām al-ṣulūb* (system of the crosses).[81] This system is well known thanks to the *Libro de las cruzes* (*Book of the crosses*), which Alfonso the Wise would translate in the thirteenth century. Samsó affirms that this text is "one more item in the long series of contacts between Isidorian-Latin and Arabic culture in Muslim Spain."[82]

76 David Porreca, "Hermes Mercurio Trismegisto en el 1300," in Valeria Buffon and Claudia D'Amico (eds), *Hermes Platonicus. Hermetismo y platonismo en el Medioevo y la Modernidad temprana* (Santa Fe: Universidad Nacional del Litoral, 2016), 18–19 and 26–7.

77 Charles Burnett, "Ṭhābit Ibn Qurra the Ḥarrānian on Talismans and the Spirits of the Planets," *La corónica: A Journal of Medieval Hispanic Languages, Literatures, and Cultures* 36, no. 1 (2007): 18–19.

78 Burnett, "Establishment of Medieval Hermeticism," 134.

79 Vernet and Samsó, "Development of Arabic Science," 249.

80 Miquel Forcada, "Astronomy, Astrology and the Sciences of the Ancients in Early al-Andalus (2nd/8th–3rd/9th Centuries)," *Zeitschrift für Geschichte der Arabisch-Islamischen Wissenschaften* 16 (2007): 4–6.

81 Forcada, "Astronomy," 4.

82 Vernet and Samsó, "Development of Arabic Science," 244.

After al-Ḍabbī, there is evidence that a group of astrologers were active in the Córdoban court during the reigns of al-Ḥakam I (796–822), ʿAbd al-Raḥmān II, and Muḥammad (852–86). The activities of this group – including suggestions that they dabbled in the Hermetic sciences – can be reconstructed thanks to the recent availability of the first part of the second book of the *Muqtabis* by Ibn Ḥayyān (d. 1076), the most significant chronicle of early Andalusian history,[83] and to the *Treatise on Stars*, written by the *faqīh* and polymath ʿAbd al-Malik b. Ḥabīb (d. 853), one of the earliest astrological treatises written in al-Andalus.[84]

Their activities are linked to the beginning of al-Andalus's cultural development and a new wave of Eastern influences I associate with Hermes Trismegistus's "second coming" to the Iberian Peninsula. This cultural flourishing was the result of earlier events in the east. After defeating the Umayyads in 750 CE, in 762 the Abbasid dynasty established its capital in newly founded Baghdad. The Abbasids undertook a vigorous process of translation, especially from Greek and Syriac, and adopted many cultural traditions from the Persians, whom they had just defeated.[85] Van Bladel has studied how the figure of Hermes and his traditions developed and spread due to this cultural environment.[86] The "last of the Umayyads," the future ʿAbd al-Raḥmān I (r. 756–88), escaped the massacre of his family and fled to the Iberian Peninsula. There, helped by his family's clients (*mawālī*), he founded an independent emirate.[87] Despite military successes, during his reign and in the decades that followed, al-Andalus was "little more than a rural society and a cultural desert."[88]

However, between the rules of al-Ḥakam I and ʿAbd al-Raḥmān II the court imported a huge amount of cultural and institutional practices from Baghdad, including a wealth of books. This process has been called the "orientalization of al-Andalus."[89] The goal of this "baghdadization" was to strengthen the bases of their own government by emulating the era's most successful empire.[90] In addition to being a successful warrior, al-Ḥakam I was also a learned ruler who wrote poetry and brought Eastern sophistication and urbanite glamour to al-Andalus – personified by the musician-courtesan Ziryāb, whose relevance the historian

[83] See Luis Molina Martínez, "Ibn Ḥayyān," *Real Academia de la Historia: DB-e*, available online at: https://dbe.rah.es/biografias/16692/Ibn-hayyan (last accessed September 19, 2022).

[84] Due to lack of space, for the available manuscripts, facsimiles, and editions of the different parts of the *Muqtabis* and the *Treatise on Stars* I refer to Forcada, "Astronomy," 2–3.

[85] See Dimitri Gutas, *Greek Thought, Arabic Culture* (New York: Routledge, 1998).

[86] Kevin van Bladel, *The Arabic Hermes: From Pagan Sage to Prophet of Science* (Oxford: Oxford University Press, 2009).

[87] On the Umayyad dynasty's arrival and consolidation in al-Andalus, see Eduardo Manzano Moreno, *Conquistadores, emires y califas: Los omeyas y la formación de al-Andalus* (Barcelona: Crítica, 2006), 189–238.

[88] Forcada, "Astronomy," 7.

[89] For this process, the standard study is Mahmūd ʿAlī Makkī, *Ensayo sobre las aportaciones orientales en la España musulmana y su influencia en la formación de la cultura hispano-árabe* (Madrid: Instituto de Estudios Islámicos, 1968).

[90] Forcada, "Astronomy," 7.

Ibn Ḥayyān emphasizes.[91] According to Soravia, Ibn Ḥayyān makes Ziryāb the "semi-historical/semi-mythological hero of an authentic pedagogical epic in 'Abd al-Raḥmān II's times" – someone who transformed every aspect of the court, from etiquette to dressing and even diet.[92] Although al-Ḥakam I died just before Ziryāb arrived in Córdoba, his heir allocated vast financial resources to Ziryāb and his cultural dynamization activities.[93] In this way, al-Andalus benefitted from the earlier translation movement in Baghdad, where Hermetic sciences, such as alchemy, magic, and astrology, had been prominent; thus, Hermes Trismegistus became part of the cultural advances al-Ḥakam I imported from Baghdad. Ibn Ḥayyān narrates how al-Ḥakam I educated his heir ʿAbd al-Raḥmān II

> in the most elevated sciences until he succeeded in the knowledge of wisdom and in reading the treatises of the ancients. He sent the Algeciran ʿAbbās b. Nāṣiḥ to Iraq with a substantial amount of money to search for and copy ancient books, and he brought him the *Kitāb al-Zīj*, the *Qānūn*, the *Shindhind* and the *Arkand*, the *Mūsīqā* and the rest of treatises on philosophy and science, books on medicine and others of the ancients as well. 'Abd al-Raḥmān was the first to introduce them in al-Andalus and made them known to its inhabitants. He himself studied them [...] obtaining a thorough knowledge.[94]

These are reminiscent of Alfonso the Wise's cultural deeds; four centuries later, he disseminated the same kinds of books to his Christian subjects. The list of books cited by Ibn Ḥayyān is representative of the mix of Greek and Oriental sciences brought to al-Andalus from Baghdad, a blend that echoes the Hellenistic world in which Hermes was born. The *Qānūn* is a version of Ptolemy's *Handy Tables* produced by Theon of Alexandria, whereas the *Shindhind* and *Arkand* are Hindu astronomical works.[95] These books would become part of the legendary library of Córdoba. Other fragments of *Muqtabis II/1* demonstrate ʿAbd al-Raḥmān II's enthusiasm for Hermetic-related sciences, such as astrology, and reveal him to be a true believer: "He was knowledgeable of [...] philosophical sciences, of the computing of the planet's positions, of the science of astronomy, and of upper influences [*al-āthār al-ʿulwiyya*]."[96]

Eastern sciences also reached al-Andalus through the Near Eastern scholars who moved there. The aforementioned musician Ziryāb left Baghdad with his whole library and was extremely well-educated in the ancient sciences, especially astrology.[97] Another immigrant was the physician al-Ḥarrānī, about whom not much is known, but whose name "opens up a wide range of possibilities regarding the transmission of science," because "he was surely knowledgeable of the materials that made up the Sabian culture of Ḥarrān, which included worship of the stars,

91 Bruna Soravia, "Une Histoire de la 'Fitna.' Autorité et légitimité dans le 'Muqtabis' d'Ibn Hayyan," *Cuadernos de Madinat al-Zahra* 5 (2004): 86.
92 Soravia, "Une Histoire de la 'Fitna,'" 87.
93 See Manzano Moreno, *Conquistadores*, 306–8.
94 Ibn Ḥayyān, *Muqtabis II/1*, 139r, cited in Forcada, "Astronomy," 10.
95 Forcada, "Astronomy," 21.
96 Ibn Ḥayyān, *Muqtabis II/1*, 140r., cited in Forcada, "Astronomy," 10.
97 Ibn Ḥayyān, *Muqtabis II/1*, 150v, cited in Forcada, "Astronomy," 24.

magic, talismans, Hermetic doctrines and so on."[98] As we will see below, al-Ḥarrānī's grandsons traveled to the east between 941 and 962 and studied with the son of the famous Ḥarrānian Thābit Ibn Qurra; for this reason it has been suggested that they brought talismanic magic techniques back with them to al-Andalus.[99]

ʿAbd al-Raḥmān II gathered a circle of astrologers around him, and he consulted with them before making important decisions. One of them was ʿAbbās b. Firnās, who, according to the *Muqtabis*, was an expert in alchemy and magic, specifically in a discipline called *Ṣāḥib al-nīranjāt*.[100] The *nīranjāt* are a category of charms specifically related to a genre of books called the Pseudo-Aristotelian *Hermetica*.[101] We will see how these books and the *nīranjāt* are constantly mentioned in the Andalusi magical treatise the *Ghāya*. ʿAbbās b. Firnās was said to have practised magic and alchemy, which subjected him to suspicion and indictments for heresy.[102] He also wrote astronomical poems that referenced the lunar mansions, which were not known to the Greeks but were related to several Eastern astronomical traditions, and they also appear in the *Ghāya*.[103] The last noticeable member of this group of astrologers/poets is Yaḥyā al-Ghazāl, whose poems include references to the Neoplatonic doctrines of union with the One and bear a resemblance to the famous Muslim philosopher al-Kindī's (d. 873) epistles about the soul.[104] In fact, al-Kindī was also inspired by Hermetic doctrines, which he probably received through Ḥarrānian traditions.[105]

The members of this network of learned courtiers/astrologers have also been labelled as *udabāʾ*, practitioners of *adab*, the difficult-to-define epitome of Muslim education and culture that was introduced into al-Andalus through this process of orientalization. I will explain this concept in Chapter Two, as well as its occasional relationship with Hermetic traditions. Ibn Ḥayyān uses the biographies of famous *udabāʾ*, such as the abovementioned ʿAbbās b. Nāṣiḥ, ʿAbbās b. Firnās, and al-Ghazāl,

98 Forcada, "Astronomy," 24.

99 Vernet and Samsó, "Development of Arabic Science," 249. On the Ḥarrānians, see the comprehensive study by Tamara M. Green, *The City of the Moon God: Religious Traditions of Ḥarrān* (Leiden: Brill, 1992). Van Bladel (*Arabic Hermes*, 64–118) questions the Ḥarrānian origin of many Arab Hermetic sources, including those who relate them to Sabaean traditions, and he goes against the opinion of Arabists such as Pingree and Cottrell. However, a large number of references to Ḥarrān and the Sabaeans that are related to Hermetic materials go unmentioned by Van Bladel, such as some in the *Ghāya* and other Andalusi works. On the influence of Ḥarrān in al-Andalus, see Maribel Fierro, "Plants, Mary the Copt, Abraham, Donkeys and Knowledge: Again on Bāṭinism during the Umayyad Caliphate in al-Andalus," in Hinrich Biesterfeldt and Verena Klemm (eds), *Differenz und Dynamik im Islam, Festschrift für Heinz Halm zum 70* (Geburtstag, Würzburg: Ergon Verlag, 2012), 136–7.

100 Ibn Ḥayyān, *Muqtabis II*/1, 130v–31r., cited in Forcada "Astronomy," 24.

101 See Charles Burnett, "*Nīranj*: A Category of Magic (Almost) Forgotten in the Latin West," in C. Leonardi and F. Santi (eds), *Natura, scienze, e società medievali: Studi in onore di Agostino Paravicini Bagliani* (Florence: SISMEL, 2008), 37–66.

102 Ibn Ḥayyān, *Muqtabis II*/1, 130v–32r., cited in Forcada, "Astronomy," 39.

103 Forcada, "Astronomy," 33.

104 Forcada, "Astronomy," 43–4.

105 See C. Genequand, "Platonism and Hermetism in al-Kindī's *Fi al-Nafs*," *Zeitschrift für Geschichte der arabisch-islamischen Wissenschaften* 4 (1987), 14–16.

to describe a spirited intellectual life and to characterize *adab* as a community developer.[106] Ibn Ḥayyān points to a model of the cultivated courtesan that combined the sophistication of the *udabā'* with knowledge of the "science of the ancients," including astrology and magic. This model was sponsored by Andalusi rulers to enhance the culture of the emirate; a model that, I suggest, is not so dissimilar from the one that Alfonso would pursue for his own court.

ʿAbd al-Raḥmān II was succeeded by his son Muḥammad I (852–86), whose rule was plagued with war and rebellions. This turbulence would grow under al-Mundhir (886–8) and ʿAbd Allah (888–912), but ʿAbd al-Raḥmān III (912–61) established a new era for al-Andalus by declaring an independent caliphate in 929. This peak of Andalusi power coincided with two figures, Ibn Masarra (883–931) and Maslama b. Qāsim al-Qurṭubī (906–64) – author of the *Ghāya* – who were connected with *bāṭinism*, Islamic occultism – the field of those who look for the *bāṭin* (inner, esoteric) meaning of sacred texts. As Forcada points out, these figures' thought might have "bloomed in the breeding ground prepared by Yaḥyā al-Ghazāl, Abbās b. Firnās and their fellows."[107] In her study of *bāṭinism* during this period, Fierro highlights that the followers of the heterodox philosopher Ibn Masarra were prosecuted after his death, and this could have been one of the reasons why the author of the *Ghāya* hid his identity.[108]

The famous historian Ibn Khaldūn (d. 1406) regarded the *Ghāya* as "the best and most complete treatise on magic ever written in Arabic."[109] Like many other learned men of his time, Ibn Khaldūn believed that it had been written by the famous Andalusi astronomer Maslama al-Majrīṭī (d. *c.* 1004), because most manuscripts attributed it to him. This erroneous identification lasted until Fierro pointed to Maslama b. Qāsim al-Qurṭubī as the probable author,[110] and most contemporary specialists agree with her. Al-Qurṭubī was a *muwallad*[111] who, in his early years, followed the path to become a Sunni scholar in al-Andalus, which included studying with Maliki jurists and traditionalists. Al-Qurṭubī undertook a trip to the east prior to 932, which allowed him to visit the most important Islamic sites and study with renowned teachers.[112] Al-Qurṭubī returned to al-Andalus after 936 and became blind

106 Soravia, "Une Histoire de la Fitna," 87.

107 Forcada, "Astronomy," 38.

108 Maribel Fierro, "*Bāṭinism* in al-Andalus. Maslama b. Qāsim al-Qurṭubī (d. 353/964), author of the *Rutbat al-Ḥakīm* and the *Ghāyat al-Ḥakīm* (*Picatrix*)," *Studia Islamica* 84 (1996): 103–8.

109 In Godefroid de Callataÿ and Sébastien Moureau, "Towards the Critical Edition of the *Rutbat Al-Ḥakīm*: A Few Preliminary Observations," *Arabica* 62 (2015): 386.

110 For detailed arguments, as well as al-Qurṭubī's biographical data, see Fierro, "*Bāṭinism* in al-Andalus."

111 As Fierro reminds us, "the Muwalladūn were Arabized indigenous inhabitants of the Iberian Peninsula, whose Islamization came about as a result of that Arabization." Maribel Fierro, "*Mawālī* and *Muwalladūn* in al-Andalus," in Monique Bernards and John Nawas (eds), *Patronate and Patronage in Early and Classical Islam* (Leiden: Brill), 239.

112 For the details of this transformative *riḥla* (trip), see Godefroid de Callataÿ and Sébastien Moureau, "A Milestone in the History of Andalusī Bāṭinism: Maslama b. Qāsim al-Qurṭubī's Riḥla in the East," *Intellectual History of the Islamicate World* 5 (2017): 86–117.

shortly thereafter. Back in Córdoba, he had many students, including the prince ʿAbd Allāh. According to his biographers, al-Qurṭubī wrote works on women, *ḥadīth*, and the casting of lots, and he also translated a book on the interpretation of dreams, and another on religious matters by Dhūl-Nūn al-Miṣrī (d. *c.* 862), an Egyptian mystic, alchemist, and *bāṭinī*. Al-Qurṭubī's two most important works are the *Rutbat al-ḥakīm* (*The rank of the sage*), the first known book of alchemy written in the Iberian Peninsula, and the *Ghāyat al-ḥakīm*, which focuses on magic.

The *Ghāya* is primarily a work about astral magic; that is, how to perform magic through rituals and other procedures that manipulate the stars' influence on terrestrial things. The principal tools of the magician are talismans and the charms known as *nīranj*.[113] Ibn al-Faraḍī indicates that al-Qurṭubī mastered enchantments and *nīranjāt* (*ṣāḥib ruqan wa-nīranjāt*).[114] Al-Qurṭubī affirms that he looked at 224 books while composing the *Ghāya*,[115] and he masterfully quotes the most important Arab sources on astrology, magic, and alchemy up to the tenth century. The sources include:[116] 1) the pseudo-Aristotelian *Hermetica*; 2) *Rasāʾil Ikhwān al-Ṣafāʾ* (*Epistles of the Brethren of Purity*), a collection of about fifty letters-treatises, probably compiled in Basra between the ninth and tenth centuries by a Shiʿi-Ismaʿili esoteric brotherhood of philosophers-scribes, that al-Qurṭubī might have brought to al-Andalus;[117] 3) the doctrines of the Sabaeans of Ḥarrān, the city of pagan star worshippers – Hermes was their prophet; 4) other important authorities on the sciences of the ancients, such as the astrologer Abū Maʿshar,[118] Jābir b. Ḥayyān, the legendary compiler of alchemical books, and Ibn Waḥshiyyah, the author of *Kitāb al-filāḥa al-nabaṭiyya* (*Book of Nabatean agriculture*, a famous treatise on agriculture, astrology, and magic).[119]

113 Burnett, "*Nīranj*."

114 Fierro, "*Bāṭinism* in al-Andalus," 84.

115 *Ghāya* III.5, 182.

116 On the sources and intellectual background of the *Ghāya*, see David Pingree, "Some of the Sources of the *Ghāyat Al-Hakīm*," *Journal of the Warburg and Courtauld Institutes* 43 (1980): 1–15; Liana Saif, *The Arabic Influences on Early Modern Occult Philosophy* (New York: Palgrave Macmillan, 2015), 27–45; Liana Saif, "A Preliminary Study of the Pseudo-Aristotelian Hermetica: Texts, Context, and Doctrines," *Al-ʿUṣūr al-Wusṭā* 29 (2021): 20–80; and Liana Saif, "From *Ġāyat Al-Ḥakīm* to *Šams al-maʿārif*: Ways of Knowing and Paths of Power in Medieval Islam," *Arabica* 64, nos 3–4 (2017): 299–309; Burnett, "Ṭhābit Ibn Qurra," 13–18; and Burnett, "*Nīranj*."

117 On this tradition and its relationship with the *Ghāyat al-Ḥakīm*, including complete and recent bibliography, see Godefroid de Callataÿ, "Magia en al-Andalus. Rasāʾil ijwān al-Ṣafāʾ, Rutbat al-ḥakīm y Ghāyat al-ḥakīm (Picatrix)," *Al-Qanṭara* 34 (2013): 297–344.

118 On Abū Maʿshar, see the editions of his books by David Pingree, *The Thousands of Abū Maʿshar* (London: Warburg Institute, 1968); Abū Maʿshar, *The Abbreviation of The Introduction to Astrology: Together with the Medieval Latin Translation of Adelard of Bath*, trans. Charles Burnett, Keiji Yamamoto, and Michio Yano (Leiden: Brill, 1994); Abū Maʿshar, *The Great Introduction to Astrology by Abū Maʿšar*, eds Keiji Yamamoto and Charles Burnett, with an edited Greek version by David Pingree, 2 vols (Leiden: Brill, 2019).

119 Even though, as Hämeen-Anttila affirms, "there are some undeniable similarities between the Hermetic tradition and the Nabatean Agriculture," they are not conclusive enough to

Many of the Eastern authors that al-Qurṭubī used recognize the aforementioned concept of an "oriental Plato," who transmitted the revelation of the ancient cultures he had access to during his travels.[120] Like their Hellenistic predecessors, Arab philosophers embraced older and foreign traditions (Indian, Sassanid) as receptacles of the ancient wisdom for which they were searching.[121] As Saif has demonstrated, learned Arab men did not limit themselves to translating and transmitting Greek knowledge; they also elaborated on it and created a comprehensive system.[122] Muslim thinkers continued the process of reconciling Platonic, Aristotelian, and Stoic thought that had started in late antiquity. Thus, theories such as the Neoplatonic microcosm-macrocosm, Aristotelian causality, and Stoic *sympatheia* were harmonized by Arab philosophers. Traces of all these theories are present in the *Ghāya*.[123] Not surprisingly, the *Ghāya* mentions Hermes Trismegistus as an authority on magic and astrology, and more or less ambiguously associates him with the planet Mercury. Hermes and Mercury are both connected to charms for the specific use of the *kuttāb* (scribes working for the caliphal administration) and the *udabā*ʾ (specialists in *adab* and learned courtiers, such as the circle of astrologers mentioned above).[124]

Hermes Trismegistus and Medieval Networks of Translators

The cultural glory of the Caliphate of Córdoba reached the height of its splendor with al-Ḥakam II, whom the chronicles say gathered hundreds of thousands of volumes in his library. If this were true, the number of books in the libraries of Córdoba exceeded that of all the other libraries in Europe combined. But the Caliphate collapsed in 1031 after a period of turbulence, or *fitna*, which led to it being divided into various independent, Muslim-ruled principalities, the *ṭāʾifa* kingdoms. These kingdoms competed among themselves, both militarily and culturally, and often for the same skilled men and scholars, regardless of their religion. Lacking military power, they hired Christian mercenaries – such as the celebrated Cid Campeador – and also patronized famous poets, artisans, and scholars. Some weaker *ṭāʾifa* kingdoms, along with their libraries, soon fell into the hands of Christian conquerors. The fall of the *Ṭāʾifa* of Toledo in 1085 had a dual symbolic meaning: it had been the capital of the "lost" Visigothic kingdom, and its libraries represented a significant part of the former Caliphate's richness.

---

warrant any final conclusions on a direct influence, see Jaakko Hämeen-Anttila, *The Last Pagans of Iraq. Ibn Waḥshiyyah and the Nabatean Agriculture* (Leiden: Brill, 2006), 171.

120 This idea is supported by Dan Attrell and David Porreca, Introduction to *Picatrix: A Medieval Treatise on Astral Magic,* trans. David Porreca and Dan Attrell (University Park: The Pennsylvania State University Press, 2019), 2.

121 See Walbridge, *Wisdom of the Mystic East,* 11–13.

122 Saif, *Arabic Influences,* 196. On the "Neoplatonic" Aristotle received in the Middle Ages, see John Marenbon, *Medieval Philosophy: An Historical and Philosophical Introduction* (New York: Routledge, 2006), 3.

123 See Saif, *Arabic Influences,* 3–45.

124 For these reasons, in an earlier work I argued that the *kuttāb* and *udabā*ʾ were the main addressees of the *Ghāya*. For these claims and further information on the *Ghāya*, see Udaondo Alegre, "If You Want to Pray to Mercury."

The lack of a powerful unified authority in Iberia created interesting cultural and political phenomena in which "political associations and power relations between Iberian domains manifest shifts in a malleable, polycentric formation comprised of interaction networks."[125] In this context, the Islamicate cultural landscape was encroached upon by a progressively stronger "Hispanicate" influence coming from the northern Christian kingdoms; however, these realignments cannot be reduced to a simple Christian–Muslim struggle, but rather, "reflected larger changes in the Islamicate world-system and in Europe." Economic and political influence from Europe in Spain was bolstered by religious groups such as Cluny and later Cîteaux.[126] At the end of the eleventh century, religious and political contact with France was prioritized thanks to the *Camino de Santiago* (pilgrimage road to Compostela).

In this environment, the cultural wealth of al-Andalus was first available to learned men from the peninsula, and then to erudite scholars from Europe who flocked there due to the promise of new and endless sources of knowledge; they soon created new networks of scholars or joined the existing ones. A network can be defined "as a series of decentralized, interconnected nodes that are adaptable and flexible rather than fixed and static"; nodes are significant, "not for their inherent characteristics or qualities, but because of their contribution to the network's goals."[127] This logic can be applied to networks of elite scholars from the three religions active on the peninsula during this turbulent period when political circumstances were in constant flux. Since no strong, hierarchized state controlled them, scholars benefitted from patrons and small leaders and were able to develop their own systematic goals. Since scholars from beyond the Pyrenees began to collaborate in a formidable translation process, the Arabs of Spain became "the principal source of the new learning for western Europe."[128] Burnett classifies some of these erudite teams' productions as Hermetic, as well as the sources with which they worked.[129] From the beginning of the translation process "we find the exact sciences inextricably mixed up with astrology and magic and their transmission hedged with language redolent of a mystery religion."[130] I am going to introduce some scholars who participated in this process, particularly those associated with Hermetic wisdom.

Hugo de Santalla was a prominent translator and part of a network of scholars operating within the Ebro River valley during the twelfth century. Although some of his works have been preserved, not much is known about his life, except that his

[125] Jean Dangler, *Edging Toward Iberia* (Toronto: University of Toronto Press, 2017), 93.

[126] Dangler, *Edging Toward Iberia*, 94

[127] Dangler, *Edging Toward Iberia*, 94.

[128] Charles Haskins *Studies in the History of Mediaeval Science* (Cambridge: Harvard University Press, 1924), 5. For information about the translation process, see the works by Burnett in the Bibliography.

[129] See Charles Burnett, "A Hermetic Programme of Astrology and Divination in mid-Twelfth-Century Aragon: The Hidden Preface in the *Liber novem iudicum*," in Charles Burnett and W. F. Ryan (eds), *Magic and the Classical Tradition* (London: Warburg Institute, 2006), 99–100.

[130] Charles Burnett, "The Translating Activity in Medieval Spain," in S. K. Jayyusi (ed.), *The Legacy of Muslim Spain* (Leiden: Brill,1992), 1038.

second name is probably a demonym from Galicia.[131] As Burnett points out, Santalla "made a point, above all, of translating works attributed to Hermes or depending on Hermes' authority."[132] The only addressee of his works was Michael, bishop of Tarazona from 1119–51. Michael established a centre of study in Tarazona to which diverse scholars were attracted.[133]

Close to Tarazona there is another town, now called Rueda de Jalón, which at that time hosted the Banū Hūd, a learned Arab dynasty who ruled the *ṭāʾifa* of Saragossa from 1038–1110. In 1110 the Banū Hūd were expelled from Saragossa by the Almoravids, a rigorous Berber dynasty of warrior monks who came to help defend the *ṭāʾifa* against the Christians but instead ended up conquering most of them for themselves. The Aragonese king Alfonso the Battler defeated the Almoravids, conquered Rueda de Jalón in 1118, but allowed the Banū Hūd to stay. There, Sayf al-Dawla, the last of the Banū Hūd, was the neighbour of Michael, bishop of Tarazona (only 55km away);[134] the two of them established a friendship and engaged in cultural exchange. Sayf al-Dawla brought part of the wondrous library his family had gathered in Zaragoza to Rueda de Jalón and offered some books to Bishop Michael; Hugo de Santalla would translate several of them, one of which was the *Astronomical Tables* of al-Khwārizmī (*c.* 780–850).

Santalla affirms that he found the original Arabic version of al-Khwārizmī's text in the library of Rueda de Jalón (*in Rotensi armario*) "among the more secret inner reaches of the library" (*inter secretiora bibliotece penetralia*).[135] Santalla's words suggest "a part of the library specially designated for non-Muslim sciences and magic," and that he "certainly wishes to foster the impression that he is passing on secret knowledge which must not be divulged to other than worthy individuals."[136] This keenness towards secrecy is also found in other prefaces by Hugo de Santalla; for instance, in that of the *Centiloquium* by Pseudo-Ptolemy – a book of astrological aphorisms – where Hugo advises his master "not to commit the secrets of such a great wisdom to somebody unworthy or to allow anyone who rejoices in the number of his books – rather than being pleased with the knowledge in them – to share in the secrets."[137]

As I mentioned above, there is a suggestive connection between Hugo de Santalla and Isidore of Seville. One of Santalla's goals was to find the four kinds of divination mentioned in the *Etymologies* within those Arabic books. There is a treatise on geomancy (divination through earth), which Santalla authored, that is based on a

131 In Galicia (north-western Spain) there are many small villages and towns called Santalla, which derives from a contraction of the popular saint, Santa Eulalia or Santa Olalla (in Galician).

132 Burnett, "Establishment of Medieval Hermeticism," 134.

133 Haskins, *Studies*, 68.

134 Until 1140, when he was forced to relinquish Rueda de Jalón in exchange for some lands near Toledo. Burnett "Translating Activity," 1041.

135 I translate the original Latin reproduced in Haskins, *Studies in Mediaeval Science*, 73.

136 Burnett, "Translating Activity," 1042.

137 "Ne tante sapiencie archana cuilibet indigno tractanda commictas et ne quemlibet participem adhibeas qui pocius gaudet librorum numero quam eorum delectetur artificio," cited in Haskins, *Studies*, 70.

work on Arabic sand divination by the unknown Tripolitan Alatrabulucus.[138] In this book's prologue, Burnett finds a reference to a "secret society of an intellectual elite" and "a special bond between men who have been privileged to receive God's gift or intuitive knowledge"; this bond would produce "a state of peace in human society [...] parallel to the bonds which govern and preserve the universe."[139] I suggest that Santalla refers to a network of learned men or "philosophers," blessed by God regardless of their religion – such as Bishop Michael, Sayf al-Dawla, Abraham Ibn Ezra, or himself – who shared knowledge with each other in the region around Tarazona. Thus, Vernet called the Ebro Valley the "nexus between East and West."[140]

An elite category of men are later described in this prologue as "wise men inclined to philosophizing" (*sapientes ad philosophandum pronos*) and "all the professors of philosophy" (*universos philosophie professores*). Their knowledge must be kept secret because, among the sages of antiquity there are reports of as many worthy as unworthy men who practise philosophy (*apud sapientium quamplurimus dignos et indignos in usu fuisse philosophorum antiquitas refert*); for this reason, Santalla only offers a small part of the wealth of wisdom gained from ancient wise men to his worthy contemporary philosophers (*ex priscorum opulentia huiusmodi munusculum adporto*).[141] Hermes Trismegistus is among those wise men of antiquity whose knowledge Hugo de Santalla is sharing with worthy philosophers. In the prologue of his treatise on spatulamancy (divination through the shoulder blades of sheep) Santalla affirms that Hermes was read (or chosen) among the Greeks (*aput Grecos Hermes fuisse legitur*).[142]

The most important of Santalla's translations is closely related to Hermes: *Hermetis Trimegesti liber de secretis naturae et occultis rerum causis ab Apollonio translatus* (*The book of Hermes Trismegistus on the secrets of nature and the occult causes of things translated from Apollonius*).[143] It is a translation of the *Sirr al-khalīqa wa-ṣanʿat al-ṭabīʿa* (*The secret of creation and the art of nature*), which probably had a lost Hellenistic original and was translated into Arabic from Greek or Syriac.[144] It includes the *Tabula smaragdina* (*Emerald table*), the most celebrated alchemical treatise. According to the text, Apollonius, the aforementioned legendary sage, found the *Tabula smaragdina* in the tomb of Hermes Trismegistus.[145] Burnett highlights how throughout this work there is an emphasis "on the idea of an underlying unity in nature and of bonds connecting every level of creation. For all things derive from one substance and one seed."[146] This translation, first into Latin, would long remain

138 Haskins, *Studies*, 77.
139 Burnett, "Translating Activity," 1043.
140 Juan Ginés Vernet, "El valle del Ebro como nexo entre Oriente y Occidente," *Butlletí de la Reial Acadèmia de Bones Lletres de Barcelona* 23 (1950): 249–86.
141 Original Latin in Haskins, *Studies*, 78. My translation.
142 Original Latin in Haskins, *Studies*, 79. My translation.
143 Cited in Haskins, *Studies*, 79–80.
144 Mohammad Karimi Zanjani Asl, "*Sirr al-Khalīqa* and Its Influence in the Arabic and Persianate World: ʿAwn b. al-Mundhir's Commentary and Its Unknown Persian Translation," *Al-Qantara* 37, no. 2 (2016): 442.
145 Asl, "*Sirr al-Khalīqa*," 443.
146 Burnett, "Translating Activity," 1043.

popular among aspiring alchemists. As we will see, Apollonius or Balinus (his Arabic nickname) would appear along with Hermes in many Latin and Castilian works.

Tudela, a town near Tarazona and Rueda de Jalón – all within Michael's bishopric – was the birthplace of two important Jewish scholars: the philosopher and poet Judah Halevi (1075–1141), and the abovementioned philosopher, astronomer, and biblical commentator Abraham Ibn Ezra (1089–1167). Ibn Ezra translated the *Astronomical Tables* of al-Khwārizmī into Hebrew. According to Haskins, it shares some parallels with Santalla's Latin translation.[147] This connection suggests the involvement of Jewish scholars in a network around this intellectual node of Tarazona. Like Santalla, Ibn Ezra frequently refers to Hermes Trismegistus in his works, but he calls him Enoch, the biblical character identified with Hermes since antiquity;[148] for instance, in one work Ibn Ezra affirms that "there are many things in Enoch's *Book of Secrets* whose reason is not clear to us."[149]

Other illustrious translators came from beyond the Pyrenees to work in the area; among them, the Istrian Hermann of Carinthia (d. after 1144) and the Englishman Robert of Ketton (*c.* 1110–60). Ketton became canon in Tudela, knew several of the same sources as Santalla, and perhaps had access to the library of the Banū Hūd – and most probably, Hermann and Santalla worked together.[150] In his main original work, a cosmogony called *De essentiis* (*On the essences*), Hermann of Carinthia cites the *Emerald Tablet* from the *Secret of Creation* – translated by Santalla – and mentions several other Hermetic works, including the *Asclepius*.[151] However, Hermann distinguishes between "the ancient oriental sage Hermes (associated with Persia and India) and Tri(s)megistus, the author of the Latin *Asclepius*," associated with Plato's wisdom.[152]

In the preface of *De essentiis*, addressed to his friend Ketton, Hermann notes that both have been working night and day on the "intimate treasures of the Arabs" (*intimis Arabum thesauris*) in the "inner sanctuaries of Minerva" (*adytis Minerve*), and Hermann is now considering whether it is appropriate to make the fruits of their research public.[153] Hermann is afraid of being as guilty as Numenius, who divulged the Eleusinian mysteries and consequently "saw the Eleusinian goddesses in a dream dressed as prostitutes available for use to all and sundry." However, the goddess Minerva reassures Hermann in another dream that "her attributes are not

147 Haskins, *Studies*, 74.

148 See Shlomo Sela, Introduction to *Abraham Ibn Ezra on Elections, Interrogations, and Medical Astrology*, ed. and trans. Shlomo Sela (Leiden: Brill, 2010), 20.

149 Book of Elections 5.5.1, in *Abraham Ibn Ezra on Elections*, 67.

150 Burnett, "Translating Activity," 1044.

151 See Charles Burnett, "Hermann of Carinthia and the *Kitāb al-Isṭamāṭīs*: Further Evidence for the Transmission of Hermetic Magic," *Journal of the Warburg and Courtauld Institutes* 44 (1981): 167.

152 Burnett, "A Hermetic Programme," 103.

153 Burnett, "Translating Activity," 1044; and Hermann of Carinthia, *De essentiis: A Critical Edition with Translation and Commentary*, trans. Charles S. F. Burnett (E. J. Brill., 1982), 70–3.

diminished by being made freely available and should be given out liberally."[154] It is difficult to know the extent of Hermann's intended disclosure, but both he and Ketton were well connected to the most important European Church authorities. Ketton promised Peter the Venerable, abbot of Cluny, who was in charge of promoting the Cluny reform in Spain, "a celestial gift which embraces within itself the whole of science," and Hermann sent one of his translations (Ptolemy's *Planisphere*) to Thierry of Chartres, "the foremost educator in France of the second quarter of the twelfth century."[155] In the preface of his translation of Ptolemy's *Planisphere*, Hermann refers to his "most beloved teacher Thierry" (*diligentissime preceptor Theodorice*) and he "who accommodates Plato's soul from heaven among mortals again" (*Platonis animam celitus iterum mortalibus accommodatam*).[156] The school of Chartres was influenced by Platonic thought, and the Hermetic *Asclepius* was one of his main references.[157] The *Cosmographia* by Bernardus Silvestris (d. after 1159) also refers to the Latin *Asclepius* and other books of Hermes. Silvestris dedicated his *Cosmographia* to Thierry as well, and in its preface Hermann recounts how Thierry was engaged in compiling an annotated library of texts on the seven liberal arts – the future *Heptateuchon* – for which he needed Arabic texts.[158]

Another important English translator, Adelard of Bath (*c.* 1080–1152), travelled extensively throughout the Near East, France, and Sicily – where Emperor Frederick II (1197–1250) sponsored translations from Arabic[159] – and possibly also to Spain. As Burnett explains, Bath became acquainted with three Arabic works which included Hermetic wisdom: the *Abbreviation of the Introduction to Astrology* of Abū Maʿshar (787–886), which mentions some "lots" of Hermes that are used for astrological divination; the *Centiloquium* of Pseudo-Ptolemy, of which the ninth verbum gives the opinions of the *domini prestigiorum* (the masters of talismans); and the *Liber prestigiorum* of Thābit, following Ptolemy and Hermes.[160]

As we can ascertain, the node around Tarazona–Tudela–Rueda del Jalón in the twelfth century worked as a portion of a network that was larger than the individual kingdoms of which these towns were part. Parts of this region – including its inhabitants – changed ownership from Aragon to Castile several times, and many inhabitants came from across Europe and belonged to different religious confessions. Since Michael, the bishop of Tarazona, was a member of the network rather than its head, his patronage was less decisive than that of ʿAbd al-Raḥmān II in Córdoba or Alfonso X in Castile.

I have given a brief glimpse into this group of translators and their activities[161] and emphasized the influence Hermes Trismegistus and his tradition exerted on

154 See Burnett "Translating Activity," 1044; and Hermann of Carinthia, *De essentiis*, 70–3.

155 See Burnett, "Translating Activity," 1044.

156 Hermann of Carinthia, *De essentiis*, 348.

157 See Winthrop Wetherbee, *Platonism and Poetry in the Twelfth Century: The Literary Influence of the School of Chartres* (Princeton: Princeton University Press, 2015), 69.

158 See Burnett, "Translating Activity," 1044.

159 See Francesco Gabrieli, "Frederick II and Moslem Culture," *East and West* 9, no. 1/2 (1958): 53–61.

160 Burnett, "Establishment of Medieval Hermeticism," 127.

161 See the works of Haskins and especially Burnett for a more complete picture.

them. In this connection, Wasserstrom affirms that in multi-religious Iberian circles at that time "the figure of Hermes stood for a transconfessional wisdom, a universal revelation, which doctrine further endorsed Muslim study of Jewish works"; Hermes provided "an elite interconfessionalism in which terminology and mythical constructs are shared across religious boundaries."[162] These guiding principles could be extended to Spanish Jews abroad – such as Ibn Ezra, Judah Halevi, and Maimonides – and then in the diaspora, and also to Andalusi philosophers and mystics who died in the Near East – such as Ibn Sab'īn and Ibn al-'Arabī.[163] Figures like Maimonides and Ibn al-'Arabī mark the epochal greatness of the Spanish emigrants, which may be sensed "as a matter of thresholds: they operated between East and West, between ancient and modern, between philosophy and mysticism, and between Muslim and Jew. This export of *convivencia* (coexistence), with its veritable connoisseurship of thresholds (*Schellenkunde*), unmistakably reshaped the Mediterranean intellectual world."[164]

The cultural and political conditions in Iberia triggered the best possible conditions for these interconfessional circles and networks; Hermetic ideas allowed an – at least intellectual – *convivencia*. Even though the reality of a real *convivencia* between the three cultures has been discussed by scholars many times,[165] a period of relative harmony seemed to have existed between Muslim, Christian, and Jewish intellectual elites, all of whom made reference to Hermes. But throughout the thirteenth century this exchange progressively waned. In Christian Castile, Alfonso the Wise embraced the figure of Hermes and divulged the "secrets" that previous erudite men wanted to keep hidden; by contrast, in Jewish and Muslim circles Hermes became part of mystical currents – Kabbalah and Sufism – where "esoterism flourished among elites who believed that they alone actualized the theory of philosophy and perfected the practice of mysticism" – as Wasserstrom has observed.[166] This mystical drift, as well as the role that Hermetic magic and thought had within it, has been thoroughly explained by Saif.[167]

Among those Muslim Iberian mystics, Ibn Sab'īn (1217–70) stands out. His lost treatise, *Sharḥ kitāb Idrīs* (*Commentary of the book of Idrīs*) interpreted a scripture attributed to the Quranic prophet Idrīs[168] – whom Muslims scholars identified with

[162] Steven Wasserstrom, "Jewish-Muslim Relations in the Context of Andalusian Emigration," in Mark D. Meyerson and Edward D. English (eds), *Christians, Muslims, and Jews in Medieval and Early Modern Spain: Interaction and Cultural Exchange* (Notre Dame: University of Notre Dame Press, 1999), 73.

[163] Wasserstrom, "Jewish-Muslim Relations," 73 and 78.

[164] Wasserstrom, "Jewish-Muslim Relations," 78.

[165] For an analysis and summary of the main stages and points of the discussion, see Ryan Szpiech, "The Convivencia Wars: Decoding Historiography's Polemic with Philology," in Suzanne Conklin Akbari and Karla Mallette (eds), *A Sea of Languages: Rethinking the Arabic Role in Medieval Literary History* (Toronto: University of Toronto Press, 2013), 135–61.

[166] Wasserstrom, "Jewish-Muslim Relations," 73.

[167] Saif, "From *Ġāyat al-Ḥakīm*," 307–8 and 344.

[168] Vincent Cornell, "The Way of the Axial Intellect: The Islamic Hermetism of Ibn Sab'īn," *Journal of the Muhyiddin Ibn 'Arabi Society* 22 (1997): 54.

both the biblical Enoch and Hermes Trismegistus, probably influenced by Ḥarrān.[169] Ibn Sabʿīn's *Budd al-ʿārif* (*The prerequisites of the gnostic*), begins in this way:

> I petitioned God to propagate the wisdom which Hermes Trismegistus [*al-harāmisa*] revealed in the earliest times, the realities that prophetic guidance has made beneficial, the happiness that is sought by every person of guidance, the light by which every Fully-Actualized Seeker wishes to be illuminated, the knowledge that will no longer be broadcasted or disseminated from [Hermes] in future ages and the secret [*sirr*] from which and through which and for the sake of which the prophets were sent.[170]

Ibn Sabʿīn makes it clear that Hermes Trismegistus is the source for his doctrines. As a prophet, Hermes reaffirms a primordial wisdom that transcends all revealed religions. These lines contain themes we saw in the texts by Hugo de Santalla and Hermann of Carinthia, such as calling upon privileged men who are "enlightened" by God – regardless of their religion – and who are able to distill wisdom from the teachings of the wise men of the past, starting with Hermes. In fact, Cornell also demonstrates the relationship between some of Ibn Sabʿīn's doctrines and the ancient and Arabic *Hermetica*.[171] I suggest that a close examination of Ibn Sabʿīn's network in al-Andalus and then in North Africa would reveal more commonalities between those interested in Hermes in Muslim and Christian domains; however, the focus of this work is on Hermetic activity within medieval Iberia, which at some point was concentrated in Toledo, to where we are now moving.

After its conquest in 1085, Arabic intellectual treasures were available to the Christian conquerors of Toledo. Church authorities, and then the crown – committed to the translation task – began lifting the veil of secrecy that had concealed Hermes and took advantage of previous and existing interconfessional contact. When translation activity around the node of Tarazona–Tudela–Rueda del Jalón started to disappear, a more comprehensive and "official" programme was undertaken and planned in Toledo in the mid-twelfth century.[172] Toledo's cathedral was constructed on top of the main mosque of Arabic Toledo. A library and school would have been connected to the mosque, enabling the new rulers to utilize already existing resources and traditions. The authorities decided to take advantage of the city's cultural capital: many Jews and Muslims lived there and could be recruited. This was the case with successive archbishops, such as Raymond de Sauvetât, also known as Raimundo de Toledo (d. 1152), a monk of Cluny who allegedly launched the school of translators, and the philosopher and translator Dominicus Gundissalinus, also known as Domingo Gundisalvo (*c.* 1115–90). Gundissalinus translated important Arabic works and wrote five important treatises, which incorporated Jewish and Arab philosophical

169 Philip S. Alexander, "From Son of Adam to Second God: Transformations of the Biblical Enoch," in Michael E. Stone and Theodore A. Bergen (eds), *Biblical Figures Outside the Bible* (Harrisburg: Trinity Press International, 1998), 118.

170 In Cornell, "Way of the Axial Intellect," 54.

171 Cornell, "Way of the Axial Intellect," 61–3.

172 See Charles Burnett, "The Coherence of the Arabic-Latin Translation Program in Toledo in the Twelfth Century," *Science in Context* 14, nos 1–2 (2001): 249–88.

achievements – such as those of Ibn Sina, al-Ghazāli, al-Fārābī, and Ibn Gabirol – into the Latin tradition.[173] Gundissalinus also abandoned secrecy and the restrictiveness of previous translators. As Jolivet points out, Gundissalinus seemed to react "to a secret intellectual elite" and considered that "it is no longer possible to be a sage (*sapiens*); one can only aspire to be proficient in certain sciences, or at least to know something about a few of them."[174] To facilitate this task, Gundissalinus describes each of the sciences in his *De scientiis* (*On the sciences*) which largely draws on his translation of al-Fārābī's *Iḥṣāʾ al-ʿulūm* (*Enumeration of the sciences*).

This work was also translated by Gerard of Cremona (1114–87),[175] the most prolific Arabic-to-Latin translator at that time, who was attracted to Toledo while looking for, or rather, "because of his love for [Ptolemy's] *Almagest* (according to his students' biography) and discovered there a large quantity of Arabic texts, which he proceeded to translate into Latin."[176] Similarly, Daniel of Morley – who had previously gone to Paris in pursuit of masters but was disappointed with what he found there – heard that the *doctrina Arabum*, which "consisted almost entirely of the quadrivial arts," flourished in Toledo; Morley hurried there to attend the lectures of the "wiser philosophers in the world."[177]

Thus, a new generation of translators – including Christians, Mozarabs (Christians who had lived under Muslim power), Arabs, and outstandingly courtly Jews – joined the programme of translations in Toledo. In the first stage of the School of Translators of Toledo, it was primarily Jews – who spoke Romance dialect and Arabic – who helped produce translations into Castilian, which an educated cleric then rendered into Latin.[178] A definitive shift happened when Alfonso the Wise decided to promote a vernacular culture in Castile, and many translations remained in Castilian, without being further translated into Latin. This means that Hermes and his tradition also passed from a Latin to a Castilian milieu, which I will focus on throughout the rest of this book. But before turning to Alfonso's cultural enterprise, I will talk about Hermes's presence in a genre of Castilian works produced at the cusp of these two periods.

Hermes in Castilian Sapiential Literature: *Bocados de Oro* and its Antecedents

In the last part of this chapter, I investigate Hermes Trismegistus's role in thirteenth-century Castilian wisdom literature and some quintessential works: *Bocados de oro*, *Libro de los buenos proverbios*, and *Poridat de las poridades*. These texts were preceded by the seminal *Disciplina clericalis*, a Latin work by a Jew who converted to Christianity,

173 See, for instance, Alexander Fidora, "Dominicus Gundissalinus and the Introduction of Metaphysics into the Latin West," *The Review of Metaphysics* 66, no. 4 (2013): 691–712.

174 Jean Jolivet, "The Arabic Inheritance," in Peter Dronke (ed.), *A History of Twelfth-Century Western Philosophy* (Cambridge: Cambridge University Press, 1988), 135–6.

175 See Burnett, "Translating Activity," 1049; and Burnett, "Coherence."

176 See Charles Burnett, "Gerard of Cremona," in Kate Fleet et al. (eds), *Encyclopaedia of Islam, THREE*, https://referenceworks.brill.com/display/entries/EI3O/COM-27411.xml?rskey=8uwZLa&result=1 (last accessed June 23, 2021).

177 Burnett, "Institutional Context," 218.

178 Francisco Márquez Villanueva, *El concepto cultural alfonsí* (Barcelona: Bellaterra, 2004), 66–70; and Burnett, "Coherence," 250–1.

Petrus Alphonsi. Since I pay particular attention to the transformation and reworkings Hermes experienced after his passage through Arabic culture, I will demonstrate how this literature has traces of important trends developed in the Arabic *Hermetica*. In this way, we will see how the Hermetic tradition found an unexpected course of diffusion in Castilian culture, which was interested in the figure of Hermes not only as a transmitter of arcane arts and transcendent wisdom but also as a model for everyday reflections on quotidian problems and government issues.

Even though the technical *Hermetica* – with its capacity to grant wondrous skills and power – seduced translators and powerful men, Hermes was also the alleged author of writings that granted more spiritual than temporal benefits. This philosophical and spiritual dimension was reworked in sapiential or wisdom literature. Initially, Hermes embodied esoteric wisdom, but eventually he also became one of the sages who spread easily acceptable and widely applicable aphorisms. Like other sages, in the wisdom literature Hermes's sayings are closer to common knowledge than to secretly transmitted knowledge.

When Castilian interpreters translated this Arabic nomologic literature, they presented a Hermes that had inherited the tension between esoteric and exoteric wisdom, which served the philosopher as much as it did the king and layman. However, scholars have dedicated much less attention to Hermes in translations of wisdom literature than in technical, astrological, alchemical, and magical treatises. Written in old Castilian, these works present a formidable barrier for specialists who are much more comfortable working with Latin or Arabic, which has hindered the construction of a nuanced perspective on medieval Hermetic knowledge. In this sense, even Burnett suggests that there was an impasse in Hermetic developments in Europe between the previously mentioned Latin translators and Renaissance magi such as Marsilio Ficino and Pico della Mirandola.[179] I hope this book will help fill this gap by discussing vernacular works in Castilian.

A direct precursor of Castilian wisdom literature is *Disciplina clericalis* by Petrus Alfonsi or Petrus Alphonsi of Huesca, a converted Jew formerly called Moses Sephardi (*c.* 1062–1140). The work was intended to be a "rulebook for clerics" – in the Middle Ages, cleric or clerk also referred to a man of letters, since the majority of intellectual education was administered by the Church. It introduces the novelty that its sources were Christian, Arab, and Jewish, which Petrus Alphonsi was able to read in Hebrew and Arabic. This uniqueness ensured the work's incredible success throughout Europe. *Disciplina clericalis* contains a prologue and thirty-three examples (or exemplary stories). The stories are framed as lectures given by a father to his son, or from a master to his disciple, and they are sprinkled with sayings, attributed to various philosophers, that came from Arab wisdom texts. This book, as well as the sapiential genre in general, is also related to educational and moralistic works within the genre of Arabic *adab*.[180]

The first philosopher cited by Alfonsi is Hermes Trismegistus, but he uses his Arabic and Jewish names: "The philosopher Enoch, who in Arabic is called Idrīs, says to his son: the fear of God should be in your work, and in this way, blessings

[179] Burnett, "Establishment of Medieval Hermeticism," 140.
[180] Jolivet, "Arabic Inheritance," 133.

come to you without work."[181] The fact that Enoch spoke to his son seems to echo Hermetic writings in which Hermes addressed his son Tat. This work also hints at the coeval existence of the "secrets" evoked in Hermetic writings and a "natural" wisdom that does not need books to be developed but can be transmitted by them.

The dialogue between the master and his disciple that frames the fifteenth exemplum is of particular interest: an intelligent woman helps a Muslim Spaniard (*hyspanus*) recover his money. Before his pilgrimage to Mecca, he had entrusted it all to a malicious man who would not give it back to him upon his return. Astonished by the astuteness of the woman, the disciple says: "I think that any philosopher would have thought in such an ingenious manner."[182] His master responds: "A philosopher would have been able to do well with both natural and acquired intelligence in combination with scrutiny of the secrets of nature, what the woman achieved with only her natural intelligence."[183] A non-education-based wisdom that is the product of everyday experience – as demonstrated by the woman in the story – is compared to the wisdom of the philosopher and sage, which has been acquired in two ways: by natural intelligence (*ingenio naturali*) and through books (*artificiali*, or the rules of art or technique). The latter includes the close study of the "secrets of nature" (*secreta naturae*), which might be a reference to the abovementioned Hermetic *Sirr al-khalīqa* by pseudo-Apollonius – translated into Latin as *Liber de secretis naturae.*

For the twenty-fifth exemplum, Petrus Alfonsi uses a source that comes from the Hermetic *Libro de prophetiis* (*Book of prophecies*) attributed to Plato,[184] which also circulated under the name *Liber vaccae* (*Book of the cow*). This book contains numerous magical recipes similar to those that appear in *Picatrix*.[185] The hero of this tale is the legendary alchemist Marianus, whose alleged work, *Liber de compositione alchemiae* (*The book on the composition of alchemy*), was translated into Latin by Robert of Chester in 1144 and was diffused widely – especially through Chester's prologue on the three Hermeses, as we will see in Chapter Four.[186] Marianus prophesies the fall of a king based solely on his own experience and knowledge of humanity, which indicates that Alphonsi deliberately put aside the "technical" aspects of the *Hermetica* and kept the sapiential ones.

181 "Enoch philosophus qui lingua arabica cognominatur Edric, dixit filio suo: Timor Domini sit negociatio tua, et ueniet tibi lucrum sine labore." Petrus Alfonsi, *Disciplina Clericalis*, eds Esperanza Ducay and María Jesús Lacarra (Zaragoza: Guara Editorial, 1980), 110.

182 "[...] nec puto quod aliquis philosophus subtilius cogitaret." Petrus Alfonsi, *Disciplina Clericalis*, 127.

183 "Bene posset philosophus suo facere naturali ingenio et artificiali, secreta eciam naturae rimando, quod mulier solo fecit naturali ingenio." Petrus Alfonsi, *Disciplina clericalis*, 127.

184 This is how the twenty-fifth example begins: "Plato tells in *Book of Prophecies* that there was a king in Ancient Greece who was cruel to the people." ("Plato retulit in *Libro de propheciis* quod quidam rex erat in Grecia senex, gentibus crudelis.") Petrus Alfonsi, *Disciplina clericalis*, 139.

185 On this work, see Saif, "Cows and the Bees."

186 On this translation, see Marion Dapsens, "De la *Risālat Maryānus* au *De compositione alchemiae*: Quelques réflexions sur la tradition d'un traité d'alchimie," *Studia Graeco-Arabica* 6 (2016): 121–40.

Alfonsi was well acquainted with wisdom literature's relationship with the Bible, specifically with the biblical wisdom books. Wisdom literature was a common genre throughout the ancient Near East; notably in Egypt, with famous works such as *The Maxims of Ptahhotep* and the *Instruction of Amenemhet*. In fact, the similarities between certain Hermetic collections of aphorisms enabled Mahé to suggest that Hermetic treatises developed as elaborations of these aphorisms.[187] Perhaps because of this affinity with the Bible, clerics and men of medieval letters were able to seamlessly assimilate translated Arabic wisdom literature into their Christian cultural outlook, despite drawing on frowned-upon traditions – including Hindu, Persian, Syrian, Greek, and Byzantine. As Alvar has noted, even though the intended audiences for these works are clear (clerics, common people, nobles, princes), it is not always easy to discern their origin because the stories and aphorisms passed through a multitude of traditions and languages, so much so that the majority of the time the links in the chain of transmission escape us.[188] The dating and authorship of Castilian translations, as well as the relationship between them, pose enormous problems.[189] For my purposes, I will simply mention that the works I address below were translated in the thirteenth century during the reign of Ferdinand III (1217–52) and at the beginning of the reign of Alfonso X the Wise (1252–84).[190]

The *Bocados de oro* (hereafter *Bocados*) contains the most interesting appearance of Hermes. This work is a translation of *Mukhtār al-ḥikam wa-maḥāsin al-kalim* (*The most select maxims and the best sayings*), written between 1048 and 1049 by the Syrian-Egyptian scholar al-Mubashshir Ibn Fātik (1012–97).[191] He was born in Damascus but spent most of his life in Fatimid Egypt. The date of the Castilian translation is not known, but the most accepted hypothesis dates it around the end of Ferdinand III's reign or the beginning of Alfonso X's, perhaps towards 1260, since a section of the *Bocados* has parallels with a section of Alfonso's legal code, *Las siete partidas*, which was written between 1256 and 1265.[192] The *Bocados* establishes the conventions of most varieties of wisdom genre: it is written in prose, has a narrative frame, and contains a brief biography of each philosopher followed by the maxims attributed to him – Hermes's section follows this structure. This composition connects the book to

[187] See Jean-Pierre Mahé and Joseph Paramelle, "Extraits hermétiques inédits d'un manuscrit d'Oxford," *REG* 104 (1991): 108–39; and a discussion on this theory in Bull, *Tradition of Hermes*, 9.

[188] Carlos Alvar, *Traducciones y traductores. Materiales para una historia de la traducción en Castilla durante la Edad Media* (Madrid: Centro de Estudios Cervantinos, 2010), 84.

[189] For information on this, refer to the works by Haro Cortés and Bizzarri quoted here.

[190] For a complete definition of wisdom literature, see Marta Haro Cortés, *Los compendios de castigos del siglo XIII: Técnicas narrativas y contenido ético* (Valencia: Universitat de València, 1995), 15–21.

[191] On his life, see Emily Cottrell, "Al-Mubashshir Ibn Fatik," in H. Lagerlund (ed.), *Encyclopedia of Medieval Philosophy* (Dordrecht: Springer, 2011), 1: 815–18.

[192] *Partidas* II.5.17, cited in Marta Haro Cortés, "Bocados de Oro," in José Manuel Lucía Megías and Carlos Alvar Ezquerra (eds), *Diccionario filológico de literatura medieval española. Textos y transmission* (Madrid: Castalia, 2002), 224.

Greek doxographies, the most famous example of which is Diogenes Laertius's *Lives and Opinions of Eminent Philosophers*, not available to the Arabic-speaking world.

The *Bocados* includes Greek personalities, such as Pythagoras, Socrates, Aristotle, Homer, Alexander of Aphrodisias, and Hermes Trismegistus, as well as three figures associated with him in the *Hermetica*: Ammon, Asclepius, and Tat. Hermes occupies the second chapter of the book, coming immediately after Seth. In Hermes's section, the Castilian translator presents a selection from the original Arabic, in which he kept pagan and Arabic Hermetic components; however, he refined – or censored – other elements connected to Islam. To illustrate this elaboration, I use Van Bladel's English translation of this section of al-Mubashshir's *Mukhtār*[193] and my own translation of the *Bocados*. In the second, this section opens with: "Hermes was born in Egypt. In Greek, Hermes means monk, and the Hebrews call him Enoch. He was the son of Jared, son of Mahalalel, son of Kenan, son of Enos, son of Seth, son of Adam."[194] The *Mukhtār* actually says that, in Greek, Hermes means *ʿUṭārid* (the Arabic name for the planet Mercury). Different manuscripts say *monge* and *menje* (monk), but also *mege* (mage).[195] It is difficult to know why the translator changed *ʿUṭārid* to monk. Perhaps this gives Hermes an appearance of religiosity.

Al-Mubashshir also mentions that "he was also named, upon him be peace, 'Ṭrismīn' among the Greeks; among the Arabs, 'Idrīs', among the Hebrews, 'Enoch'."[196] The translator eliminated the Quranic reference to Idrīs, as well as the reference to Trismīn, which, as Van Bladel mentions, seems to be a corruption of Trismegistus[197] – something the translator may not have understood. However, the Jewish reference to Hermes as Enoch, reinforced by the inclusion of Enoch's genealogy from Genesis, was retained. Even if the translator is attempting to portray a Hermes that is relatable to Ferdinand III's and Alfonso X's Arab, Jewish, and Christian subjects, much care was taken to eliminate specific references to the Quran.

In the next excerpt, the *Bocados* faithfully renders: "He lived before the great flood that destroyed the world, and this was the first flood. And after that, another flood ravaged only Egypt."[198] This seems to relate Hermes's genealogy to the most

[193] Not only because it is an exact and elegant translation but also because Van Bladel (*Arabic Hermes*) used the only published edition of *Mukhtār al-ḥikam*, carried out by Badawī [Abū l-Wafā'al-Mubaššir Ibn Fātik, *Muḫtar al-ḥikam wa-maḥāsin al-kalim / Los Bocados de Oro (Mujtār al-ḥikam)*, ed. ʿAbdarraḥmān Badawī, (Madrid: Publicaciones del Instituto Egipcio de Estudios Islámicos, 1958), whose notes, like those of Rosenthal's manuscripts in his studies of this work, clarify many of the obscure passages.

[194] "Nasció Hermes en Egipto. E Hermes en griego quiere tanto dezir como monje, e disen los Ebraicos Enoh. E fue fijo de Xaret, fijo de Mabalet, fijo de Qina, fijo de Enes, fijo de Sed, fijo de Adam." *Bocados de Oro: kritische Ausgabe des altspanischen Textes* (Romanistische Versuche und Vorarbeiten, 37), ed. Mechthild Crombach (Bonn: Romanisches Seminar der Universität Bonn, 1971), 5.

[195] *Bocados*, 5a.

[196] In Van Bladel, *Arabic Hermes*, 185.

[197] Van Bladel, *Arabic Hermes*, 185.

[198] "E fue ante del grant deluvio, el que destruyó el mundo, e éste fue el primer diluvio. E después ovo otro diluvio que astragó a Egipto solamente." *Bocados*, 6.

widespread one given to him in the Arab world; it originated with Abū Maʿshar's lost work *Kitāb al-ulūf*, which was transmitted by Andalusi scholars such as Ibn Juljul (*c.* 944–94 CE) and Sāʾid al-Andalusī (1029–70 CE). I will thoroughly examine the version of this story in Alfonso's *GE* in Chapter Four; for now it is enough to remember that Abū Maʿshar distinguishes between three Hermeses: Hermes I, who lived in Egypt and taught the arts and the sciences before the Flood, which he predicted; Hermes II, who was Babylonian; and Hermes III, who was also born in Egypt and a disciple of Pythagoras.[199]

Kahane and Pietrangeli affirm that "the *vita* of Hermes presented in the *Bocados* contains essentially the same features which have been attributed in Islamic tradition, since Abū-Maʿshar, to Hermes."[200] However, I suggest that when the translator reworked the *Mukhtār* he put the two versions of the Arab Hermes, which initially diverged, in greater harmony. Al-Mubashshir presents an alternate genealogy for Hermes, which contradicts Abū Maʿshar's and was removed in the Castilian version. The *Mukhtār* states: "In the beginning of his career [Hermes] was a student of Agathodaemon the Egyptian. Agathodaemon was one of the prophets of the Greeks and the Egyptians; he is for them the second Ūrānī, and Idrīs is the third Ūrānī, upon him be peace. The explanation of Agathodaemon is 'he of happy fortune.'"[201] An excerpt from the previous section of the book – also left out of the Castilian translation – says that Seth was the first of the Ūrānī. As Van Bladel and Cottrell explain, even though we do not know the exact meaning of "Ūrānī" this genealogy and terminology appears in other Arabic works, which can often be traced back to the pagan city Ḥarrān and its Sabean inhabitants.[202]

For example, in his encyclopedic *Kitāb al-fihrist*, Ibn al-Nadīm (d. *c.* 990 CE) refers back to a testimony of al-Kindī, the Arab philosopher, via one of his disciples. Ibn al-Nadīm writes that the main luminaries of the Sabeans are Ūrānī, Agathodaemon, and Hermes (which also corresponds with other authors), but no author after al-Nadīm was able to explain this "trinity" or the etymology of Ūrānī.[203] However, both versions share some details. For instance, Abū Maʿshar affirmed that "Hermes I" was Enoch and Idrīs, like al-Mubashshir's Hermes. By removing the reference to the three "Ūrānīs," the Castilian translator eliminates the main difference between Mukhtār's version of the story of Hermes and that of Abū Maʿshar. Since the *Bocados* retains the detail that Hermes lived before the Flood, it is possible to identify him with Abū Maʿshar's first Hermes – in reality, al-Mubashshir refers to three Ūrānīs, not to three Hermeses. For this reason, the Hermes of the *Bocados* ceased being "the only

199 See for instance, Sāʾid al-Andalusī, *Historia de la filosofía y de las ciencias o libro de las categorías de las naciones [Kitāb Ṭabaqāt al-umam]*, eds Eloísa Llavero Ruíz and Andrés Martínez Lorca (Madrid: Trotta, 2000), 77–8 and 105–6.

200 Henry Kahane, Renée Kahane, and Angelina Pietrangeli, "Hermetism in the Alfonsine Tradition," in David Ross (ed.), *Mélanges Offerts À Rita Lejeune* (Gembloux: Éditions J. Duculot, 1969), 445.

201 In Van Bladel, *Arabic Hermes*, 188.

202 See Van Bladel, *Arabic Hermes*, 188–9; and especially Emily Cottrell, "Adam and Seth in Arabic Medieval Literature," *Aram* 22 (2010): 526–30.

203 See the discussion in Van Bladel, *Arabic Hermes*, 188–9.

successful alternative to Abū Maʿshar's,"[204] as it originally appeared in the *Mukhtār*, and became its companion in Castilian. The story of Hermes in the *Bocados* is more compatible with that in Alfonso's *GE* – as we will see. Al-Mubashshir includes the son of Hermes, Tat, as does the *Bocados*. However, Abū Maʿshar does not include reference to Tat. I will return to Hermes's different lineages in Chapter Four.

The *Bocados* continues: "And Hermes left Egypt and wandered all over the earth for eighty-two years."[205] Here the Castilian translator committed a considerable error, because the *Mukhtār* says: "Hermes left Egypt and went around the whole earth. He returned to Egypt and God raised him to Himself there. God the Exalted said, 'And We raised him to a high place.' That was after [he had lived] eighty-two years."[206] Here Al-Mubashshir quotes Quran 19:57; Idrīs is introduced one verse earlier, in 19:56: "And mention in the Book the account of Idrīs. Indeed, he was a man of truth and a prophet." The translator removed the Quranic reference and quotation, but besides that, al-Mubashshir did not say that after leaving Egypt Hermes travelled the earth for eight-two years but that after his entire life on earth God raised him to the sky. Later in the text, he insists that Hermes was on the earth for eighty-two years.

The *Bocados* does accurately translate that Hermes not only discovered sciences like astronomy, but he also played a fundamental role in spreading them around the world, and to these teachings he also added faith in God: "And he invited all men of the earth to obey God in seventy-two languages. And he populated one hundred and eight towns and showed them the sciences. And he was the first to define the sciences of the stars."[207] The *Mukhtār* then says: "and he established for each region [*iqlīm*] a model of religious practice [*sunna*] for them to follow which corresponded to their views. Kings were his servants, and the whole earth's population and the population of the islands in the seas obeyed him."[208] Al-Mubashshir speaks about *sunna* – in Islam a term referring to one of two primary sources of the revelation, the other being the Quran. The *Bocados* eliminates the religious nature of the original by stating: "And he established in every town of every part of the earth the law that suited them and pertained to their views. And the kings of the entire earth obeyed him, as well as those of the islands and the seas."[209] Therefore, Hermes is categorized simply as a legislator, a tradition that he inherited from the Egyptian Thoth and was recorded by Isidore, as we saw above. In line with the separation of civil and canonical law in Christian lands, the reference in the *Bocados* is much more religiously "neutral" than the original, which contains clear Islamic connotations. The same occurs in the following passage, in which al-Mubashshir mentions elements

[204] Van Bladel, *Arabic Hermes*, 193.

[205] "E salió Hermes de Egipto e anduuo por toda la tierra ochenta e dos años." *Bocados*, 5.

[206] See Van Bladel, *Arabic Hermes*, 86.

[207] "E convidó a todos los omes de la tierra para obedescer a Dios con setenta e dos lenguajes. E pobló ciento e ocho villas e mostró les las sciencias. E él fue el primero que falló las sciencias de las estrellas." *Bocados*, 5.

[208] In Van Bladel, *Arabic Hermes*, 186.

[209] "E establesció a cada pueblo de cada partida del mundo la ley que les conviníe e que pertenescíe a sus opiniones. E obedesciéron-le los reyes e toda la tierra e los de las islas de los mares." *Bocados*, 5.

of Hermes's preaching, curiously similar to the five pillars and other fundamental elements of Islam:

> He preached God's judgment [*dīn*], belief in God's unity, mankind's worship [of God] [*Ibādat al-khalq*] and saving souls from punishments. He incited [people] to abstain piously [*al-zuhd*] from this world, to act justly, and to seek salvation in the next world. He commanded them to perform prayers that he stated for them in manners that he explained to them, and fast on recognized days of each month, to undertake holy war [*al-Jihād*] against the enemies of the religion, and to give charity [*al-zakāt*] from [their] possessions and to assist the weak with it. He bound them with oaths of ritual purity from pollutants, menstruation, and touching the dead.[210]

It is evident that such a "religion of Hermes" could have developed only after the emergence of Islam and its laws, not before.[211] The *Bocados* lightens the Islamic references of the original in such a way that, by insisting on the piety and monotheism of Hermes, it is reminiscent of passages of the Latin *Asclepius* that pleased early Christian thinkers:

> He exhorted us to follow the law of God, to acknowledge the unity [of God], to abhor the world, to do justice, and to demand salvation in the next life. And he commanded them to pray and to fast on certain days in each month, to fight with their enemies of faith, and to give means to God's people to help the poor among them.[212]

The *Bocados* does reproduce the alcohol and food restrictions from al-Mubashshir, which can be traced back to Leviticus and Deuteronomy, as well as to Islamic law: "He forbade them to eat pork and zebra, camel, and other such foods. And he forbade them all to drink any wine."[213] The preservation of the clearly Islamic prohibition of wine, as well as the following passage with clear pagan connections, is striking:

> And he established many festivals on specific days, and to make sacrifices at the entrance of the sun in the heads of the [zodiac] signs, when the signs are at the sight of the moon, at the times of the planets' conjunctions, when the planets enter in their houses, are in their apogees, or align with other planets. And he commanded them to make sacrifices of all things: of flowers, such as roses; of grains, such as wheat and barley; of fruits, such as grapes; and of beverages: such as wine.[214]

210 Van Bladel, *Arabic Hermes*, 186.

211 Van Bladel, *Arabic Hermes*, 95.

212 "E convidó a la ley de Dios e a otorgar la unidat e aborrescer el mundo e fazer justicias e demandar salvación en el otro mundo. E mandó-les fazer oraciones e ayunar días sabidos en cada mes e lidiar con sus enemigos de la fe e dar a los de Dios averes para ayudar con ellos a los flacos." *Bocados*, 5.

213 "E vedó-les comer carne de puerco e de zebra e de camello e otros tales comeres. E vedó-les enbeudar de todo vino." *Bocados*, 5.

214 "E establescíó-les muchas fiestas en tienpos sabidos, e fazer sacrificios a la entrada del sol en las cabeças de los sinos, e d'ellos a vista de la luna e a los tienpos de las conjunciones de las planetas e quando las planetas entran en sus casas e en sus exaltaciones o quando cataren a otras planetas. E mando-les que fiziesen sacrificios de todas las cosas, de las

Both the *Bocados* and the Arabic original recall Arabic writings about the pagan customs of the city of Ḥarrān. Due to its resonances with the *Bocados* and other wisdom literature, I summarize some of these testimonies. In *al-Fihrist* (*The catalogue*), Ibn al-Nadīm refers to the testimony about the Sabeans of Ḥarrān by al-Kindī, whose disciple, al-Sarakhsī (d. 899 CE), had collected in his *Risāla fī wasf madhāhib al-Sābiʾīn* (*Description of the Sabeans' doctrine*).[215] Mattila has studied the references to the Sabeans in both al-Sarakhsī and the *Rasāʾil ikhwān al-Ṣafāʾ* – one of the abovementioned sources of the *Ghāyat al-Ḥakīm* – and comes to the conclusion that "their primary frame of reference is clearly the religion practised in Ḥarrān."[216] Al-Kindī signalled that some Sabean practices were similar to those found in Islam, such as orations, fasting, and dietary restrictions, but other practices are not connected with and even contradict Islam, which resemble those retained by the translator of the *Bocados*. For the month of *Nisan*, for instance, Ibn al-Nadīm names sacrifices to the planets on certain dates, holidays dedicated to astral conjunctions and to the sun when it enters into the different houses of the zodiac, feasts to deities, devils, jinn, etc., and even a sacrifice to Hermes.[217]

Ḥarrān was located south-east of present-day Turkey, between Damascus, Carchemish, and Nineveh. It had a lengthy history that dates back to the second century BCE – it even appears in Genesis – gaining occasional prominence during the successive empires that occupied the region.[218] According to what Ibn al-Nadīm narrates, during Caliph al-Maʾmūn's reign, pagans from the city of Ḥarrān who had resisted conversion to Christianity adopted the name Sabean (in Arabic: *ṣābiʾa*) with the goal of protecting their religion. Sabeans appear in the Quran as *al-Sābiʾaūn*, one of the religious cults or "people of the book" acknowledged by Muhammad. While it is not clear to whom the Quran refers, it most likely implies Mandean or Gnostic groups. Furthermore, for many Muslim scholars, the Sabeans are simply pagans who preceded the monotheistic religions. For instance, Ṣāʿid al-Andalusī affirms that "all Greeks were Sabeans, venerated the stars and practised the worshipping of idols."[219] Numerous Arabic traditions claim that in Ḥarrān, Hermes Trismegistus was honoured and considered their main prophet. Some scholars speculate whether or not these beliefs were preserved in a Neoplatonic philosophical environment; according to this theory, which is contested, a Neoplatonic school survived there and preserved books and planetary cults related to Hermes. According to scholars such as Hadot and Tardieu, in the wake of the Justinian decrees against paganism and philosophical schools (529 CE), the Neoplatonic philosopher Simplicius of Cilicia

flores: las rosas, e de los granos: el trigo e la cevada, e de la fruta: las huvas, e de los brevajes: el vino." *Bocados*, 5.

215 In Van Bladel, *Arabic Hermes*, 86–7. As Green (*City of the Moon God*, 144) gathers, another important relation about the Sabeans is found in *Kitab al-Āthār al-Bāqīyah ʿan al-Qurūn al-Khālīyah* (*Chronology of Ancient Nations*) by al-Bīrūnī (973–1050 CE).

216 Janne Mattila, "Sabians, the School of al-Kindī, and the Brethren of Purity," in Ilkka Lindstedt, Nina Nikki, and Riikka Tuori (eds), *Religious Identities in Antiquity and the Early Middle Ages* (Leiden: Brill, 2021), 95.

217 See the relation in Green, *City of the Moon God*, 150.

218 For more about the history and religion of Ḥarrān, see Green, *City of the Moon God*.

219 Al-Andalusī, *Historia de la filosofía*, 80.

(490–560 CE) emigrated to Sasanian territory, where he supposedly established himself in the city of Ḥarrān. There, he worked with Damascius (*c.* 458–538), the last leader of the Academy of Athens.[220] Critics of this theory, such as Van Bladel, argue that none of Hermes's books from Ḥarrān have been found.[221] Cottrell has questioned Van Bladel's criticism, since it is irrefutable that many Arabic sources – including several not examined in *The Arabic Hermes* – refer to the astrological wisdom of the Sabeans in such a way that it evokes both the Hermetic tradition and what we know about Ḥarrān.[222] For instance, *Picatrix* III.vii contains a large passage titled: "On the attraction of the virtues of the planets, and in what way we can speak of them, and how their effects are divided between planets, figures, sacrifices, orations, incense, and propositions; and the states of the sky needed for each planet."[223] The passage begins by quoting "the wise Athabary" (al-Ṭabarī) on the "operations of the wise men" (*sapientibus*). Thus, the chapter includes "copious instructions for the adoration of the planets," the most characteristic feature of the Sabeans.[224] If we turn to the original in the *Ghāya*, we find that those wise men were *al-Ṣābiʾaīn*, whom Pingree identified as from Ḥarrān.[225] Later on, the *Picatrix* declares that "The wise men made determined prayers and sacrifices to the planets in mosques," and "they say that Hermes commanded them to do this in their mosques or churches"[226] – something that calls to mind the temples of Ḥarrān, which al-Masʿūdī described in his visit to the city, rendered by Alfonso in his *GE*.[227]

Another Arabic source in the *Hermetica* that is related to Ḥarrān and mentioned in the *Picatrix* is *De imaginibus* by Thābit ibn Qurra al-Ḥarrānī (826–901 CE), named for his origins in the city. Thābit Ibn Qurra was the main figure of the Sabeans of Ḥarrān who lived and worked in Baghdad. Syriac works on religion, rites, and the burial practices of the Sabeans – sadly, all lost – are attributed to him.[228] Although

220 Michel Tardieu, "Ṣābiens coraniques et 'Ṣābiens' de Ḥarrān," *Journal Asiatique* 274 (1986): 1–44; and Ilsetraut Hadot, "Dans quel lieu le néplatonicien Simplicius a-t-il fondé son école de mathémathiques , et où apu avoir lieu son entretien avec un manichéen?," *The International Journal of the Platonic Tradition* 1 (2007): 42–107.

221 Van Bladel, *Arabic Hermes*, 64–118.

222 Emily Cottrell, "'L'Hermès Arabe de Kevin van Bladel' et la question du rôle de la literature Sassanide dans la presence d'écrits hermètiques et astrologiques en langue arabe," *Bibliotheca Orientalis* 72 (2015): 349–53.

223 "De attractione virtutis planetarum, et quomodo loqui possumus cum eis, et quomodo effectus dividitur per planetas, figuras, sacrificia, oraciones, suffumigaciones, proposiciones; et status celi necessarii cuilibet planetarum." *Picatrix*.III.vii.1.

224 Plessner, "Summary," lxx.

225 *Ghāya* III.7, 195. See David Pingree, "Al-Ṭabarī on the Prayers to the Planets," *Bulletin d'études orientales* 44 (1992): 105–6.

226 "Sapientes autem qui oraciones et sacrificia fecerunt planetis in moschetis faciunt predicta [...] Et dicunt quod Hermes hoc iussit facere in moschetis sive in eorum ecclesiis." *Picatrix*. III.vii.35.

227 For this passage, see *GE*3 I, 319–22; and for that of al-Masʿūdī, see *Al-Masʿūdī*, 4:61–100; and Ahmad M. H. Shboul, *Al-Masʿūdī & His World: A Muslim Humanist and His Interest in Non-Muslims* (London: Ithaca Press, 1979), 11–12. See also Green, *City of the Moon God*, 214–15.

228 See Van Bladel, *Arabic Hermes*, 93.

he is known primarily for his important Arabic translations and original astronomy and mathematics works, Thābit ibn Qurra also wrote *De imaginibus*, a work on astrological magic that explains how to create talismans to attract the power of celestial bodies. This text is non-extant in Arabic but is known from two twelfth-century translations, the first by John of Seville as *De imaginibus* and the second by Adelard of Bath as *Liber prestigiorum*.[229]

As I mentioned earlier, al-Andalus developed direct contact with the legendary city when the physician al-Ḥarrānī immigrated to Iberia in the ninth century. His descendants visited the Ḥarrān community in Baghdad and studied with Thābit Ibn Sinān, son of Thābit Ibn Qurra.[230] Van Bladel suggests that Thābit Ibn Sinān translated a lost Syriac work by his father, *The Laws of Hermes and the Prayers that The Sabeans Use When Praying*, and this book might have been al-Mubashshir's source for the section on Hermes that is translated in the *Bocados*.[231]

The translator of the *Bocados* decided to limit the reference to specifically Islamic parts of al-Mubashshir; nevertheless, he respected other references – just as unorthodox or even more so – to the city of Ḥarrān. However, the translator does remove some details regarding the order Hermes established at the beginning of time, such as the tripartite division of society: "He ordered people into three classes: priests, kings, and subjects."[232] This partition, just after the description of Sabean rituals, reminds me of that in Plato's *Republic* III.3, which could be used as further evidence for the connection between the last Neoplatonists and Ḥarrān.[233]

Furthermore, the *Bocados* does not include al-Mubashshir's suggestive physical description of Hermes, nor the description of the religion that he founded, described as *al-milla al-ḥanīfiya* (the *ḥanīfī* community), a term that has several different connotations in Islam. The Quran qualifies Abraham as a *ḥanīf*, probably meaning "a believer in a religion which existed before Judaism, Christianity, and Islam."[234] Mattila points out that although the aforementioned al-Sarakhsī and the *Rasāʾil ikhwān al-Ṣafāʾ* typically associate the term Sabean with the residents of *Ḥarrān*, "the wider extension of the term, entangled with the term *ḥanīf*, allows them to expand its meaning to encompass also the religion practised by the ancient Greek philosophers."[235] Al-Mubashshir possibly adheres to some sources from Ḥarrān interested in linking Hermes's religion with both the Sabeans (mentioned in the Quran as a legal sect) and those that followed the *ḥanīfī* religion (also revalidated by the Quran) – equally connected with an imaginary prehistory of Islam. Moreover, Fowden suggests that the Ḥarrānians may have called their religion *ḥanputa* ("paganism" in Syriac),[236] possibly related to the Arabic *ḥanīfiya*. Al-Mubashshir

229 Saif, *Arabic Influences*, 27–8.
230 Fierro, "Plants, Mary the Copt," 136.
231 Van Bladel, *Arabic Hermes*, 95.
232 In Van Bladel, *Arabic Hermes*, 187.
233 Al-Masʿūdī (*c.* 896–956 CE) mentions inscriptions from Plato in the temples and streets of Ḥarrān during his visit in 946 CE.
234 See Cottrell, "Adam and Seth," 530.
235 Mattila, "Sabians," 95–6.
236 Garth Fowden, *Empire to Commonwealth: Consequences of Monotheism in Late Antiquity* (Princeton: Princeton University Press, 1993), 530.

would have been interested in distinguishing between the *ḥanīfī* and Sabeans – who would be saved – and true polytheists (*mushrikūn*) – who would be condemned to hell.[237] The translator of the *Bocados* was not interested in presenting clarifications that somehow "aligned" Hermes's doctrine with Islam. Rather, it was more important to depict him as an ancient sage whose teachings were compatible with Christianity, perhaps even a vague precedent of it. Furthermore, in the more secular context of the courts of the late Fernando III and Alfonso X, around the time the *Bocados* was translated, the pagan heritage of the sages of antiquity was a lesser issue.

After the section on the *fechos* (facts) of Hermes, the *Bocados* includes his *dichos* (sayings). At first glance, it seems as if these sayings are not substantially distinct from those of other philosophers. Nevertheless, a detailed analysis allows connections to be made between it and the philosophical *Hermetica*. Comparative work between the doctrine of Hermes in the *Bocados* and the *Corpus hermeticum* has been carried out by Kahane and Pietrangeli. They recognize the mixture of Christian and Hermetic elements that Rosenthal identified in al-Mubashshir's Arabic original[238] and state that "various of the sayings attributed to Hermes convey clear and direct reflections of the treatises [of the *Corpus hermeticum* and the *Asclepius*]."[239]

Although they ignored the original Arabic, these authors did conduct research on the direct citations of the *Corpus hermeticum* and the *Asclepius* in the *Bocados*, discovering obvious similarities. For example, regarding the saying "The best thing that is in man is intellect [*seso*],"[240] they assert that *seso* in Castilian "is the equivalent, frequently appearing in the treatise *Asclepius*, of the basic Hermetic concept of *nous* in some such meaning as 'faculty of intuition of the divine'."[241] As we will see, this idea is further substantiated in the Hermetic passages of *Poridat de las poridades* (to which these authors do not allude). *Seso* would be equivalent to the Greek word *nous* ("mind, intellect") stemming from the Neoplatonic background of the *Hermetica* – later translated into Latin as *intellectus*.[242] However, as Hanegraaff explains, even though *nous* is a term that is perfectly common in Greek philosophical discourse, in the *Hermetica* it has a much more complex meaning, closer to a spiritual apprehension that can lead humans to salvation.[243] Some of these implications are clearly expressed in the Castilian term *seso* used in this context.

In this sense, the sentence immediately before this quote of *Bocados*, upon which Kahane and Pietrangeli do not remark, states: "The best thing that God made in this world is man."[244] This declaration recalls the famous passage in *Asclepius* 6 that begins: "Magnum, o Asclepi, miraculum est homo." It was quoted by Pico della Mirandola at the beginning of *Oratio de hominis dignitate* and became a motto of

237 Van Bladel, *Arabic Hermes*, 190–1.
238 Franz Rosenthal, "Al-Mubashshir Ibn Fātik. Prolegomena to an Abortive Edition," *Oriens* 13–14 (1960–1): 135.
239 Kahane and Pietrangeli, "Hermetism," 446.
240 "La mejor cosa que es en el ome es el seso." *Bocados*, 14.
241 Kahane and Pietrangeli, "Hermetism," 446.
242 As with with *intellectus agens*, "agent intellect" (*nous poietikos*) from Aristotle.
243 Hanegraaff, *Hermetic Spirituality*, 8–9.
244 "La mayor cosa que Dios fizo en este mundo es el ome." *Bocados*, 14.

the Renaissance. Therefore, in the *Bocados* the best aspect of God's creation is man, and the best aspect of man is *seso*. In fact, in the *Hermetica*, *nous* provides man with the reverence (*eusebeia*) for God's creation that can lead him to salvation.[245]

This sentence in the *Bocados* might appear casual enough if not for an identical quote by Hermes that appears in *Poridat de las poridades*, along with others that also mention *seso* in a Hermetic context, as I will show below. These coincidences seem to point to common sources, and even to a Hermetic background. Other sayings echoing specific passages of the *Hermetica* that Kahane and Pietrangeli gathered include: "Do not squander your will with the sweetness of the world, that twists you from the thought of your soul!"[246] This certainly evokes the primacy of the spiritual over the material in the *Hermetica*, and it is compatible with Christian morals. The following is another example that emphasizes merit and personal improvement as prerequisites for wisdom: "He who wishes to arrive at wisdom must be of good acts, and he must be rid of foolishness"[247] – this mixture of knowledge and ethics is compatible with both the *Hermetica* and *adab*, as we will see in Chapter Two.

Other than aphorisms that can be immediately digested by the common reader without any intermediation, the *Bocados* includes some maxims that ask for help from a prophet. Kahane and Pietrangeli identify this prophet as the mystagogue – found in mystical cults and Hermetic literature – who guides the initiate through the various stages of their spiritual training. The *Bocados* states that "men only know God's grandeur because they were guided to serve him by the prophets and those loved by him who spoke through the Holy Ghost";[248] and God "[...] instilled the Holy Ghost in his prophets and messengers, and He uncovered the secrets of the faith and the truths of wisdom."[249] Therefore, there is an explicit reference to the "secrets" to which we must be guided by someone blessed by God. Kahane and Pietrangeli suggestively place this figure of the prophet in relation to the herald mentioned in the fourth treatise of the *Corpus hermeticum*.[250] It states that even if all humanity shares reason, not everyone has intellect (*nous*), therefore God: "[...] filled a great mixing pot with intellect [*nous*] and sent it below, appointing a herald whom he commanded to make an announcement to the hearts of humans."[251]

The *Bocados* includes other Hermetic characters in sections dedicated to Hermes's advice for King Amun, Tad, and Çagalquius.[252] All of them appear throughout the *Corpus hermeticum* and are joined together in the *Asclepius*, where we are told, for instance, that: "When [Tat] entered, Asclepius suggested that Hammon also join

245 See Hanegraaff, *Hermetic Spirituality*, 8–10.

246 "¡Non te tires con tu voluntad e con el dulçor del mundo, que te destorva del pensamiento de tu alma!" *Bocados*, 6.

247 "El que quisiere llegar al saber ha de ser de buenas obras, e ha-se de quitar de la nescedat." *Bocados*, 6.

248 "Non conoscen los hombres la grandeza de Dios, si non por que los guió a su servidumbre por sus prophetas e los sus amados que fablaron por spíritu santo." *Bocados*, 6.

249 "[...] aproprió a sus profetas e sus mandaderos con el spíritu santo, e descubrió las Poridades de la fe e las verdades de la sabiduría." *Bocados*, 7.

250 Kahane and Pietrangeli, "Hermetism," 448–9.

251 *Corpus Hermeticum* IV.4, in Copenhaver, *Hermetica*, 15.

252 *Bocados*, 15, 18, and 20.

them."[253] A brief gloss of sections of the *Bocados* where these characters appear reveals some interesting passages. I would like to examine what Hermes says to Amun, for instance: "For it suits you to clean your soul through good will and speaking the truth."[254] This recalls the insistence of purifying the soul found in both the *Hermetica* and the theological rites related to Hermes that Iamblichus describes in *On the Mysteries*. This is also the case when the *Bocados* says: "And pay attention to those who practise the higher alchemy, and be of good heart to them: and those are the farmers, because there is no greater alchemy than breeding the earth by seeding and planting."[255] Hermes's reference to a "higher alchemy" (*alquimia mayor*) seems to recall the *opus magnum*, as alchemy was also known. I also see the possible influence of Ibn Waḥshiyya's *Nabatean Agriculture*, which appears in the *Picatrix* and constitutes an extraordinary mixture of magical and agricultural practices.[256]

Çagalquius is easy to identify as Asclepius, because the *Bocados* refers to him as "the sage that was a disciple of Hermes."[257] Finally, in Ṭāṭ's section, al-Mubashshir includes a reference to the Sabeans: "The lessons of Ṭāṭ, who is Ṣāb son of Idrīs – peace be upon him. The pagans [*al-ḥunafā'*] are named after Ṣāb, so they are called the Sabeans [*al-Ṣābi'aūn*]."[258] Although the translator of the *Bocados* did include the Sabean rituals, he omitted this relationship mentioned in the section on Tad – perhaps because it is incomprehensible once translated into Castilian. In fact, the *Bocados* omits this entire introduction to Tad, including the statement that he is the son of Idrīs.[259]

Despite occasional lapses, the *Bocados* contains the most substantial references to Hermes of any piece of Castilian wisdom literature. According to my analysis, the translator took the original material from al-Mubashshir and integrated it into new cultural frames for Castile, where not only wisdom literature but also history, astrology, and the rest of the Hermetic sciences were of interest. For this reason, the translator pays close attention to the Hermes section. On the one hand, he reduces the references to Islam and harmonizes different Arabic traditions about Hermes; on the other hand, the *Bocados* respects the pagan references to the Sabeans of Ḥarrān who, as we saw, were not only known in Baghdad but also in al-Andalus. Despite these elaborations, Hermes's sayings in the *Bocados* evoke the syncretic cultural environments in which the *Hermetica* appeared.

253 "Quo ingresso Asclepius et Hammona interesse suggessit. Trismegistus ait." *Asclepius*, 1.

254 "Pues conviene-te a ti que alinpies tu alma por buenas voluntades e por dezir verdat." *Bocados*, 15.

255 "E para mientes a los que fazen el alquimia mayor, e faz-les buenos coraçones: E éstos son los labradores, que non ay atal alquimia como poblar la tierra con senbrar e plantar." *Bocados*, 16.

256 On this treatise, see Hämeen-Anttila, *The Last Pagans of Iraq*.

257 "[...] el sabio que fue diciplo de Hermes." *Bocados*, 30. Çagalquius is also known as Catalquius, Gagalquius, Catalqus, Zacalquis, or Catalpius in different manuscripts of the *Bocados de Oro*; see Mechthild Crombach (ed.), *Bocados de Oro: kritische Ausgabe des altspanischen Textes* (Romanistische Versuche und Vorarbeiten, 37) (Bonn: Romanisches Seminar der Universität Bonn, 1971), 20a.

258 See Van Bladel, *Arabic Hermes*, 95.

259 *Bocados*, 18.

Latin, French, Provençal, and English translations – the latter is considered the first printed work in English – were produced based on the Castilian *Bocados*.[260] Thus, through this translation process Hermes's fame as sage spread throughout Europe. Haro Cortés stresses the foundational role of the *Bocados*: "There is no doubt that *Bocados de Oro* and *Libro de los buenos proverbios* were the most widespread works of wisdom literature translated from Arabic in the Middle Ages – it must not be forgotten that they share common material and sources."[261] These two works not only provided "a suggestive arsenal of wisdom" but were also susceptible to "different ways of compilation, selection, combination, reduction or amplification; giving rise, thus, to new anthologies of universal value, such as *Dichos y castigos de sabios* (*Sayings and advice of sages*) or the *Libro de los treinta y cuatro sabios* (*Book of thirty four sages*)."[262] Quotes from Hermes found in the *Bocados* appear in *Tratado que hizo El Tostado de cómo al ome es necesario amar* (*Treatise that El Tostado made on how man needs to love*); for instance: "The great philosopher Hermes says: the stupid is small, although old, and the wise is big, although young."[263]

Castilian Versions of Aristotle's Hermetic Teachings to Alexander

Hermes's prominence in the *Bocados* makes his absence in the other seminal Castilian wisdom text mentioned by Haro Cortés, *El Libro de los buenos proverbios*, more noticeable. This work is the Castilian translation of *Kitāb ādāb al-falāsifa* (*The book of the sentences of the philosophers*). *Adab* (plural *ādāb*) has a broad meaning in Arab culture, as we will see in Chapter Two. This work was allegedly written by the Nestorian Christian Ḥunayn Ibn Isḥāq (*c.* 803–73), who was director of the *Bayt al-Hikma* (House of Wisdom) in Baghdad, the legendary Abbasid centre of translation. *Ādāb al-falāsifa* is one of the oldest collections of gnomology in Arabic, and it influenced numerous later works – including the *Mukhtār*, the source for the *Bocados*. For this reason, both texts share content,[264] none of which mentions Hermes. This could be due to various reasons. For instance, Ḥunayn's original text has not survived intact; all that remains is a selection or summary prepared by Muḥammad al-Anṣārī, of whom nothing is known.[265] Of course, al-Mubashshir used many other sources, some Hermetic, as we saw above.[266] Ḥunayn (803–73) is from the generation

[260] See Cottrell, "Al-Mubashshir Ibn Fatik," 816–17.

[261] Marta Haro Cortés, "*Dichos y castigos de sabios*: Compilación de sentencias en el manuscrito 39 de la colección San Román (RAH) I Edición," *Revista de Literatura Medieval* 25 (2013): 16.

[262] Haro Cortés "*Dichos y castigos de sabios*," 16.

[263] In John K. Walsh, "Versiones peninsulares del '*Kitāb Ādab al-falāsifa*' de Ḥunayn Ibn Isḥāq. Hacia una reconstrucción del 'Libro de los buenos proverbios'," *Al-Andalus* 41, no. 2 (1976): 378–9; this quote is from *Bocados*, 13.

[264] Hugo O. Bizzarri, "Libro de los buenos proverbios," in José Manuel Lucía Megías and Carlos Alvar Ezquerra (eds), *Diccionario filológico de literatura medieval española. Textos y transmisión* (Madrid: Castalia, 2002), 796.

[265] Mohsen Zakeri, "*Ādab al-falāsifa*: The Persian Content of an Arabic Collection of Aphorisms," *Mélanges de l'Université Saint-Joseph* 57 (2004): 176.

[266] Such as those suggested by Van Bladel, *Arabic Hermes*, 95.

immediately before Thābit Ibn Qurra (836–901), so it is plausible that he worked in Baghdad before many of the works on Hermes from Ḥarrān became popular there.

However, the *Libro de los buenos proverbios* does include components from Aristotle's teachings to Alexander, which has Hermetic connections. In the Castilian text, these teachings appear in the form of the master's letters to his disciple and follow the schematics of a *regimine principum* or mirror of princes; they include references to the qualities of a good ruler as well as to general human relationships.[267] The parts from *Libro de los buenos proverbios* and the *Bocados* that reference Alexander the Great date back to a tradition about him that was arguably developed by Pseudo-Callisthenes (*c.* 200 BCE). Pseudo-Callisthenes is the original source for most medieval literary traditions about Alexander, including Arabic, Persian, Latin, and Romance versions – although an independent Syriac version could have influenced the Quranic, and later Arabic/Islamic, mention of a "two horned" Alexander.[268]

This tradition was eventually divided into two. According to Sturm, one would furnish the details on Alexander that are found in the *Bocados*, while the contents of the *Libro de los buenos proverbios* are related to the *Epistola Alexandri ad Aristotelem*.[269] As I explained earlier, a genre of pseudo-Aristotelian *Hermetica* exists in which Aristotle's teachings to Alexander are based on the wisdom of Hermes Trismegistus, and it includes books of talismanic magic and astrology. This tradition was known in the Alfonsine *scriptorium* since, as previously indicated, some of the essential sources of the *Ghāya/Picatrix* come from it.

The connection to the pseudo-Aristotelian *Hermetica* is clearer in two Castilian translations: *Secreto de los secretos* and *Poridat de las poridades*. The original Arabic source of these works, *Sirr al-asrār* (*The secret of secrets*), has been lost, but it was translated from Greek by Yahye abn Aluitac. Kasten and other authors identify abn Aluitac with the Syrian Yahya al-Baṭrīq (or al-Biṭrīq), a Nestorian Christian and translator who lived in Baghdad during the caliphate of al-Maʾmūn (813–33).[270] As with Ḥunayn and the *Libro de los buenos proverbios*, a Christian facilitated the diffusion of wisdom literature in the Arab world. However, Bizzarri disagrees with this version and states that the work emerged from Christianized and Hellenized Arab circles in the east, probably between 950 and 970.[271]

The *Sirr al-asrār* claims it is a letter written by Aristotle to Alexander to instruct him on many different topics – some of which are close to the technical *Hermetica*,

267 Harlan Sturm, *The Libro de los buenos proverbios: A Critical Edition (Studies in Romance Languages)* (Lexington: The University Press of Kentucky, 2014), 28.

268 See Kevin van Bladel, "The Alexander Legend in the Qurʾān 18:83–102," in Gabriel Said Reynolds (ed.), *The Quran in Its Historical Context* (Abingdon: Routledge, 2008), 175–80. On this tradition and its relation to Arabic wisdom literature, see Emily Cottrell, "Al-Mubaššir Ibn Fātik and the α Version of the Alexander Romance," in Richard Stoneman, Kyle Erickson, and Ian Richard Netton (eds), *The Alexander Romance in Persia and the East* (Eelde: Barkhuis, 2012), 234–41.

269 Sturm, *Libro de los buenos proverbios*, 16.

270 Lloyd A. Kasten, "*Poridat de las poridades*: A Spanish Form of the Western Text of the Secretum Secretorum," *Romance Philology* 5 (1951–2): 183.

271 Hugo Bizarri (ed.), *Secreto de los secretos. Poridat de las poridades* (Valencia: Universidad de Valencia, 2010), 13.

such as physiognomy, astrology, alchemy, and magic – during his campaigns in Asia. As Gaullier-Bougassas points out, the text serves a dual purpose as a mirror of princes and Hermetic treatise, revealing "scientific" secrets. The transmission and translation of the book in Latin and then vernacular languages fluctuated between these two statuses.[272] According to Bizarri, the tradition of *Sirr al-asrār* was soon divided into two branches, which he labels SS/A and SS/B; this division corrects the previous and inaccurate – so he argues – denomination posited by Kasten of short or Western and long or Eastern.[273] The transmission of different versions of *Sirr al-Asrār* is a complex issue. The version titled SS/A was translated from Arabic into Persian, twice into Hebrew, and finally into Castilian in the middle of the thirteenth century under the title *Poridat de las poridades*. This Castilian translation is probably from the end of Fernando III's or the beginning of Alfonso X's reign, and it has not been determined if it was translated using the Arabic version or an intermediary Hebrew translation.[274] The fact that it was translated into Castilian limited its spread to the rest of Europe.[275]

The branch titled SS/B, long, or Eastern, had a widespread diffusion. In the twelfth century, fragments were translated into Latin by Johannes Hispalensis (d. 1157).[276] According to his prologue, an unidentified Queen Theresa, or Tarasia, commissioned him to write a book to preserve health; thus Hispalensis simply translated the sections about dietetics in the *Sirr al-asrār* and titled it *De regimine sanitatis* (*The guidance of health*) or *Epistula Alexandro de dieta servanda* (*Letter to Alexander on the diet that must be kept*). Johannes Hispalensis also translated *De imaginibus*, the abovementioned book of talismanic magic by Thābit Ibn Qurra. This could explain some information about the discovery of the book that Johannes includes in his prologue:

> Suddenly, a fragment of this work that the philosopher Aristotle prepared for King Alexander came to my mind. In Arabic, it is called *Cyretesar*, that is, *Secreto de los secretos*, that Aristotle made (I say what they say) for King Alexander about the organization of government. The text contains many useful things for the king [...]. About its discovery [Aristotle] says thus: "I make known the search that was diligently given to me by the emperor. I did not stop incessantly visiting

[272] Catherine Gaullier-Bougassas, "Révélation hermetique et savoir occulte de l'Orient dans le Secretum secretorum et les Secrets des secrets français," in Catherine Gaullier-Bougassas, Margaret Bridges, and Jean-Yves Tilliette (eds), *Trajectoires européens du Secretum secretorum du pseudo-Aristote (XIIIe–XVIe siècle)* (Turnhout: Brepols, 2015), 63. For more information on the complex European transmission of the book, I refer to the other works included in the same collective volume, and also to Steven J. Williams, *The Secret of Secrets. The Scholarly Career of a Pseudo-Aristotelian Text in the Latin Middle Ages* (Ann Arbor: The University of Michigan Press, 2003).

[273] Bizarri, *Secreto de los secretos*, 14; Kasten, "*Poridat de las poridades*," 180–3.

[274] Kasten, "*Poridat de las poridades*," 182.

[275] Bizarri, *Secreto de los secretos*, 14.

[276] For a comparative study and commentary on the Arabic text and Johannes Hispalensis's translation, see Regula Foster, *Das Geheimnis der Geheimnisse: Die arabischen und deutschen Fassungen des pseudo-aristotelischen "Sirr al-asrār / Secretum secretorum"* (Wiesbaden: Ludwig Reichert Verlag, 2006).

> places and temples in which I believed that the work of the philosophers would be located and hidden, or in which they could have deposited their doctrines, when I arrived at a certain temple that Hermes had constructed for himself, in which the sun was venerated by certain men. And there I found a certain wise and religious elder, graced with science, doctrine, and experience. I addressed him and diligently strove to please him. I showed him kindness and persuaded him with sweet words until he revealed to me a secret place in which I found many writings and secrets from the philosophers. Amongst them, I found a book written in golden letters, and thus, with the help of God and the fortune of the emperor, once I had achieved and found that which the emperor had commanded me and for which I had spent much time searching, I returned with joy, carrying with me what I desired.[277]

The motif of the search for wisdom is a common topic in wisdom and Hermetic literature, but here we also find a place where "the work of the philosophers would be located and hidden," and where there is a temple that Hermes built to the sun, which might be an allusion to the city of Ḥarrān. Not all versions of this work follow this narration, and they set out to "Christianize" the original.

This is what happened when the enigmatic Philip of Tripoli found in Antioch and then translated some form of this long Eastern, or SS/B version of the work as *Secretum secretorum*, which he dedicated to the bishop of the city, Guy of Valence (bishopric around 1228–37). He watered down some parts related to Hermetic sciences such as magic, alchemy, and geomancy.[278] The first mention of *Secretum secretorum* in Spain is made by Petrus Alphonsi in *Disciplina clericalis*.[279] The legal code of Alfonso X, *Las siete partidas* (*The seven parts*), includes various quotes from the *Secretum secretorum* in its second part – which is partly a mirror of princes. Some of those quotes are closer to *Poridat de las poridades*, the Castilian translation from the Arabic SS/A version, and to the *Bocados* – who also used the *Sirr al-asrār*. Other quotes are different than any of the known versions – including the other Castilian

277 "Dum cogitarem vestre iussioni obedire, huius rei exemplar ab Aristotile philosopho regi Alexandro mango de disposicione regiminis, in quo multa continentur regi utilia [...] de cuius invencione sic ait: "Egressus sum diligenter inquirere quod michi preceptum est ab imperatore, et non cessavi sollicite circuire loca et templa in quibus suspicabar opera philosophorum sita et abscondita esse, vel in quibus commendaverant suant doctrinas, donec pervenirem ad quoddam altare quod sibi edificaverant Hermes, in quo sol venerabatur a quibusdam, ibique inveni quendam senem prudentem et religiosum, sciencia et doctrina moribusque ornatum. Huic adhesi et huic cum suma diligencia placere studui et amabilem me exhibui illi et verbis dulcissimis eum linivi, quousque michi locum secretum detegeret, in quo inveni plura philosophorum scripta et secreta. Interque hunc librum aureis litteris inscriptum inveni, et sic deo auxiliante et fortuna imperatoris vel merito invento quod ab imperatore michi preceptum fuerat et quod diu quesiveram, reversus sum cum Gaudio portans mecum desiderium meum." Cited in Bizzarri, *Secreto de los secretos*, 168. My translation.

278 Kasten, "*Poridat de las poridades*," 181; Bizzarri, *Secreto de los secretos*, 13.

279 In example IV: "Vt, inquid, Aristotiles in epistola sua quam Alexandro regi composuit, meminit" and XXIV. "Aristotiles in epistola sua castigauit regem Alexandrum ita dicens" Petrus Alfonsi, *Disciplina clericalis*, 116 and 139.

translation, *Secreto de los secretos*. This suggests that perhaps other translations existed and that *Secreto de los secretos* might not yet have been produced.[280]

Secreto de los secretos only includes one reference to Hermes: "Oh Alexander, avoid spilling human blood as much as you can. In truth, you do not want to take the divine work, because the resplendent doctor Hermogenes wrote this: [...]."[281] Of course, Hermogenes is a confused rendering of Hermes. *Poridat de las poridades*, translated from the SS/A, short, or Western branch, offers a more abundant flow of scientific and Hermetic knowledge. For example, treatise VII includes a physiognomy, a description of the seasons of the year – including astronomical details – and a lapidary.[282] The prologue of the book explains the last moments of Aristotle: "And some say that he died a natural death. And that his grave is known. And others said that he went to heaven."[283] There is an obvious similarity to Enoch/Idrīs/Hermes's ascent to heaven, narrated by the Quran and recounted in numerous Hermetic sources, as we will see later in this book. The Castilian translator explains the transmission of the book in this way:

> Said he who translated this book, Yahye abn Aluitac: I did not abandon the search for any temple among all temples where the philosophers distilled their books of secrets, nor did I refuse to ask for advice from any thoughtful man I knew, until I reached a temple called Abodenxenit, which Hermes, the older, constructed. There I asked and pleaded with a wise hermit until he showed me all of the books of the temple. And amongst them was a book that Miramamolin asked to be discovered written in golden letters, and I, very pleased, devoted myself to studying it. And I began with the help of God and with the blessing of Miramamolin to translate it from the language of the gentiles into Latin, and from Latin into Arabic.[284]

Thus, Yahye assumes the search – which in other versions is undertaken by Aristotle – as commanded by Miramamolin – a distorted combination of the word *amīr* and al-Maʾmūn, Caliph of Baghdad between 813 and 833. Yahye explains that he visited temples where the philosophers hid their secrets, which, once again, bear strong resemblances to Ḥarrān. The "supreme" temple of wisdom is none other than that of Hermes and is called "Abodenxenit" – we do not know where this name comes from. Bizzarri compares this narrative with the legend of

280 Bizarri, *Secreto de los secretos*, 19–20. *Partidas* II.8.2, II.9.5, and II.10.3.

281 "O Alexandre, esquiua e esquiuate quanto podieres la sangre humanal derramar. En verdat, no quieras a ty tomar el diuinal oficio por que el doctor resplandeçiente, Hermogenes, escriuio assi [...]." Bizarri, *Secreto de los secretos*, 75.

282 Bizarri, *Secreto de los secretos*, 31.

283 "Et algunos dizen que murió su muerte natural. E que su sepulcro es sabido. Et otros dixieron que subiera al cielo." Bizarri, *Secreto de los secretos*, 100.

284 "Dixo el que trasladó este libro Yahye abn Aluitac: Non dexe templo de todos los templos o condensaron los philosophos sos libros de las Poridades que non buscasse nin omne de horden que yo sopiesse que me conseiasse de lo que demandaua a quien no preguntasse fasque uin a un templo quel dicen Abodenxenit que fizo Hermes, el mayor, pora si. Et demande a un hermitanno sabio e roguel e pedil merçed fasta que me mostro todos los libros del templo. E entrellos falle un libro que mando Al Miramomelin buscar escripto todo con letras doro. E torneme pora el muy pagado. E comence con ayuda de Dios e con uentura de Miramomelin a trasladarlo de lenguage de los gentiles en latín e de latín en arauigo." Bizarri, *Secreto de los secretos*, 102–3.

the discovery of the abovementioned *Emerald Table* by Balinus in the *Kitāb sirr al-halīka*:[285] Balinus enters a crypt below the statue of Hermes Trismegistus and finds the emerald tablet, along with a book, in the hands of an old man who is seated there.

Kasten commented on the possible influences in *Poridat de las poridades* from the *Rasā'il Ikhwān al-Ṣafā*,[286] which I mentioned above as one of al-Qurṭubī's sources – who probably brought them to al-Andalus – included in the *Ghāya*. Among many other things, the *Rasā'il* synthesizes Arabic Neoplatonism with Hermetic elements. Treatise IV of *Poridat*, dedicated to the "clerks of the court and governors" (*alguaciles y adelantados*), begins with a philosophical digression. Aristotle wants to teach Alexander "what intellect [*seso*] is and how it is gathered and discovered and many celestial secrets that I cannot avoid to show you what true intellect is and how God granted it to men."[287] In this context of a "revelation of celestial secrets," *seso* (intellect) seems to be used in a Hermetic manner as *nous*, especially because it is followed by an explanation of the Neoplatonic doctrine of emanation – derived from Plotinus and elaborated on in the *Rasā'il*. Aristotle explains: "Know that the first thing that God did was a simple, spiritual, and very accomplished thing, and contained in it are all things of the world, and he gave it the name of *seso* [intellect], and from it came something else not as noble that they call the soul. And God placed them with his virtue in the body of man."[288] The Neoplatonism derived from Plotinus that the *Rasā'il* develops speaks of three hypostases or primordial realities: the One – which monotheistic religions identified with God – from which emanated the *nous* or intellect, and from this the Soul, or Soul of the World. In this passage, we can also see an allusion to the aforementioned theory of the microcosm/macrocosm, which is prominent in the *Rasā'il*. *Poridat* explains that the hierarchy of God–Intellect–Soul is equivalent to the hierarchy of God–rule–court clerk (*alguacil*). The first authority on this matter is Hermes: "And for this reason Hermes, when they asked him why the advice of the advisor was better than the one who asked for it, said thus: 'Because the advice of the advisor is free of will and this is the word of truth.'"[289] Other quotes from Hermes in the treatise use technical vocabulary that, like *seso*, can be related to the *Hermetica*.[290] For instance: "And this is what the great Hermes

285 Bizarri, *Secreto de los secretos*, 50. See also Didier Kahn, *La table d'émeraude et sa tradition alchimique* (Paris: Les Belles Lettres, 1994).

286 Kasten, "*Poridat de las poridades*," 184.

287 "[…] qué es el seso e como se ayunta e descubre y muchas poridades celestiales que non pude escusar por mostrar vos el seso verdadero qual es e commo lo puso Dios en los hombres." Bizarri, *Secreto de los secretos*, 123.

288 "Sepades que la primera cosa que Dios fizo fue una cosa simple spirital e mui conplida cosa e figuro en ella todas las cosas del mundo e púsole nombre seso e del salió otra cosa non tan noble quel dicen alma. E púsolos Dios con su virtud en el cuerpo del omne." Bizarri, *Secreto de los secretos*, 123.

289 "E por esto dixo Hermes quandol demandaron que por que era el conseio del conseiador meior que el del que lo demanda. Dixo assy: 'Porque es el conseio del conseiador libre de la uoluntad e esta es la palabra uerdadera.'" Bizarri, *Secreto de los secretos*, 124.

290 As suggested by Kahane and Pietrangeli, "Hermetism," 446.

said in one of his counsels, that the well-accomplished king, he who has natural intellect [*seso*] and pursues the fulfillment of his reign and the permanence of his law, must excuse himself to seize his subjects' possessions."[291] Since it follows that Neoplatonic passage from the *Poridat*, it is clear that when the Castilian translator speaks of *seso*, it is in relation to *nous* or intellect, the second of the Neoplatonic hypostases. Finally, the *Poridat* includes a quote very similar to that in the *Bocados*, which I think is reminiscent of the Latin *Asclepius*: "Know, Alexander, that man is of a higher nature than all other living things in the world, and there is no quality in any creature out of all the ones God made that is not in him."[292]

Many earlier scholars have focused on the general and inclusive aspect of knowledge in sapiential literature, and often they simply mention Hermes in brief notes to their editions of his works. In fact, as we have seen, Hermetic tradition is consubstantial to some of those works, because Hermetic content appears in the sapiential genre in different doses depending on the text. The importance of Hermes in this sapiential literature, which began to be translated at the end of Fernando III's reign, can partly explain the eminence that the old sage acquired in the works of Alfonso the Wise, and particularly in the *GE*, which used as sources several of the sapiential works discussed here.

Conclusion

This chapter briefly summarizes how Hermes and his traditions originated in Hellenistic Egypt and then developed to eventually reappear in the Iberian Peninsula. From the beginning, the history of Hermes is a history of translation, from Egyptian languages into Greek; from Greek into Latin, Syriac, Coptic – among other languages of ancient Christianity – and Persian; from most of these languages into Arabic; and finally, in the Iberian Peninsula, from Latin and Arabic into Latin and Castilian. After Hermes's arrival in the peninsula, Christian scholars negotiated his pagan culture. Aside from sparse archaeological evidence, the first strong traces of the Hermetic sciences – astrology, talismanic magic, *melothesia* – are in the heresy of Priscillian. The Church prosecuted the practices of Priscillianism, but a segment of the clergy found great fascination in the sciences that Priscillian nurtured. This fascination is embodied by Isidore of Seville, who, through his *Etymologies*, influenced how Hermes would be characterized in the Middle Ages. Isidore also classified magic, included Hermes as one of its main representatives, and mentioned a concept related to the Hermetic tradition for the first time in Latin: the microcosm. Isidore kept his influence after the Arab conquest of Spain in 711 CE; however, Arabic culture developed their own Hermetic tradition and imported it to the Iberian Peninsula.

291 "Et esto dixo el grant Hermes en uno de sos castigos que el bien complido pora rey e el seso natural e el complimiento de su regno e duramiento de su ley es escusar de tomar aueres de sus yentes." Bizarri, *Secreto de los secretos*, 108.

292 "Sepades Alexandre que el omne es de más alta natura que todas las cosas biuas del mundo. E que no a manera propria en ninguna creatura de quantas Dios fizo que no la aya en él." Bizzarri, *Secreto de los secretos*, 130.

In the ninth century, the rulers of al-Andalus tried to imitate the height of Baghdad's splendour and even imported many of the books of the "Sciences of the Ancients," which had been translated from Greek, Persian, and Syriac. I suggest that Hermes came to the Iberian Peninsula for a second time with those books. Hermetic sciences developed in al-Andalus during the ninth century in the circles of courtier-astrologers patronized by al-Ḥakam I and ʿAbd al-Raḥmān II, but they really flourished in the next century after al-Qurṭubī wrote the *Ghāya*, which incorporated most Arabic Hermetic traditions. During the tenth century the circumstances changed and ʿAbd al-Raḥmān III began to prosecute heterodox thinkers. Things temporarily improved during the period of cultural splendor of al-Ḥakam II, who gathered an immense library; however, his weak son, Hishām II (976–1009), delegated all his power to the implacable Almanzor, who removed and burned all the books he considered unorthodox in 979.

The need to hide all Hermetic knowledge and sciences under a veil of secrecy continued after the fall of Córdoba's Caliphate in 1031. During the ensuing period of the *ṭāʾifa* kingdoms, scholars from different religions and countries flocked to Iberia, attracted by Arabic cultural treasures. Some of them collaborated in networks that clustered in nodes. In the middle of the twelfth century, one of these nodes operated in the bishopric of Tarazona, located across several Iberian kingdoms. Erudite men working there shared a common interest in the sciences and teachings of Hermes. This interest continued when the epicentre of translation activity moved to Toledo, where translation was supported by archbishops and high Church dignitaries. Toledo kept attracting translators and talent from all over the Christian world. Arabic works were initially translated into Latin, but throughout the thirteenth century the Castilian language reached a point of maturity. Thus, during the reigns of Fernando III, and then his son Alfonso X the Wise – who furthered the universal access to culture that his father aimed to establish – the bulk of the translations were made into Castilian, the shared language of all subjects of his kingdom. It was at this moment that Hermes Trismegistus started "to speak" a vernacular language. Thus, the medieval Hermetic tradition has a vernacular strand that many specialists in the field have commonly overlooked. The first works in which the "Castilian Hermes" appeared were translations of Arabic sapiential literature. In this genre, Hermetic wisdom was sometimes merged with universal or "common sense" advice, but at other times it contained a secret message.

Castilian political culture eventually chose to reveal Hermes and make his *poridades* or secrets accessible to those who had the intellect and language skills to understand them. Castilian wisdom literature offered an optimal perspective on the interrelation between different Hermetic traditions that had developed throughout the centuries; they presented the figure of the wise Hermes in a way that justifies the key role that Alfonso would give him in his oeuvre. Wisdom literature was often dedicated to educated kings, princes, and courtiers. Thus, it is no surprise that in the *GE* – his ambitious universal history – Alfonso presented Hermes/Mercury as an exemplary courtier, wise in all kinds of sciences and whose education was, in part, inspired by Arab *adab*. In this way, the *Hermes arabicus* that was translated and homogenized in Castile became an essential ingredient for the creation of a veritable *Hermes hispanus* by Alfonso the Wise, as we will see in the rest of this book.

2

Hermetic History in the Arabic Sources of Alfonso the Wise's *General Estoria*

Introduction

Hermes Trismegistus's journey on the Iberian Peninsula reached a crucial tipping point during the reign of Alfonso X the Wise of Castile (1252–84). The learned king blended diverse Eastern and Western Hermetic traditions and presented a new incarnation of Hermes that fitted within the social and political circumstances of thirteenth-century Castile. Hermetic traditions resonate prominently across various genres in Alfonso's oeuvre, not only those related to Hermetic sciences – such as astrology and magic – but also to historical ones such as the *GE*. The *GE* incorporates sources from past traditions as well as from productions of the royal *scriptorium*; therefore, focusing on this historical work will allow me to offer a comprehensive portrait of Hermes during this complex and culturally fruitful period. In this chapter, I will briefly introduce Alfonso and the *GE*; then I will explore the origin and Hermetic core of the most important Arabic sources that were translated and included – or rather deeply interpreted – in the *GE*; finally, I will offer specific examples of how Alfonso renders tales from those sources that have been qualified by Arabists as "Hermetic history." These works served both as an innovative historical component – from a European perspective – and as fertile ground for incorporating Hermes Trismegistus as a character in such an ambitious universal history.

Alfonso X and the *GE*

Alfonso's father, Fernando III, became king of Castile in 1217. He inherited the kingdom of León from his father, Alfonso IX, in 1230, and then conquered a vast number of Muslim territories in the south – the significant city of Córdoba fell in 1236, and Seville in 1248. Seville had been the capital of the Almohad empire in al-Andalus for almost a century.[1] The once extensive Muslim lands in Spain were reduced to the kingdom of Granada in the south-east, and the kingdom of Castile became larger than all the other territories in the peninsula combined. When Fernando III died in 1252, Alfonso X inherited an immense kingdom that had recently incorporated

1 On Fernando III's conquests, see Ana Rodríguez López, *La consolidación territorial de la monarquía feudal castellana: expansión y fronteras durante el reinado de Fernando III* (Madrid: Consejo Superior de Investigaciones Científicas, 1994).

hundreds of thousands of Arabic-speaking vassals. Alfonso never equalled his father when it came to military conquests, but his cultural achievements would become unparalleled in Castilian and Spanish history.[2]

Alfonso led the Iberian process of translating Arabic texts – a process that had started centuries earlier – but he decided to use Castilian, rather than Latin, as the target language. With this shift, the king not only imbued the main language of his kingdom with prestige but also aided a political centralization project, which intended to integrate all members of his kingdom, regardless of their religion, through a common language. A clearly defined cultural project accompanied the political one.[3] Alfonso did not seek to diminish or eliminate Islamicate power but to integrate Muslim culture within a common endeavour;[4] as Dangler has explained, the king's centralizing goals "represented a novel, large-scale political and cultural project, carried out in collaboration with the largest and most erudite group of Christian, Jewish, and Muslim intellectuals of his time in all of western Europe."[5] Regarding the influence of Muslim culture, Márquez Villanueva has raised an important question: what should we make of Alfonso, a Christian king who founded universities using a Western model and a madrasa-like centre to study Arabic and Arab sciences?[6] Fierro has pointed out the similarity between Alfonso the Wise's political and cultural project and that of his former rivals, the Almohad rulers, whom he effectively succeeded; the Almohad project of sapience, which was to ultimately achieve "a radical political transformation," served as the framework for Alfonso X's political and cultural goals.[7] This ideal of *sapientia* also had Christian influences,[8] but in this work I will focus on its Arabic roots, as they are closely connected with Hermetic sources.

Thus, following both European and Arab models, Alfonso led a diverse team of scribes and scholars who not only translated works into Castilian but also produced many original works in different genres, such as literature, science, law, and history. According to most specialists, the royal *scriptorium* was divided into different teams that each worked to translate separate works and topics. Some of these translations were later produced as independent Castilian translations, but others were dissected, elaborated on, and compiled into new products. The sources mention how Alfonso

2 On the life of Alfonso X see Salvador H. Martínez, *Alfonso X el Sabio: una biografía* (Madrid: Polifemo, 2003).

3 See Francisco Márquez Villanueva, *El concepto cultural alfonsí* (Barcelona: Bellaterra, 2004).

4 According to Maribel Fierro ("Alfonso X 'the Wise': The Last Almohad Caliph?," *Medieval Encounters: Jewish, Christian, and Muslim Culture in Confluence and Dialogue* 15, nos 2–4 (2009): 192), Alfonso belongs to an Islamicate world in the sense coined by Marshall G. S. Hodgson (*The Classical Age of Islam*, vol. 1 of *The Venture of Islam* (Chicago: The University of Chicago Press, 1974, 57–60)). Thus, the wise king, although Christian, was influenced by Islamic culture and even furthered it.

5 Dangler, *Edging Towards Iberia*, 95–6.

6 Márquez Villanueva, *El concepto cultural alfonsí*, 18.

7 See Fierro, "Alfonso X 'The Wise'," 194.

8 See Manuel Alejandro Rodríguez de la Peña, "*Imago sapientiae*: los orígenes del ideal sapiencial medieval," *Medievalismo* 7 (1997): 11–40.

supervised the process, and sometimes even the proper use of Castilian.[9] This was the case with works related to astrology and magic – Hermetic sciences the wise king was particularly fond of. For instance, at the beginning of his reign, Alfonso ordered translations of the *Picatrix* and the *Libro de las cruzes* (*Book of the crosses*) – works I mentioned in Chapter One – as well as the compilation of the *Lapidario*. Later in his life, he used these and other astrological books to compose original works such as the *Astromagia*, *Libro de las formas e de las imágenes* (*Book of the forms and the images*), and the *Libro del saber de astrología* (*Book on the knowledge of astrology*); all contain references to Hermes Trismegistus.[10]

This compilation procedure was used to create two grand historical projects commissioned by the Castilian king: the *Estoria de España* (*History of Spain*, a chronicle about the rulers of the Iberian Peninsula) and the *GE*. The latter, which I will focus on in this book, was an ambitious endeavour aiming to trace the history of the world from the beginning of time to Alfonso's era. Even though the project did not come to fruition in its entirety, the result is still an impressive achievement. We do not know exactly when the compilation process began, but specialists agree that it started before 1272, but was unfinished at the time of the king's death in 1284.[11] In the prologue, Alfonso asserts his prominent role in the project:

> I, Don Alfonso, by the grace of God king of Castile, Toledo, León, Galicia, Seville, Córdoba, Murcia, Jaén, and the Algarve, son of the very noble King Don Fernando and the very noble Queen Doña Beatriz, after I collected many writings and many stories of the ancient facts, I selected the truer and better among them to the best of my knowledge, and thus made this book.[12]

We do not have much information about the many qualified specialists who worked on this project. However, the fourth part reveals at least one of those workfellows when it states that it was finished in 1280 and "I Martín Pérez de Maqueda, scribe of

9 See Gonzalo Menéndez Pidal, "Cómo trabajaron las escuelas alfonsíes," *NRFH* 5 (1951): 363–80; Diego Catalán, "El taller historiográfico Alfonsí. Métodos y problemas en el trabajo compilatorio," *Romania* 84, no. 335 (3) (1963): 354–75; Inés Fernández-Ordóñez, *Las estorias de Alfonso el Sabio* (Madrid: Istmo, 1992), 47–68; and Irene Salvo García, "'E es de saber que son en este traslado todas las estorias.' La traducción en el taller de la *General Estoria* De Alfonso X," *Cahiers d'Études Hispaniques Médiévales* 41, no. 1 (2019): 139–54.

10 Throughout this book I reference these works and their bibliographies, which are also included in the Bibliography. For Hermetic elements in Alfonso's astrological production, I recommend Ana Domínguez Rodríguez, *Astrología y arte en el "Lapidario" de Alfonso X el Sabio* (Murcia: Real Academia Alfonso X el Sabio, 2006).

11 Carlos Alvar Ezquerra, "*La Grande e General Estoria*," in Patrizia Botta et al. (eds), *Rumbos del hispanismo en el umbral del Cincuentenario de la AIH* (Roma: Bagatto, 2012), 2:19.

12 "Yo don Alfonso, por la gracia de Dios rey de Castiella, de Toledo, de León, de Gallizia, de Sevilla, de Córdova, de Murcia, de Jaén e del Algarbe, fijo del muy noble rey don Fernando e de la muy noble reína doña Beatriz, después que ove fecho ayuntar muchos escritos e muchas estorias de los fechos antiguos escogí d'ellos los más verdaderos e los mejores que ý sope e fiz ende fazer este libro." *GE*1 I, 5.

the books of the very noble King Alfonso, wrote this book along with some of my other scribes that I had by his mandate."[13]

The *GE*'s chronology follows that of Jerome's Latin version of the Greek *Chronicle of Eusebius*, which had served as a pattern for many Christian historical works for centuries – some of which became sources for the *GE*. For instance, Alfonso organized the contents and parts of the *GE* according to Augustine's six ages of the world. The fifth part is incomplete, and only the prologue and a few pages of the sixth part have been preserved. Sánchez Prieto-Borja, assisted by other scholars, has published the only complete edition of all existing parts of the *GE*.[14]

Regarding the project's intellectual framework, the research conducted by Martínez is worth noting. He conceives Alfonso as the ultimate representative of a specific medieval humanism that existed in Castile and was characterized by its: 1) multiculturalism; 2) use of the vernacular; and 3) secularism.[15] I will discuss these three characteristics in relation to the *GE*: as we saw in Chapter One, by Alfonso's time, pagan, Christian, Arab, and Jewish traditions collided with and influenced each other; the *GE* integrates sources from these traditions in a unique way. Up until this point, most European scientific, literary, and historical works were written in Latin; however, Alfonso decided to produce the vast majority of his works – including the *GE* – in his still-developing vernacular language, Castilian. The enhancement of its stylistic and syntactic resources enabled Castilian to express content that until then was the domain of the great cultural languages (i.e., Latin and Arabic).[16] At a time when Christian dogma prevailed in all intellectual domains, Alfonso adopted a much more secular approach and was occasionally criticized for it.[17] In both his juridical and historical works, Alfonso displays a desire to promote a secular culture.[18]

The *GE* takes a surprisingly secular approach, especially compared to other historical works, both earlier and contemporary. At the time, the contemporary prototype used by Latin Christendom was the *Historia scholastica* by Petrus Comestor (1100–79). Despite its enormous success as a textbook across Europe – including in Castile – the *GE* only partially imitated the model established by the *Historia scholastica*.[19] Like the *Historia scholastica*, the *GE* follows the Bible's chronology: starting with the creation of the world and finishing in Jesus's times. However, as

13 "Yo, Martín Pérez de Maqueda, escrivano de los libros de muy noble rey don Alfonso, escribí estte libro con otros mis escribanos que tenía por su mandado." *GE4* II, 620.

14 I refer to the extensive bibliography on the *GE* included in this edition.

15 See Salvador H. Martínez, *El humanismo medieval y Alfonso X el Sabio: Ensayo sobre los orígenes del humanismo vernáculo* (Madrid: Polifemo, 2016), 13–18.

16 Sánchez-Prieto Borja, introduction to *GE1* I, xxx.

17 See Ana M. Montero, "Reconstrucción de un ideal de espiritualidad en los hombres del saber de la corte de Alfonso X," in Lillian von der Walde, Concepción Company, and Aurelio González (eds), *Temas, motivos y contextos medievales* (México: El Colegio de México, 2008), 519–20.

18 Sánchez-Prieto Borja, introduction to *GE1* I, xxiv–xxv.

19 Francisco Rico, *Alfonso el Sabio y la General Estoria: Tres Lecciones* (Barcelona: Ariel, 1972), 45–60.

Sánchez-Prieto points out, Alfonso decided to take the Bible as the "tree" to grow his work around just because there was no other option at the time.[20] Due to unforeseen circumstances the *GE* concludes at the end of the Old Testament, yet the initial plan was to continue until Alfonso's reign. But the most substantial difference lies in the amount of non-Christian content the *GE* contains. The *Historia scholastica* summarizes and comments on the historical parts of the Bible, and some chapters include a brief appendix of *incidentia*, a listing of contemporary secular facts and figures – in which it follows the model of Eusebius's *Chronicle*. However, biblical facts in the *GE* form a mere tenth of the total content,[21] the inverse of Comestor. This proportion gives a secular flavour to the work, not to mention that Alfonso used Arabic sources extensively, which Comestor would never have imagined doing. Specialists have pointed out other possible precedents to Alfonso's innovative model for history;[22] however, as Montero establishes that "there was nothing that resembled the *GE* in Europe"[23] – we must look elsewhere.

To understand why Alfonso detached himself from Latin Christendom's historical works we have to look at his intentions, and a good place to start is the *GE*'s prologue. It is significant that it starts with the opening sentence of Aristotle's *Metaphysics*: "all men by nature desire to know." But Alfonso quickly adapts this idea to the discipline of history: "[to know] the facts that happen at all times, as much in past times, as in [the times] in which they live, as in the times to come."[24] Thus from the beginning, Alfonso articulates a new universal and secular conception of history, in which the main objective is not to grasp how God's providential will plays out over time. Instead, the *GE* transmits an idea of knowledge as a totality and discloses a hierarchized universe that binds man to the world and God.[25] This view connects the *GE* with the rest of Alfonso's projects, especially the scientific ones. Martin points out that history's new epistemological dignity corresponds with the view that it is a depository and celebration of knowledge.[26] In addition to emphasizing his own agency, in the *GE* Alfonso connects himself and his ancestors with the most important rulers the world has known. For this reason, the project has been interpreted as a way of justifying his legitimacy as emperor of the Holy Roman Empire, a title he spent numerous years attempting to claim. In the *GE*, exemplary rulers and learned men – like himself – are presented as models for his courtiers. Martínez affirms that the wise king's model of the courtier or learned man was directly influenced by

20 Sánchez-Prieto Borja, introduction to *GE*1 I, xliv.

21 See Rico, *Alfonso el Sabio*, 55.

22 For a good summary, see Georges Martin, "El modelo historiográfico Alfonsí y sus antecedentes," in Georges Martin (ed.), *La historia alfonsí: El modelo y sus destinos (siglos xiii–xv)* (Madrid: Casa de Velázquez, 2000), 9–40.

23 Ana M. Montero, "A Possible Connection between the Philosophy of the Castilian King Alfonso X and the *Risālat Ḥayy Ibn Yaqẓān* by Ibn Ṭufayl," *Al-Masāq: Islam and the Medieval Mediterranean* 18, no. 1 (2006): 11.

24 "Natural cosa es de cobdiciar los omnes saber los fechos que acaecen en todos los tiempos, tan bien en el tiempo que es passado como en aquel en que están como en el otro que á de venir." *GE*1 I, 5.

25 See Rico, *Alfonso el Sabio*, 142.

26 See Martin, "El modelo historiográfico Alfonsí," 39.

the Arabs and specifically related to *adab*, a complex educational concept in Arabic culture that I will explain below. He builds upon Maravall's earlier research about *adab* and courtesy in Castilian sapiential works – a genre derived from Arab sources, as we have seen – and relates it to the ideal of the courtier that Alfonso presents in various works, including the *GE*.[27]

In short, the *GE* is a polyhedric work – impossible to explain using a single source or exogenous factor (including Alfonso's political and imperial agenda).[28] Alfonso's goals in the *GE* include: 1) interpreting history in line with his personal principles; 2) providing the kingdom's diverse vassals with a tailored historical work; 3) satisfying his own curiosity and that of many of his subjects; 4) including all types of information in an encyclopedic format; 5) making Castilian a true language of culture; 6) integrating biblical and gentiles' histories in a new way;[29] 7) incorporating Arab and Jewish materials from diverse genres, including historiography and astrology/magic; 8) presenting history as a discipline dependent on moral philosophy;[30] 9) offering a particular model of the courtier and an implicit mirror of princes, thus contributing to the education of all Castilians.

The most pertinent question for my research is discovering how Hermes Trismegistus and his tradition fits into these varied influences and Alfonso's goals. As we saw in Chapter One, Hermetic traditions came to the learned king and his Castilian court mostly in their Islamic form. For these reasons, even though Arabic books were not Alfonso's main sources, nor were they the only way through which Hermetic materials reached him, their influence is evident in the Hermetic elements found in many passages of the *GE*. Alfonso sponsored a large number of translations from Arabic, and many of them – some still unknown to us – became sources for the *GE*. Fraker emphasizes how "it is beyond doubt that many of these Spanish texts are full of allusions to things Hermetic";[31] and he also speculated that "certain strains in the Alfonsine historical writing might also be Hermetic."[32] To discern how the Hermetic traditions filtered into the *GE*'s narrative, I focus on a specific subgenre of geographic and historical books containing Hermetic components that are the *GE*'s main Arabic sources. Even though these books were not addressed by Fraker, they undoubtedly confirm his conclusions. These books contain educational and cultural elements of Arabic *adab*, and so they are also important for understanding how Hermetic traditions travelled from an Arabic to a Castilian cultural environment.

27 Martínez, *El humanismo medieval*, 176–84; Jose Antonio Maravall, "La cortesía como saber en la Edad Media," *Cuadernos Hispanoamericanos* 62 (1965): 528–38.

28 Sánchez-Prieto Borja, introduction to *GE*1 I, xlix.

29 For a thorough elaboration on analogous points, see Sánchez-Prieto Borja, introduction to *GE*1 I, l–lxxxv

30 See Martínez, *El humanismo medieval*, 27–8.

31 Charles F. Fraker, *The Scope of History: Studies in the Historiography of Alfonso el Sabio* (Ann Arbor: University of Michigan Press, 1996), 173.

32 Fraker, *Scope of History*, 173.

Adab and Wondrous and Hermetic Components in the *GE*'s Arabic Sources

Studies on the Arabic material in the *GE* have increased substantially in recent years. Arabic historiography is a fundamental component of the historical and literary canon Alfonso used to compose the *GE*; so much so that Muslim materials are used to interpret Christian ones, including the Bible.[33] While not all Arabic sources have been identified, Alfonso extensively employs and references some, which greatly facilitates their identification by scholars. However, leading experts on Alfonso's oeuvre have not yet investigated from which specific genres within the diverse Muslim historical tradition those sources originate. Sánchez-Prieto Borja suggests that, despite some traces in Christian sources, "it is possible that we need to relate the *GE*'s interest in including all kinds of picturesque events and wonders of the world to Arab historiography."[34] As I will show, these characteristics are specific to some *adab* genres, which occasionally, and depending on the author, also include magical, astrological, and Hermetic motifs. In fact, this is occurring in the *GE*'s most widely used Arabic sources. This Hermetic content does not always derive from Arabic works, but it is prevalent in those used by Alfonso. Let us see how these features are related to *adab* and its historical genres.

Initially, *adab* had the same meaning as *sunna* (path, custom, habit, pattern of conduct, etc.),[35] but *sunna* eventually came to refer to religious customs inherited from the Prophet, while *adab* expressed secular ones.[36] Thus, *adab* was presented as a secular alternative to *sunna* and comprised "practical ethics separated from all Koranic and traditional teachings and also the sum of educational elements needed by a man who wanted to behave appropriately in all circumstances of life."[37] In the Abbasid period, *adab* conveyed a secular Arab culture that rendered a man urbane, but contact with other cultures – especially through translations in Baghdad – expanded *adab* to include non-Arabic literature, and this led to it expressing a more universal humanism through its philanthropic and educational components. Classical Islamic thought absorbed the ancient principles of humanism – including its ethical, social, and intellectual message – and *paideia* (the system and ideal of education in Greece).[38] This suggests that the Latin scholarly tradition was not the only route through which ancient humanism influenced Alfonso's thought. It could have also travelled via an Arab route alongside *adab*. Therefore, while

33 Sánchez-Prieto Borja, introduction to *GE*1 I, lvi–lvii.

34 Sánchez-Prieto Borja, introduction to *GE*1 I, lvi and ci.

35 On the ancient concept of *adab* as an ancestral custom related to *sunna*, see Carlo Alfonso Nallino, *La littérature arabe des origines à l'époque de la dynastie umayyade: Leçons professées en arabe à l'Université du Caire* (Paris: G. P. Maisonneuve, 1950), 7–28.

36 Charles Pellat, "ADAB, ii. Adab in Arabic Literature," in *Encyclopædia Iranica*, available online at: http://www.iranicaonline.org/articles/adab-ii-arabic-lit_(last accessed September 28, 2022); see also Seger Adrianus Bonebakker, "Adab and the Concept of Belles-Lettres," in Julia Ashtiany et al. (eds), *ʿAbbasid Belles-Lettres* (Cambridge: Cambridge University Press, 1990), 17.

37 Pellat, "ADAB."

38 Joel L. Kraemer, "Humanism in the Renaissance of Islam: A Preliminary Study," *Journal of the American Oriental Society* 104, no. 1 (1984): 156.

the *adab* present in the translated wisdom literature may have inspired Alfonso's courtly ideal – as Maravall and Martínez emphasize – it is worth exploring how geographical and historical *adab* genres could have also influenced his humanistic and educational project.

General treatises of *adab* always include amusing anecdotes on historical characters, and provide their readers with information about important events that cultivated citizens can use to entertain their peers. Edifying historical content also fulfills the ethical purposes of *adab*; as Hodgson explains, historical writing "from which could be drawn examples piquant or cogent to enliven every point" merged with the *adīb*'s thinking in a variety of ways.[39] Despite the concept's complexity, *adab* always entails a correlation between knowledge/education and morals – which, as we will see, is consistent with many historical characters in the *GE*. The two Arabic words usually associated with history, *taʾrīkh* and *khabar* (pl. *akhbār*), articulate different understandings of the genre: *taʾrīkh* expresses a sense of dating and periodization, whereas *khabar* is closer to "story, anecdote" and holds "no notion of the fixation of time at all."[40] The oldest historical reports are known as *akhbār*. They were compiled and introduced through *isnād* (chains of transmitters) and follow the model of *aḥadīth* (records of the traditions and sayings of the Prophet) from the *sunna*. After the eighth century, and especially in the writings of al-Ṭabarī (839–923), *taʾrīkh* became the common name for historical works. Over time a new distinction between *taʾrīkh*, "chronologically dated history," and *akhbār*, then understood as "literary history," was established. The first was usually characterized by straightforward prose, like that of al-Ṭabarī, whereas the second was understood as "a further dimension of *adab*"[41] that used rhetorically inflected language, encompassed a moral aspect, and eventually incorporated amusing and wondrous elements. Historians who were also scribes and *udabāʾ* (specialists in *adab*, sing. *adīb*) created *adab*-minded history, which integrated *akhbār* and other genres, such as biography and geography.[42] This close relationship between geography and *akhbār* is particularly relevant here because the *GE*'s main Arabic sources come from geographical genres associated with *adab* that have a substantial historical component.

Fernández-Ordóñez has tracked the *GE*'s Arabic sources and concludes that the two most frequently used are both referred to as *Estoria de Egipto* (*History of Egypt*).[43] Their original Arabic titles are: the *Kitāb al-masālik wa-l-mamālik* (*Book of the roads and the kingdoms*) by Abū ʿUbayd al-Bakrī (*c.* 1014–94) and *Kitāb al-ʿadjāʾib al-kabīr* (*The great book of marvels*) by al-Waṣīfī (*c.* tenth century). I argue that at least a third (alleged) *History of Egypt* can be added to this list: *Kitāb murūj al-dhahab* (*Book of the prairies of gold*) by al-Masʿūdī (d. 956), which contains characteristics similar to the first two and whose importance has thus far been underestimated. Alfonso calls each book *History of Egypt* because they dedicate large sections to that

39 Hodgson, *Classical Age of Islam*, 1, 454.

40 Li Guo, "History Writing," in Robert Irwin (ed.), *The New Cambridge History of Islam* (Cambridge: Cambridge University Press, 2010), 4: 444.

41 Francis Robinson, "Education," in Irwin (ed.) *The New Cambridge History of Islam*, 4: 503.

42 Guo, "History Writing," 446.

43 See Fernández-Ordóñez, *Las estorias de Alfonso*, 173–202.

country; however, their Arabic titles are meaningful. As we will see below, *al-Masālik wa-l-mamālik* refers to a specific genre that encompasses Arab geography up to the eleventh century; whereas the *ʿadjāʾib* (wonders) referenced in the second title are a component of *adab* works frequently connected to magical, astrological, and Hermetic material. *ʿAdjāʾib* encompass a wide range of topics: monuments from antiquity, portents in the animal and vegetable world, finds from famous characters, magic, etc. In his study on the *maravillas del mundo* (*wonders of the world*) in the *GE*, Sánchez-Prieto acknowledges that these wonders come from different authors, but perhaps those from Arab sources "have a definitive weight in the Alfonsine conception of history."[44] Thus, the Arabic concept of *ʿadjāʾib* provides us with clues about the *GE*'s features.

Reflecting on the *ʿajīb* (wonderful, strange; this adjective is related to *ʿadjāʾib*) in Arab geography, Miquel highlights that, despite its inherently irrational essence, it is susceptible to rational analysis. The *ʿadjāʾib* is an opportunity for an author to engage in research; what previous traditions would have explained with a myth, some Muslim authors interpret through any available science, including magic.[45] Similarly, we will observe how Alfonso interprets what he deems as historical information, like the supernatural abilities depicted in the Ovidian tales, as a form of magic that can be logically explained by drawing upon Arabic sciences. The predilection for *ʿadjāʾib* in geographical *adab* opened the door to including Hermetic elements, in which can be found traces of Hermes Trismegistus, his writings, those who transmitted his knowledge, and associated disciplines – alchemy, astrology, and magic. Not all *adab* writers embraced those components – in fact, some of them strongly abhorred magic or astrology – but they are widespread throughout the genre. Due to Alfonso's fondness for Hermetic and astrological topics, it is reasonable to assume that he selected Arabic geographical and historical books that not only complemented his Latin sources but also were related to other aspects of his intellectual endeavours. Understanding how these geographical genres flourished, evolved, and accommodated Hermetic components can help us identify how their content influenced Alfonso's historical writings.

From the Heyday of Arabic Geography to al-Bakrī's *Kitāb al-Masālik wa-l-Mamālik*

Arab geography is in part a result of the translation movement from Greek into Arabic that took place during the cultural splendour of the Abbasid Caliphate. Ptolemy (100–170 CE) became the unequalled authority on geography. Using him as a foundation, Muslim writers developed *ṣūrat al-arḍ* (the science of the form or representation of the earth), which initially combined astrological and astronomical

44 Pedro Sánchez-Prieto Borja, "Las maravillas del mundo en la General Estoria de Alfonso X," in Constance Carta, Sarah Finci, and Dora Mancheva (eds), *Edad Media*, vol. 1 of *Antes se agotan la mano y la pluma que su historia = Magis déficit manus et calamus quam eius historia: Homenaje a Carlos Alvar* (San Millán de la Cogolla: Cilengua, 2016), 337.

45 A. Miquel, *La géographie humaine du monde musulman jusqu'au milieu du XXe siècle*, 4 vols (Paris: Mouton & Co, 1973–80), 1:42–3.

data, geodesy, and the "science of the climes."[46] Arab astronomy adopted Ptolemy's system of the seven climes (*aqālīm*, from the Greek *climata*) latitudinally distributed on the earth's surface. Authors such as al-Masʿūdī placed each clime under the influence of a planet, while others, for instance al-Muqaddasī, preserved a tradition attributed to Hermes Trismegistus that used fourteen climes, with seven climates north of the equator and seven to the south.[47] The most influential book on this science was the *Kitab ṣūrat al-arḍ* (*Book of the representation of the earth*) by the famous mathematician Muḥammad Ibn Musā al-Khwārizmī (*c.*780–*c.*850) – from whom "algorithm" derives – who also had a great interest in geography, which introduces some historical and *adab* topics.[48]

It is no surprise that geographical subjects soon entered into the general cultural knowledge of the educated citizen, and then into general or encyclopedic works related to *adab*, including those by the great representatives and developers of the genre, al-Jāḥiẓ (*c.* 776–869) and Ibn Qutayba (828–89). Al-Jāḥiẓ's *Kitāb al-tarbīʿ wa al-tadwīr* (*Book of the treatise of the quadrature and the circumference*) includes a universal history that contains biblical and mythological information and is supported by sciences such as astronomy, astrology, geography, geology, zoology, ethnography, and magic – including references to Hermes Trismegistus.[49] Geographical and historical subjects are also a significant part of al-Jāḥiẓ's most famous work, *Kitāb al-ḥayawān* (*Book of the animals*) and are central to his *Kitāb al-amṣār wa ʿadjāʾib al-buldān* (*Book of the metropolises and wonders of the world*). In this last work we also find the concept of *ʿadjāʾib* (wonders), which al-Jāḥiẓ cultivated throughout his works. As Shboul explains, al-Jāḥiẓ's works embody the ninth-century enrichment of the Arabic humanities.[50]

Even though *adab* takes many shapes according to the particular readership to which it is addressed, among their main readers we can single out the *kuttāb* (sing. *kātib*), scribes and secretaries in the caliphal administration, who ideally needed to know a little about every science. Consequently, specific manuals for *kuttāb* were developed. The most influential of these manuals – particularly in al-Andalus[51] – was the *Kitāb adab al-kātib* (*Book of the scribe's adab*) by Ibn Qutayba, which included history and geography in its "curriculum." Ibn Qutayba also wrote the *Kitāb al-maʾārif* (*Book of secular knowledge*), which "contains all the historical information needed by cultivated men"[52] and classifies famous characters of history by placing them in their geographical contexts,[53] and the *Kitāb ʿuyūn al-akhbār* (*Book of the sources of history*), which focuses on highly literary accounts (i.e., *akhbār*) of important personalities.

46 See Miquel, *Géographie humaine*, 1:12.
47 Miquel, *Géographie humaine*, 1:11 and 82.
48 Miquel, *Géographie humaine*, 1:75.
49 Miquel, *Géographie humaine*, 1:38–9; al-Jāḥiẓ (Ǧāḥiẓ), *Le Kitāb al-tarbīʿ wa-t-tadwīr de Ǧāḥiẓ*, ed. Ch. Pellat (Damas: Institut français de Damas, 1955), index, 18–19.
50 Shboul, *Al-Masʿūdī & His World*, 30.
51 Bruna Soravia, "Entre bureaucratie et littérature: La kitāba et les kuttāb dans l'administration de l'Espagne Umayyade," *Al-Masāq* 7 (1994): 166–7.
52 Pellat, "ADAB."
53 Miquel, *Géographie humaine*, 1:66.

General manuals and *adab* encyclopedias included geographical content. However, a specific category was soon developed that popularized geographical and geodesical[54] technical procedures and made them applicable to the particular duties of the *kuttāb*: *masālik wa-l-mamālik* (roads and kingdoms). These works stopped using the division of *aqālīm* (climes) and focused on a more useful one: *mamlaka* (region, province). In the tradition of the Roman *itineraria*, they describe different *masālik* (roads) in every *mamlaka*, including useful information, such as cities that the *masālik* cross, distances, and populations.[55] The name of this genre (or group of related works),[56] *masālik wa-l-mamālik*, is also the title of many books – including that of al-Bakrī, one of the *GE*'s main Arabic sources. Despite the rigid expositive structure of these works, from the beginning they incorporated *adab*-related topics. The first important author to write a book with this title was Ibn Khurdādhbegh (820–912), a high-ranking *kātib* in the Abbasid Caliphate who was responsible for the postal service (*bārid*), which facilitated the exchange of information (and intelligence) between Baghdad and its most remote provinces. Ibn Khurdādhbegh organized the topics of his book into three categories: 1) geographical records (*ṣūrat al-arḍ*), routes, and taxes; 2) *adab*; and 3) historical and geographical topics of interest to the *kuttāb*. The second version of the book – written some forty years later – substantially increased the *adab* and wondrous content.[57]

The genre reached the height of its development with Yaʿqūbī (d. 898) and his *Kitāb al-buldān* (*Book of countries*), which incorporated many socio-historical details of interest to the caliphal administration, such as the local implementation of power and tax distribution.[58] Yaʿqūbī is the oldest historical source to mention the Hermetic-related tradition of Apollonius of Tyana and his talismans,[59] which reached medieval Spain – as we saw in Chapter One. Yaʿqūbī's text makes it evident that the *masālik wa-l-mamālik* genre is the product of "the great empire of Islam" (*mamlakat al-Islām*), which is understood as comprising all Muslim nations. In the tenth century the genre was further developed by al-Balkhī (850–934), al-Iṣṭakhrī (850–957), Ibn-Ḥawqal (943–88), and al-Muqaddasī (946–91). Al-Muqaddasī's *Aḥsan al-taqāsīm fī maʿrifat al-aqālīm* (*The best division for the knowledge of the regions*) represents the pinnacle of the genre. The *Aḥsan al-taqāsīm* consolidates the esteem for the geographer's *ʿiyān* (personal observations) during his *riḥla* (travels), which would define Arabic geography from then on. Importantly for us, al-Muqaddasī does

54 Geodesy comes from the Greek γεωδαισία or *geodaisia* (literally, "division of Earth") and was initially understood as the science of measuring and understanding the geometric shape of the Earth.

55 See Francisco Franco-Sánchez, "*Al-masālik wa-l-mamālik*: Precisiones acerca del título de estas obras de la literatura geográfica árabe medieval y conclusiones acerca de su origen y estructura," *Philologia Hispalensis* 2, no. 31 (2017): 40.

56 For a discussion on the academic classification of this genre and its controversies, see Franco-Sánchez, "*Al-masālik wa-l-mamālik*," 38–43.

57 Miquel, *Géographie humaine*, 1:89–90.

58 Miquel, *Géographie humaine*, 1:102.

59 Asl, "*Sirr al-Khalīqa*," 439.

not disregard wondrous, even magical, sources – including a book of talismans (*kitāb al-ṭilismāt*).[60]

The waning of the genre after the eleventh century coincides with the disappearance of the *mamlakat al-Islam* concept. This is clear in the last important book associated with this tradition, the Andalusi Abū ʿUbayd al-Bakrī's *Kitāb al-masālik wa-l-mamālik* – one of the *GE*'s sources. Al-Bakrī was the son of ʿAbd al-ʿAzīz al-Bakrī, who came from an aristocratic family that belonged to the Córdoban caliphal court. This is why *GE*1 refers to al-Bakrī as Abul Ubeyt and introduces him as the son of Abda Albaziz Albacrí.[61] When the Caliphate fell, ʿAbd al-ʿAzīz al-Bakrī became king of the cities of Huelva and Saltés – close to Niebla – but soon was deposed and went to Córdoba with his son and family.[62] Later in the *GE* Alfonso confuses members of the family by affirming that:

> But we find that a wise king, who was the lord of Niebla and Salces [...] made a book in Arabic that they call the *History of Egypt*, and his nephew gave it another name in Arabic, *Quiteb almazahelic uhalmelich*, which in our language of Castile means [...] *Book of the Ways and the Kingdoms.*[63]

The transliteration and translation of the title are accurately rendered, as is the description of the *masālik* genre: "in it he talks about how many journeys and leagues, both far and wide, there are in the lands of the kingdoms [...] according to where the tolls must be located in the territories."[64] The *History of Egypt* by the "king of Niebla" is mentioned several times in the *GE*.[65] The period of the *taifas* coincided with the political and cultural apogee of the scribes (*kuttāb*) who administered the courts. We can assume that al-Bakrī received an exemplary *adab* education, because he became a courtly intellectual, poet, and scribe who served in the *taifas* of Córdoba and Almería, where he would be raised to the rank of *wazīr*.[66] He was also known for his philological works and interest in mundane pleasures.[67] Ibn Ḥayyān (d. 1076), considered the most important historian of al-Andalus, whose stylish writing also came from *adab*-oriented instruction, was among al-Bakrī's masters.[68] Al-Bakrī was

60 Miquel, *Géographie humaine*, 1:321–2.

61 *GE*1 I, 160–1.

62 See Antonio García Sanjuán, "Al-Bakrī," *Real Academia de la Historia: DB-e*, available online at: https://dbe.rah.es/biografias/24083/al-bakri (last accessed September 28, 2022).

63 "Mas fallamos que un rey sabio, que fue Señor de Niebla e de Salces [...] e fizo un libro en arávigo, e dízenle la Estoria de Egipto, e un su sobrino pusol otro nombre en arávigo, Quiteb almazahelic uhalmelich, que quiere dezir en el nuestro lenguage de Castiella tanto como [...] Libro de los caminos e de los regnos." *GE*1 1, 409–10.

64 "[...] fabla en él de todas las tierras de los regnos cuántas jornadas á ý e cuantas leguas en cadaúno d'ellos en luengo e en ancho [...] en razón de los portadgos en qué logares deven seer por las tierras." *GE*1 I, 410.

65 For the different ways in which Alfonso refers to al-Bakrī and his work, and possible reasons for this, see Fernández-Ordóñez, *Las Estorias de Alfonso*, 178–85.

66 See García Sanjuán, "Al-Bakrī."

67 See García Sanjuán, "Al-Bakrī."

68 See Luis Molina Martínez, "Ibn Ḥayyān," *Real Academia de la Historia: DB-e*, available online at: https://dbe.rah.es/biografias/16692/Ibn-hayyan (last accessed September 19, 2022).

also taught by the geographer Abū-l-ʿAbbās al-ʿUdhrī (d. 1085), who wrote another *al-Masālik wa-l-mamālik*. This book has been preserved in very fragmentary form, but quotations from later authors justify the opinion that al-ʿUdhrī specialized in prodigies and wonders.[69]

Al-Bakrī's *Kitāb al-masālik wa-l-mamālik* offers a geographical description of the entire Muslim-known world – including Egypt – yet is focused on al-Andalus in particular, of which he offers the most original material; however, this book has been transmitted in incomplete form.[70] In addition to geographical information, it also provides numerous historical, ethnographical, and marvellous details in an amusing and educative, and thus *adab*, fashion. Al-Bakrī is used to support key passages in the *GE* that contain marvels and wise men learned in astrology. Just before incorporating al-Bakrī as a source for Abraham's life, Alfonso includes a chapter entitled: "On the place and time of Abraham's birth according to the Arabs."[71] He knew this was a bold step and proceeds to justify the use of Arabic sources to explain biblical characters. The learned king argues that, if the Church Fathers could use gentile and Jewish authors to discuss events during Christ's birth, he can use the Arabs to do the same with Abraham – and implicitly for any other biblical event. After all, "even though their faith is mistaken," Arabs "said many good, true, and reasonable words about the deeds of the Bible and other knowledges, and they were great wise men, and still are nowadays."[72] Immediately following this, Alfonso relies on Abul Ubeyt (al-Bakrī) in the "twenty-first chapter of his book, on Abraham's birth,"[73] for a quotation that includes *ʿadjāʾib* related to astrology:

> Abul Ubeyt says in that chapter that, at the time of Abraham's birth, a very bright star that had never been seen before appeared in the sky, in the same way as the stars called comets do. As we have told you before, King Nino was an astronomer, because he had learned this art from King Nemprot of Yonito in the Orient. Later, he made his heirs learn it too. Despite this, when Nino saw the star he had doubts about what the newly visible star was and its meaning, thus he sent for the kingdom's astrologers and asked them what that star signified.[74]

69 See Miquel, *Géographie humaine*, 1:269; Luis Molina, "Las dos versiones de la geografía de al-ʿUḏrī," *Al-Qantara* 3 (1982): 250.

70 See Abū ʿUbayd al-Bakrī, *Kitāb al-masālik wa-l-mamālik*, eds Adrien van Leeuwen and André Ferre, 2 vols (Qarṭāj: Dār al-ʿArabīya li-l-Kitāb, 1992).

71 "Del logar e del tiempo del nacimiento de Abraham segund los arábigos." *GE*1 I, 160–2.

72 "E comoquier que ellos anden errados en la creencia, [...] buenas palabras e ciertas e con razón dixieron en el fecho de la Biblia e en los otros saberes, e grandes sabios fueron e son aún oy." *GE*1 I, 160.

73 "[...] el XXI capítulo de su Libro sobr'el nacimiento de Abraham." *GE*1 I, 160.

74 "E cuenta aquel Abul Ubeyt en aquel capítulo que al tiempo en que Abraham ovo de nacer que pareció en el cielo una estrella muy luzia, como nacen las estrellas a que llaman cometas, e aquella estrella non solié ý parecer d'antes. E víola el rey, e maguer que era él astronomiano, como vos avemos contado, que lo aprendiera el rey Nemprot de Yonito en oriente e fízolo él después aprender a los sos herederos, dubdó qué querié seer o qué querié significar aquella estrella que assí parecié de nuevo, que non solié ý parecer d'antes, e envió por los estrelleros del regno e preguntóles que aquella estrella nueva qué mostrava." *GE*1 I, 161–2.

Even though this passage from al-Bakrī is lost, it is similar to other biblically connected *ʿadjāʾib* that he relates in his extant accounts about the Holy Land.[75] Alfonso includes many other quotations from al-Bakrī that are linked to astrological phenomena and knowledge. The *GE* explains that Nino – like Herod – killed all the male newborns in his kingdoms, because his astrologers prophesied that Abraham would come to wipe out belief in pagan gods. However, according to al-Bakrī, Abraham's family hid in a cave, where the patriarch was born and grew strong and healthy. When his father Tare exited the cave, he saw the star of Jupiter standing over his head, and soon Abraham "started to read and then also to learn the knowledge of the stars."[76] Notice that "knowledge of the stars" is a literal Castilian rendering of an Arabic idiom for astrology: *ʿilm al-nujūm*, which appears in Arabic magical books.[77] Alfonso supplements this information from Arabic sources with Josephus's well-known account in *Judean antiquities* about young Abraham learning astrology and other sciences in Chaldea – which the *GE* subsumes under the *quadrivium*[78] – and then teaching them to the Egyptians later in his life.[79] The internal consistency of the *GE* is preserved: Alfonso, agreeing with his Arabic sources, presents Egyptians as well-versed in astrology, which is in agreement with Arabic sources – as I will show in the next section – but the origin of this knowledge is biblically justified by a prestigious source, Josephus.

Alfonso continues to navigate between biblical, Jewish, and Arabic sources in a similar manner. For instance, Genesis 12 narrates how Abraham went to Egypt due to a famine in Canaan. When the *GE* presents this episode, it adds that according to Abul Ubeyt (al-Bakrī), Abén Avez, and Abén Acelim – the latter two authors remain unidentified – the name of the reigning pharaoh was Caduf.[80] Here the *GE* also includes al-Bakrī's elaboration on the episode of Pharaoh's lustful desires for Sarah, the wife of Abraham, whom he had introduced as his sister:

> Abul Ubeyt says that it happened in this way: When the Pharaoh had the chance, he extended his hand to seize Sarah and bring her closer to him, but then his hand shrunk and was paralyzed and dry. When he realized that his god would not heal

75 Ducéne provides several examples from al-Bakrī's account about Palestine, including a river of fire and previously unknown miracles of Jesus; see Jean-Charles Ducène, "La description géographique de la Palestine dans le Kitāb Al-Masālik Wa-l-Mamālik D'abū ʿUbayd Al-Bakarī (m. 487/1094)," *Journal of Near Eastern Studies* 62, no. 3 (2003): 181–4.

76 "[…] començó de luego a leer e aprender otrossí de luego el saber de las estrellas." *GE*1 I, 164.

77 For instance, *Ghāya* III.7, 201 and III.7, 222.

78 See *GE*1 I, 165.

79 *GE*1 I, 212. In Flavius Josephus, *Judean antiquities*, ed. Louis H. Feldman, books 1–4 (Leiden: Brill, 2004), 1.154–68. On this topic, I recommend Annette Yoshiko Reed, "Abraham as Chaldean Scientist and Father of the Jew', Josephus, 'Ant.' 1.154–168, and the Greco-Roman Discourse about Astronomy/Astrology," *Journal for the Study of Judaism in the Persian, Hellenistic, and Roman Period* 35, no. 2 (2004): 119–58.

80 *GE*1 I, 213.

> it, he begged Sarah to pray to her god to cure his hand. So did she, then Pharaoh's hand healed, and he did not seize her anymore.[81]

This is a biblical and miraculous *ʿadjāʾib*. Even though it has not been preserved in al-Bakrī's extant fragments, I did find an identical narration in al-Waṣīfī.[82] Al-Bakrī relied on authors who wrote in the *masālik* genre and specialized in *adab* literary traditions and wonders – such as al-Faqih and al-Waṣīfī – which could explain the Abraham story coincidence. As we will see below, in the case of al-Waṣīfī, wonders acquire a Hermetic tone, which also happens in the last reference to al-Bakrī that I want to discuss.

Just before narrating Abraham's death, *GE1* stops referring to Abul Ubeyt by name and starts quoting his source as *Estoria de Egipto*. This change happens in a particularly wondrous section dedicated to the flying ark that King Nimrod built. This wonder led him to heaven where, according to the *Estoria de Egipto*, "he saw where the God of Abraham was, knew the power of God more than he had before, and rejoiced."[83] As I mentioned in Chapter One – and will discuss further in Chapter Five – ascending to heaven for knowledge is a characteristic Hermetic theme related to the Neoplatonic ascent of the soul and is closely associated with Hermes's Jewish and Arab counterparts, Enoch and Idrīs.

We have seen how the *masālik wa-l-mamālik* were geography books that contain *adab*, particularly its more literary and wondrous elements. In other geography books, *adab* equals or surpasses geography in importance. Not surprisingly, in some of those works the astonishing and Hermetic components are even more prevalent, and the *GE* profited from them.

Hermetic History in the *GE*'s Sources: al-Waṣīfī and al-Masʿūdī

Al-Waṣīfī and al-Masʿūdī illustrate Arabic geography books' tendency to exaggerate and overemphasize the *adab* components, especially the wondrous and historical/anecdotal (*akhbār*) aspects, as we will see below. Occasionally, this propensity included Hermetic features, particularly in the passages rendered in the *GE*. These two authors developed a trend forged by the Persian Ibn al-Faqīh (869–*c*. 951), one of the most influential and quoted Muslim geographers. As I pointed out earlier, al-Bakrī quotes Ibn al-Faqīh profusely, as does al-Waṣīfī and al-Masʿūdī, whom al-Bakrī also uses. This link, which can be traced back to al-Faqīh, is key to exploring Alfonso's taste when it came to picking Arabic sources.

Ibn al-Faqīh's *Kitāb al-buldān* (*Book of countries*, *c*. 903) was a five-volume encyclopedia of the Islamic world that has only survived in fragments from a

81 "E cuenta Abul Ubeyt que fue d'esta guisa: que Faraón, luego que tovo tiempo, tendió la mano pora echarla en Sarra pora llegarla assí, e que se le encogió la mano, e que se le paró como seca. E pues que sintió que sus dios nol sanavan que rogó él a Sarra que rogasse ella a su Dios quel sanasse. E ella fízolo, e fue luego sano el rey, e non travó más d'ella." *GE1* I, 214.

82 *L'Abrégé des merveilles*, trans. Carra de Vaux (Paris: Librairie C. Klincksieck, 1898), 323–4.

83 "[…] él subrié al cielo e verié ó estaba el Dios de Abraham. E coñoció más que solié el poder de Dios, e folgó." *GE1* I, 298–9.

summary (*Mukhtaṣar kitāb al-buldān*) composed one century later and extensively quoted by other authors. The preserved materials have allowed Miquel to brand Ibn al-Faqīh's work as a "systematization of the spirit of *adab* in the actual interior of geography" and a "geographical, idealist, and universalizing humanism," which "do not seek as much to know man as to educate a certain kind of man."[84] It frames Ibn al-Faqīh's humanism as similar to that of Alfonso, for whom the education of all the kingdom's subjects was a priority.[85] They both share a predominately secular approach, where God plays a relatively minor role.[86] Ibn al-Faqīh encourages the reader to welcome his work because it "encompasses all kinds of histories [*akhbār*] of the different countries, and of the monuments and other wonders [*ʿadjāʾib*] that we can see in the provinces."[87] In this way, geography leads to history, and history – along with all the other disciplines that constitute a cultured man's wealth – to the *ʿadjāʾib*.[88] For Ibn al-Faqīh it is also important to identify certain exemplary historical "heroes" in every human epoch – who frequently coincide with those in the *GE* – for instance, Abraham, Moses, and Solomon in Israel, and Alexander, Aristotle, and Hermes Trismegistus in Greece.[89]

Among the Hermetic-related topics in al-Faqīh, one is especially relevant for the passages of the *GE* that I will examine below: Apollonius of Tyana (*c.* 3 BCE–*c.* 97 CE) and the tradition of using talismans to magically defend cities. As we saw in Chapter One, Apollonius was a wandering Neo-Pythagorean philosopher, about whom Philostratus wrote a famous and novelistic biography (completed *c.* 230). This and others' colourful accounts turned Apollonius into a celebrity among pagans and Christians. Byzantine sources describe how he travelled through the Near East and made talismans, or *telesmata* (*τελέσματα*), "to protect different cities from pests and other dangers," and they are described as "small statues or effigies moulded in different metals."[90] The Arabic tradition called him Balīnās or Balīnūs, considered him the "master of talismans" (*ṣāḥib al-ṭilasmāt*), and associated him with alchemy, magic, and astrology.[91] Muslim authors translated works, such as the Byzantine *Great book of talismans* (sixth century), where Apollonius's talismans "seem to have a monumental character (statues mounted on a pillar and protected by a shrine-like architectural structure), and mark the landscape of the city that has requested

84 Miquel, *Géographie humaine*, 1:xxii, 182 and 184.
85 Martínez, *El humanismo medieval*, 89.
86 Miquel, *Géographie humaine*, 1:187.
87 Ibn al-Faqīh, *Compendium libri Kitāb al-boldān*, 1–3, cited in Miquel, *Géographie humaine*, 153–4 and 283.
88 Miquel, *Géographie humaine*, 1:179.
89 Miquel, *Géographie humaine*, 1:165 and 169 n. 3.
90 Lucia Raggetti, "Apollonius of Tyana's *Great Book of Talismans*," *Nuncius* 34, no. 1 (2019): 158.
91 See Martin Plessner, "Balīnūs," in P. Bearman et al. (eds), *Encyclopaedia of Islam, Second Edition*, website: http://dx.doi.org/10.1163/1573-3912_islam_SIM_1146 (last accessed September 19, 2022).

them."[92] These protective talismans soon became a major topic in Arabic literature,[93] and they also appear in the *GE* – as we will see below. According to Coulon, who provides an extensive account of Balīnūs and his talismans in Ibn al-Faqīh and other *adab* and geography authors, Balīnās's importance in Muslim occult sciences is a logical consequence of his popularity in geography and history treatises.[94] For instance, Balīnūs appears in the *Ghāya/Picatrix* several times. Hence, Alfonso could find "historical" and "practical" accounts of the talismans used by ancient rulers and learned men in Arabic geography books; ones the *Picatrix* teaches its readers how to make. In the *Ghāya/Picatrix*, Balīnūs is an authority on the construction of talismans and is associated with Mercury/Hermes Trismegistus.[95]

As Raggetti explains, many of these texts related to Balīnūs can be called "Hermetic," since "either Hermes is explicitly mentioned as the author, or the text is inscribed in his line of transmission, which includes Apollonius, Aristotle, and Alexander."[96] The texts usually attributed to Apollonius in the Islamic period can be divided into two groups: 1) philosophical-alchemical works and 2) works on astrology and talismans. The most popular work in the first group is *Sirr al-khalīqa wa-ṣanʿat al-ṭabīʿa* (*The secret of creation and the art of nature*), which probably had a lost Hellenistic original and was translated into Arabic from Greek or Syriac.[97] As we saw, the *Sirr al-khalīqa* includes the famous alchemical treatise *Tabula smaragdina* (*Emerald table*). According to the text, Apollonius received the *Tabula smaragdina*, along with *Sirr al-khalīqa*, from Hermes Trismegistus.[98] These features make Apollonius a paradigmatic character in this geographical *adab* genre that was influenced by Ibn al-Faqīh, which is sometimes called *kutub al-ʿadjāʾib* (books of wonders), and includes references to Hermetic lore and talismans.[99] As Miquel explains, when geographical books focus on *adab* they present it in one of two ways: one is in the manner of Ibn al-Faqīh that we have just seen, where *adab* and history depend on a geographical classification system and fit into the accounts of different countries; the other is that of al-Masʿūdī, where information is integrated into history and geography is subordinated to a chronological presentation.[100]

Despite his widespread fame and influence, we do not know much about al-Masʿūdī's life. From his writings we can deduce that he studied with eminent teachers and was "endowed with an extraordinary intellectual curiosity which impelled him, on the one hand, to educate himself with books, and, on the other, to enrich his human experience by undertaking long journeys both within and outside the Muslim

92 Raggetti, "Apollonius," 162.

93 On talismans as an important defensive asset in medieval Arabo-Islamic sources, see Giovanna Calasso, "Les remparts et la loi, les talismans et les saints: la protection de la ville dans les sources musulmanes médiévales," *Bulletin d'études orientales* 44 (1992): 87–92.

94 Jean-Charles Coulon, *La magie en terre d'Islam au Moyen Age* (Paris: Comité des travaux historiques et scientifiques, 2017), 92–8.

95 *Picatrix* II.x.10, 12, 15, 19, 22, 26, 31, and 36.

96 Raggetti, "Apollonius," 175; see also 182.

97 Asl, "*Sirr al-khalīqa*," 442.

98 Asl, "*Sirr al-khalīqa*," 443.

99 See Coulon, *La magie*, 92–8.

100 Miquel, *Géographie humaine*, 1:211.

world."[101] Only two of his thirty-six works have survived. His most important work was the *Akhbār al-zamān* (*Histories of time*), an enormous thirty-volume universal history, now lost; then he wrote the *Kitāb al-awsaṭ* (*Middle book*), an abridgement of and supplement to the *Akhbār al-zamān*; and finally he wrote the book that has given him universal fame: *Kitāb murūj al-dhahab wa-ma ʿādin al-jawhar* (*Book of the prairies of gold and mines of gems*), a summary and revision of the two previous works, which also includes numerous geographical, biographical, philosophical, and wondrous notes. I will show how the *GE* echoes some of its passages.[102] His other extant book is the *Kitāb al-tanbīh wa ʾishrāf* (*Book of admonition and revision*), which corrects and clarifies aspects of his previous works. Shboul underlines "the importance of geographical considerations in *al-Mas ʿūdī*'s view of universal history, and his awareness of the inter-relations between geographical factors and historical and cultural aspects."[103]

Shboul also presents al-Masʿūdī as "one of those outstanding Arab scholars whose life and works vividly reflect the humanistic aspects of Islamic intellectual life of his age."[104] This view is shared by Pellat, who considers al-Masʿūdī the paradigmatic *adīb* (possessor of *adab*) in the tradition of al-Jāḥiẓ.[105] Magical and Hermetic aspects are also part of al-Masʿūdī's humanistic discussions. Green reminds us that al-Masʿūdī visited the mysterious city of Ḥarrān in 943 and offered "the only Muslim eye-witness account" of it.[106] And Sánchez Prieto-Borja points out that in *GE*3 Alfonso takes from al-Masʿūdī information on the gentiles' temples.[107] This passage of *GE*3 appears to be a summarized interpretation of a longer section by al-Masʿūdī. In his work, al-Masʿūdī provides context regarding the religion of Ḥarrān along with other pagan beliefs. He also describes the temples and rituals he observed in the city.[108] I find in the passage of *GE*3 an undeniable Ḥarrānian and Hermetic flavor when Alfonso explains how ancient Arabs – presumably still not Muslim – and other peoples, "stated that the planets were living and rational entities, more adept than others at approaching God, and that angels served as intermediaries between the planets and God;" and for this reason, they "held the planets in high esteem and would offer sacrifices to receive rewards from them when needed" and even "built houses and temples and named them after the planets."[109]

[101] See Charles Pellat, "al-Masʿūdī," in Bearman et al. (eds), *Encyclopaedia of Islam, Second Edition*.

[102] I quote this book using the celebrated Arabic edition and French translation by Barbier de Meynard and Pavet de Courteille, *Al-Mas ʿūdī: Les prairies d'or*. Translations of Arabic terms into English are mine, for which I also looked at the French rendering.

[103] Shboul, *Al-Mas ʿūdī*, 79.

[104] Shboul, *Al-Mas ʿūdī*, xv.

[105] Pellat, "al-Masʿūdī."

[106] Tamara M. Green, *The City of the Moon God: Religious Traditions of Ḥarrān* (Leiden: Brill, 1992), 115.

[107] Sánchez Prieto-Borja, introduction to *GE*3 I, lxxviii–lxxix.

[108] For this passage, see *GE*3 I, 319–22; and for that of al-Masʿūdī, see *Al-Mas ʿūdī*, 4:61–100; and Shboul, *Al-Mas ʿūdī*, 11–12. See also Green, *City of the Moon God*, 214–15.

[109] "[…] dizién que las planetas eran cosas bivas y razonables, y que ellas eran más guisadas que otras cosas de llegarse a Diós, y que los ángeles eran mensajeros entre Diós y ellas […]

In his *Tanbih*, al-Masʿūdī distinguishes between different kinds of pagan Sabeans, including the Egyptian Sabeans, who honoured Hermes Trismegistus and the Agathodaimon as their prophets – the remnants of whom would become the Ḥarrānian people.[110] According to Green, al-Masʿūdī's descriptions of belief in Ḥarrān correspond to "a Hermeticism enlivened by a heavy dose of Neoplatonic and Neopythagorean doctrine."[111] This idea implies that ancient Egyptians practised a form of Hermetic cult. Alfonso's descriptions of Egyptian rituals and doctrines that use al-Masʿūdī as a source reflect this Hermetic essence – as we will see below. It is also remarkable that in a chapter of this section entitled "On the temples that the gentiles made for the planets," Alfonso names his source as *Istoria de Egipto*, and mentions the Egyptians, along with the ancient Arabs, among those who worshipped the planets and named temples after them; I will clarify the *GE*'s view of gentiles/pagans in Chapter Three.[112] This leads me to think that Alfonso considered the *Murūj* another *History of Egypt*. In the section of the *Murūj* that corresponds to ancient Egypt, al-Masʿūdī includes a succession of legendary kings associated with magic and talismans not found in original sources from those periods or later recensions by Christian historiographers. Al-Masʿūdī's accounts of those kings are based on Coptic sources or informants.[113] Coulon suggests that various Muslim dynasties in Egypt – such as the Tulunids, Ikhshidids, and Fatimids – used those imaginative Coptic stories of autochthonous ancient kings to support their legitimacy.[114] These fictional kings appear in the *GE* because Alfonso uses not only al-Masʿūdī's stories but also those of al-Waṣīfī, another author who depicts a legendary and "Hermetic" Egypt even more prominently.

Al-Waṣīfī's *Kitāb al-ʿadjāʾib al-kabīr* (*Book of great marvels*), also known as *Mukhtaṣar al-ʿadjāʾib* (*Summary of the wonders*) is a further development of the trend towards accumulating wonders in *adab*. De Vaux notices that even though the main manuscript on which he based his celebrated edition was attributed to Ibrāhīm Ibn Waṣīf Shāh al-Misrī, al-Masʿūdī is given as the author in other copies; however, al-Masʿūdī does not mention this book in the *Murūj*, and his style is different.[115] Al-Waṣīfī – the most probable author of the book – is known by several different names; some Arabic authors refer to Ibrāhīm b. Waṣīf Shāh, others call him Ibn Waṣīf al-Ṣābiʾ, which betrays a Sabean/Ḥarrānian origin, and others, al-Waṣīfī – such as Ṣāʿid al-Andalusī. Jamāl al-Dīn al-Idrīsī (d. 1251), a contemporary of Alfonso,

tovieron por bien a las planetas y de fazerles sacrificios porque les fiziesen pro y honra cuando menester lo oviesen [...] labraron casas y templos, y posiéronles los nombres de las planetas." *GE*3 I, 319–20.

110 See Green, *City of the Moon God*, 115. See also Michael Cook, "Pharaonic History in Medieval Egypt," *Studia Islamica*, no. 57 (1983): 96.

111 Green, *City of the Moon God*, 115.

112 "De los templos que los gentiles fizieron a las planetas." *GE*3 I, 319 and 320.

113 See Shboul, *Al-Masʿūdī*, 15 and 121–2. On Arabic writings on ancient Egypt and their use of Coptic sources, see Okasha El-Daly, *Egyptology: The Missing Millenium. Ancient Egypt in Medieval Arabic Writings* (London: Routledge), 60–4.

114 Coulon, *La magie*, 160.

115 Carra de Vaux, introduction to *L'Abrégé des merveilles*, xxvii–xxxvi.

bears witness to al-Waṣīfī's renown in al-Andalus and quotes and describes him as an author "who had written books on the temples and sciences of the ancient Egyptian sages."[116] Al-Bakrī mentions al-Waṣīfī's "visits to Egypt, where he tested the magical efficacy of images and statues in temples."[117] Since the *Kitāb al-ʿadjāʾib* "displays a perhaps disproportionate interest in Spain and its neighborhood," Cook argues that this work could be an Andalusi forgery.[118] Sezgin thinks that al-Waṣīfī actually existed and was Ibn Waṣīf al-Ṣābiʾ, an erudite ophthalmologist who was active in Baghdad in the middle of the tenth century and had Andalusi connections.[119] His *nisba* (*al-Ṣābiʾ*) indicates he was a Sabean, something consistent with the *Kitāb al-ʿadjāʾib*'s insights on "the ancient Sabean paganism of Spain."[120] Cook acknowledges the possibility of al-Waṣīfī's "Ḥarrānian connection with Spain" because "we know of two Ḥarrānian brothers in Spain in the tenth century" and "their long voyage to the East where they conferred with Sabean scholars – one of them an oculist named Ibn Waṣīf."[121] He is referring to the grandsons of al-Ḥarrānī – who, as we saw in Chapter One, emigrated from Baghdad to the court of ʿAbd al-Raḥmān II. The brothers' trip would have been between 941–2 and 951–2, and for this reason Sezgin thinks that Ibn Waṣīf would have "become well known in Spain early on."[122] Al-Qurṭubī, the author of the *Picatrix*, travelled to the east between 932 and 936, visited Baghdad, and studied with noteworthy teachers. Therefore, I believe it is possible that al-Qurṭubī met with or studied under al-Waṣīfī.[123] This feasible contact reinforces the connections between the two works. Cook highlights some of the *Kitāb al-ʿadjāʾib*'s content: "priests learned in astrology and magic, sage rulers, marvellous constructions, talismans, treasures, ancient wisdom, and occasional glimpses of monotheism,"[124] features that I see as completely compatible with the *Ghāya/Picatrix* and sections of the *GE* we will see below. This relationship is also supported by two quotations from the *Kitāb al-ʿadjāʾib* that Ritter notes in his edition in the *Ghāya*.[125] The *Ghāya* even calls this source *Akhbār Miṣr*[126] (*History of Egypt*), as does the *GE*.

The *Kitāb al-ʿadjāʾib* has two distinct parts: the first is comprised of various elements, such as a history of creation and some biblical characters, a description of

116 In Cook, "Pharaonic History," 82.

117 See Ursula Sezgin, "al-Waṣīfī," in Bearman et al. (eds), *Encyclopaedia of Islam, Second Edition*.

118 Cook, "Pharaonic History," 98.

119 See Sezgin, "al-Waṣīfī."

120 See Cook, "Pharaonic History," 98.

121 See Cook, "Pharaonic History," 98.

122 See Sezgin, "al-Waṣīfī."

123 In their paper on al-Qurṭubī's transformative *riḥla* (trip), Callataÿ and Moureau do not mention al-Waṣīfī among the personalities he met, but of course it is impossible to reconstruct every step of his journey. Callataÿ and Moureau, "A Milestone in the History of Andalusī Bāṭinism," 86–117.

124 Cook, "Pharaonic History," 71.

125 *Ghāya* III.11, 278–80 and IV.2, 309–15, cited in Cook, "Pharaonic History," 81. On passages from the *Ghāyat al-ḥakīm* containing descriptions of talismans and statues used to defend cities, which are reminiscent of al-Waṣīfī's style, see also Coulon, *La magie*, 159–60.

126 *Ghāya* IV.2, 310; cited in Cook, "Pharaonic History," 82.

jinn (genies), giants, and Arab seers, and a cosmography, including faraway seas and islands; the second and longest part is a history of Egypt, hence its title in the *GE* and the *Ghāya*. Cook calls the *Kitāb al-ʿadjāʾib* a "Hermetic history," a label supported by its references to Hermes, its "overall atmosphere," and some implicit Hermetic links.[127] This label applies to the section of the *GE* that I focus on in the next section: the story of Queen Doluca. In this section Alfonso draws heavily on components from al-Waṣīfī's "Hermetic history" and similar ones from al-Masʿūdī.

Queen Doluca and the Magical Defence of Egypt: "Hermetic History" in the *GE*

A close reading of Doluca's story allows us to assess how Alfonso renders the Arabic sources we have just discussed, as well as their Hermetic components. To understand the *GE*'s version, it is important to remember that, while Alfonso introduces many translated sources in his historical works, he does not treat all of them with the same level of fidelity.[128] Of course, translations from the *Vulgate* Bible are relatively faithful. However, when passages from Ovid's *Metamorphoses* are introduced – as we will see in Chapter Three – frequent excursus, digressions, and interpretations are included. In this instance, the *GE* interprets as much as it translates. My analysis of the *GE*'s Arabic historical sources in this chapter allows me to conclude that Alfonso translates, interprets, mixes, and even reorganizes them more freely than any other genre of sources. For this reason, it is not always possible to compare original segments and discuss the fidelity of their translation and interpretation in the *GE*; moreover, sometimes we can identify characters and stories that are derived from a particular passage in an Arabic source and then relayed throughout various sections of the *GE*. I will begin by examining the influences from al-Waṣīfī, whom previous scholars – following the *GE*'s statements – have regarded as the main source of Doluca's section.

Al-Waṣīfī grabs the reader's attention on the first page of the *Kitāb al-ʿadjāʾib*. He promises to reveal everything he knows about "the secrets of nature" – here I see an implicit reference to *Sirr al-khalīqa wa-ṣanʿat al-ṭabīʿa* (*The secret of creation and the art of nature*), the abovementioned book by Apollonius of Tyana. Al-Waṣīfī also promises to describe "the histories [*akhbār*] of the kings of the earth and the wonders they made, as well as the marvels that the diverse regions contain, magical instruments, talismans, temples, laws, countries, and inscriptions carved in stone."[129] All this is present in the *GE*'s story of Doluca, yet not all of it comes from al-Waṣīfī. The legendary Queen Doluca appears in many Arabic authors.[130] Her association with talismans, astrology, and magic seems to make her very attractive to Alfonso, who gives her a prominent place. In *GE*1, Doluca succeeds the pharaoh mentioned in

127 Cook, "Pharaonic History," 71.

128 Rico, *Alfonso el Sabio*, 178–9.

129 *L'Abrégé des merveilles*, 1.

130 For different sources on Doluca, see José María Bellido Morillas, "Dos visiones hispano-medievales de un cuento del Egipto faraónico: Variaciones de Abū Ḥāmid Al-Garnāṭī y Juan Ruiz De Alcalá, Arcipreste de Hita, sobre El príncipe predestinado," *Revista de literatura* 71, no. 141 (2009): 202. See also El-Daly, *Egyptology: The Missing Millenium*, 130 and 133.

Exodus who drowns in the Red Sea. Alfonso indicates that "a wise man of the Arabs who was called Alguazif and wrote the *Estorias de Egipto*" says that the pharaoh's name was Talme.[131] Alguazif is the Castilian version of al-Waṣīfī. Fernández-Ordóñez alleges that, beginning with this first mention of Alguazif's *Estoria de Egipto* in *GE*1 and extending all the way to *GE*4, Alfonso uses Alguazif as the reference for events in that country and in Babylon; whereas the work of al-Bakrī, which is still used to supplement some biblical narratives, is never referred to by that title after this point.[132] There are some issues with this assertion. Talme can indeed be found in al-Waṣīfī, who affirms that Ẓalmā was the pharaoh during Moses's time and that "historians called [Ẓalmā] al-Walīd, son of Muṣʿab, and believed that he was [an] Amalekite";[133] the problem is that Ẓalmā is the last pharaoh to appear in al-Waṣīfī's work, which means this book is not the source of all information in the *GE*. Fernández-Ordóñez notices this mismatch and has also observed that the passages based upon Alguazif do not coincide with al-Waṣīfī's preserved work. This has led her to suggest that Alfonso could have used a different and longer version of the *Kitāb al-ʿadjāʾib*, or a completely different book. Similar views are shared by other prominent specialists.[134] However, a close examination of some passages leads me to disagree with Fernández-Ordóñez and posit that while Alfonso did use al-Waṣīfī, al-Masʿūdī is actually a more relevant source for Doluca's story – even though the Castilian king elaborated on it and combined it with other works. In my view, Alfonso perceived al-Masʿūdī's work as an additional *Estoria de Egipto*, parallel to the works of al-Waṣīfī and al-Bakrī. Thus, Alfonso amalgamated all of them to create a coherent narrative. This means there are at least three *Estorias de Egipto* in the *GE*, not two, as has been previously suggested. In his preserved work al-Masʿūdī attaches greater importance to Doluca than al-Waṣīfī and provides details that are closer to the *GE*'s account. Pharaoh Talme also appears in al-Masʿūdī, who affirms that "al-Walīd, son of Muṣʿab, is Moses's pharaoh," and his alias was Ẓalmā (the "tyrannical" or "unrighteous").[135] Fernández-Ordóñez notices this detail[136] but does not point out this more important clue: in al-Masʿūdī, Ẓalmā (Talme) comes just before Doluca, like in the *GE*, while al-Waṣīfī makes Doluca appear centuries earlier than Ẓalmā. This indicates that Alfonso might have given priority to al-Masʿūdī as a source for Doluca's story, but without completely disregarding al-Waṣīfī.

In fact, Al-Waṣīfī barely dedicates two pages to Dolaīfa (Doluca). These pages focus on the war she waged against the Amalekites, in which both sides display

131 "E dize un sabio de los arávigos que ovo nombre Alguazif, e escrivió las estorias de Egipto […]." *GE*1 II, 132.

132 Fernández-Ordóñez suggests that these changes happened because Alfonso used a different team of collaborators, *Las estorias de Alfonso*, 181–3.

133 *L'Abrégé des merveilles*, 388. This was pointed out by Fernández-Ordóñez, *Las estorias de Alfonso*, 180.

134 A. G. Solalinde, introduction to *General estoria*, part I, vii–lxxxi, particularly xiii, note 1; Fernández-Ordóñez, *Las estorias de Alfonso*, 180–5; and, with nuances, Sánchez-Prieto Borja, introduction to *GE*4 I, xxi.

135 *Al-Masʿūdī*, 2:398.

136 Fernández-Ordóñez, *Las estorias de Alfonso*, 180.

plenty of magic and other *ʿadjāʾib*. In the end, the queen loses and poisons herself.[137] *GE1* says that Talme – the pharaoh Moses defied – was succeeded by the princess Munene, who declined to rule and appointed Doluca instead.[138] Alfonso states that "Some writers who wrote histories of Egypt" – a hint that he consulted several – "narrate that Lady Doluca was Pharaoh's cousin, and others that [she was] his niece, the daughter of his sister."[139] Even though al-Waṣīfī's version situates Queen Dolaīfa (or Dolaīka) significantly earlier than Moses, in his account Queen Huriā, the daughter of Ṭūṭīs, the pharaoh in Abraham's time, picked her cousin Dolaīfa, the daughter of her uncle Māmūn, as successor.[140] Thus, Alfonso was aware that in some versions Doluca was the cousin of the daughter of a pharaoh (as in al-Waṣīfī) but situates her in Moses's times (like al-Masʿūdī) and not in those of Abraham (like al-Waṣīfī). Let us now examine how Doluca's Hermetic history develops in the *GE* and construct its plausible use of several Arabic sources.

Doluca's story is divided into three sections in *GE1* that are inserted between biblical narratives. The first focuses on Doluca's architectural constructions containing magical protections, the second on the new wedding customs the queen instituted in Egypt, and the third on how she died after appointing a successor.[141] According to my scrutiny, the first section is supported in al-Masʿūdī and not in al-Waṣīfī. Let us contrast al-Masʿūdī's account of the queen with that of the *GE*. Al-Masʿūdī introduces Queen Dalūka as the successor to Ẓalmā and immediately begins to explain the wonders she built. For instance, she ordered the *ḥāʾiṭ al-ʿajūz* (wall of the old woman) to be built, which included *mahāris* (watchtowers) placed closely together. This wall was built to protect Egypt against foreign enemies following the debacle of the pharaoh and his army drowning in the Red Sea. Dalūka also built Egypt's *barābī* (temples, sing. *barbā*). Helped by her knowledge of magic, as a protective measure Dalūka placed images of all possible enemies who might attack Egypt, either from land (riding horses and camels) or from sea (sailing from Rome or Syria), in the *barābī*. She also gathered all the *asrār al- ṭabīʿa* (secrets of nature) and *khawāṣṣ* (occult properties or virtues) of minerals, plants, and animals in the *barābī*. Both the talismanic protections and the mention of the "secrets of nature" are reminiscent of the abovementioned Hermetic traditions from Apollonius of Tyana. However, regarding this passage of al-Masʿūdī, El-Daly indicates that we can find similar scenes at the temple of the historical Queen Hatsheptut (1507–1458 BCE) at Deir El-Bahri, and also at her Red Chapel at Karnak, In these scenes, enemy boats, animals, and soldiers are magically destroyed by fire.[142] These similarities indicate that real Egyptian practices may have been interpreted through Hellenistic Hermetic traditions by the Arabs.

Al-Masʿūdī also explains how Dalūka performed these operations during the appropriate conjunction of celestial bodies and how the images of the temples

137 *L'Abrégé des merveilles*, 339–40.
138 *GE1* II, 191–4.
139 "E unos de los escrividores de las estorias de Egipto dizen que doña Doluca era prima cormana de Faraón, e otros á ý que dizen que su sobrina, fija de su hermana." *GE1* II, 193.
140 *L'Abrégé des merveilles*, 338–9.
141 *GE1* II, 194–7, 259–67, and 747–51, respectively.
142 El-Daly, *Egyptology: The Missing Millenium*, 77.

effectively defended against successive invasions; for instance, when the Yemenis attacked Egypt while mounted on camels, the images of camels in the *barābī* fell to the earth, as did the real camels.[143] Zeilabi explains that in the Islamic world, especially in Egypt, there were "talisman houses known as *barābī* in which human and animal images were made and kept for various talismanic purposes." *Barābī* is apparently a Nabataean word that is also used in Coptic and originally meant "a strong building for magic."[144] Thus, Doluca is one of the legendary rulers of Egypt who, as Coulon argues, embodies Frazer's idea about the magical origins of royalty: rulers practised magic and made talismans to ensure the prosperity and security of their kingdoms.[145] This also seems to describe Alfonso's ideal ruler.

The first section about Doluca in the *GE* is longer than what I believe is its source for this passage in al-Masʿūdī that I have just described, and the descriptions of astral magic and its devices and procedures are significantly more elaborate. This could mean that Alfonso used a longer version or a related source, or that he expanded upon al-Masʿūdī's account using the material on magic available to him. Comparing both versions, we see that the *GE* also narrates how Queen Doluca, a wise astrologer, ordered a temple with protective images called *barbe* to be built. However, it seems that there was some confusion when translating the original source: "They put the name of *barbe*, in Egyptian, to that temple with its images. This history later relates – as you will find out – that *barbe* in Egyptian means 'wall of the old woman' in Castilian."[146] *Barbā* means talismanic house or temple, but al-Masʿūdī calls the wall *ḥāʾiṭ al-ʿajūz* (literally, the wall of the old woman). Thus, the translators of *GE*1 erred by saying that *barbe* (*barbā*) means "the wall of the old woman"; the same mistake is repeated many times until *GE*4.

Then *GE*1 narrates how Doluca made her subjects bring pillars (*pilares*) from a quarry to build the *barbe*. These pillars might be Alfonso's interpretation of the *mahāris* (watchtowers) on the wall that are described by al-Masʿūdī, but the *GE* portrays them using an astrological lens, specifying that there were twenty-eight, "according to the number of the moon's houses, and then they erected a temple on them."[147] The description and use of the twenty-eight mansions of the moon is consistent with the books of astrological magic Alfonso translated and developed from Arabic sources, such as the *Picatrix*, *Astromagia*, and *Libro de las formas e imágenes que son en los cielos* (*Book of the forms and images that are in the sky*).[148] The latter's name is reminiscent of a book mentioned later in this first passage of *GE*1 on Doluca. Doluca placed an idol in the fourth wall of each temple. The details of how the statues were suffumigated and

143 This description appears in *Al-Masʿūdī*, 2:398–400.

144 Negar Zeilabi, "Talismans and Figural Representation in Islam: A Cultural History of Images and Magic," *British Journal of Middle Eastern Studies* 46, no. 3 (2019): 433.

145 Coulon, *La magie*, 160.

146 "[…] e pusieron nombre en su egipciano a aquel tiemplo con sus imágenes el Barbe. E segund fallaredes que cuenta esta estoria adelant barbe en egipciano quiere dezir tanto como en castellano pared de vieja." *GE*1 II, 197.

147 "[…] segund que son XXVIII las mansiones o las posadas de la Luna, e fizo sobr'ellos un tiemplo." *GE*1 II, 194.

148 For a discussion of the *Picatrix*'s dependence upon the *manāzil al-qamar* (lunar mansions), see Pingree, "Some of the Sources," 8.

consecrated with animal blood according to astrological rituals are also reminiscent of rituals described in the *Picatrix*.[149] Alfonso explains the process of suffumigating the idols for twenty-eight days in accordance with the phases of the moon. The main instruments for these rituals were seven *sofumerios* (incense burners), which were used for suffumigations and prayers to the planets throughout the seven days of the week[150] – we must remember that the association of each day of the week with a planet dates back to the origins of astrology in Babylon (Sunday with the sun, Monday with the moon, etc.). *Ghāya* III.7 describes similar planetary rituals used by the Sabeans, whom Pingree identifies as from Ḥarrān.[151] Hence, this section of *GE1* is in line with al-Masʿūdī's statement above that the city of Ḥarrān was the last remnant of Egyptian paganism. Alfonso refers to the books of Ileo and Miniamín, two unknown wise men, as the sources that describe these buildings and rituals. Miniamín allegedly describes how Afrondítiz, the wisest astrologer and diviner in Egypt at the time, built the four idols and the images accompanying them. The idols worked as protective talismans following the Hermetic tradition of Apollonius of Tyana. For instance, Afrondítiz placed an idol made of red copper (*arambre Bermejo*) in the eastern wall. This idol served as protection against enemies coming from the sea,[152] something we also saw in al-Masʿūdī. According to Miniamín, Afrondítiz ordered the carving of letters from the *Libro de las imágenes* (*Book of images*) – this title echoes Alfonso's *Libro de las formas e imágenes que son en los cielos* – in the idol. In the *GE*, this book "was a very precious book made by the wise astrologers of Egypt, in which they gathered all the characters, figures, and letters for charms found in their science."[153]

A passage from al-Masʿūdī that comes after the description of Dalūka's constructions provides a clue to Miniamín's identity in the *GE*. Al-Masʿūdī complements the information about her temples with his own experiences as a traveller. He reports that when he was visiting Ikhmīm (or Akhmīm) he heard about the famous early Sufi Dhū l-Nūn al-Miṣrī al-Ikhmīmī (d. *c.* 862), whom I consider a probable inspiration for the *GE*'s Miniamín. According to al-Masʿūdī, al-Ikhmīmī was a *zāhid* (an ascetic initiated into Sufism) and *ḥakīm* (wise man) who had his own *ṭarīqa* (Sufi school or order).[154] Like Alfonso's Miniamín, and like Apollonius of Tyana, al-Ikhmīmī was associated with inscriptions and images in temples, which he studied while visiting them. Some of the inscriptions collected by al-Masʿūdī reveal that the men who built *barābī* knew astrology and magic, such as one who says: "He who queries the stars knows nothing; he who commands the stars does what he wants."[155] These stories are founded on reality. As Wiet explains, many Arab writers "have enthused over the ancient temple

---

[149] On the efficacy of animal sacrifice combined with astrological rituals in the *Ghāya/Picatrix*, see Saif, *Arabic Influences*, 36–7. On suffumigation in the *Picatrix*, see Attrell and Porreca, introduction to *Picatrix*, 28.

[150] *GE1* II, 196–7.

[151] Pingree, "Al-Ṭabarī on the Prayers," 105–6.

[152] "[…] pora'l defendimiento de la mar." *GE1* II, 195.

[153] "[…] fue una obra muy preciada que fizieron los sabios estrelleros de Egipto en que ayuntaron todas las karactaras e todas las figuras e letras que fallaron por su ciencia pora sus espiramentos e sos encantamientos que fizieron." *GE1* II, 195.

[154] *Al-Masʿūdī*, 2:401.

[155] *Al-Masʿūdī*, 2:402.

of Akhmīm (of which no trace now remains), which was particularly famed owing to its traditional association with Hermes Trismegistus."[156] This association goes back to Hellenistic times, when Akhmīm was called Panopolis. One of the first famous alchemists, Zosimos of Panopolis (d. beginning of the fourth century), was from there, and "the oldest reference to Apollonius of Tyana in the Islamic world is found in a treatise attributed to Zosimus of Panopolis."[157] Not surprisingly, Dhū l-Nūn al-Miṣrī al-Ikhmīmī was also associated with alchemy and Hermetic traditions.[158] Knysh suggests that parts of his doctrine closely mirror Coptic mysticism and Neoplatonic ideas, which have gained him a reputation as a theurgist and expert in "hieroglyphs, alchemy, astrology, and magic."[159] In al-Andalus, al-Qurṭubī transmitted a work by Dhū l-Nūn al-Miṣrī.[160] Thus, al-Masʿūdī used this historical figure to support the stories of Dalūka's temples, and Alfonso might have reinterpreted this figure as Miniamín.

Immediately after discussing Doluca and the knowledge he acquired during his travels through Egypt, al-Masʿūdī refers to one of his lost works, the *Kitāb al-qaḍāyā wa al-ṭajārib* (*Book of problems and experiences*), which, according to Khalidi, seems to have provided "the most valuable information" on al-Masʿūdī's scientific method and his views on geographical, chemical, and alchemical phenomena.[161] Al-Masʿūdī offers a succinct account of all the knowledge he was able to obtain in Egypt and the contents of the *Kitāb al-qaḍāyā*, which included a chapter "containing everything that [I] could not include here" on chemical qualities and the *khawāṣṣ* (occult properties) of things and talismans.[162] Since this book appears immediately after mentioning al-Ikhmīmī, I posit that al-Masʿūdī's *Kitāb al-qaḍāyā* was the inspiration for *GE*1's *Libro de las formas*, a book in which the Egyptians placed all their occult knowledge.

Alfonso also describes the protective images of armed warriors and their mounts that al-Masʿūdī mentions: "[Doluca] ordered them to make images of horsemen and to place them at the foot of the idols. They were depicted in many ways and armed with different weapons."[163] *GE*1 also assures readers of the efficacy of those images and specifies that "while that temple and those images, produced through stars and charms, were present there and in an unblemished state, no enemy could do the Egyptians wrong or enter Egypt."[164] These extensive descriptions of wondrous

[156] G. Wiet, "Akhmīm," in Bearman et al. (eds), *Encyclopaedia of Islam, Second Edition.*

[157] Asl, "*Sirr al-khalīqa*," 438.

[158] Jawid Mojaddedi, "Dhū l-Nūn al-Miṣrī," in Fleet et al. (eds), *Encyclopaedia of Islam, THREE.* See also Coulon, *La magie*, 177–9.

[159] Alexander Knysh, *Islamic Mysticism: A Short History* (Leiden: Brill, 2000), 41.

[160] Fierro, "*Bāṭinism* in al-Andalus," 89–90.

[161] See Tarif Khalidi, "Masʿūdī's Lost Works: A Reconstruction of Their Content," *Journal of the American Oriental Society* 94, no. 1 (1974): 37.

[162] *Al-Masʿūdī*, 2:408–9. Saif points out that works such as the *Picatrix* include the idea that "various types of magic receive their potency from the celestial bodies that instilled occult properties into natural things." Saif, *Arabic Influences*, 167.

[163] "[...] e mandó fazer a pie de cada ídolo muchos cavalleros por imágenes que estavan por sí ant'essos ídolos, e que eran de muchas guisas e armados de muchas maneras de armas." *GE*1 II, 196.

[164] "[...] en cuanto aquel tiemplo e aquellas imágenes obradas por sus estrellas e por sos encantamientos, como avedes oído, estidieron en aquel logar guardadas e enteras que

buildings are undoubtedly inherited from Arabic geography's relish for wondrous monuments: one kind of *ʿadjāʾib*. Only at the end of the section does Alfonso depart from al-Masʿūdī and establish a connection between those wonders and future events in *GE*4. The wise king clarifies that over time the images deteriorated and then finally were ruined by the magician Drimiden, who by doing so helped his lord, Nebuchadnezzar, conquer Egypt.[165]

The second section on Doluca in *GE*1 describes how the queen solved the terrible problem created in Egypt after most of the noble men perished with the former pharaoh in the Red Sea; as a consequence, Egyptian ladies were widowed or were unable to find suitable candidates within their rank to marry. I cannot find the origin of this story in either al-Masʿūdī or al-Waṣīfī. Unless a better source is discovered, I think it likely that it originated from a short reference in *Tuḥfat al-albāb wa nukhbat al-ʿadjāʾib* (*The gift of the intellects and the selection of wonders*) by the Andalusi Abū Ḥāmid al-Garnāṭī (1080–1170); he affirms that after God sank the pharaoh and his men, Dalūkā "made the women marry slaves in order to multiply their offspring."[166] Al-Garnāṭī is compatible with al-Masʿūdī and al-Waṣīfī. He was also a geographer with a particular interest in wonders, as we observe from the title of this book and also from his *al-Muʿrib ʿan baʿd ʿadjāʾib al-maghreb* (*The praise of some of the wonders of the west*). In his works, al-Garnāṭī describes the stories behind the wonders that he witnessed on his journeys, which is in line with al-Masʿūdī and the geographer-traveller type that became prominent after the tenth century.

The version of this story in *GE*1 is much less radical than al-Garnāṭī's. Alfonso does not go so far as to suggest that noble Egyptian women married slaves; after all, he was a king in charge of his own nobility and their conduct. But Alfonso develops the story in a psychologically interesting way, expressing the Egyptian women's frustration at the lack of men and the ban on marrying those who were not their equals. In a women's assembly, a lady named Tada asks: "Tell me, ladies, if you had permission to marry shopkeepers, servants, and labourers who work to earn their money, would you want them?" The rest of the ladies reply: "How could we not want to [marry them]!? We are aging, and we cannot wait for a man to have us and make children, and we feel so miserable due to all this and cannot bear it anymore. Are not those men similar to our noblemen, and of the same nature?"[167] Faced with these needs, Tada goes to see Doluca and cleverly negotiates by warning her that many of the women are at risk of shaming themselves and their families. Doluca agrees to

---

enemigo ninguno que mal les pudiesse fazer que les non pudo entrar en Egipto." *GE*1 II, 197.

165 *GE*1 II, 197.

166 Abū Ḥāmid al-Garnāṭī, *Tuḥfat al-albāb (El regalo de los espíritus)*, ed. Ana Ramos (Madrid: CSIC, 1990), 123.

167 "Dezidme, dueñas, si vos diessen suelta que casássedes con tenderos e con sirvientes o omnes obreros que labrassen por sos dineros ¿querer los yedes? Dixiéronle todas: – Pues ¿cómo lo non querriemos?, ca nos fazemos ya mugeres de días e caraças, que nos salimos de tiempo de ser pora varón e fazer fijos, e tan lazradas en tod esto que lo non podemos sofrir. ¿E cuidades que non son estos varones como los otros nuestros nobles e omnes en su natura como ellos?" *GE*1 II, 261.

permit unequal marriages but wisely sets out a procedure for this and also navigates new problems that come to her kingdom; for instance, some men no longer worked because they were busy with "disputes with their women and their vices."[168] Here, Alfonso illustrates how the queen, who is learned in astrology, is also a wise ruler.

Even though in this passage Alfonso refers to an unknown *Libro de la estoria de Jairón el adivino* (*Book of the history of Jairón the diviner*), I suspect that most of this long passage was developed as a response to a question raised in al-Garnāṭī or a related work: what would happen if noble women were forced to marry their inferiors? The *GE*'s answer fulfills one of the main functions for "wonders" that we saw earlier: to push the limits of rational understanding, especially for a king such as Alfonso, who was deeply concerned about his kingdom's laws and wrote several legal codes.

Alfonso closes the story of Doluca with a section describing how she determined her succession before she died; he also describes the magnificence of her sepulchre. These events of Doluca's reign are not directly recorded in either al-Masʿūdī or al-Waṣīfī. Until a direct source is discovered, I assume that these are Alfonso's own elaborations, built upon other specific episodes that I will describe below, from the two authors. Through this embellishment Alfonso develops his own "wonders" and closes the reign of his admired Doluca in an honourable and peaceful way – very different from the end of his own rule, which was preceded by his son Sancho and many nobles rebelling.

Al-Masʿūdī talks about Dalūka's architectural constructions and the wisdom locked in them, but does not discuss the end of her reign. However, Alfonso plausibly took the name of Doluca's successor from al-Masʿūdī. After discussing Dalūka's buildings, al-Masʿūdī says that he is now returning to the history of Egypt's kings, and lists "the kings who succeeded the old queen Dalūka." The first is Darkūs, son of Bulūtis.[169] Similarly, Alfonso says that when Doluca grew older she appointed her nephew Darcón, son of Bolotez, as successor, in what looks like a Castilian transliteration of the Arabic names.[170] The rest of the information (how she picked astrologers and wise men to be Darcón's advisors, made him pharaoh, died peacefully three years later, and was buried in a magnificent sepulchre) – all absent in al-Masʿūdī – is likely Alfonso's own creation; however, I think these details were inspired by another passage by al-Waṣīfī. Up to this point, the only thing Alfonso could have borrowed from him is the fact that Doluca was picked as queen because she was the cousin and niece of Egyptian royalty, because al-Waṣīfī situates Doluca in Abraham's time and has her die in battle after a short account of her reign.

But I suggest that, since Alfonso wanted to peacefully pass power from Doluca to Darcón, he took inspiration from how al-Waṣīfī describes the succession from Huriā to Doluca, which includes a description of Huriā's burial and sepulchre. Al-Waṣīfī informs us that "Huriā had decreed that her body would be buried in a city that she ordered to be built in the desert in the west. In that city she had prepared a wondrous sepulchre that had been ornamented in a magnificent way, where she had erected

168 "[…] en pleito de sus mugieres e en sos vicios." *GE*1 II, 265.

169 *Al-Masʿūdī*, 2:410.

170 *GE*1 II, 747.

the idols of the stars."[171] Similarly, Alfonso explains that when Doluca died, "they took her to a sepulchre that she had made for herself in the west when she was still alive"; thus, both sepulchres were in the west. In the *GE* the sepulchre is also very ornate because "she had it covered with gold, silver, many images, and many precious stones," and on it, "they put her body in a golden litter that had many precious stones."[172] Al-Waṣīfī only talks about the "idols of the stars" in Doluca's sepulchre, but Alfonso may be elaborating on this when he explains that her litter "was in a golden tower that had figures of the seven planets, the twelve zodiacal signs, and the twenty-eight houses of the moon, and these things belong to the *knowledge of the stars*" (my emphasis). Once again, we find similar imagery in Alfonso's *Picatrix* and *Astromagia*, as well as the idiom for astrology that was borrowed from Arabic.[173]

Alfonso assimilates the style of geographical *adab* in such a way that he elaborates and expands on his sources' detailed literary stories (*akhbār*) and wonders (*ʿadjāʾib*) using his own knowledge of Arab culture. I do not think we should interpret this as forgery, even if he takes events associated with one queen and attributes them to another. Rather, Alfonso expresses the essence of the "Hermetic history" of Egypt produced by Muslim authors in a "creative" way and articulates it inside the narrative of the *GE* while also being guided by the biblical account. In addition, Alfonso's priority is describing Doluca as an exemplary ruler, as well as discussing her broad wisdom, on astrology and magic in particular; the last words of Doluca's story, which also establish a connection with Nebuchadnezzar's future conquest in *GE*4, are intended to convey this. Alfonso reiterates that Doluca had them put those images in the sepulchre, as she had done earlier in the "wall of the old woman" because she was "a very wise astrologer," and that this was the most precious knowledge for "kings, queens, princes, and the bishops of the gentiles in Egypt and all the lands to the south and west."[174] Thanks to this knowledge "the whole of Egypt was defended until the deeds of Drimiden the wise and King Nebuchadnezzar, which we will tell you about later."[175] This connection is not directly mentioned in the *GE*'s identified Arabic sources, but as we will see, it could have been inspired by them and then re-elaborated by Alfonso.

171 *L'Abrégé des merveilles*, 339.

172 "[…] leváronla a un sepulcro que avié ella fecho pora sí en su vida en ell occidente […] cubriól todo de oro e de plata, e muchas imágenes, e muchas piedras preciosas […] e pusieron a ella en lecho de oro que avié puestas a logares muchas piedras preciosas." *GE*1 II, 748–9.

173 "[…] e el lecho yazié en un crochel todo dorado e figurado en él las VII planetas, e los doze signos e las XXXVIII mansiones, e estas cosas al saber de las estrellas pertenece." *GE*1 II, 749.

174 "E fízolo allí imaginar todo aquella reína Doluca, lo uno porque era ella muy sabia estrellera […] reis e regnas e infantes e los obispos de sos gentiles e todos los otros grandes omnes de Egipto e de todas las tierras d'aquellas partes de mediodía e los de orient el saber e la cosa que ellos más preciavan e por que más se exaltavan el saber de las estrellas era." *GE*1 II, 749.

175 "[…] fue toda Egipto defenduda fasta'l fecho de Drimiden el sabio e fasta'l rey Nabucodonosor, como vos contaremos adelant en su tiempo […]." *GE*1 II, 749.

Nebuchadnezzar and the "Magical Conquest" of Egypt

*GE*4 narrates the life of Nebuchadnezzar. Even though this long section provides information on other topics, such as the whereabouts of the Jews after the Fall of Jerusalem, the first Romans, etc., a substantial part of it focuses on the famous king's conquest of Egypt.[176] Historically speaking, Nebuchadnezzar II did not conquer Egypt, although there exist some biblical, Arabic, and Judaic/Midrashic traditions on this topic, to which the *GE*'s account is related.[177] In *GE*4, the conquest entails a "magical war" that employs talismans, idols, and magical devices, which clearly aligns with al-Waṣīfī's "Hermetic history." Alfonso quotes the *Estoria de Alguazif*, *Estoria de Egipto*, or *Ystoria caldea de Alguaziph*, as a main source; thus, everything seems to point to al-Waṣīfī. However, as we saw above, the last pharaoh in al-Waṣīfī's *Kitāb al-ʿadjāʾib* is Ẓalmā, a contemporary of Moses who lived many years before Nebuchadnezzar's invasion. We also saw above how this inconsistency has led many specialists to believe that Alfonso used a longer version of this work, or a completely different book. I suggest that, when describing this conquest, Alfonso drew inspiration from passages that we can find spread across the *Kitāb al-ʿadjāʾib* but combined them with accounts by other authors. He then brought everything together into Nebuchadnezzar's era. In this way, the Castilian king formulated his own narrative regarding the conquest of Egypt and ensured coherence with the story of Doluca from *GE*1.

This hypothesis is hinted at in the passage from al-Waṣīfī in which he describes the city where Huriā was buried. At the end of this account, right before introducing Doluca, al-Waṣīfī indicates that the city was prosperous "until Bukht-Nāṣṣar came to ruin it and took ownership of its treasures."[178] Thus, if Alfonso took inspiration for Doluca's burial from here, he also found a reference to Nebuchadnezzar's legendary conquest when looking at this passage. There is another hint in the section on King Manāūs by al-Waṣīfī. This tyrannical king squandered the treasures of Egypt, took away men's honour by snatching their wives, and cruelly suffocated rebellions by sending the ruthless captain Qarmās – a giant who was a descendant of Idrīs (i.e., Hermes Trismegistus) – to quell them.[179] Manāūs was succeeded by his son Afrāūs, a wise ruler who built wonders and was his father's complete opposite – he acted as a learned and exemplary king following the *adab* tradition. However, a series of disgraces arose in Afrāūs's kingdom: women became sterile, lions and crocodiles started to attack people, floods and heavy rains were succeeded by droughts, and so on. Afrāūs tried to counteract these calamities with talismans and prodigious machines, but they all proved useless. Finally, the cause was discovered: Afrāūs's father had stolen the wife of a powerful magician named Ajnās and thereby infuriated him. According to al-Waṣīfī: "Helped by his art's resources, this magician gradually nullified the virtues of Egypt's talismans, because against each talisman there exist powers and other talismans able to combat and destroy its strength." Then – and this

176 Nebuchadnezzar's life and deeds, including the conquest of Egypt, extends throughout *GE*4 I, 13–249.

177 See Israel Ephal, "Nebuchadnezzar the Warrior: Remarks on His Military Achievements," *Israel Exploration Journal* 53, no. 2 (2003): 178–91.

178 *L'Abrégé des merveilles*, 339.

179 *L'Abrégé des merveilles*, 219–20.

is significant for my argument – he adds: "and this is what allowed Bukht-Nāṣṣar the Persian to conquer Egypt, despite it being defended by all its princes."[180] Eventually Afrāūs reached an agreement with the magician, but the important point here is that according to al-Waṣīfī's chronology, this king lived centuries before Nebuchadnezzar – who appears in this episode as part of an explanation. If Alfonso introduced a version of this story in *GE*4, as I will argue below, he might also have discovered that Egypt's talismanic defences were disabled by Nebuchadnezzar. In my opinion, Alfonso interpreted the defenses as referring to those built by Doluca – and he used a different source, al-Masʿūdī, for them.

*GE*4 states that Nebuchadnezzar's conquest began to take shape when, according to Eusebius and Sigebert of Gembloux (*c.* 1030–1112), Egypt had a king called Vafre, son of King Samnetico; however, Alfonso clarifies that Alguazif the Arab calls these kings Gomez and Lucas, names that sound suspiciously Castilian.[181] Another striking factor is that Alfonso tells a story about these two kings that is very similar to the tale about the dishonoured magician in al-Waṣīfī. *GE*4 says that according to Alguazif, in the times of King Lucas/Samnetico

> a lad among those astrologers, wizards, and sorcerers of Egypt [...] married a beautiful woman and loved her dearly. This woman knew a lady in the king's house and went to see her many times. One day the king noticed this woman and took a liking to her, because she was very beautiful, so he ordered in secret that she not be allowed to leave. Since she had to stay with the king, the lad lost her and was very wretched.[182]

Just like in al-Waṣīfī, the sorcerer unleashes his revenge, and with similar consequences. In the *GE* he even joins forces with his magician colleagues: using charms, "they harmed the power of many images [talismans]" that protected Manip, the kingdom's capital; among other abominations, they caused "fishes and sea monsters to come to the Nile's riverbanks [...], birds damaged bread and people [...], savage beasts abandoned jungles and wastelands and came to the roads, where they killed and ate people [...], the waters flooded the lands," and, worst of all, while this was happening, "a piece of the *barbe*, the wall of the old woman, fell."[183] Soon King Lucas/Samnetico died and left these problems to his son, Gomez/Vafre.

180 *L'Abrégé des merveilles*, 222.

181 *GE*4 I, 31–2.

182 "[...] un mancebo d'aquellos estrelleros e fechizeros e daquellos encantadores de Egipto [...] casara con una mugier muy fermosa e amávala mucho. E avié esta su mugier coñocencia con una dueña de casa del Rey e ívala veer muchas vezes. E víola el Rey un día et pagos mucho d'ella de cómo era muy fermosa, e mando en su poridad que la non dexassen ir, e fiziéronlo. E ovo ella a fincar con el Rey, e perdióla el mancebo d'esta guisa e fue muy cuetado." *GE*4 I, 35–6.

183 "[...] tollieron luego por sos encantamientos el poder a muchas ymagenes [...] venir los pescados e los bestiglos del mar a la Ribera del Nilo [...] las aues que dannassen los panes et a los omnes [...] encantaron luego las bestias salvages, e que las fazién salir de las selvas e de los yermos e venir a los caminos, e mataban a los hombres e comiénselos [...] esparzién ell agua sin recabdo por tierra más que non solié [...] entonces cayó un pedazo de Barbe, d'aquella pared de la vieja." *GE*4 I, 36–8.

There are several important points I want to highlight: 1) The story Alfonso attributes to Alguazif parallels that in al-Waṣīfī's book, which takes place during the reigns of two earlier kings of Egypt; 2) Al-Waṣīfī's story compares the magician's destruction of the images and talismans with the destruction Nebuchadnezzar would cause centuries later, but Alfonso places the story of the wronged magician in the time of the conqueror; 3) The most important talismans protecting Egypt are those erected by Doluca, which Alfonso describes in *GE*1; 4) Doluca is constantly mentioned in these sections of *GE*4, and they refer back to specific details in *GE*1; however, all make the same translation mistake: in Arabic *barbā* is an Egyptian temple, not the wall of the old woman (*ḥāʾiṭ al-ʿajūz*). Thus, when it comes to Egypt's magical defences, I argue that *GE*4 is referencing and elaborating on the material Alfonso created in *GE*1, not an Arabic source. In fact, Alfonso makes this clear:

> the wall of the old woman was the temple that we talked about in the reasons for the third age. They called it *barbe* in their language, and it means exactly that: the wall of the old woman. We told you that it was made by Queen Doluca, who reigned after Pharaoh Talme, who died in the Red Sea chasing Moses. She put the four images with horsemen, rattles, and many other things made with smoking rituals, sacrifices, and charms by astrologers [in the temple], as it was said. The history of the Arab Alguazif [written] in Arabic says that this *barbe* was carved by a wise master called Bodura.[184]

Everything has been mentioned in *GE*1 with the exception of Bodura. I think Bodura is a device Alfonso uses to follow up on the decay of Egypt's protections causing its future defeat, which is mentioned at the end of Doluca's story. Bodura is also a way to introduce a new development: a prophecy about Egypt's fall. *GE*4 explains something new about Doluca: she rewarded Bodura by commissioning his lineage to take care of the images and protections for Egypt from then on, and she assigned a perpetual income for this. Despite astrologers having prophesied that Egypt would be conquered when those images lost their power, later kings would neglect their duty. Among these kings is Samnetico/Lucas, who not only places guards who were not from Bodura's lineage in charge of the images but does not pay them properly, and all this leads to an image falling. Lucas is frightened when the image falls because he knew the prophecy. Even though he then tries to improve Egypt's defences, his offence towards the magician worsens the danger.[185] *GE*4 also narrates that, when King Samnetico/Lucas feels he is going to die, he calls for his son Vafre/Gomez, with whom he has a long conversation.[186] The father tells his son about many things

184 "[...] la pared de la vieja fue el tiemplo que vos dixiemos en las razones de la tercera edad que llamaron ellos Barbe en so lenguaje, que quiere dezir esto mismo que dixiemos, la pared de la vieja, la que vos contamos que mandara fazer la reína Doluca, que regnó empós el faraón Talme, que murio en el mar Vermejo yendo tras Moisén. E puso las cuatro imágenes con cascaveles e con cavalleros e con otras cosas muchas fechas con sufumerios e con sacrificios e con encantamientos muchos de estrelleros como es ya contado. E diz aquella estoria de Alguazif del aravigo que a este barbe que le labrara un maestro sabio que dixieron Bodura." *GE*4 I, 33.

185 These events are narrated in *GE*4 I, 34–5.

186 *GE*4 I, 41–8.

related to Egypt's history, particularly about Doluca, the protections she built, and the prophecy about Egypt's fall if the temples are destroyed and the images and statues in them neglected:

> Believe that, while those images have the power to make spirits talk through them and tell the kings of Egypt what is coming, Egypt will be in a good place. But it is written that these images will lose this power, and a wise man of Babylon will harm the power in them, and a king from that land [...] will come, destroy, and ravage Egypt.[187]

I have not found a similar prophecy in either al-Waṣīfī or al-Masʿūdī. However, it is highly evocative of Hermes Trismegistus's famous lament to Asclepius in the *Asclepius*. In this Hermetic treatise, the looming ruin of Egypt is connected to disregard for the cult of the statues, which also prophesize and have spirits in them. Hermes Trismegistus says:

> I mean statues ensouled and conscious, filled with spirit and doing great deeds; statues that foreknow the future and predict it by lots, by prophecy, by dreams and by many other means [...] a time will come when it will appear that the Egyptians paid respect to divinity with faithful mind and painstaking reverence – to no purpose. All their holy worship will be disappointed and perish without effect, for divinity will return from earth to heaven, and Egypt will be abandoned. The land that was the seat of reverence will be widowed by the powers and left destitute of their presence. When foreigners occupy the land and territory [...] then this most holy land, seat of shrines and temples, will be filled completely with tombs and corpses.[188]

There is no proof that the Arabic-speaking world had direct knowledge of the *Asclepius*, other than indirect and vague quotes, but it was well-known in medieval Christianity by authors that Alfonso held in high esteem, including Augustine, who quotes this exact passage,[189] and authors from the Platonist School of Chartres, who, as we saw, were very influential on Alfonsine thought. Since there is no trace of this prophecy in either al-Waṣīfī or al-Masʿūdī, it is possible that the prophecy of Egypt's fall in *GE*4 is Alfonso elaborating on his direct, or indirect, knowledge of the *Asclepius*. Alfonso did at least know that Asclepius was an important character in the Hermetic tradition. As we will see later in this book, in the famous passage of the three Hermes in *GE*2 it is "Esculapius" (the Castilian name for Asclepius) who discovers the book of Hermes Trismegistus.[190] In any case, the similarities with the passage from the *Asclepius* reinforces the presence of Hermetic elements in *GE*4.

However, I do not see any possibility of this also being the inspiration for an important element in Samnetico's prophecy to Vafre: a wise man of Babylon who would harm the

[187] "[...] crey tú que en quanto aquellas imágenes aquel poder ovieren de fablar los espíritos en ellas e dezir a los reis de Egipto lo que les á de venir, estará Egipto en buen logar. Mas escrito es que a perder an estas imágenes aquel poder, e que un sabio de Babiloña gele á de taller, e que un Rey d'allá [...] verná, e destroíra a Egipto e hermarla á." *GE*4 I, 46.

[188] *Asclepius* 24, translation by Copenhaver, *Hermetica,* 81.

[189] Augustine, *Civitate Dei* VIII.xxxiii–xxxiv. On medieval knowledge about the *Asclepius*, see Copenhaver, *Hermetica*, xlvii–xlviii.

[190] *GE*2 I, 49.

power of the statues. This prophecy is repeated several times. Some pages later, *GE4* mentions an astrologist who visits King Vafre and tells him the same prophecy, including that the four statues "would lose the virtue that they had, because a strange man would make them lose it."[191] This man is Drimiden, who in *GE4* provides invaluable help for the conquest of Egypt in *GE4* – perhaps Alfonso's inspiration came from the maltreated magician that we saw earlier in al-Waṣīfī. Angered because Egypt sheltered some Jews who had escaped Babylon, Nebuchadnezzar decides to conquer this land. He consults his wise men, who warn him about Egypt's magical defences, but then Drimiden, the kingdom's wisest magician, proposes a plan: he will travel in disguise to Egypt in an "undercover" mission and, dodging the guards – almost like a "magical commando" – he will penetrate the enchanted *barbe* compound and magically sabotage the statues' power.[192] The surprising fact is that Nebuchadnezzar knows – because his astrologist father had told him – the magical rituals Doluca used to build and consecrate the statues in *GE1*, which included suffumigation, animal sacrifices with blood, and the observance of astrological requirements.[193] This information facilitates the execution of Drimiden's plan, whose advancements are described in detail by Alfonso. To enter Egypt, Drimiden disguises himself as a diviner who is making a pilgrimage (*romería*) to the *barbe* and the holy places of Egypt.[194] Truth be told, this pilgrimage resembles the pilgrimage to Santiago de Compostela that was at its peak in Alfonso's time – as we can ascertain in several lyrical compositions in Alfonso's *Cantigas de Santa María* and the pictures that accompanied them.[195] Helped by an old woman – who is reminiscent of the woman who helps Asclepius understand the book of Hermes in *GE2*, as we will see in Chapter Five – Drimiden evades the guards and finally enters the sacred place. The magician comes prepared for his mission, carrying blood and ointments made with astrological ceremonies and cooking procedures, which he applies to the idols in a counter-ritual to Doluca's in *GE1*. As Attrell and Porreca affirm in the *Picatrix*, "ointments, confections, and pills made of strange mixtures are not so rare."[196] Thus, Drimiden "soiled them in such a way that harmed all the power and strength that they had earlier, when the spirits came and talked through them."[197] Alfonso suspiciously states that "we will neither tell you which ointments they were nor with which astral conjunctions and charms they were made, because we did not find them in the books of the wise men from which we take this evidence; for we found that the Book of Alguazif lacks a folio in this place."[198] Thus, Alfonso mentions the counter-rituals and

191 "[…] perderién la virtud que avién e que omne estraño gelo farié perder." *GE4* I, 64.
192 The consultation and plan are described in *GE4* I, 67–9. Of course, the emphasis on the thrilling details of the ancient "mission impossible" are mine.
193 *GE4* I, 68–9.
194 *GE4* I, 84.
195 See, for instance, María Victoria Chico, "La vida como un viaje: viaje y peregrinación en la composición pictórica de las Cantigas De Santa María de Alfonso X El Sabio," *Revista de filología románica*, anejo IV (2006): 129–33.
196 Attrell and Porreca, introduction to *Picatrix*, 28.
197 "Ensuziólas de guisa que les tollió tod el poder e la fuerça que avién antes de venir los espíritos e fablar en ellas." *GE4* I, 94.
198 "[…] d'estas melezinas cuáles fueron e en cuáles estrellaciones fechas e por cuáles encantamientos, non vos lo diremos, ca non fallamos en los libros de los sabios don estas

ointments – which turn out to be similar to those in his *Picatrix* and *Astromagia* – but declines to provide details, giving a convenient excuse. This, along with the exhaustive references to Doluca's constructions in *GE*1 and the iteration of the same translation mistakes that we found in *GE*4, leads me to think that Alfonso creatively constructed the long conquest of Egypt from minor references in al-Waṣīfī, al-Masʿūdī, and perhaps other authors, along with contextual elements from biblical, Midrashic, and Christian sources, as I pointed out earlier. Thus, I favour this as the origin of the long account about Nebuchadnezzar's conquest in *GE*4 rather than Alfonso using a lost work by Alguazif/al-Waṣīfī – a position defended by previous scholars.

The only work that offers an alternative explanation, and even the remote possibility of being *GE*4's source, is one of al-Masʿūdī's lost works. We saw how the *Murūj* lists the kings after Dalūka, starting with Darkūs (Darcón in *GE*1). The last king in that list is Kabil who, according to al-Masʿūdī, "must battle the kings of the West. Bukht-Nāṣṣar, satrap of the king of Persia in the west, came to attack him, ravaged his lands, destroyed his army, and went back to the west."[199] Al-Masʿūdī mentions that he narrated this conquest in *Kitāb rāḥat al-arwāḥ* (*Book of the repose of souls*), another of his lost works.[200] Earlier I claimed that Alfonso was following this part of the *Murūj* when writing the story of Doluca in *GE*1 – the mention of Darcón demonstrating that he might have reached at least this page – but then al-Masʿūdī, although he mentions Nebuchadnezzar's conquest, also adds that it happened in Kabil's times, who does not coincide with any of the Egyptian kings in *GE*4. Thus, until the *Kitāb rāḥat* is found, I defend the hypothesis that Alfonso found a reference to Nebuchadnezzar's conquest of Egypt in al-Masʿūdī that could be added to those he found in al-Waṣīfī. When Alfonso reached Nebuchadnezzar's reign in *GE*4, based on his sources, he assumed that the famous king had conquered Egypt and that it was an important matter. Consequently, Alfonso reconstructed the conquest in a plausible way using the hints that he found in his sources and keeping the details consistent with and connected to Doluca's story in *GE*1. In doing this, Alfonso made himself worthy of continuing the "Hermetic history of Egypt" that his sources had begun.

Conclusion

Specialists have identified the most important Arabic sources named in the *GE* and have pointed out their wondrous elements, but they have not significantly explored the cultural background in which those books were written and how they brought together their disparate characteristics. I have contextualized these Arabic sources within Muslim scholarly production, concluded that they actually belong to *adab*-related geographical genres, and traced their evolution from their origins to Alfonso's times. We saw how these works also incorporate historical knowledge, ethical advice, and wondrous elements. Even though "marvels" (*mirabilia*) can also be found in some Christian sources, the comprehensive inclusion of astrological, magical, and

razones tomamos. E fallamos que mingua en este logar de la razón d'esto en el Libro de Alguazif una foja." *GE*4 I, 94.

199 *Al-Masʿūdī*, 2:411.

200 *Al-Masʿūdī*, 2:411. On this book, see Khalidi, "Masʿūdī's Lost Works," 40.

Hermetic elements is specific to certain Arabic sources that Alfonso used. As we saw, *adab* and Hermetic components – which are not necessarily related – came together in some geographical and historical Arabic sources.[201] These Hermetic insertions are also prominent features of the *GE* as a whole, yet oddities in most of its Latin models; therefore, I suggest that Arabic geographical and historical sources helped to fit astrology, magic, and the Hermetic tradition into the *GE* and, in a sense, made the whole work a sort of continuation of those genres. Alfonso portrays himself as "a bearer of civilization"[202] who is not so different from the wise men and rulers in his Arabic sources, who were endowed with astrological knowledge that allowed them to accomplish exemplary deeds. This is what occurs in the stories of Abraham and Doluca. In the writings of al-Bakrī, al-Waṣīfī, and al-Masʿūdī, Alfonso found "historical evidence" for the ancient usefulness of the astro-magical sciences he had been translating and developing since the beginning of his reign. These sources were also elaborated on in the *GE*, as can be ascertained in the story of Doluca, along with its later ramifications during the conquest of Nebuchadnezzar. According to my interpretation, Alfonso did not limit himself to faithfully rendering Arabic sources, "Alguazif" in particular, despite what he affirms in these sections and what previous specialists have believed. To tackle the contradictions found within his Arabic sources, Alfonso decided to re-elaborate and enhance them in order to place them within a more coherent historical narrative. In the *GE* events are often explained in a more extended and detailed way than in the Arabic sources, where they are briefly reported or sometimes just mentioned in passing. Even more importantly, characters taken from biblical, pagan, Arabic, and Jewish sources – Abraham, Moses, Doluca, Nebuchadnezzar, etc. – interact throughout history in a comprehensible and exemplary way. Not surprisingly, Hermes also appears in the *GE*'s narrative, and in Chapter Three I will introduce one of his embodiments: the god Mercury. I will argue that in this incarnation in particular, Hermes is also presented as an exemplary courtier – including *adab* features – for the *GE*'s Castilian readers. As we will see, in the *GE*, renderings of Ovid's *Metamorphoses* are interposed with the Arabic sources discussed in this chapter. Not surprisingly, the Ovidian Mercury (i.e., Hermes), comes into play in a world consistent with the Arabic Hermetic history that we have just seen.

201 Coulon, *La magie*, 92–8.

202 Márquez Villanueva, *El concepto cultural Alfonsí*, 39; Rico, *Alfonso el Sabio*, 113–14; Fierro, "Alfonso X 'the Wise'," 190.

3

Interpreting Ovid's *Metamorphoses* in the *General Estoria* through Hermetic Motives and *Adab*

Introduction

Throughout the Middle Ages in Europe, classical works were read and interpreted through a Christian lens, and Alfonso X's *GE* is no exception. This large historical work uses biblical narratives as a frame; however, extensive passages from classical mythology, in particular from Ovid's *Metamorphoses*, are intermingled with the biblical characters and stories.[1] The *GE*'s interpretation of the pagan gods and heroes is consistent with Ovid's reception in the Middle Ages.[2] Nevertheless, it is remarkable that no other historical work from this period gave such a prominent role to classical sources – especially to the *Metamorphoses* – and that Alfonso's approach does not place greater emphasis on the Christian interpretation. These features of the *GE* demonstrate that Alfonso's intellectual endeavours were much more secular than those of his European contemporaries.[3]

The *GE* refers numerous times to the writings of the "gentiles" that we must understand as a synonym for "pagans," including not only ancient peoples like the pre-Islamic Arabs and the Egyptians – as we saw in Chapter Two – but also the Greeks and Romans. But who was the Castilian king – as well as most of his contemporaries – referring to with these words? How are Roman authors such as Ovid related to them? Marenbon has dedicated a thorough study to the medieval "problem" of paganism, and provides us with a definition of pagans/gentiles, which "correspond to how beliefs were classified by educated Christians in Western Europe in the Middle Ages"; those educated Christians – among whom we must include Alfonso – regarded as pagans "anyone, at any period, who is not a Christian, a

1 See Martínez, *El humanismo medieval*, 385–7.

2 My main reference for the study of Ovid and his medieval commentators in the *GE* are Salvo García's studies, which are included in the Bibliography. See also Martínez, *El humanismo medieval*, 416–17 and 431; Benito Brancaforte, *Las "Metamorfosis" y las "Heroidas" de Ovidio en la "General Estoria" de Alfonso el Sabio* (Madison: The Hispanic Seminary of Medieval Studies, 1990); M. Rosa Lida de Malkiel, "La 'General estoria': Notas literarias y filológicas (I)," *Romance Philology* 12 (1958): 111–42; and María Luzdivina Cuesta Torre, "Los Comentaristas de Ovidio en la General Estoria II, Caps. 74–115," *Revista de literatura medieval* 19 (2007): 137–69.

3 See Martínez, *El humanismo medieval*, 16.

Jew or a Muslim."[4] In this sense, it is significant that for Aquinas, a contemporary of Alfonso, "'pagans' or 'gentiles' were a distinctive subgroup of the wider class of unbelievers [*infideles*] that also included Jews and heretics."[5] In this way, when the *GE* refers to the "gentiles" or "pagans," it includes the first humans – whose customs and beliefs are described[6] – to the Greeks and Romans – and in this it aligns with the New Testament in the *Vulgate*. In his Latin translation of the Bible, Jerome used the adjective *gentiles* (nominative plural of *gentilis,-e*) – derived from the noun *gens, gentis* (clan, tribe, people, family) – to translate the Hebrew word *goy* and the Greek *éthnē* (*ἔθνη*), which the New and Old Testaments, respectively, use to designate the non-Jews. When Christianity became the religion of the Roman Empire, the religious change happened quickly in the cities but much slower in less populated rural areas. For this reason, from the fourth century the Church Fathers used the term *paganus*, which means "of the country, rustic, peasant" (form *pagus*, "the country"), to designate the people whose beliefs were neither Christian nor Jewish. In the centuries to follow, pagans were assimilated with gentiles, likely due to the ongoing reading and commentary of the *Vulgate*, and both groups also excluded Muslims upon their arrival – possibly because they too were monotheistic, whereas pagans practised polytheism. To facilitate my analysis, I will use "gentile" or "pagan" in the same sense as Alfonso, including Roman, Greeks, and previous civilizations, but excluding Muslims and Jews. It is crucial to consider these distinctions in the *GE*, as will be seen in this chapter.

Thus, to support the secular approach of the *GE*, as well as the widespread presence of non-Christian sources, Alfonso frequently asserts that "although they were gentiles" (*mager que gentiles*) they were also "good and wise men" (*omnes buenos e que fueron sabios*),[7] which justifies his use of gentile writings in a similar manner to his justification of the use of Muslim authors, as we saw in Chapter Two. I also explained earlier that Arabic sources are utilized not only as historical references but also to interpret Christian content, including the Bible. Moreover, as I will discuss below, Arabic sources are also used to explain pagan authors, something that other specialists have barely touched upon. What is even more remarkable is that the Arabic sources used for interpretation include not only historical works but also *adab*, scientific, magical, and even Hermetic ones; all of them contain traces of Hermes Trismegistus.

In this chapter, I am going to examine Arabic elements in the *GE*'s retelling of Ovid's *Metamorphoses*,[8] focusing specifically on a section that historicizes and

4 John Marenbon, *Pagans and Philosophers. The Problem of Paganism from Augustine to Leibniz* (Princeton: Princeton University Press, 2015), 5.

5 Marenbon, *Pagans and Philosophers*, 5. As Marenbon expertly explains throughout this monograph dedicated to the topic, this definition was not consistently applied by every medieval author, and not even by Aquinas in all his works. However, it is entirely applicable to the book of Alfonso, so I refer to Marenbon's work for more nuanced considerations.

6 See, for instance, *GE*1 I, 117–22.

7 For instance, in *GE*1 I, 117.

8 In this way I follow recent approaches by Erik Ekman, "Ovid Historicized: Magic and Metamorphosis in Alfonso X's *General Estoria*," *La corónica. A Journal of Medieval*

interprets "the story of Io" (hereafter *TSOI*).[9] First I will contextualize this passage within the historical narrative of *GE*1, showing how it is closely preceded and followed by sections in which the use of Arab sources is evident. Then I will examine the three stages of interpretation that Alfonso adopts from his contemporaries, how he uses them to interpret Ovid, and how the Castilian king introduces his own particularities, including contributions from the Arab sciences and a special treatment of the figure of Mercury. Understanding how the figuration of Mercury emerges out of classical and Arabic source texts in Spain at this time will allow us to reassess how previous scholars viewed the reception of Ovid in medieval Castile. Using this new perspective, I will also elucidate on the profound originality of Alfonso's hybrid interpretation of classical materials, despite his apparent allegiance to techniques inherited from contemporary European authors. These processes of cultural syncretism in the *GE*'s Ovidian stories are embodied by the god Mercury – who displays features that make him similar to the Arabic Hermes.

I propose that this interweaving of sources and interpretations not only makes Mercury an archetypical character within the hierarchy of knowledge that Alfonso is defending but also an example of the multicultural dimension of Alfonsine medieval humanism.[10] I also defend the position that for Alfonso, Mercury/Hermes Trismegistus could be used as a shared point of reference for the three religious traditions of his kingdom because he was respected by all of them. This mythical sage was an intellectual model for Iberian elites, regardless of their faith, because his ancient wisdom came before the advent of their faith traditions. Rereading Roman mythology through the lens of the Hermetic material in *TSOI* also brings old Mediterranean traditions, such as the bonds between Hermes and Isis in Hellenistic Egypt, to the surface. In addition, I also argue that Mercury is presented as a model courtier, who in thirteenth-century Castile was imbued with elements of *adab*. When Alfonso identifies Mercury as the "Arabic Hermes," he imbues him with distinct features of Arab culture that were highly valued in his court: a noble lineage, an ideal courtly education, extensive understanding of the liberal arts, and expertise in astral magic. In what follows, I will connect these three areas of knowledge to Arabic books of education and astrological magic, as well as to Alfonso's cultural programme as a whole. In Chapter Two I discussed the impact of *adab*, an Arab educational concept, on Alfonso's oeuvre, and specifically on the *GE*. In this chapter I will explore these *adab* notions in *TSOI* and point to specific references to the liberal arts (the *trivium* and *quadrivium*) that are closely related to Hermes-Mercury and that I will fully develop in Chapter Five. In sum, in this chapter we will see how Alfonso incorporates Roman literary stories into the *GE* with the aid of new historical, scientific, and magical ideas obtained from Arabic material and how he coherently blends them into his cultural project and body of work.

Hispanic Languages, Literatures, and Cultures 42, no. 1 (2013): 23–46; and Ana M. Montero, "A Possible Connection."

9 *GE*1 I, 300–23. The story of Io is in *Met*.I.567–745.

10 Martínez, *El humanismo medieval*, 45–86.

Alfonso's Placement and Interpretation of the Story of Io

Inserting *TSOI* into the historical narrative of *GE*1 stands out as an example of Alfonso's thorough shaping of the *GE*. As we saw, the *GE* is organized following the structure of the Bible.[11] *TSOI* is located in book VI of the *GE*'s account of *Genesis*, chapters XVIII–XXIX,[12] and it comes just after a long section in which Alfonso recounts the life of Abraham.[13] Alfonso inserts *TSOI* just before narrating the patriarch's death and introducing Isaac's deeds. However, this pagan episode is not isolated between biblical stories.

The biblical contents before and after *TSOI* are elaborated using a diverse array of material – including Arabic sources that describe aspects of Abraham's life, the lands he travelled through, and their rulers (of Babylon, Egypt, etc.). As we saw in Chapter Two, one significant source is the *Kitāb al-masālik wa-l-mamālik* (*Book of highways and kingdoms*) by the Andalusi polymath al-Bakrī, which Alfonso quotes several times using its Arabic name but also refers to it as the *Estoria de Egipto* (*History of Egypt*).[14] This source is referenced throughout the narration of Abraham's life, including directly before *TSOI*, in a transitional chapter where Alfonso briefly summarizes some pagan events that "happened in Abraham's time."[15] There we find al-Bakrī's *Estoria de Egipto* listed alongside Christian sources, including Eusebius. As I pointed out in Chapter Two, al-Bakrī's works belong within an *adab* genre that includes geographical histories containing plenty of wondrous, and even Hermetic, elements. The last quotation before *TSOI* describes the aforementioned Nimrod's ascent to heaven in a marvellous ark.[16] As we saw, the ascent to heaven for knowledge is a characteristic Hermetic theme related to the Neoplatonic ascent of the soul. It is also closely associated with Hermes's Jewish and Arab counterparts, Enoch and Idrīs.

The anecdote of Nimrod's ascent to heaven appears immediately before *TSOI*, where we will find gods and magic with features of Arabic culture. As we will see below, at the end of *TSOI*, there are similar motifs when Io travels to Egypt, where she transforms into Isis. The veneration of Hermes Trismegistus was connected to that of Isis in antiquity – a bond to which the *GE* alludes. Besides, Egypt's connections with astrology during Abraham's visit to the country are introduced immediately before *TSOI*, and shortly afterwards Alfonso presents the story of Queen Doluca. As we saw in Chapter Two, Doluca was another Egyptian queen closely associated with magic and astrology, which she used to build magical defences in Egypt. The sources for Doluca's story are the *Kitāb murūj al-dhahab* (*Book of the prairies of gold*) by al-Masʿūdī and the *Kitāb al-ʿadjāʾib* by al-Waṣīfī.[17] As we saw below, al-Waṣīfī's book is described by modern scholars as a "hermetic history of Egypt."[18] Alfonso's version

11 On Ovid and the Bible in the *GE*, see Sánchez-Prieto Borja, introduction to *GE*1 I, li–lvi.

12 *GE*1 I, 300–23.

13 *GE*1 I, 155–297.

14 As we saw in Chapter Two. See Fernández-Ordóñez, *Las estorias de Alfonso*, 173–92.

15 "De las cosas que contecieron en tiempo de Abraham." *GE*1 I, 298–300.

16 *GE*1 I, 298–9.

17 Alfonso introduces Queen Doluca and how she rose to power in *GE*1 II, 191–4; and develops her reign in *GE*1 II, 194–7, 259–67, and 747–51.

18 Michael Cook, "Pharaonic History in Medieval Egypt," *Studia Islamica*, no. 57 (1983): 71.

of *TSOI* is coloured by wondrous and Hermetic elements, which make the Ovidian fable suitable for its place in the *GE*. Since Alfonso uses Arabic sources to illustrate and interpret the biblical narrative of Abraham, it does not seem odd that he also uses them in his analysis of *TSOI*, as it is placed in the middle of the patriarch's story in *GE*1. Moreover, Alfonso follows the three-stage Christian interpretation of Ovid that was prevalent in the Middle Ages, and below I will examine how he manages to introduce Arab magical and Hermetic components in each stage.

Ovid's works were not forgotten during the Middle Ages, and their influence in twelfth-century Europe, and especially in France, was so prominent that the century has been called *aetas ovidiana*.[19] During this century, scholars successfully developed two ancient methods of interpretation to Ovid: euhemerism and allegory. Euhemerism is the method of interpreting mythology articulated by Euhemerus of Messene (third century BCE), according to whom ancient gods were actually historical kings and exemplary men. Allegory reveals that texts might contain a hidden meaning. Philo of Alexandria (first century CE) adapted allegorical analysis from Stoic and Platonic commentators on Homer and applied it to the Bible, because he thought that in the holy writings, "when rightly interpreted, the apparently circumstantial narrative contains a moral, and sometimes a metaphysical, meaning."[20] Philo influenced two early Greek Christian thinkers, Justin Martyr (d. *c*. 165) and Clement of Alexandria (*c*.150–before 215), and after them allegorical interpretations of the Bible continued throughout the Middle Ages. Paradoxically, in the twelfth century thinkers from the most important schools in France – Chartres, Orléans, and Paris – once again used allegory to interpret pagan writers, and they combined it effectively with euhemerism and a fitting moral interpretation to accommodate Ovid within the Christian culture of this time. Alfonso took advantage of these developments to integrate the myths of the *Metamorphoses* into the narrative and biblical framing of the *GE*, where they are also translated into a vernacular language for the first time. Ovid had been used in historical works occasionally, but never to such an extent and in such a thorough way as in the *GE*; this would have not been possible without the tools of euhemerism and allegory. Alfonso refers to them directly in a passage from *GE*2:

> The friar explains that some reasons for those transformations are explained through allegory – which is to say one thing but signify another – some through the customs of the matters that are explained, and others through history. Thus, all the transformations that Ovid talks about are explained in these three ways: allegory, customs, and history.[21]

[19] Cristina Noacco, "Lire Ovide au xiie siècle: Arnoul d'Orléans, commentateur des *Metamorphoses*," *Troianalexandrina* 6 (2006): 132.

[20] Marenbon, *Medieval Philosophy*, 26.

[21] "Et departe el fraire que las razones d'essos mudamientos que las unas se esponen segunt allegoria, que es dezir uno e dar ál a entender; las otras segunt las costumbres d'essas cosas de que son dichas las razones. Las otras segunt la estoria. E por estas tres maneras, allegoría, costumbres, estoria, se esponen todos los mudamientos de que Ovidio fabla." *GE*2 I, 368.

Here, Alfonso's source is Arnulf of Orléans (twelfth century), whom Alfonso usually refers to as "the friar" when he quotes from him. Arnulf defined these three ways of interpretation (allegorical, moralistic, and historical): "Modo quasdam allegorice, quasdam moraliter exponamus, et quasdam historice."[22] Both Arnulf and Alfonso understood "history" as euhemeristically interpreting the stories of gods as events associated with historical kings, and for Alfonso, "customs" (*costumbres*) refer to moralistic readings. As Noacco explains, Arnulf usually does not use all three interpretations for the same myth but rather focuses on one at a time.[23] However, in some myths collected in the *GE*, Alfonso uses all three in a systematic way, as in the section on *TSOI*, probably because it is the first myth from the *Metamorphoses* that he extensively develops.[24] Let us consider how Alfonso understands each of these stages and how Arabic influences, particularly the figure of Mercury, filtered into them.

Historical/Euhemeristic Interpretation of the Story of Io

Since the *GE* is a historical work, the historical stage of interpretation is understandably the most developed one. Alfonso explicitly justifies including the *Metamorphoses* alongside the Bible and also harmonizes *TSOI* with the general features and aims of the *GE*. The *GE* is divided into six parts, according to the six ages of the world outlined by Augustine in *The City of God*, and Ovid's *Metamorphoses* and *Heroides* are the main sources for pagan kings and events in the first three ages, from Creation to the end of the Trojan War. The criteria for inserting Ovid's material in between biblical narratives is inspired by the two main historiographic sources that Alfonso used to develop the structure of the *GE*: Eusebius's *Chronicle* or *Chronikoi kanones* (Canonical canons, early fourth century) and Petrus Comestor's *Historia scholastica* (c. 1170).[25] These authors included brief passages (*incidentia*) about pagan events, which Eusebius organized into tables that synchronized biblical facts with the histories of different pagan nations. Even though the original Greek is lost, the work has been preserved in a Latin translation by Jerome. This is why Alfonso introduces *TSOI* in a historical narrative that he claims is supported by both Eusebius and Jerome.

In the *GE*, following Nimrod's ascent to heaven, Alfonso turns to Eusebius as a source and lists diverse pagan events that happened during the lifetimes of Abraham and Isaac. At the end of this list, Alfonso explains that "In the meantime, just as Eusebius relates in Greek and Jerome in Latin, the reign of the Argives started, and it

22 Arnulf of Orléans, *Arnulphi Aurelianensis Allegoriae super Ovidii Metamorphosis*, in Fausto Ghisalberti, "Arnolfo d'Orleans, un cultore di Ovidio nel secolo XII," *Memorie del Reale Istituto Lombardo di Scienze e Lettere* 24 (1932): 201.

23 Noacco, "Lire Ovide," 137.

24 As Salvo García indicates, only two of the *Metamorphoses*'s myths are translated and interpreted in *GE*1: Io (*GE*1 I, 301–23) and Callisto (*GE*1 II, 630–54). Irene Salvo García, "Ovidio y la compilación de la General estoria," *Cahiers d'Études Hispaniques Médiévales* 37, no. 1 (2014): 55–6.

25 See Irene Salvo García, "L'Ovide connu par Alphonse X (1221–84)," *Interfaces (Milano)* 3, (2016): 201.

was seated in the city of Argos, in Greece. The first king who ruled there was Inachus, whose daughter was Io, who was turned into a cow according to the gentiles."[26] Thus, the insertion of pagan authors between stories from the Bible is justified based on the precedent of the most important Christian authorities,[27] including Eusebius, who is considered the first historian of Christianity,[28] and Jerome, the translator of the Bible. As Alfonso explains, both were good and wise Christians who wrote about ancient authors:

> Since Eusebius, who was bishop of Caesarea and a holy man, and Jerome, a bishop and also a saint who translated the Bible into our Latin, talk about these subjects in their chronicles, we want to tell you about them here, in the same way as gentile authors do, and then we will say what they mean.[29]

Alfonso abandons the Bible's chronology and jumps into Ovid's, but finds nothing wrong with this procedure since Eusebius and Jerome had done the same. The difference is that those illustrious fathers briefly mentioned *TSOI* and other episodes from the *Metamorphoses* to harmonize them within a Christian chronology, whereas the *GE* includes and comments on some of them extensively. Alfonso announces that he will first tell the story – the historical interpretation – and then reveal the meaning – the allegorical and moralistic interpretations. Furthermore, Alfonso also claims that the writings of the gentiles can be subjected to allegorical interpretations in the same manner as the Bible:

> we consider that gentiles said words and thoughts that express one thing and imply other, just as our Old and New Testaments do. The Old Testament always presents things in figure, but the New Testament not as much, since it is already presenting facts."[30]

26 "En esta sazón, assí como cuenta Eusebio en el griego e Jerónimo en el latín, se començó el regnado de los argueos, que es de la cibdad de Argos de Grecia, e el primero rey que ý regnó fue Ínaco, cuya fija era Ío, que fue mudada en costumbres de vaca, segund sos gentiles." *GE*1 I, 300.

27 The notice about *TSOI* is effectively taken from Eusebius/Jerome. "Incidentia: His temporibus primus aput Argos regnauit Inachus a. L. (Incidens e, 161 of Abraham and one of Jacob): Inachi filia Io quam Aegypti mutato nomine Isidem colunt." Eusebius of Caesarea, *Chronicorum canonum*, ed. Alfred Schöne, 2 vols (Dublin: Weidmannos, 1967), 2, 15–16.

28 And he still is, as Pope Benedict XVI acknowledged recently: https://www.vatican.va/content/benedict-xvi/en/audiences/2007/documents/hf_ben-xvi_aud_20070613.html (last accessed May 23, 2023).

29 "E pues que Eusebio, que fue obispo de Cesarea e santo omne, e Jerónimo, otrossí obispo e santo, e que trasladó la Biblia en este nuestro latín, fablan d'estas razones en sus crónicas, querémosvos contar aquí d'ellas, segund las cuentan los autores de los gentiles, e desí diremos en cabo lo que quieren decir." *GE*1 I, 300.

30 "[…] fallamos que tan bien dixieron los gentiles palabras e razones que dizen uno e dan ál a entender como lo fazen los nuestros testamentos, el de la nueva ley e el de la vieja, que andudo siempre en figura, lo que non faze tanto el nuevo, que anda ya en el fecho de la cosa." *GE*1 I, 300.

The wise king is referring to how facts and characters in the New Testament are prefigured in the Old, an essential feature of medieval Christian interpretations of the Bible.[31] Alfonso goes on to state that some works of the gentiles, such as those of Ovid, can be interpreted figuratively (allegorically) as well.

Once Alfonso has demonstrated that the *Metamorphoses* comprises historical materials endorsed by the highest Christian authorities, he can give them shape according to the *GE*'s structural principles. One of these principles is *señoríos* (lordships), which describes how world supremacy rotated between biblical, pagan, and Christian lords until it reached Alfonso.[32] This is his interpretation of the *translatio imperii* theory, according to which the *señorío* belonged to Israel until the captivity in Babylon. Besides, as Martin explains, Alfonsine history is all about *reyes, prinçipes, y altos omnes* (kings, princes, and noble men) within ancient and medieval history.[33] Therefore, throughout a single *señorío* the *GE* follows important men and rulers from both the biblical and gentile realms. In short, the *GE* determines that *TSOI* takes place during the *señorío* of Israel,[34] where the most important man was Abraham. However, since Alfonso decides to insert a passage from the *Metamorphoses* that took place in Greece, it is important for him to explain who the lofty men were there, and why this was the case.

We are informed that Inachus, father of Io, was the king of Argos, one of the seven lands of Greece, which counted "among the noblest who existed there in the time of Abraham."[35] Ovid introduces Inachus as one of the vassals of the river god Peneus – indeed, Inachus is still a river that flows in Argos. Alfonso tries to make sense of the fact that a river was considered a god, king, and father and thus tidily sets out the euhemerism that underpins the historical interpretation: a powerful man called Inachus was the king of Argos, where there was a large river, thus both received the same name.

> In the early days, when the gentiles were doubtful about their beliefs, it was their custom to call the wise and powerful kings gods, and also the wise and powerful ladies goddesses, and the big rivers were called gods, and the springs goddesses, that is to say, the rivers and springs contained the virtues and powers of gods and goddesses.[36]

Here we can observe a peculiar feature of Alfonsine euhemerism that differentiates it from previous Christian interpreters: the use of Arab magical theory. The Castilian king implies that, if powerful people were historically considered river gods or river goddesses, it was because somehow they were associated with specific "virtues and

31 As Erich Auerbach explained in his seminal work *Mimesis: The Representation of Reality in Western Literature* (Princeton: Princeton University Press, 1968).

32 See Fernández-Ordóñez, *Las estorias de Alfonso*, 19.

33 Martin, "El modelo historiográfico Alfonsí," 22.

34 *GE*1 I, 300–1.

35 "[…] e una de las más nobles que ý avié en tiempo de Abraham […]." *GE*1 I, 301.

36 "E era costumbre de los gentiles en el primero tiempo en que ellos andavan en dubda en sus creencias que llamavan dioses a los reyes sabios e poderosos, e otrossí a las dueñas sabias e poderosas deessas, e a los grandes ríos dioses, e a las nobles fuentes deessas, fascas que avié en los ríos e en las fuentes virtudes e poderes de dioses e deessas." *GE*1 I, 301.

powers." The *GE* elaborates on this idea some pages later in the allegorical section – also talking about Inachus: "the gentiles called gods those who deserved it by reason of the power and knowledge that they had over things and their natures."[37]

This specific vocabulary about knowledge of the virtues, powers, and natures of things comes directly from Alfonso's translations of Arabic books of magic. Since they inform not only Alfonsine euhemerism, but also the entire unveiling of the *TSOI*, I will examine these astral magic theories and how they apply to the Ovidian characters being discussed here. In particular, this vocabulary appears in the *Ghāya/Picatrix*. In his studies on the *GE*, Fraker considers that the *Picatrix* "was well within the Alfonsines's range, was translated in their circle, and was therefore probably accessible to the compilers of the *GE*."[38] As Saif explains, the *Ghāya/Picatrix* contains a "comprehensive corpus on theories of astrology and natural/astral magic,"[39] which includes the idea that "various types of magic receive their potency from the celestial bodies that instilled occult properties into natural things";[40] therefore, the wise man or magician must know about the occult properties or virtues (*khawāṣṣ*) inherent in the nature of things, which allows him to channel magical powers. It is due to this magic that powerful kings were considered gods. As we will see, Alfonso associates all the gods in *TSOI*, especially Mercury/Hermes, with Arabic magic. The Castilian words *virtud y poder* (virtue and power) at the beginning of *TSOI* can be associated with their Latin cognates, *virtus et potencia* – both *poder* and *potentia* derive from the Latin verb *posse*. In the *Picatrix* these two words appear together many times,[41] most often in contexts where the practitioner of magic is advised on how to attract the virtues and powers of the planets; for instance: "When the moon is in Capricorn, and you want to attract its virtues and powers [...]."[42] If we contrast the Latin with the Arabic original, we find that whereas most times *virtutes* (virtues) corresponds to *khawāṣṣ*, sometimes *virtus et potencia* is a translation of the Arabic magical term *rūḥāniyya*,[43] which refers to the spiritual and volitional power of the planets being invoked;[44] occasionally the *Picatrix* also translates the Arabic term *quwwa* (power) as *vis* (power, strength).

At other times, the *Ghāya* talks about the power (*quwwa* or *qawiya*) of spirituality (*rūḥāniyya*), as when the book teaches the reader how to invoke this power from the planet Jupiter, but in this instance the *Picatrix* translates the Arabic as *spiritu et*

37 "[...] por poder e saber que avién algunos d'ellos en las cosas e en las naturas d'ellas más que los otros omnes llamaron los gentiles sos dioses a aquellos que lo merecieron d'esta guisa." *GE*1 I, 316.

38 Fraker, *Scope of History*, 173.

39 Saif, *Arabic Influences*, 73.

40 Saif, *Arabic Influences*, 167.

41 For instance, I found them used five times in the nominative case, *virtus et potencia* (e.g., *Picatrix* II.iii.7, II.v.5, and III.vii.22), and nineteen times in the accusative case, *virtutem et potentiam* (e.g., *Picatrix* I.vi.46, III.x.14, and IV.2.9).

42 "Cum Luna fuerit in Capricorno et eius virtutem et potenciam attrahere volueris." *Picatrix* IV.II.12.

43 On *rūḥāniyyāt*, see Saif, *Arabic Influences*, 27–45; and Saif, "A Preliminary Study," 60–3.

44 This happens, for instance, in *Ghāya* III.7, 210, corresponding to *Picatrix* III.7.22.

virtute (spirit and virtue).[45] Thus, the word *virtus* and its various declensions appear hundreds of times in the *Picatrix*, and most times it is used to translate the Arabic word *khawāṣṣ*, referring to occult properties; for example, in *Ghāya/Picatrix* II.vi, which explains how the powers of the planets influence the virtues in the natures of things, and thus illustrates the vocabulary used in *TSOI*. *Picatrix* II.vi adapts the Arabic original to show that the virtues (*khawāṣṣ*) can be empirically demonstrated, which is in line with Alfonso's scientific taste: "Know that what is called virtue is what can be proved through nature and experiment,"[46] whereas a literal translation of the Arabic reads: "The point, God strengthen you, of mentioning the virtues/ properties [*khawāṣṣ*] is for you to know that the active thing in nature [*ṭabīʿa*] can change and reduce its activity."[47] In this chapter we observe how medicines and talismans are used to exert magic:

> It is also clear that when simple medicines are to some extent operated by the virtue and similitude of nature existing in them, then that operation is more manifest, true, and apparent. And in this way talismans [*ymagines*] are operated by virtue and similitude, because a talisman [*ymago*] is nothing other than the power [*vis*] of the celestial bodies influencing [terrestrial] bodies.[48]

Again, to better explain how magic operates, Alfonsine translators elaborate on the Arabic original, which I translate with the key Arab terms in parentheses: "When the medicine used has the nature [*ṭabīʿa*] of the virtue [*khāṣṣ*], the action coming from it is more powerful [*ʾaqwā*, comparative of *qawiyy*, strong], and the talisman [*ṭilasm*] more prodigious."[49] Arabic theories of magic elaborated on Greek philosophical and scientific sources, for instance, the Aristotelian dichotomy of φύσις (nature) and δύναμις (power, strength, capacity, etc.) is usually translated as *ṭabīʿa* and *quwwa*, as in Avicenna,[50] and these categories were later used for magical models. Therefore, the *GE* uses specific words to explain the knowledge kings had that made them appear as gods: on the one hand, virtue, nature, and power, which refer to specific properties, and on the other, image, figure, and similitude, which refer to the microcosmic-macrocosmic theory that explains how events in the stars have effects on earth and allow talismans to work. As we will see, image, figure, and similitude are used by Alfonso in a variety of ambiguous ways.

Thus, one of the main features of distinguished gentiles in the *GE*, especially those in the *Metamorphoses*'s stories, is their knowledge of magic. However, Alfonso bestows

45 *Ghāya* III.7, 208 and *Picatrix* III.vii.21.

46 "Et scias quod istud quod dicitur virtus est id quod natura et experimento comprobatur." *Picatrix* II.vi.1.

47 *Ghāya* II.6, 86.

48 "Et patet eciam in medicinis simplicibus que quando aliquid operantur virtute et similitudine natura existentibus in eis, tunc illa operacio esset manifestior, veracior et magis apparens. Et isto modo ymagines operantur virtute et similitudine quia ymago nihil aliud est quam vis corporum celestium in corporibus influencium." *Picatrix* II.vi.1.

49 *Ghāya* II.6, 86.

50 See Andreas Lammer, *The Elements of Avicenna's Physics* (Berlin: De Gruyter, 2018), 47 and 64–8; see also Saif, "From *Gayat al-Ḥakim*," 343–4.

on the gentiles other positive characteristics, which, along with magic, contribute to them reflecting the image of an ideal courtier as a member of a learned nobility. Many specialists have emphasized how Alfonso held the gentiles in the highest esteem, and this can be appreciated in many places in his oeuvre.[51] For instance, in the legal code *Las siete partidas* (*The seven parts*), Alfonso compares gentiles with *fijosdalgo* (sons of good), a kind of nobility at that time, and affirms that *gentileza* (which in Spanish means both gentility and courtesy) is acquired in three different ways:

> The first one through lineage, the second through knowledge, and the third through skill in [i.e. being good at] weapons, customs, and manners. Since those who obtain gentility through wisdom and goodness are rightfully called nobles and gentiles, those who have gentility through lineage bear a good life mostly because it has come to them since ancient times by inheritance.[52]

Applying this to the *GE*, we observe that most gentiles taken from the *Metamorphoses* are nobles with important lineages. This is true for Jupiter in particular, the character introduced in *TSOI* after Inachus. Many specialists have highlighted Alfonso's appreciation of Jupiter, whom he considers his ancestor and an image of himself.[53] This appreciation explains why at the beginning of *TSOI GE*1 deviates from Ovid and introduces Jupiter "in history" in a separate chapter. Jupiter had already appeared in *GE*1 briefly,[54] but now Alfonso deems it necessary to explain his lineage, wisdom, and customs, which are in line with the explanation in *Las siete partidas*. We will see how Jupiter's gentility has Arabic influences when it comes to his knowledge and customs.

To justify inserting Jupiter's lineage here, Alfonso refers to Godfrey of Viterbo. According to this chronicler, when Abraham married Keturah, Janus, who was the same age as Isaac, was the king of Italy, and the king of Crete was Celio.[55] Jupiter's lineage begins with Celio – Caelus, Roman god of the sky – father of Saturn and grandfather of Jupiter.[56] Once the lineage is clear, the *GE* goes on to explain Jupiter's knowledge and the goodness of his customs, the other two requirements for gentility. When he was young and at his father's house:

51 See Irene Salvo García, "Autor frente a auctoritas: La recreación de Júpiter por Alfonso X en la General estoria I parte," *Cahiers d'Études Hispaniques Médiévales* no. 33 (2010): 646; and Martínez, *El humanismo medieval*, 384–90.

52 "E esta gentileza aviene en tres maneras; la una por linage, la segunda por saber et la tercera por bondat de armas, de costumbres et de maneras. Et como quier que estos que la ganan por su sabidoria ó por su bondat son con derecho llamados nobles e gentiles, mayormiente lo son aquellos que la han por linage antiguamiente, et facen buena vida porque les viene de lueñe por heredat." *Partidas* II.21.2.

53 On the bonds between Jupiter and Alfonso in the *GE*, see Rico, *Alfonso el Sabio*, 97–120; and Salvo García, "Autor frente a auctoritas."

54 In the first quotation from Ovid, when Alfonso presents the *Gigantomachia*.

55 *GE*I 1, 302. Salvo García notices that Alfonso prefers Godfrey's chronology to that of Eusebius or Comestor, his common sources, because it allows him to justify explaining the lineage of Jupiter at this precise moment. Gotefridi Viterbientis, *Pantheon*, Pars IV, 71; Eusebius, *Chronicorum canonum*, 15; Pierre le Mangeur, *Scholastica Historia*, 125; cited in Salvo García, "Autor frente a auctoritas," 66–7.

56 *GE*1 I, 302–5.

> [Jupiter] started to appreciate, breed, and teach birds to hunt. Every time he came [in] from hunting, he strove to acquire knowledge and put it in writing. He grew tall and handsome, of very good customs, appreciative of the finest cuisine, very wise, gentle, moderate, honest, fond of elegance, and very gallant. Saturn took notice of the customs of his son. Since his father saw that he was interested in higher and nobler things than those of the water and the ground – the domains of Neptune and Pluto, respectively – and knew about birds, the knowledge of the stars, and the *quadrivium* – the things higher than anything else – [Saturn] gave [Jupiter] power over the air and the sky.[57]

This account of Saturn's three sons, the distribution of the realms between them, and the later dispute between Jupiter and his father is material well known to medieval compilers, including the Vatican Mythographers, whose works Alfonso might have known directly or through *glossae* that used them. However, the description of young Jupiter's deeds appears to be a unique development of the *GE*.[58] Indeed, Jupiter is presented in the guise of one of the *adab*-inspired courtiers that I claim the *GE* is theorizing: a noble lineage, exquisite education, and knowledge of the liberal arts, including astrology and magic. Actually, this passage could well be used to describe Alfonso, who loved the sciences and patronized the production of books on them. Besides, just like the highest noblemen of Alfonso's time, Jupiter eagerly practised falconry. It is worth remembering that even though the origins of falconry in the Iberian Peninsula cannot be determined exactly, it was most likely introduced by the Arab conquerors;[59] and then Muslims influenced its practice in the Christian kingdoms.[60] Alfonso's nephew, Don Juan Manuel, states in the prologue of his *Libro de la caça* (*Book of hunting*) that his uncle ordered several books on hunting, including falconry, to be composed, all of which, regrettably, have been lost.[61] However, we still have the *Libro de los animales que caçan* (*Book of the animals that hunt*), translated from Arabic in 1250, two years before Alfonso became king. According to most specialists, the Castilian king ordered the translation when he was still a prince. This translation would have been made around the same time he ordered the translation

57 "[…] començó a amar aves e criarlas e enseñarlas e ir a caça con ellas. E cada que vinié de la caça e de ál que fuesse e pudié trabajávasse de los saberes de aprenderlos e saberlos e averlos por escrito. E salió grand e fermoso, trabajávasse de los saberes de aprenderlos e saberlos e averlos por escrito. E salió grand e fermoso, e muy bueno en sus costumbres, e amador de todas las cosas guisadas, e muy sabio e muy manso, muy mesurado, muy franco e cobdiciador de toda apostura, e muy doñeador. E Saturno su padre paró mientes en las costumbres d'aquel fijo. E pues que vío que se trabajava de cosas más altas e más nobles que los de las aguas, como Neptuno, e que los de las tierras, como Plutón, e entendió con las aves e con los saberes de las estrellas, e del cuadruvio, que son más altas cosas que tod esto ál, asmó cómol diesse el poder del aire e del cielo." *GE*1 I, 304.

58 Salvo García has thoroughly tracked the similarities between Saturn's narrative in the *GE* and the Vatican Mythographers, but she did not find any possible source for this account of Jupiter's youth. Salvo García, "Autor frente a auctoritas," 69–71.

59 Francisco Juez Juarros, "La cetrería en la iconografía andalusí," *Anales de historia del arte* 7, (1997): 71.

60 Juarros, "La cetrería en la iconografía andalusí," 71.

61 Don Juan Manuel, "Libro de la caza," in Jose M. Blecua (ed.), *Obras completas* (Gredos: Madrid, 1981), 1: 549–50.

of *Calila e Dimna* – a work deeply influenced by *adab*.[62] This further justifies the claim that Alfonso projects a portrait of himself onto the depiction of young Jupiter, as both princes were enthusiastic about falconry and produced written works – in Alfonso's case, translations from Arabic. The other features of Jupiter presented in this passage are closer to a description of the urbanite and sophisticated courtier proposed by the *adab* culture, making him a refined individual who appreciates mundane pleasures, such as cooking and dressing.

But Jupiter is also fond of the lofty arts of the *quadrivium*, especially "the knowledge of the stars"; this is a literal Castilian translation of an Arabic idiom for astrology: *ʿilm al-nujūm*, which appears several times in the *Ghāya*.[63] In this manner, Alfonso is developing a unique way of interpreting Ovidian characters, combining euhemerism with explanations influenced by translations from Arabic.

Next, the *GE* describes how Jupiter took his kingdom by overthrowing and mutilating Saturn, which led to the birth of Venus.[64] Then there is an explanation of why these characters were considered planets and gods and how the story of Saturn's dethronement is a depiction of the astrological processes of generation. Since the planet Jupiter has a benefic nature (*de buena natura e bien querenciosa*), and Saturn a malefic (*malquería*) one, the first overthrowing the second means that "Jupiter tempers the evilness of the planet Saturn,"[65] and so he helps "produce the things and raise the fruits of the earth, helped by Venus together with the sun's warmth."[66] These are well-known astrological processes of generation that have an Arabic origin and are also described in the *Picatrix*.[67] Once Inachus and Jupiter, the main gods in Ovid's story, have been placed in history based on their lineages, and a magical theory has been used to explain why they were considered powerful gods, Alfonso proceeds to the narrative substance of the myth. Let us examine how it is narrated in the *Metamorphoses* and the nuances that the *GE* version introduces.

In the *Metamorphoses*, Ovid describes how Jupiter saw Io returning from her father's stream, immediately fell in love, and tried to win her over with enticing words. However, the nymph rejects him and flees. To seize the maiden Jupiter produces a mist that detains Io, and then he rapes her.[68] Episodes like this in the *Metamorphoses* can be troubling to modern sensibilities, and traditional narrative theorists have not done much to ease their reception by explaining them with terms like "active subject"

62 See Martínez, *El humanismo medieval*, 179–80.
63 For instance, *Ghāya* III.7, 201 and III.7, 222.
64 *GE*1 I, 304.
65 "Júpiter atiempra la maldad de la planeta de Saturno." *GE*1 I, 305
66 "[…] criar las cosas en la tierra, e otrossí crecer los frutos con la planeta Venus ayuntada con la calentura del sol." *GE*1 I, 305.
67 On the negative and positive natures of Saturn and Jupiter respectively, and their relationship with the corruption and generation of things on earth, see *Picatrix* III.vii.9–10; and *Ghāya* III.7, 198–9. I will elaborate on the idea of corruption and generation in relation to an even more significant reference in *TSOI* later.
68 *GE*1 I, 305–6.

and "passive object."[69] Not surprisingly, feminist critics have articulated a vigorous critique of this overly simplified tradition of Western narrative and theory. In this sense, de Lauretis has proposed an influential and more nuanced interpretation of Ovidian myths:

> The hero, the mythical subject, is constructed as human being and as a male; he is the active principle of culture, the establisher of distinction, the creator of differences. Female is what is not susceptible to transformation, to life or death; she (it) is an element of plot-space, a topos, a resistance, matrix, and matter.[70]

Even though Jupiter is a god, this theory of the gendered subject for the most part applies to him – an active principle of culture, a creator – and to Io – part of a (fluvial) plot-space, resistant, and objectified. However, as we will see, when Alfonso interprets the story using the resources available to him, the relevance of Io gradually grows until she ultimately becomes a true heroine of culture and civilization. In fact, Io is one of those female characters whom Alfonso empowers by allowing them to share with men what he believes are the two most important ancient sources of power: education and magic. Both become central in the Castilian version of *TSOI* and have undeniable Arabic influences.

Early in the story, we can appreciate this elaboration through the use of magic. Where Ovid simply says that Jupiter "threw a mist over the wide earth,"[71] Alfonso interprets that "with his spells and through the stars, about which he was very wise, Jupiter produced a heavy mist, which fell upon that valley."[72] Therefore, in the *GE* the mist is a product of Jupiter's knowledge of astral magic. Euhemerism often reaches its limits when it must explain a supernatural god's powers, yet Alfonso uses Arabic concepts of natural magic to explain them. But in the *GE* Jupiter is not the only one to possess supernatural powers or magical knowledge, and these abilities are not exclusive to males. Ovid narrates how Juno sees the mist of an unknown origin spread over Argos. Since Jupiter was not in heaven, the jealous wife, distrustful of him, descends through the air to earth and dispels the mist.[73] To explain these prodigies, Alfonso clarifies that "Juno was a lady who strove to know the natures of the earth, the air, and the sky, therefore the gentiles called her a goddess" because "she knew a lot about spells and stars."[74] Therefore, Juno turns out to be an accomplished magician herself, a rank that she acquired through her own study and effort, similar to Jupiter. Ovid's Roman readers did not need these explanations, but they are necessary for Alfonso to transpose the actions of these mythical beings into a historical narrative

69 Teresa de Lauretis, *Alice Doesn't: Feminism, Semiotics, Cinema* (Bloomington: Indiana University Press, 1984), 105.

70 de Lauretis, *Alice Doesn't*, 105–6.

71 "Cum deus inducta latas caligine terras/ occuluit tenuitque fugam rapuitque pudorem." *Met.*I.598–9.

72 "[...] le guisó por sus encantamentos e por las estrellas dond era muy sabio que decendió una grand niebla en aquel val." *GE*1 I, 306.

73 *Met.*I.601–9.

74 "Juno fue dueña que se trabajó de saber las naturas de la tierra e del aer e del cielo, e llamáronla por ende sos gentiles deessa [...] sabié mucho de encantamientos e de las estrellas." *GE*1 I, 307.

through the use of scientific, cultural, and philosophical concepts of his own age. Juno was able to use the elements in the manner she did because she had studied and knew their natures and their special virtues or properties, exactly what Arabic books of magic promise the industrious practitioner will learn. Thus, it does not come as a surprise when Juno, "with her spell climbed into a cloud, reached the place where Jupiter and Io were, conjured the mist, rushed there, and discovered them."[75]

Now we reach the crucial moment of the story: Io's transformation. The *Metamorphoses* only says that Jupiter, "anticipating the coming of his wife, had transformed the daughter of Inachus into a white heifer."[76] In Latin "anticipated" (*praesenserat*) can mean having a presentiment or divine premonition. Alfonso does not waste the opportunity to expand on this and rationalizes that Jupiter foresaw the coming of Juno thanks to his astrological skills and acted accordingly, which seems congruent with medieval judicial astrology:

> King Jupiter was so wise that through his great knowledge of the stars he grasped the things that would come, both the playful and the lofty ones, and especially those things that the gentiles' gods were going to do or did to others. Jupiter foresaw the coming of his wife, but before she could see him, with his knowledge of spells [he] turned Io into a heifer and made her look like [*semejasse*] a very beautiful cow.[77]

Thus, magic is used to foresee Juno's arrival, and also to transform Io. The choice of words in this and other passages have made some specialists wonder about the reach of the magic described by the *GE*. Ekman proposes that when Alfonso expresses the transformations operated by the gods using the words *figura* (figure) and *semejança* (resemblance) – as is the case here – it could convey that the gods' magic is based "on a visual illusion" that "tricks the eyes of viewers into thinking they have seen a true transformation."[78] This is clearly the case in the *GE*'s version of the *Gigantomachia*, where it first presents material from the *Metamorphoses*;[79] there, Alfonso explains that the gods were "very wise from the knowledge they had about the stars and charms, which is a magical art," so they "transfigured" (*transfiguraron*) themselves into figures, such as Jupiter into a ram, "and they transformed in such a way that whoever saw them would believe that Jupiter's ram was a true ram."[80] I think that

75 "[…] por su encantamiento subió en una nuve, e púsose luego en aquel logar ó Júpiter e Ío estavan. E conjuró otrossí la niebla, e tirós d'allí luego, e fincaron descubiertos Júpiter e Ío." *GE*1 I, 307.

76 "Coniugis adventum praesenserat inque nitentem/ Inachidos vultus mutaverat ille iuvencam." *Met.*I.609–10.

77 "El rey Júpiter tan sabio era que tan bien en las cosas jogosas como en las otras de grandes fechos escogié por el so grand saber de las estrellas las cosas que avién de venir, tan bien en lo uno como en lo ál. E esto sobre todo en las cosas que los unos de sus dioses de los gentiles avién de fazer o fazién a otros. E Júpiter sintió d'antes la venida de la reína Juno su muger, e ante quel ella huviasse veer mudó él por sos encantamientos e su saber a Ío en noviella, e que semejasse vaca, e fízola muy fermosa." *GE*1 I, 307–8.

78 Ekman, "Ovid Historicized," 28.

79 *GE*1 I, 151–62.

80 "[…] eran muy sabios por el saber que avién de las estrellas e por el arte mágica, que es el saber de los encantamentes […] E de guisa se trasmudaron que los qui los viessen que

since this is the first reference to the *Metamorphoses* in the *GE*, Alfonso might have been doubtful about presenting a transformation that was "not very orthodox to [the] Catholic faith," as Sánchez-Prieto Borja understands it, and thus he implied a definition of *encantamiento* (charm) as conjuring a mental state in the viewer.[81] However, on other occasions the *GE* depicts "real magical powers" over matter and persons thanks to astral magic, as we have just observed in *TSOI*. Alfonso could also make use of the ambiguity that the term *semejança* (similitude) still has in Spanish to describe the magical powers of the gentiles and be vague, but without denying their existence. We saw earlier that in the *Picatrix* talismans are called *ymagines* (images), a word very close in meaning to "figure" in both Latin and Spanish, and they "are used by virtue and similitude [*similitudine*]."[82] The Latin *similitudo* was translated into Spanish as *semejança*, which can refer to the theory of the microcosm-macrocosm,[83] which explains that things happening in the sublunar (earthly) world are mirrored in the stars. In this same sense, the *Lapidario* talks about *figuras del cielo* (figures of the sky).[84] In addition, *semejança* (similitude), and especially *figura*, are significant terms in allegorical interpretations. As we will see, Alfonso concludes the introductory chapter of the allegorical part of *TSOI* by assuming that "everything is said in figure and similitude [*semejança*] of other things."[85] Therefore, I posit that at times, Alfonso remains calculatedly ambiguous when using these words, as happens here: Jupiter "transformed" (*mudó*) Io into a heifer so she "would look like" (*semejasse*) a cow, and "made her" (*fízola*) very beautiful.[86] *Semejasse* is ambiguous, but *mudó*, and especially *fízola*, have factual connotations that could make readers think this was an actual transformation.

In any case, after the transformation, the relentless Juno is still suspicious, and to test Jupiter, she asks him if she can have the heifer for herself. He acquiesces. Still distrusting her husband, the goddess orders Argus – the shepherd taking care of her cattle and earthly possessions – to guard Io. With his 100 eyes, Argus is uniquely equipped for the task, because even when he sleeps some eyes remain open. Under the care of Argus, Io starts her new life as a cow. She wanders sadly through her former places, but nobody recognizes her, neither her sisters – the Naiads – nor her father. To let her father know who she is, Io uses a hoof to write her name, as *Yo*, in the sand, something that provokes Inachus to despair.[87] When Argus sees this, he takes Io farther away to distant pastures and climbs up a mountain to watch over her.[88] This is when Jupiter, unable to endure his sorrow for this lost object of desire, calls on Mercury to rescue Io. However, in the *GE* this Mercury is different from the one described by Ovid and displays new attributes.

creyessen que aquel carnero de Júpiter que verdadero carnero era [...]." *GE*1 I, 171.

81 Sánchez-Prieto Borja, introduction to *GE*1 I, liii.

82 "[...] ymagines operantur virtute et similitudine." *Picatrix* II.vi.1.

83 On the application of this theory in the *Picatrix*, see Saif, *Arabic Influences*, 196.

84 Alfonso X el Sabio, *Lapidario*, 274.

85 "Mas todo es dicho en figura e en semejança de al." *GE*1 I, 316.

86 *GE*1 I, 307–8.

87 *GE*1 I, 309–10. On the medieval interpretative tradition and this episode, see Salvo García, "L'Ovide connu par Alphonse," 211.

88 *GE*1 I, 307–8, which is a version of *Met*.I.612–67.

Jupiter summons Mercury, his son with Maia (Atlas's daughter), to kill Argus. Mercury shows up with the traditional features of his iconography: winged feet, a hat, and a snake-twined caduceus (*virga* in the *Metamorphoses*, *verga* in the *GE*). Mercury quickly obeys Jupiter's command, goes to where Argus is, and disguises himself by removing his hat and wings and using his sleep-inducing wand as a shepherd's staff. Alfonso completes Mercury's portrait by pointing to his magical skills, something absent in Ovid. Ovid writes that, when approaching Argus, Mercury, "with [the staff], as a shepherd, through devious fields, drives goats that he gathered while coming [here], and sings with [a flute of] reeds set together."[89] Alfonso offers a different explanation of the story by clarifying that Mercury "brought the staff in his hand and assembled in front of him a herd of goats, which it is said that he made with his spell, because Mercury was very wise in the *trivium*, and even in the *quadrivium*."[90] In this way, the *GE* associates Mercury with two things: the liberal arts and magic – the second cogently derived from the first. Alfonso's epistemology, inspired by translations from Arabic, makes it clear that magic was considered an extension of the *quadrivium* – which included astronomy. Ovid's Mercury gathers a herd, while Alfonso's Mercury magically creates one.

Immediately after characterizing Mercury "as wise in the *trivium*, and even in the *quadrivium*," Alfonso reinforces this connection between Mercury and astronomy by saying that "now his name is that of one of the planets, the one called Mercury."[91] I interpret these successive claims that Mercury is an ancient god, a master in the liberal arts, a magician, and a planet, as another indication that Arabic astro-magical works directly influenced Alfonso's historical narrative. As we saw in Chapter One, in the *Picatrix* the magician is invited to invoke the personified planet Mercury, who is ambiguously associated with Hermes Trismegistus and presented as a patron of *adab* education and refinement. This is echoed here but with further refinement of Mercury's character: that of a graceful courtier. Ovid says that Mercury "sings with a flute of reeds set together," and Argus was "enraptured" (*captus*) by it.[92] Alfonso is much more emphatic about Mercury's singing skills and the enthusiastic reaction of Argus; thus, Mercury "was singing wonderfully and very well with that instrument. When Argus saw and heard him, [he] was very much delighted by the sound."[93] This description completes the portrait of a courtier and depicts someone skilled in music and playing – similar to how Alfonso gently describes his own father in the *Setenario*.[94]

The Castilian king continues the story in keeping with Ovid: Argus asks Mercury to sit beside him and continue playing. Mercury tries to make Argus go to sleep with his song in order to kill him, a very difficult task due to Argus's 100 eyes. The

89 "Hac agit, ut pastor, per devia rura capellas, dum venit, adductas et structis cantat avenis." *Met.*I.675–6.

90 "[E] acogió ante sí una manada de cabras que dizen que fizo él por su encantamiento, ca era Mercurio muy sabio en el trivio e aun en el cuadruvio." *GE*1 I, 311.

91 "E es agora el su nombre d'una de las planetas, e es a la que dizen Mercurio." *GE*1 I, 311.

92 *Met.*I.676–7.

93 "E cantava muy bien a maravilla con aquel instrumento. E Argo cuandol oyó yl vío pagós mucho del son." *GE*1 I, 311.

94 Alfonso X el Sabio, *Setenario*, 13.

god has a chance when Argus asks him about the new instrument he is playing, and Mercury replies with a long and entrancing song. Alfonso reveals that "the flageolet [*caramillo*] with which Mercury was singing was a new instrument that had on it seven small reeds."[95] Later, during the allegorical interpretation of the passage, we will see that this number is related to the seven liberal arts. Mercury answers Argus's question "through long explanations and details, in order to calm him down, put him to sleep, and then kill him."[96] Here Ovid and the *GE* both introduce a digression about the instrument's origin: the story of the nymph Syrinx – who was turned into a musical instrument to avoid the lust of the god Pan. The sung story has the intended effect, and Mercury puts Argus to sleep. As well as his musical and rhetorical skills, Mercury relies on a magical device. Alfonso explains that Mercury's *verga* (staff):

> had such a nature that when he touched with it anything alive, one of its ends made it sleep, and the other woke it up. Mercury touched Argus with the end that made him sleep in such a way that he could not wake up even if he wanted to, because that was the nature and power of the staff.[97]

This is a much more detailed explanation than in the *Metamorphoses*, where Ovid only mentions Mercury's *medicata virga* (healing wand).[98] In the Hellenistic period, Mercury's wand with two intertwined serpents, also known as the caduceus, was associated with both the healing god Asclepius and Hermes Trismegistus.[99] Alfonso elaborates on this feature, which is only briefly mentioned in Ovid, to emphasize that Mercury is a magician who employs charmed objects that are not dissimilar to the talismans described in the *Picatrix*. Besides, in connection with the magical caduceus, we find the same two technical words related to Arabic astral magic that we saw earlier: nature (*ṭabīʿa*) and power (*quwwa*).

In the *Metamorphoses*, when Argus falls asleep, Mercury seizes the opportunity to cut off his head with a curved sword (*falcato ense*).[100] It is well known in literature and art that Mercury carried a curved sword, known in Greek as a *harpe*. It is significant that Alfonso calls this weapon *alfange*, the curved weapon typically used by Muslims in the Iberian Peninsula – a term taken from the Andalusian Arabic word *al-khanjar*. Alfonso had experienced long years of war against Muslims from his youth onwards, thus it does not seem that it is by chance that he describes Mercury as having an Arab weapon. The *GE* makes the following remarks about Mercury's weapon: "He drew the *alfange* that he had brought, since that was the name of Mercury's sword;

95 "E aquel caramiello con que cantava Mercurio era nuevo, e avié en él VII cañiellas." *GE*1 I, 311.

96 "E respondiól assí por sus razones luengas porque oviesse quel dezir e en qué se detener, e adormirle, e desí matalle." *GE*1 I, 311.

97 "[...] avié natura que a la cosa viva que tañié con el un cabo que la adormié, e con el otro la espertava. E tanxo a Argo con la parte que adormié, e firmó en éll el sueño, de guisa que maguer que Argo quisiesse espertar non pudiesse, ca tal era la natura e el poder de la verga." *GE*1 I, 311.

98 *Met.*I.715.

99 See Walter J. Friedlander, *The Golden Wand of Medicine: A History of the Caduceus Symbol in Medicine* (Westport: Greenwood, 1992), 61–81.

100 *Met.*I.716.

in Latin it is called *arpe*, and it has a curved shape, as the edge has the form of an arc."[101] Thus, Alfonso is aware of the "original" name of Mercury's sword; however, he decides to provide an Arabic name for it as well. Moreover, Alfonso only uses the word *alfange* in one other passage of the *GE*, also in relation to Mercury's weapon. When talking about Perseus's deeds, Alfonso says that Mercury grants the hero his sword, with which he would kill Medusa and other enemies, and Alfonso mentions several times that it was an *alfange* or *alfanhe*.[102] Moreover, Ovid does not call Mercury's sword *harpe* in *Metamorphoses* 1, but later in the story of Perseus in *Metamorphoses* 4 and 5, he describes the hero killing an enemy in this way: "Pointed upon him the *harpe* proved with Medusa's slaughter."[103] In turn, Alfonso does not mention the name *harpe* in Perseus's story in *GE*2, as he does in *TSOI* in *GE*1. These correlations demonstrate the internal coherence of the *GE*.

After Mercury kills Argus, Juno sadly picks out the eyes of her shepherd and puts them in the tail of a peacock – Alfonso takes this etiological origin of the peacock's feathers from Ovid. But then the goddess unleashes her revenge and spurs one of the Erinyes (Furies) against Io. The infernal deity, interpreted by Alfonso as something that provokes "turmoil and horror in both eyes and heart,"[104] chases the terrified Io from her land to Egypt. Once there, Jupiter, taking pity on Io, begs his wife for forgiveness, and she allows him to turn Io back into a woman. During the transformation, Alfonso presents something that does not appear in Ovid: "and Io was turned in such a way from bad customs to good ones that nothing from the cow remained on her, neither on her limbs nor on her customs."[105] A reference to bad customs has already appeared several times, including in the title of the chapter: "On Argus's death, the event of the peacock and Queen Juno, and how Io improved her customs and was made a goddess."[106] It is mentioned again in Alfonso's rendering of Io's transformation into Isis: "And from then onwards Io was so much instructed in Egypt, and kept away from any bad custom, and devoted herself so much to good customs and to be good, that [she] was deemed as a goddess in all the Nile's riverbanks of Egypt. And changed her name from Io to Isis."[107] Ovid does not directly mention Isis, but briefly says that in Egypt Io was considered to be a famous goddess (*dea celeberrima*).[108] Alfonso may have drawn this connection between Io and Isis

101 "Sacó el su alfange que trayé, ca assí avié nombre la espada de Mercurio; en el latín le dize arpe, e era d'una fechura corva como que querié venir en arco d'aquella parte de lo agudo." *GE*1 I, 313.

102 See especially *GE*2 I, 386–90.

103 "Vertit in hunc harpen spectatam caede Medusae." *Met.*V.69.

104 "[...] un tan mal talant e tan mal espanto en los ojos e en el coraçón." *GE*1 I, 313.

105 "E de guisa fue Ío tornada toda de malas costumbres en buenas que ninguna cosa de la vaca non fincó en tod ella nin de los miembros nin de las costumbres." *GE*1 I, 314.

106 "De la muerte de Argo e del fecho del Pavón e de la reína Juno, e de Ío cómo mejoró sus costumbres e fue fecha deesa." *GE*1 I, 313.

107 "E d'allí adelant tanto fue Ío castigada en Egipto e partida de toda mala costumbre, e tanto se dio a buenas costumbres e a seer buena que la otorgaron en Egipto por deessa en todas las riberas del Nilo. E mudáronle el nombre, e de Ío que la llamavan antes llamáronla después Isis." *GE*1 I, 314–15.

108 *Met.*I.746.

from his use of Latin commentators or glosses to these texts; however, the insistence on good customs, study, and education is specific to the *GE*. Another innovative aspect is closely related to the transformation of Io into a powerful female ruler of Egypt with Hermetic characteristics, which Alfonso presents in a completely original section. As we will see below, the medieval Christian interpretation of *TSOI* is one of sin and redemption, a derogatory pattern typically reserved for female mythological characters. However, in the allegorical and moralistic parts of Alfonso's presentation we find a secular emphasis on education that will allow Io to transcend not only the limitations of the female gendered subject in Ovid – according to the abovementioned De Lauretis's terminology – but also the misogynistic portrayal of women as sinners in Christian exegesis.

Allegorical Interpretation: *Integumenta*, *Glossae*, and Etymology

By the end of chapter XXV – of Genesis 6 – *GE1* has interpreted *TSOI* in a "historical" way, using a euhemeristic approach tinted with magical theory to rationalize the supernatural phenomena. The second interpretative method is the allegorical one, which Alfonso announces as follows: "Now we will say what these reasons and transformations signify according to how we find them discerned by wise men."[109] Alfonso proposes a deeper interpretation that is supported by respected authorities he has not yet introduced. Thus, chapters XXVI and XXVII contain a specific allegorical interpretation. As we saw, for centuries this method had only been used for the Bible; perhaps for this reason, at the beginning of chapter XXVI the Castilian king once more justifies the use of allegory when interpreting pagan writings. According to Alfonso, the gentile authors "were very wise men who talked about very great things, and on many occasions did it in figure and resemblance [*semejança*] of one thing for another,[110] in the same way as the writings of our holy Mother Church does."[111] Thus, the figurative interpretations that medieval exegetes applied to the Bible can also be used for pagan authors. To Alfonso, this seems to be a particularly valid and worthwhile approach to Ovid's *Metamorphoses* which, he argues, was "the theology and the Bible of the gentiles."[112] Then Alfonso briefly summarizes the astonishing events of *TSOI* that he elaborated on in the historical part, but at the end emphasizing that they should not be considered false or spurious (*flabiella*), because "whoever understands the reasons of Ovid, he finds there is nothing spurious there."[113] Thus, Ovid had some hidden reasons for writing such a bizarre story. According to Alfonso, looking for these reasons is not a heterodox deviation, because otherwise,

109 "Agora diremos estas razones e estos mudamientos qué dan a entender segund los fallamos departidos de omnes sabios." *GE1* I, 314–15.

110 Notice the use of *semejança* in an allegorical context.

111 "[...] fueron muy sabios omnes, e fablaron de grandes cosas e en muchos logares en figura e en semejança d'uno por ál, como lo fazen oy las escrituras de la nuestra Santa Eglesia." *GE1* I, 315.

112 "[...] la teología e la Biblia d'ello entre los gentiles." *GE1* I, 315.

113 "[...] el que las sus razones bien catare e las entendiere fallará que non á ý fabliella ninguna." *GE1* I, 316.

"Dominicans and Franciscans would not be converting [Ovid] into our theology."[114] These two recently founded religious orders were the most intellectually prestigious in the thirteenth century, and Alfonso thought – wrongfully, as we will see – that the commentator of Ovid from which he was primarily drawing his material was associated with the Franciscans.

As I pointed out earlier, the Castilian king concludes this supporting chapter by reaffirming that in Ovid, "everything is said in figure and resemblance [*semejança*] of other thing, and now we will explain to you how."[115] This explanation is included in the next chapter (XXVII), which at the beginning specifies the allegorical technique that it is going to be used: "We read in the *integumenta* of the wise men who exposed the obscure secrets of the gentiles [...]."[116] Since Alfonso is introducing a new and important term, he immediately explains it: "*integumentum* [*integumento*] means discovery, because it distinguishes, discovers, and clarifies the words, the reasons, and what the wise men among the gentiles wanted to express with them, because they used to say one thing for another."[117] This definition clarifies the relationship between allegorical interpretation and the concept of *integumentum* within the intellectual history of twelfth- and thirteenth-century Europe. Through this construct, I will track how Alfonso gathers the influence of the most renowned philosophical schools that preceded him in medieval Europe and adds to them his own novelties – mostly nurtured by his programme of translation from Arabic.

The concept of *integumentum* originated in the School of Chartres, which was deeply embedded in the Platonic tradition – that, for them, included the Hermetic treatise *Asclepius*. This school was very influential on Alfonso's intellectual endeavours.[118] Chartres is considered a focal point in the so-called Renaissance of the twelfth century and in medieval humanism.[119] According to John of Salisbury (d. 1180), a renowned student of the school, Bernard of Chartres (d. 1130), its academic head, used to expound texts in the classroom as "an 'image of all the arts' in which grammar and poetry served to set off the truths of mathematics, physics, and ethics."[120]

[114] "Nin freires predigadores e los menores que se trabajan de tornarlo en la nuestra teología non lo farién si assí fuesse." *GE*1 I, 316.

[115] "[...] todo es dicho en figura e en semejança de al. Agora departir vos emos cómo." *GE*1 I, 316.

[116] "Leemos en los integumentos de los sabios que espusieron oscuros los dichos de los gentiles [...]." *GE*1 I, 316.

[117] "[...] e es integumento por descobrimiento, porque departe e descubre e apaladina las palabras e razones sobre lo que quisieron dezir en ellas los sabios de los gentiles, en que dixieron encubiertamientre uno por ál." *GE*1 I, 316.

[118] See Martínez, *El humanismo medieval*, 57–63. On Chartres see Wetherbee, *Platonism and Poetry*.

[119] The groundbreaking and now classic studies on these concepts are those of Haskins, *The Renaissance of the Twelve Century*; and R. W. Southern, *Medieval Humanism and Other Studies* (New York: Harper and Row, 1970), which Salvador Martínez applies to Castile in *El humanismo medieval*, 45–86.

[120] In Winthrop Wetherbee, "Philosophy, Cosmology, and the Twelfth-Century Renaissance," in Peter Dronke (ed.), *A History of Twelfth-Century Western Philosophy* (Cambridge: Cambridge University Press, 1988), 35.

William of Conches (d. 1154), another of Bernard's students, furthered this method, and in his *glossae* on the classical *auctores* pursued "an underlying wisdom largely by analyzing the figurative language, what he calls the *integumenta* in their texts."[121] This technique allowed commentators "to deal with passages outwardly at odds with Christian truth" and to characterize their authors as philosophers who expressed the deepest meanings in their works.[122] Alfonso aligns with these theories when he portrays Ovid as one of the gentiles' wisest men (i.e., an authentic philosopher). The influence of Chartres' intellectual developments extended to the other two great centres of learning in twelfth-century France, Orléans and Paris, homes to two of the key writers from whom Alfonso draws his own work: Arnulf of Orléans and John of Garland.

Towards the end of the twelfth century, the centre of medieval humanism shifted from Chartres to Orléans,[123] where teaching was particularly focused on the Latin classics. *Lectio* (teaching according to institutionalized norms) developed into *exegesis* (the explanation and critical interpretation of texts). Teachers in Orléans accompanied Ovid's verses with *glossae* and *scolia* – notes explaining the meaning of the text, clarifying grammar, and addressing geographical, historical, or poetical allusions.[124] Among these teachers Arnulf, a famous grammarian and poet, stood out. Arnulf followed the doctrine of Bernardus Silvestris, who aimed to lift the *involucrum* (the deceiving veil of the fable) to show the *integumentum* (occult meaning), understood as the true intention of the author.[125] Bernardus Silvestris (*c.* 1100–*c.* 1165) was a poet and philosopher closely connected with Chartres, hence the intellectual transfer from Chartres to Orléans. As Wetherbee points out, in Arnulf of Orléans's commentaries on Ovid, "the ancient authors appear as philosophers-poets."[126] It is important to highlight this exegetical, Platonic, and Chartrian flavour, because Arnulf's *Allegoriae super Ovidii Metamorphosis* (*c.* 1170) is the most prominent critical source in the *GE*'s presentation of the *Metamorphoses*. As I said earlier, Alfonso borrows the three interpretive methods that he applies to *TSOI* from Arnulf: the historical, allegorical, and moralistic.

John of Garland (*c.* 1195–1272) was an English-born teacher at the University of Paris. Following Arnulf's parameters, John composed his own commentary in verse on the *Metamorphoses*, the *Integumenta Ovidii* (*c.* 1230), a title that also betrays the Chartrian origin of its philosophical theory. Throughout the thirteenth century, Arnulf's *Allegoriae* and John's *Integumenta* became increasingly joined together in manuscripts, and by the end of the century they no longer existed as independent texts.[127]

121 Wetherbee, "Philosophy," 35.
122 Wetherbee, "Philosophy," 36.
123 Salvador Martínez, *El humanismo medieval*, 63–4.
124 Noacco, "Lire Ovide," 131.
125 Noacco, "Lire Ovide," 134.
126 Wetherbee, "Philosophy," 44.
127 Noacco, "Lire Ovide," 144. These two works were edited by Ghisaberti in 1932 and 1933, respectively.

Both Arnulf and John are widely used in the *GE*. However, their integration into Alfonso's text introduces a series of problems and questions. Half of the *GE*'s glosses of the *Metamorphoses* are authorized by an unknown *freire* (friar), and they usually can be found in Arnulf's *Allegoriae*, while other glosses are attributed to "John the English" and indeed they coincide with John of Garland's *Integumenta*. Besides these, there are glosses attributed either to the *freire* or to John that cannot be found in either.[128] In several works Salvo García has defended the position that these discrepancies and lacunae can be explained by the possibility that Alfonso used a Latin *codex* of the *Metamorphoses* that included a commentary on the text.[129] After the twelfth century, interpretative glosses of the *Metamorphoses*'s myths were commonly included in the text's Latin manuscripts. Most glosses corresponded to Arnulf and John, the most popular interpreters, but some were from minor and unidentified authors. The best example is in the *Vulgate* commentary on the *Metamorphoses*, written in France around 1250 and widely circulated at the end of the thirteenth century.[130] Therefore, it is highly possible that Alfonso utilized the *Vulgate* or a comparable commentary on the *Metamorphoses* which greatly relied on Arnulf and John. The fact is that Alfonso often attributes *glossae* of Arnulf to John, and occasionally to an unknown friar without it being possible for us to determine if these are mistakes made by Alfonso or if he found them in a source unknown to us.[131] It is likely that since he thought his main interpreter was a friar, Alfonso asserted that Franciscans ("minor friars") were interpreting Ovid – as we saw above.

The Castilian king takes most of the *integumenta* from Arnulf, John, and "the friar," which he understands in a very specific way that goes back to Chartres. In this chapter the *GE* singles out the "proper names" (*nombres proprios*) of the characters in *TSOI* and focuses on analyzing them.[132] According to Wetherbee, the nature and implications of the *integumenta* were almost certainly established by William of Conches in his *Glossae super Timaeum* (a commentary on Plato's Timaeus); for Conches, "the simplest *integumenta* are etymologies of proper names from mythology."[133] This kind of etymological analysis of proper names is found in the *GE*'s allegorical section on *TSOI*, because single words can be "treated as *integumenta* and 'broken open' by etymology to yield philosophical meaning, as in Isidore or

[128] See Salvo García, "L'Ovide connu par Alphonse," 214.

[129] See, for instance, Salvo García, "L'Ovide connu par Alphonse," 214–15; Salvo García, "Ovidio y la compilación," 59.

[130] On the *Vulgate*, see Irene Salvo García, "The Latin Commentary Tradition and Medieval Mythography: The Example of the Myth of Perseus (Met. IV) in Vernacular Languages," in G. Pellissa Prades and M. Balzi (eds), *Ovid in the Vernacular: Translations of the Metamorphoses in The Middle Ages & Renaissance* (Oxford: Medium Ævum, 2021), 70; and Salvo García, "L'Ovide connu par Alphonse," 203–4.

[131] Salvo García, "L'Ovide connu par Alphonse," 215; Salvo García, "The Latin Commentary Tradition," 70.

[132] "E los nombres proprios que en estas razones de Ío á son éstos: Ínaco, Ío, Júpiter, Juno, Argo, Mercurio, Siringa, Pan, Isis, Pavón, que es nombre comunal." *GE*1 I, 317.

[133] Wetherbee, *Platonism*, 44–5.

Fulgentius."[134] For this etymological analysis, in addition to Arnulf and John, Alfonso also uses material from the Arab sciences and various authorities.

The first proper name in the story that the *GE* wants to discuss is that of Io's father, the river god Inachus. Alfonso once again explains how men could have been regarded as gods and rivers, and he bases this explanation on Arab magical theory. However, this time Alfonso attributes the explanation to "the wise men who uncovered the sayings of the gentiles in the *integumenta*," who explain that "the power and knowledge of things and their natures" is the main reason why "gentiles deemed as gods some of them who deserved it."[135] In reality, his main sources on *integumenta* (Arnulf and John), did not talk about these "scientific" – and also magical – explanations at all; they are Alfonso's own development. As I explained earlier, "powers" and "natures" are significant terms within Arab magical theory, connected to the "powers and virtues" that Alfonso used earlier to introduce the river god Inachus.[136] He provides this magic-related explanation but then adds that "when any man or god was considered a river, it was because of the coldness of the land where he ruled and the chastity of their people, and also because he was very powerful along the riverside and the neighbouring lands of that river."[137] In reality, this is a good example of an *amplificatio* that Alfonso creates from his sources. The key component of Alfonso's elaboration lies in the etymology that he provides for Inachus, who "according to master John and the friar, means coldness and chilling."[138] This is Alfonso's rough interpretation of Arnulf (and not John). The teacher from Orléans actually said that Daphne (in the myth that precedes *TSOI* in the *Metamorphoses*) "is imagined to be the daughter of the river god Peneus, because his water is cold, and chastity is the daughter of coldness, such as impudence is the daughter of heat."[139] Then, Arnulf continues to describe Io, "the virgin daughter of the river god Inachus, who therefore was thought to be cold until her nubile years."[140] Giving his own spin on Arnulf, Alfonso affirms that "virgin damsels are commonly of a cold nature until they marry, and that is why gentiles called some of

[134] Wetherbee, "Philosophy," 36.

[135] "Leemos en los integumentos de los sabios que espusieron oscuros los dichos de los gentiles [...] E fallamos que departen que por poder e saber que avién algunos d'ellos en las cosas e en las naturas d'ellas más que los otros omnes llamaron los gentiles sos dioses a aquellos que lo merecieron d'esta guisa." *GE*1 I, 316.

[136] *GE*1 I, 301.

[137] "E cualquier rey o dios que ellos dixieron que era río gelo dizién por razón de friura d'essa tierra ó él regnava e de la castidad de las yentes d'ella. E diziéngelo otrossí por seer el rey o aquel dios muy poderoso de las riberas e de las tierras vezinas d'aquel río." *GE*1 I, 316.

[138] "E Ínaco, segund maestre Juan e el fraire, quiere dezir tanto como friura e atempramiento." *GE*1 I, 317.

[139] "Io virgo filia Inachi dei cuiusdam fluvii fuit. Quod ideo fingitur quia frígida fuit ante annos nubiles." Arnulf of Orléans, *Arnulphi Aurelianensis Allegoriae* 1.9, 203.

[140] "Dane ideo filia Penei dei fluvii fingitur quia aqua est frigida, et pudicicia est filia frigiditatis sicut impudicicia caloris." Arnulf of Orléans, *Arnulphi Aurelianensis Allegoriae* 1.10, 203.

them daughters of those rivers and gods,"[141] including Daphne and Io.[142] This hints at Arnulf's originally moralistic interpretation; for him, *TSOI* is an allegory of the story of sin (the loss of chastity and virginity) and redemption. However, Alfonso shifts this emphasis when he adds that if gentiles focused on kings and their offspring it was "because they only talk in their stories about great men, some of good customs, others of bad ones."[143] Arnulf's interpretation of the story relates to Christian morals and the theme of sin and redemption, while Alfonso emphasizes education and how it can develop good customs and amend bad ones.

After he establishes these premises in his discussion of Inachus, Alfonso completes the allegorical part with etymological *glossae* on the other characters' proper names. Earlier we saw how etymological analysis was recovered by the authors of *integumenta* in the twelve century; however, this type of analysis was also characteristic of the high Middle Ages, starting with Augustine, reaching its pinnacle in Isidore, and even extending into the ninth century with Remigius of Auxerre, who wrote commentaries on the Bible and the Roman classics. Alfonso refers to all these authorities here. For instance, we find that Jupiter is the "higher air" and Juno the "lower air" ("aer the suso" and "aer the yuso"), ideas that the Castilian king refers to as coming from Augustine's *The City of God*,[144] but which he could also have found in Arnulf.[145]

This is a good example of how allegorical interpretation is related to another, older hermeneutic tool for interpreting myths: etiology. This tool was mainly used to articulate the origin of places and customs but can also be understood as a type of nature-based allegory, as we can observe here, on the basis of which characters poetically represent nature or how it works.[146] In fact, Augustine took the etymologies of Jupiter and Juno from Cicero's *De natura deorum*, where they are explained by Balbus. Herren explains that this character is the "spokesman for the Stoic position on the gods" in the book, because the philosophical school originally developed this naturalistic etymological interpretation.[147] To these old etymologies Alfonso adds that, according to Remigius of Auxerre, Jupiter's name also means "separating lord or enemy" – a strange gloss, which Alfonso later discusses in the moralistic section.[148]

141 "[…] cualquier rey o dios que ellos dixieron que era río gelo dizién por razón de friura d'essa tierra ó él regnava e de la castidad de las yentes d'ella […] el agua es madre de la friura, e la friura madre de la castidad […] porque las donzellas vírgines fasta'l tiempo de casar suelen seer de fría natura e casta más que en el tiempo de después llamaron a algunas d'ellas essos autores de los gentiles fijas d'aquellos dioses e reyes." *GE*1 I, 316.

142 *GE*1 I, 317.

143 "E ellos non fablaron en sos dichos si non de grandes omnes, quier fuessen de malas costumbres quier de buenas." *GE*1 I, 317.

144 Augustine, *Civitate Dei* IV.xi: "ipse in aethere sit Iuppiter, ipse in aere Iuno."

145 "Iunone, id est inferiori aere." Arnulf of Orléans, *Arnulphi Aurelianensis Allegoriae* I.10, 203.

146 See Guisaberti, in Arnulf of Orléans, *Arnulphi Aurelianensis Allegoriae*, 201.

147 *De natura deorum* 2.65–6. Michael Herren, *The Anatomy of Myth: The Art of Interpretation from the Presocratics to the Church Fathers* (Oxford and New York: Oxford University Press, 2017), 117.

148 "Júpiter es el aer de suso, e, segund dize Ramiro en los esponimientos de la Biblia, quiere dezir tanto como enemigo apartant o señor apartador. Juno, segund los autores, es el aer

Argus means, among other things, "argued" (*argudo*), but "according to master John, for Argus we can also understand the world"[149] – in fact, the first definition is in John,[150] while the second is from Arnulf.[151]

The *glossae* about Mercury cover a wide range of material related to the development of this figure since antiquity, so they are especially relevant here. The first note discusses the Greek Hermes: "according to what Remigius says, [Mercury] means piling up of stones in the height of the mountains."[152] Originally, the Greek *hermae* were heaps of stones or shapeless columns at the side of the road, in high places, and by land boundaries, which later would incorporate statues of Hermes, the god of travellers and merchants.[153] This information was well-known to medieval commentators. Although most of Remigius's work is lost, part of it has been preserved through the works of commentators; specialists have determined that Remigius and his followers used widely known authorities on mythology that were transmitted from antiquity to the medieval world, such as the three Vatican Mythographers, Fulgentius (early sixth century), and Isidore.[154] These sources explain the classical features mentioned here, such as that of intermediary, either between gods and men (as we see in Homer) or between men in commerce. In *The City of God* VII Augustine describes Mercury as the middle courier (*medius currens*), who can be identified with speech between men.[155] In his *Etymologies*, Isidore takes these words about Mercury, as *medius currens*, from Augustine.[156]

*GE*1 affirms that Mercury "according to Remigius, reveals a word or reason that runs among men," information that he expands upon in this way: "and he is the merchant's god or lord, because an intermediary word has to exist between those who sell and those who buy; and he was wise in many arts, and lived until Moses's time, according to what Lucas says."[157] Alfonso refers to Lucas de Tuy's *Chronicon mundi* (*Chronicle of the world*, 1236), one of the *GE*'s main sources and its closest Castilian historical forerunner. Indeed, Lucas upholds that "Mercury was the son of Jupiter, and according to Fulgentius, partly was in charge of commerce, partly

de yuso." *GE*1 I, 317.

149 "[…] e por Argo otrossí, segunt maestre Joán dize, podemos entender el mundo." *GE*1 I, 317.

150 "Argus ab arguto fertur." John of Garland, *Integumenta Ovidii*, ed. Fausto Ghisalberti (Messina and Milano: Principato, 1933), 99.

151 "Argo id est seculo." Arnulf of Orléans, *Arnulphi Aurelianensis Allegoriae* I.10, 203.

152 "[…] segund dize Ramiro, tanto quiere mostrar amontonamiento de piedras en el alteza de los montes." *GE*1 I, 317.

153 See *Hermae* in William Smith, *A Dictionary of Roman and Greek Antiquities* (New York: D. Appleton & Co., 1874).

154 Diane K. Bolton, "Remigian Commentaries, on the 'Consolation of Philosophy' and Their Sources," *Traditio* 33 (1977): 393.

155 Augustine, *Civitate Dei* VII, xiv.

156 *Etymologies*.VIII, xi, 45–9.

157 "Mercurio, segund Ramiro, tanto quiere mostrar como palabra o razón que corre medianera entre los hombres, e que éste es como dios o señor de los mercaderos, porque entre los que venden e compran siempre á de andar palabra medianera; e fue sabio de muchas artes, e alcançó fasta'l tiempo de Moisén, segund cuenta Lucas." *GE*1 I, 318.

supervised businesses, whence it is thought that he was the god of merchants."[158] Lucas adds immediately that "it is also said that this [Mercury] was Hermes, who also spoke in a prudent way, and according to Fulgentius from this reason he was thought to be the god of speech and eloquence."[159] And finally we find that he also was "the grandson of Atlas, was wise in many arts and because of that after his death he was carried across into the gods."[160] We see that for both of Mercury's aspects, as god of merchants and as god of eloquence, Lucas refers to Fulgentius (early sixth century). Indeed, this mythographer wrote that "Mercury was in charge of trading" and provided a clear etymology of his name as *mercium-curum*, which might come from the Latin *mercatus* (trading) and *cura* (care), or perhaps from the Greek *kurios* (lord, master).[161]

In Lucas de Tuy, Alfonso could find that Mercury was "the god of merchants" and "wise in many arts," and somehow also that "he lived until Moses's time,"[162] because on the same page of the *Chronicon mundi* Lucas introduces Moses in the timetable and begins the "story of Moses."[163] But the interesting part is that, if Alfonso found and read this information in Lucas, as he claims, he also might have found mention that Mercury was Hermes, and a few pages later that there were three Mercuries, and one of them was Hermes Trismegistus.[164] Even though Alfonso does not explicitly state the identification of Mercury with Hermes Trismegistus until *GE*2, he is already advancing it here in *GE*1 when he discusses the god's attributes. I will comment on the story of the three Hermeses and its meaning in Chapter Four.

I have just examined how Alfonso develops the allegorical part of *TSOI*'s interpretation and how he includes the *integumenta* as an etymological explanation of the character's names; now it is time to see how Alfonso articulates the third and moralistic part of his analysis.

158 "[...] dicitur fuisse filius Iouis and secundum Fulgentium dicitur Mercurius quasi mercium curator quasi negotiationibus indendebat unde fungitur fuisse deus mercatorum." As the editor Falque Rey explains, these sentences are only in some of the manuscripts; for instance, in those she calls "B." Lucas de Tuy, *Chronicon mundi*, ed. Emma Falque (Turnhout: Brepols, 2003), I, 26, p. 29, footnote.

159 "Iste etiam dicut est Hermes qui idem sonat quod discretus secundum Fulgentium unde fingitur fuisse Deus sermonis et eloquentie." Lucas de Tuy, *Chronicon mundi*.I, 26, p. 29, footnote.

160 "[...] nepos Atlantis multarum atrium peritus et propter hoc post mortem in deos translatus." Lucas de Tuy, *Chronicon mundi*.I, 26. This sentence is in all manuscripts.

161 Wilbur Devereux Jones, *Fulgentius the Mythographer* (Columbus: Ohio State University Press, 1972), 59–60. See also N. O. Brown, *Hermes the Thief: The Evolution of a Myth* (Lindisfarne Books, 1990).

162 *GE*1 I, 318.

163 Which extends for four pages in the modern edition, see Lucas de Tuy, *Chronicon mundi*.I. 27–8, 29–33.

164 "Tres fuerunt Mercurii. Primus fuit Hermes. Secundus iste, qui est Tremegistus philosophus. Tercius Mercurius minor in multis studiis clarus." Lucas de Tuy, *Chronicon mundi*.I. 34, 37.

Alfonso's Moralistic Reading of Ovid: Correcting Bad Customs Through Education

Chapter XXVIII is entitled "On how queen Io corrected her customs."[165] As I argued earlier, in Alfonso the term "customs" (*costumbres*) is used in a broad sense that can be related to morals but is closer to an educational ideal than to the Christian morals of other medieval Ovidian interpreters. Alfonso begins by explaining that while Io was with her father Inachus she led a chaste life. However, when she reached a marriageable age she left her father's domains (i.e., she left her chastity behind). Then, Io was seen by Jupiter, who, according to the etymology that Alfonso attributes to Remigius, is the "separating enemy" (*enemigo apartant*). And then

> [...] by charming her with mists, that is, with promises and vain words, [Jupiter] caught and forced her. And when she abandoned the path of good customs and entered into that of bad ones, the gentile authors said that Jupiter turned her into a cow; and as master John and the friar explain, he threw her into the bad customs of the beast or cow [...].[166]

Up to this point, Alfonso has been following the traditional interpretation of Christian scholars, which is often pejorative towards Io. He takes this explanation from Arnulf – as we saw, many times in the *GE* he turns out to be "the friar" – who provides a much more concise moral interpretation of the episode: "Io was loved by Jupiter, that is, by the creator god, because she was a virgin. If only those whom God loves would raise themselves to the creator by preserving their virginity! And she, once deflowered, was cast out from the number of virgins, that is, made into a beast."[167] Alfonso closely follows Arnulf but introduces several significant additions that further interpret, shape it according to his own tastes, and ultimately completely transform the role of Io in the story. Arnulf is much more sympathetic towards Jupiter, "a creator god," who apparently must follow his natural appetite for virgins. In this sense, the medieval commentator simply furthers the Ovidian idea of the mythical male hero as the creator of differences – according to De Lauretis's terminology. In Arnulf's commentary, Jupiter also bears a vague resemblance to the Christian creator God, and Io's "bestiality" seems to be a consequence of her own sinful impulses. According to Noacco, for Arnulf the most important interpretation is the moralistic one, conceived as an eternal fight between virtue and vice.[168] Io's sin – that is, lust

165 "De cómo la reína Io se emendó de sus costumbres." *GE*1 I, 319.

166 "[...] embargándola con nieblas, fascas con promessas de palabras de vanidad, alcançóla e forçóla. E saliendo ella por esta carrera de las buenas costumbres e entrando en las malas dixieron los autores de los gentiles que la mudara Júpiter en vaca. E assí como departen maestre Joán e el fraire esto es que la echó en costumbres malas como de bestia o de vaca." *GE*1 I, 319.

167 "Io virgo filia Inachi dei eiusdam fluvii fuit. Quod ideo fingitur quia frígida fuit ante anos nubiles. Amata fuit a Iove, id est a deo creatore quia virgo. Tales siquidem amat deus que virginitatem conservando ad creatorem se erigunt. Que postea divirginata de numero virginum eiecta id est bestialis facta." Arnulf of Orléans, *Arnulphi Aurelianensis Allegoriae* I.10, 203.

168 Noacco, "Lire Ovide," 140–1. On the interpretation of Io as repentant sinner in Arnulf and later *glossae* compilations, see Irene Salvo García, "Les sources de l'*Ovide moralisé* livre I.

– represents this struggle.[169] In fact, neglecting God and religion is the vice that Arnulf most often attributes to the *Metamorphoses*'s characters, which demonstrates his predominately Christian undertone.[170] In contrast, Alfonso's "morals" are much more secular. Even though Alfonso could find many more in his sources, there are only four Christian interpretations of the *Metamorphoses* in the *GE* – despite the growing tendency throughout the thirteenth century for this type of explanation, culminating with the *Ovide moralisé* (*Moralized Ovid*), the most important medieval work of this kind.[171]

Therefore, according to previous medieval commentators, the sin of Io is that of relenting to the temptation of the vice of lust; yet I see in Alfonso's interpretation not only a more secular view but also a more compassionate depiction of Io, not as a sinner but as a victim of Jupiter. As we saw earlier, throughout the *GE* Alfonso portrays Jupiter positively and even identifies the god as himself. By adding Remigius's etymological interpretation on Jupiter's name, Alfonso not only distances himself from Arnulf's view on this Ovidian episode, but also from the more general opinion of Jupiter that appears elsewhere in the *GE*. Here, Jupiter is initially a devilish figure ("separating enemy") who is directly responsible for Io's disgrace, since he "caught and forced" and then "threw her into bad customs." Alfonso does not delve into this dimension of Jupiter as "separating enemy" any further – probably because of the contradictions with the rest of the *GE*. Io being thrown into bad customs is more significant for our discussion, as she is not described in this way in Alfonso's sources. The *GE* often mentions good and bad customs (*costumbres*); of course, they have a moralistic component – most times not especially Christian but almost always educational. As I explained in Chapter Two, the Arab concept of *adab* has many aspects, but it always mixes education with good behaviour. As Gustave E. von Grunebaum explains, over time *adab* designated a "*Bildungs*-ideal which, whatever its components, was characterized by combining the demand for information of a certain kind with that for compliance with a code of behaviour."[172] Considering that in the *GE*, *TSOI* is surrounded by Arab sources that are connected to a subgenre of *adab*, I suggest that they influenced this idea of "good customs."

We saw that Io's disgrace does not end with her moral degeneration and transformation into a cow. Jupiter gives the transformed nymph to the angry Juno, who in turn entrusts her to her servant and shepherd Argus. Juno allegorically refers to the "delight of earth and wealth" (*deleit de la tierra e de las riquezas*), whereas Argus is "the world" (*el mundo*) – like the Latin *seculus* in Arnulf,[173] who interprets this part of the story in the following way:

Types et traitement," *Moyen-Âge* 124, no. 2 (2018): 323.

169 Noacco, "Lire Ovide," 148–9.

170 Noacco, "Lire Ovide," 140.

171 Salvo García, "L'Ovide connu par Alphonse," 215–16. On the *Ovide moralisé,* see also Salvo García, "Les sources de l'*Ovide moralisé,*" 308–9. See also the first translation of this work into English (and into any modern language) in *The Medieval French Ovide Moralisé. An English Translation*, trans. and eds K. Sarah-Jane Murray and Matthieu Boyd. 3 vols (Cambridge: D. S. Brewer, 2023).

172 Grunebaum, *Medieval Islam*, 250.

173 *GE*1 I, 320; and Arnulf of Orléans. *Arnulphi Aurelianensis Allegoriae* I.10, 203.

> Io was handed by Juno – (i.e., the inferior air, that is, the lower and graver vices) to Argus, which means the world, the gravest vices, because through Argus, who has multiple eyes, we are able to understand the world, or the world entangled by many enticements. And so, this world imprisoned her in such a way that the creator god was not able to recognize her.[174]

Alfonso uses this interpretation but with significant divergences. For him, Io being altered by Argus is what led to the result that "she indulged in worse vices and customs";[175] customs are a new element added by Alfonso and are a different category than Arnulf's vices. And now we come to the key part of the analysis, the meaning of Mercury killing Argus. Arnulf writes:

> But Mercury killed Argus. Through the god Mercury we have eloquence and whoever is eloquent, and [Mercury] killed the worldly lusts in her with his eloquence; and he raised her, who was better than she had ever been, to serve her creator; hence it is supposed that she was changed from a cow into a goddess.[176]

Therefore, for Arnulf, the god Mercury killed the lust in Io through his eloquence, but then he moves into ambiguous territory between the Christian and pagan – which allegory allows. The purified Io seems to be elevated to the Christian God, rather than to Jupiter, and then transformed into a "goddess" herself. According to Arnulf, Ovid not only wanted to show us exterior transformations but also the interior ones that are produced in the soul; there are two movements in the soul, one upwards and another downwards, rational and irrational, to God and to the beasts – Io's soul, degraded by sin, would have experienced the downward movement first, although finally she experiences its anagogic opposite by becoming a goddess.[177] As we saw earlier, most Christian interpretations of Io's story follow this pattern of sin and redemption. Alfonso diverges from this pious framework by emphasizing the education that Io receives from Mercury. This education enables her to transcend her "bad customs" and develop her own sense of educational power and agency.

In this sense, it is significant that Arnulf offers an independent section containing an allegorical explanation of the story of Pan and Syrinx, with which Mercury puts Argus to sleep, whereas Alfonso manages to connect the content with Mercury and his teachings. Arnulf reminds the reader that when Syrinx, daughter of the River Ladon, was transformed into reeds to escape from the lustful god Pan, he "made a pipe of seven tones" (*fecit fistulam VII vocum*) by cutting seven of the reeds, which has the following allegorical explanation:

174 "[...] Io traditur a Iunone id est inferiori aere id est viciis inferioribus et gravioribus, Argo id est seculo id est viciis gravissimis quia per Argum multiplices oculos habentem possumus mundum habere, vel seculum multiplicibus illecebris irretitum. Qui mundus ita eam incarceravit quod deum creatorem noscere non potuit." Arnulf of Orléans. *Arnulphi Aurelianensis Allegoriae* I.10, 203.

175 "[...] se dio esta Io a mayores vicios de sí e a peores costumbres." *GE*1 I, 320.

176 "Sed Mercurius Argum occidit. Per Mercurium deum facundie habemus et quemlibet facundum qui sua persuasione mundanas concupiscencias in ea mortificavit, et eam, melius quod nunquam fuit, creatore suo ad serviendum erexit. Unde fingitur de bove mutata in deam." Arnulf of Orléans, *Arnulphi Aurelianensis Allegoriae* I.11, 203.

177 See Noacco, "Lire Ovide," 135.

> The River Ladon is Greece, because the studious Greeks discovered the seven arts. Pan, that is, "everything,"[178] is clearly Rome, since the Romans wanted to have knowledge of all things. Finally, Syrinx was transformed, which means that [Pan] succeeded in transforming the Greek arts from Greek into Latin, and then sang with them.[179]

The *GE* expands this interpretation to emphasize the *translatio studii* and Mercury's patronage of the seven liberal arts. First, Alfonso offers a detailed interpretation of the transmission of the liberal arts from Greece to Rome and contextualizes this within the broader theory of the *translatio studii* passing from some *señoríos* (lordships) to others.[180] However, Alfonso ignores Arnulf's interpretation of the last transformation in *TSOI* (i.e., Argus turning into a peacock). Arnulf explains that the peacock is an arrogant bird (*superba avis*) and connects it to Argus's embodiment of the world's enticements; since Mercury is eloquence (*facundia*), the meaning of the transformation is that the worldly arrogance in Io was killed through rhetoric.[181] Alfonso goes one step further, explaining in detail how Mercury used his rhetorical and dialectical skills – a more complete display of the *trivium* – to beguile Argus, since their meeting included a contest of questions and answers. According to Alfonso: "And Mercury defeated Argus, that is, the world, by reasoning with him about the questions that Argus made and talking covertly about the reasons of the seven liberal arts. And telling him that Pan loved Syrinx, who had been transformed into reeds in the riverside of Ladon."[182] Alfonso argues that the story about Syrinx was Mercury's subterfuge, using reason and the seven liberal arts in order to "kill" the bad customs in Io, just as any good educator would do with a prince or courtier – in Arab culture, the instrument to do this was *adab*. The *udabā'* (expert on *adab*) not only would teach his pupil a complete curriculum – here, the entire *trivium* and *quadrivium* – but also would amend his behaviour, his "bad customs," and transform him into a profitable member of the court. In Alfonso's view, Io benefits so much from Mercury's education that she becomes a queen and a goddess in Egypt.

Once Mercury "kills" Argus (i.e., kills the bad customs in Io by educating her in the liberal arts), she still must escape Juno's rage. As in Ovid's original story, Io's path of escape leads her to Egypt, which is a significant place because Abraham, Isaac, Jacob, and even Jesus Christ went there too, as Alfonso points out.[183] In this way, Abraham's teachings in Egypt, which were described earlier in *GE*1 and taken from Arab sources, seem to be connected to Io. Once in Egypt, Jupiter begs Juno to

178 From the Greek Πάν.

179 "Ladon fluvius est Grecie iuxta quem greci studentes invenerunt VII. artes quas Pan id est totum, Roma scilicet que totum esse volebant id est rerum omnium habere noticiam. Tandem Siringam mutatam id est artes grecas de Greco in latinum transmutatas consecutus est, et cum eis cantavit." Arnulf of Orléans, *Arnulphi Aurelianensis Allegoriae* I.12, 203.

180 *GE*1 I, 320–1.

181 Arnulf of Orléans, *Arnulphi Aurelianensis Allegoriae* I.13, 203.

182 "E venció Mercurio a Argo, fascas al mundo razonándose con él sobre laspreguntas quel fazié Argo fablandol él encubiertamientre de las razones de las siete artes liberales, e diziendol que amara Pan a Siringa tornada en cañaveras en las riberas del río Ladón." *GE*1 I, 320.

183 *GE*1 I, 321.

forgive Io, and the jealous goddess complies. Alfonso explains how Io, once turned back into a woman, "had so much deviated from bad customs that Egyptians raised Io to a goddess and changed her name, calling her Isis."[184] Thus, the transformation of Io into Isis, which Ovid explains in a very succinct way,[185] is attributed to the complete removal of those bad customs through the teachings of Mercury. But Isis's sojourn and active role in Egypt seem to be so interesting for Alfonso that after this moralistic interpretation of the story, he dedicates an entirely original section to discussing it further.

Epilogue: Isis in Egypt

In the final chapter of *TSOI* Alfonso deviates from the Latin commentators and expands on Isis's enterprises in Egypt, which seems like an addendum to the historical/euhemeristic interpretation. Alfonso not only reconnects *TSOI* with the larger course of history in the *GE* but also with the so-called "Histories of Egypt," the Hermetic tone of which has been evoked since the beginning of the chapter:

> In Egypt, Isis was a lady accomplished in all good things. Egyptians, who were great astrologers and knowers of the nature of things, worshipped the planets and the water element more than anything else, because from the Nile came everything they had.[186]

Thus, Alfonso connects Isis's new wisdom with the Egyptians' knowledge of astrology and "the nature of things," which, as I explain below, are prerequisites for practising magic. Earlier, the *GE* talked about Egypt and astrology – Abraham taught it there – but apparently the coming of Isis made Egyptians excel further in the science of the stars. After an excerpt on Egypt's devotion to water, Alfonso insists on the importance of astrology: "And since the Egyptians worshipped the planets, they also took notice of their powers, and saw how they never stop to generate offspring and fruit in the nature of things."[187] Once again, we find magical concepts that have an Arab origin: the powers of the planets, the nature of things, and a particular emphasis on the influence of the stars in the generation and corruption of earthly things.

As Saif explains, attributing "a generative and causal role to the stars is a unique element in the Arabic theories of astral influence" developed by Abū Maʿshar.[188] This astronomer is an influential figure in Alfonso's works; for instance, the description of the three Hermeses in *GE*2 that I will examine in Chapter Four relates to him.

[184] "E Ío tanto se partió allí de todas las malas costumbres que los de Egipto que la alçaron por su deessa, e mudáronle aquel nombre Ío e llamáronla Isis." *GE*1 I, 321.

[185] *Met*.I.747–64.

[186] "Esta Isis salió en Egipto dueña muy cumplida en toda bondad, e los de Egipto, que eran muy grandes estrelleros e sabidores de las naturas de las cosas, aoravan al elemento del agua e a las planetas más que a otra cosa, e al agua por la razón del Nilo dond les vinié cuanto bien avién." *GE*1 I, 322.

[187] "E sobre aquello que los de Egipto aoravan a las planetas pararon mientes en los poderes d'ellas e vieron cómo nunca quedavan de engendrar crianças e frutos en las naturas de las cosas." *GE*1 I, 322.

[188] Saif, *Arabic Influences*, 103.

This theory on the generative power of the stars is later applied to magic by authors such as al-Kindī, the famous scientist and philosopher, and al-Qurṭubī, author of the *Ghāya*.[189] There are also many references to generation and corruption by the stars in the book of *Astromagia*, composed in the last stage of Alfonso's reign, probably around the time the *GE* was being written;[190] there we read that "all things in the world of generation and corruption must receive virtues and labors [*obras*] from the high celestial world, which oversees [all things] and gives them virtues and labours, and because of it they are generated and corrupted."[191] This is a clear rendering of Arab theories, according to which everything is inherently astral "since the stars and planets are the efficient causes of generation and corruption, and the reasons behind magical efficacy of all practices."[192] We can find clear evidence of this principle when Alfonso explains how Isis's marriage to Osiris, which echoes Egyptian mythology, was actually motivated by astral theories of generation:

> And since in their land they wanted to follow the deeds of their gods and look like them, they made everybody marry and have sons – in the same way that the planets produce things – and they did not allow any decree to impede marriage in order to not decrease their number because of fewer marriages. Therefore, they made their goddess Isis marry as well, even though they considered her a saint. They married her to a giant called Osiris, a powerful man, wise about many of the natures of things.[193]

Isis's famous marriage with Osiris was a consequence of Egyptians wanting to follow the designs of the stars and to reproduce what the stars did on a smaller scale – which seems like a version of the Hellenistic and Hermetic-related theory of the macrocosm-microcosm. Osiris was also wise about the "nature of things," a magical knowledge – as we saw earlier – not strange for a "giant" like him. Giants have an important role in the section on the three Hermeses in *GE*2. Narratives about giants in the *GE* betray the influence of both Genesis and the Book of Enoch – from heterodox Judaic traditions – as we will see in Chapter Five. Figures who came from the lineage of the giants, including Hermes Trismegistus, were closely related to astrology, because "they were the first men who measured the course of the stars, and the movements of the heavens, and discerned everything, and knew the power

189 Saif, *Arabic Influences*, 103.

190 See the edition by Agostino and its introduction.

191 "[...] deben recebir todas las cosas que son en el mundo de generación e de corrupción vertudes e obras del mundo alto celestial, que es apoderado d'ellas; e éll les da las vertudes e las obras, e por él se engendran e por él se corrompen." Alfonso X el Sabio, *Astromagia* III.2.12, 154. See other references to generation and corruption in Alfonso X el Sabio, *Astromagia* III.2.9, 152 and III.2.16, 154.

192 Saif, *Arabic Influences*, 39.

193 "E queriendo ellos seguir los fechos de sus dioses e semejarlos fazién en su tierra casar a todos e que fiziessen fijos como criavan las planetas a las cosas, e que por razón de mengua de casamiento que non menguassen, e non consintieron que orden ninguna oviesse entr'ellos que casamiento estorvasse, e fizieron por ende a esta su deessa Isis, maguer que la tenién ellos por santa, que casasse. E casáronla con un gigant a que llamavan Osiris, omne muy poderoso e muy sabio de muchas naturas de cosas." *GE*1 I, 322–3.

and the natures of the four elements."[194] Therefore, as a giant, Osiris also knows about the nature of things, and of course must be as learned in astrology as his fellow Egyptians.

To this knowledge Osiris adds an apparently surprising new component that he will transmit to his wife: "and because [Osiris] knew all mastery, subtlety, and gracefulness in the fabrics' craft, Isis was, on account of her husband, called the goddess of *lanificio* [from Latin *lanificium,* the working of wool], and *lanificio* means weaving."[195] Salvo García has located a similar *glossa* in the *Vulgate* commentary on Ovid, which could be the origin or have the same origin as that used by Alfonso. The *Vulgate* explains that Isis is called *lanigera* or *linigera,* because Isis's priests wore woolen or linen robes, or because her husband Osiris invented the craft of linen.[196] All other references to Osiris, his gigantic origins, or the astrological remarks are absent from the *Vulgate* and therefore must have been taken from another source, or developed by Alfonso, who was interested in showing a "Hermetic Egypt" that was in line with the rest of the *GE.*

However, it is evident that Alfonso endorses ancient myths that describe how Isis not only was a great magician but also an "active principle of culture," a role that Ovid reserves for male characters,[197] and a civilizing hero like Hermes, for she teaches the Egyptians various arts, such as weaving and writing.[198] In reference to this last art, Alfonso adds that Isis "was very wise and took very great care of the knowledge," and that "since the Egyptians did not have letters or an alphabet then, she invented one for them."[199] Alfonso might have taken this last piece of information from brief notes in Petrus Comestor,[200] or from Godfrey of Viterbo,[201] two of his

194 "E ellos fueron los primeros omnes que mesuraron los cursos de las estrellas e los movimientos de los cielos e lo sopieron todo, e coñocieron el poder e las naturas de los cuatro elementos." *GE*2 I, 51.

195 "E porque sabie él toda cuanta maestría e sotileza e apostura avié en fecho de paños llamáron por la razón del marido a Isis deessa de lanificio, e es lanificio filaduría." *GE*1 I, 323.

196 "Lanigera dicit quia sacerdotes Ysidis lane flosculum in signum sacerdocii in capitibus deferebant. Vel linigera propter lineum ilium quod deferebant sui sacerdotes in signum sacerdocii vel quia maritus eius Osyris scilicet usum lini dictura invenisse." *Vulgate,* v. 747, 335. Cited in Salvo García, "L'Ovide connu par Alphonse," 209.

197 See De Lauretis, *Alice Doesn't,* 105–6.

198 See Joyce Tyldesley, *Daughters of Isis: Women of Ancient Egypt* (London: Penguin, 1995), 130 and 287.

199 "Sobr'esto fue esta Isis muy sabia, e travajávase mucho de los saberes [...]. E las figuras del abc e de la leyenda de los de Egipto falló esta reína Isis, dond fue muy sabia dueña." *GE*1 I, 322.

200 "[...] Ysis in Egyptum nauigauit et quosdam apices litterarum tradidit Egyptiis." Pierre le Mangeur, *Scholastica historia. Liber Genesis,* ed. A. Sylwan (Turnhout: Brepols, 2007), 125.

201 "[...] Inachi etiam filia, nomine Isidis, ab Aegyptiis pro maxima dea est culta et venerata. Illa Isis dicitur fuisse regina Aegyptiorum, nata ex Aethiopia, quae litera Aegytiacas adinvenit." Gotefridi Viterbiensis, *Pantheon. In Germanicorum Scriptorum qui rerum a Germanis per multas aetates gestarum historias vel annales posteris reliunquerunt,* ed. Burcardo Gotthelffi o Struvio, foreword by Joannis Pistori Nidani, 3rd edn (Ratisbonae: Joannis Conradi Peezii, 1726), 4: 72–3.

main historiographical sources. However, it also echoes the ancient bonds between Isis and Hermes on the other side of the Mediterranean. The invention of writing and other knowledges was attributed to Hermes when this figure assimilated attributes of the Egyptian god Thoth, considered the inventor of writing[202] – as the famous Platonic myth of Thamus and Theuth attests.[203] Even in the *Corpus hermeticum* the inheritance of Hermes Trismegistus as Thoth, "a civilizing culture hero who gave the human race their laws and letters," surfaces.[204] In *De natura deorum*, Cicero evokes an alternative version of *TSOI*: the fifth Mercury he describes is one who actually has to escape to Egypt after killing Argus. There he gives letters and laws to the Egyptians and is called Theyt, another variant of Thoth.[205] Therefore, the transfer of the invention of letters and other attributes from Hermes/Thoth to Isis cannot come as a surprise. When Alfonso enlarges the role of Mercury as teacher of Io/Isis, and emphasizes her own agency as a developer of civilization, he is actually echoing a bond that goes back to the ancient Hellenistic and Mediterranean world.

The teacher–disciple relationship between Hermes and Isis appears in the *Hermetica*. In the *Korê kosmou*, one of the excerpts from Stobaeus's *Anthology* (fifth century), Isis informs her son Horus about Hermes, "who instructed herself and her husband, Osiris";[206] in another excerpt she tells Horus that "the king of counsel is the guide and father of all, Hermes Trismegistus," a proper epithet for a figure that assimilated features of Thoth, the vizier of the gods.[207] Throughout the *Hermetica* Isis is presented as one of Hermes's disciples, along with Tat, Asclepius, and Ammon.[208] This leads Bull to think that "Hermetism might have been found side by side with the cult of Isis and Osiris around the Mediterranean world."[209] As we saw in Chapter One, archaeologists have found temples of Isis on the Spanish coast with Hermes's name written on them. Diodorus mentions Hermes several times in relation to Isis and Osiris. The Hermes described by Diodorus "is a counsellor and sacred scribe of Osiris who invented language and letters, as well as divine rites, sacrifices, astronomy and music."[210] Diodorus also explains that "when Osiris left for his campaign of conquest he left Hermes as the advisor of Isis, and when Osiris later died and took his place among the gods, Isis and Hermes established his mysteries."[211]

202 Roelof van den Broek, "Hermes Trismegistus I: Antiquity," in Wouter J. Hanegraaff (ed.), *Dictionary of Gnosis and Western Esotericism* (Leiden: Brill, 2005), 474–5.

203 Plato, *Phaedrus*, 274b–8d.

204 Christian H. Bull, *The Tradition of Hermes Trismegistus* (Leiden: Brill, 2018), 153.

205 "Quintus quem colunt Pheneatae, qui Argum dicitur interemisse ob eamque causam Aegyptum profugisse atque Aegyptiis leges et litteras tradidisse: hunc Aegyptii Theyt appellant." *De natura deorum* 3.56.

206 *Stobaeus Hermetica* XXIII, 5–8, 25–32, 44, 48, 67–8, cited in Bull, *Tradition of Hermes*, 9. See also Copenhaver, *Hermetica*, 101–11; and M. David Litwa, *Hermetica II. The Excerpts of Stobaeus, Papyrus Fragments, and Ancient Testimonies in an English Translation with Notes and Introductions* (Cambridge: Cambridge University Press, 2018), 12–13.

207 *Stobaeus Hermetica* XXVI, 9, cited in Bull, *Tradition of Hermes*, 118.

208 See Bull, *Tradition of Hermes*, 451.

209 Bull, *Tradition of Hermes*, 454.

210 Diod. Sic., *Bib.* 1.16, cited in Bull, *Tradition of Hermes*, 92.

211 Diod. Sic., *Bib.* 1.17–20, cited in Bull, *Tradition of Hermes*, 92.

These connections between Hermes, Isis, Osiris, and the origins of writing were passed down to Christian historiography through Diodorus, because he is one of the main references on Egypt in Eusebius's *Praeparatio evangelica*.[212] Eusebius wrote that Osiris "honoured Hermes, who was endowed with an excellent genius for contriving what might benefit the common life. For [Hermes] was the inventor of letters";[213] and a little later that Osiris "passed from among men to the gods, and from Isis and Hermes received temples and all the honours which are held among the gods to be most distinguished. These two also taught men his initiatory rites and introduced many customs concerning him in the way of mysteries."[214] Although Alfonso did not know the *Praeparatio evangelica* – its first Latin translation is from the fifteenth century – Eusebius's *Canones* was his main historical authority. Thus, *TSOI* resonates with ancient pagan traditions that predate Ovid and which Christian culture had been trying to incorporate for centuries.

This last chapter dedicated to Isis demonstrates that its rendering of the Ovidian myth is closely connected to al-Bakrī's description of Egypt – a source that Alfonso uses for the lives of Abraham and Isaac. At the end of the chapter, Alfonso warns the reader that "now we will leave here her accounts and the deed of her transformation as Ovid tells it [...] and we will come back to the history of the Bible and the reasons of Abraham and Isaac."[215] However, *GE1* does not wander far from Egypt. Only three chapters later, Alfonso closes Book 1 of Genesis in *GE1* with Abraham's death, and then he also narrates the last days of Ismael – Abraham's son with Agar – in an Egypt with undeniable Arab features. The source that Alfonso quotes is again al-Bakrī:

> And his mother Agar made Ismael marry in Egypt [...] and according to the *History of Egypt*, Ismael was the first man to tame and ride horses after his father Abraham [...] and according to the *History of Egypt* in his twenty-third chapter, they buried him in Mecca close to his mother.[216]

Therefore, *TSOI* is preceded by the life of Abraham, interpreted and endorsed by Arabic sources, in which the patriarch travels to Egypt and teaches astrology, and then *TSOI* ends with the maiden being transformed into Isis in an Egypt where everybody practises astrology and cultivates all kinds of knowledge. A couple of pages after *TSOI* ends, *GE1* refers once again to the Arabic *History of Egypt* to narrate the last days of Ismael in that land.

212 *Praeparatio evangelica* 2, Preface.

213 *Praeparatio evangelica* 2 I, 3–4.

214 *Praeparatio evangelica* 2 I, 8.

215 "Agora dexamos aquí las sus razones e la fazaña del su mudamiento segund que la cuenta Ovidio [...] e tornaremos a la estoria de la Biblia a las razones de Abraham e de Isaac." *GE1* I, 323.

216 "[...] e casól su madre en Egipto [...] E segund dize la estoria de Egipto, Ismael fue después de Abraham su padre el primero omne que cavallo domó yl cavalgó [...] E segund dize la Estoria de Egipto en el XXII capítulo, soterráronlo en Meca cerca su madre." *GE1* I, 326.

Conclusion

Several specialists have thoroughly examined the influence of medieval Latin interpreters of Ovid in the rendering of Io and other stories from the *Metamorphoses* in the *GE*; only a couple of them have suggested Arab influences. In this chapter I have focused on Arab contributions that allow us to further develop the interpretation of Ovid in the *GE* and the entire production of Alfonso, including: the placement of *TSOI* between biblical sections assisted by Arabic sources; the presence of Arab cultural, magical, and scientific elements; the emphasis on Egypt; and the alter egos of Io and Mercury as the Egyptians Isis and Hermes Trismegistus.

The influence of Arab science and culture goes beyond specific details about natural magic, astrology, or weapons and is actually pervasive throughout *TSOI*. This is not strange because, as we have seen, the episode is sandwiched between Arabic geographical history sources, an *adab* subgenre with a strong educational component that allows the insertion of wondrous elements to incentivize the interest of readers. Alfonso introduces episodes from Ovid's *Metamorphoses* throughout the *GE*. Since he had to adapt pagan myths to fit within a biblical frame, Alfonso followed the pattern of contemporary Christian interpreters, who used three approaches or stages: historical/euhemeristic, allegorical/glossarist, and moralistic. However, in each of these approaches appear elements that were unfamiliar to the Latin culture of his time and can only be explained through Alfonso's work translating Arabic texts into Castilian. Therefore, the descriptions of illustrious men and women in Ovid's story of Io do not adhere to other European models: they study the liberal arts, write books on the sciences, practise astrology and magic, and excel in good customs and courtly pursuits, such as music and falconry. These components are particularly evident in the figure of Mercury, who is an accomplished magician, musician, and expert in the *trivium* and *quadrivium* – skills that he uses, along with his Arab-like *alfange*, to kill Argus and thus to allegorically educate the "bestialized" Io. Based on several allusions in the text, I suggest that Alfonso reframes Mercury as a personification of the ancient sage Hermes Trismegistus, the epitome of Mediterranean cultural and religious syncretism, and in this way he merges the reception of the Arabic and classical traditions in ways that have not been investigated in depth. In essence, Mercury becomes a *Hermes hispanus*: a summary of the Islamic Christian, Jewish, classical, and Near Eastern intellectual traditions that converged in the Iberian Peninsula. According to my interpretation, Hermes/Mercury embodies the ideal courtier presented by Alfonso in the *GE*, as well as in his production as a whole: someone from a clear lineage who has been carefully educated in all known sciences regardless of their origin and orthodoxy. Because Mercury has received this specific education, he is able to become an educator himself, who enables Io to surpass her original condition of objectified and "female" gendered subject in Ovid – according to De Lauretis's terminology – and to experience a real transformation that bestows on her the traditional attributes of the male hero or mythical subject as "active principle of culture, establisher of distinction, and creator of differences," capabilities that she exerts in a Hermetic Egypt not dissimilar to that of Queen Doluca who we saw in Chapter Two.

This education is not only present in both male and female characters in *TSOI* but is also shaped by a logic that guides the entire *GE*. In the next chapters, I will address how this particular education of the courtier, influenced by Arab *adab* and sciences, is reflected in the character of Mercury/Hermes elsewhere in the *GE*, finds echoes in other historical, biblical, and mythological characters, and relates to the actual environment of Alfonso's court. We will also see how Alfonso's works present Hermes as patron of the liberal arts, the *trivium* and *quadrivium*, in such a way that they offer a unique theory about Hermes in the Middle Ages and how this is connected to the ancient legend of the three Hermeses.

4

The Legend of the Three Hermeses in the *General Estoria*

Introduction

After several appearances in *GE*1, the god Mercury is explicitly identified as Hermes Trismegistus in *GE*2, where his role in the *GE* as a whole is explicated. This identification occurs in the same section where Mercury is also included in a catalogue of the three Hermeses. These details have intrigued specialists, especially Fraker, who has dedicated reflections to this section, its contradictions, and its possible sources. Other renowned scholars, such as Lida de Malkiel and Solalinde, also took note of this passage and pointed it out as one of the sections influenced by Arabic works, although they were not able to identify the exact sources used in it.[1] I will add new elements to this discussion, including a broader contextualization of the Arabic and Latin precedents, and suggest a credible direct source that no previous study has considered. This analysis will show how the Christian, Muslim, and Arabic sources on Hermes and the disciplines associated with him are more intertwined in the *GE* than it appears at first glance. We will ascertain how the question about the identity or multiple identities of Hermes throughout history pushed authors writing in different languages to define and reassess their intellectual models and convictions. We will also see how the Iberian blend of Hermetic sources is crucial for understanding the development of the myth of Hermes in ways that Judaic, classical, Hispanic, and Islamic studies have only partially apprehended. To assist the reader in tracing this journey through intellectual history and the complex, yet intriguing mosaic of intercultural references that converge in Alfonso's story of the three Hermeses, a diagram has been included at the end of this chapter. This appraisal once again situates Hermes in the centre of medieval Mediterranean cultural exchange and the oldest traditions on the genealogy of wisdom.

1 Fraker, *Scope of History*, 171–221; Charles F. Fraker, "Hermes Trismegistus in General Estoria II," in Ivy A. Corfis and Ray Harris-Northall (eds), *Medieval Iberia: Changing Societies and Cultures in Contact and Transition* (Woodbridge: Tamesis Books-Boydell & Brewer, 2007), 87–98; and Lida de Malkiel, "La General Estoria (I)," 121–2. Fraker had access to an index of the sources used in the *GE* that Solalinde put together; the index entry "Hermes" sends us to this passage of *GE*2 "but states that its source has not been found," Fraker, *Scope of History*, 198. In her thorough introduction to *GE*2, Belén Almeida does not mention this contentious section or its possible sources; Almeida, introduction, *GE*2 I, xxxvi–clxxii.

Hermes Trismegistus, Tat, and the Three Hermeses

This section of *GE2* begins with a short chapter entitled "On the philosopher Tat who was called Hermes, and was the son of the other Hermes Trismegistus, and who was Mercury."[2] Despite the numerous Hermetic components in the *GE*, this is the first time the name Hermes Trismegistus is mentioned. Another newcomer is his son Tat – who appears many times in the Hermetic tradition and whose name is etymologically derived from the Egyptian god Thoth. At the beginning of the chapter, Alfonso makes it clear why these names appear in this context:

> Twelve years of the reign of Joshua passed, there was announced [one who was] regarded as a great sage, he whom they called Tat, the son of Hermes, whom they called Trismegistus, as Eusebius and Jerome indicate in their chronicles. On this matter of Hermes, we find that there were three Hermeses, and all of them were wise and of great renown.[3]

The *Chronicle* of Eusebius, translated into Latin by Jerome, provides the chronological microstructure of the *GE*.[4] Eusebius introduced tables that synchronized biblical chronology with pagan events, and the *GE* uses this timeline as a guide for its historical narrative, where Alfonso inserts and elaborates on sources of diverse provenance. Sometimes, the Alfonsine compilers stitched components together in order to match a diverse array of sources with Eusebius's work. Of course, this effort does not prevent inconsistencies, as we will see with Hermes/Mercury. According to this section of the *GE*, Eusebius claimed Hermes Trismegistus lived around the time of Moses, thus Alfonso could not mention his name earlier in the *GE*; however, Hermes is now identified with Mercury, who appeared much earlier, during the time of Abraham.

According to Alfonso, Eusebius also mentioned Tat, the son of Hermes Trismegistus, who was not unknown in Castile. As we saw in Chapter Three, the sapiential book *Mukhtār al-ḥikam* (*The most select maxims*) by al-Mubashshir Ibn Fātik was translated into Castilian as *Bocados de oro* (*Morsels of gold*) around Alfonso's time. This book presents biographical sketches and maxims of ancient wise men. It includes two chapters on Hermes, one chapter on Tad (Tat), and another chapter on Çagalquius, who can be identified with Asclepius[5] – the *Bocados* refers to him as "the sage that was a disciple of Hermes."[6] Hermes, Tat, and Asclepius appear in the Hermetic treatise *Asclepius* and other ancient *Hermetica*, as well as in this section of *GE2*. I suggested in Chapter Two that, by ignoring some details from the

2 "Del philosopho Tat que ovo nombre Hermes, e fue fijo del otro Hermes Trimegisto, e fue Mercurio." *GE2* I, 48.

3 "Andados doze años del reinado de Josué fue apubliguado e tenudo por grant sabio aquel a quien dixieron Tat, que fue fijo de Hermes a que llamaron Trimegisto. assi como dizen en sus crónicas Eusebio e Jheronimo. Sobr'esta razón de Hermes fallamos que fueron tres los Hermes, e fueron todos muy sabios, e de grant fama." *GE2* I, 48.

4 Almeida, introduction, *GE2* I, xl.

5 Çagalquius is also known as Catalquius, Gagalquius, Catalqus, Zacalquis, or Catalpius in different sections of *Bocados de oro*. Crombach (ed.), *Bocados de oro*, 20a.

6 "[…] el sabio que fue diciplo de Hermes." Crombach (ed.), *Bocados de oro*, 20.

original Arabic, the unknown Castilian translator of the *Bocados* "harmonized" its description of Hermes and his followers with this section of *GE2*, although it is not possible to determine if this was actually his intent.[7]

However, the similarities between those chapters of the *Bocados* and this section of *GE2* do not go much further than mentioning Hermes, Tat, and Asclepius. Therefore, we have to reject it as a main source, although Alfonso could have been aware of the relationship between Hermes and Tat, which may indicate why he emphasizes it here. Let us see what *GE2* reveals about the three Hermeses:

> One of them was he whom they called Mercury, about whom we have already talked about in this history. We said his name means god of the merchants, because gentiles called upon him in their enterprises – in the same way as we Christians call upon our saints in our endeavours. Thus [gentiles] worshipped him and requested his assistance at all times and for everything related to commerce and regarded him as god of it. He was the son of King Jupiter and wiser than the other two Hermes, because he was a consummate master of the three knowledges of the *trivium* – grammar, dialectics, and rhetoric – as we have already told you in this history. On account of this, they called him Trismegistus, that is, a more accomplished master of these three disciplines than any other wise men at the time; and they also called him the god of the *trivium*, because those who wanted to learn something about some of these arts, or all of them, entrusted themselves to him. Now we are going to tell you about other things that happened based on the knowledge of this Hermes Trismegistus.[8]

The first thing we observe is that there are some contradictions with respect to the title of the chapter, which causes confusion when trying to determine which of the three Hermeses can be identified as Mercury, Trismegistus, or Tat, or even if two of them could be the same person. These contradictions intrigued Fraker when he studied this section; as he points out, "our text assigns the first Hermes to the time of Joshua. Pages later, indeed, this Hermes is identified with Enoch" – within the

7 As we saw, the *Mukhtār* says there were three "Ūrānī" who were considered prophets of the Greeks and Egyptians: the first was Seth, the second Agathodaemon, and the third Idrīs/Hermes; it does not include Tat and Asclepius in the triad, although it dedicates chapters to them; see Van Bladel, *Arabic Hermes*, 188–9. By eliminating the reference to the Ūrānī, *Bocados de oro* makes its version of the Hermes "dynasty" compatible with that of the *GE*. However, the *Mukhtār* indicates that Tat is the son of Hermes, whereas the Castilian translation does not.

8 "Et el uno d'ellos fue al que dixieron Mercurio, sobre cuya razón avemos ya dicho ante d'esto en esta estoria que quiere este nombre dezir tanto como dios de los mercadores, porque le llamavan los gentiles en sus mercadurías cuemo llamamos agora los cristianos a los nuestros santos en nuestras priessas, e en toda cosa e en todo tiempo que los ayudasse, e aorávanlo e teniénle por dios d'aquel mester, e fue fijo del Rey Júpiter, e más sabio que los otros dos Hermes, ca fue complidamientre maestro de los tres saberes del trivio, que son la gramática, la dialética e la rectoria, assí cuemo vos lo avemos departido en esta estoria ante d'esto. Et dixiéronle por ende este nombre Trimagisto, fascas maestro de tres saberes más complidamientre que todos los otros sabios d'aquella sazón, e llamáronle otrossí dios del trivio, e los que en alguna d'estas tres artes o en todas querién aprender algo a Mercurio se acomendauan. Agora dezir vos emos d'otras cosas que acaecieron sobre razón del saber d'este Hermes Trimegisto." *GE2* I, 48.

story of the Book of Hermes that Asclepius found.[9] I will attempt to clarify some of these details in this chapter and will show that some inconsistencies in Alfonso's text are inherited from his sources. A literal translation of the title, "On the philosopher Tat who was called Hermes, and was the son of the other Hermes Trismegistus, and who was Mercury,"[10] suggests that Tat was called Hermes, was the son of "the other Hermes Trismegistus" – implying there were several Hermeses Trismegistus – and was also Mercury. Thus, Tat is mentioned in the title of this chapter and its introductory sentence. In the chapter's final sentence, however, Alfonso announces that he is going to focus on "the knowledge of this Hermes Trismegistus." The rest of the chapters of the section follow this lead, attributing the knowledge to the book found by Asclepius and written by Hermes Trismegistus, who is identified with Enoch. Tat is not mentioned again until the brief summary at the end of the entire section, which might leave the reader confused.

Part of the problem is that the title's sentence structure is misleading. Grammar and punctuation in old Castilian are confusing, and not only due to copyists' mistakes. For example, the coordinating conjunction *e* or *et* ("and") can often be understood or translated as a comma – as happens in Latin – and other commas can be implied. Thus, we can also translate the title as: "On the philosopher Tat, who was called Hermes, and was the son of the other Hermes, Trismegistus, who was Mercury." If we interpret the title this way, Trismegistus was Mercury, but Tat was not, which solves part of the problem.

The summary at the end of the section affirms: "And this is all we told you about the knowledge of Hermes, who had the name Tat, and was the son of the other Hermes Trismegistus, who was Mercury."[11] Here it at least seems clearer that Mercury was "the other Hermes Trismegistus," and his son was Tat. However, although the title and introductory section focus on Hermes Trismegistus – with no mention of Tat – the end of the chapter claims it has been talking about the knowledge of Tat, his son. These types of summaries, which are followed by statements about what will follow, are ubiquitous in the *GE*. Since different teams working for Alfonso developed the various sections, a supervisor was needed to connect all of them. A possible explanation for this erroneous summary is that in this instance, the supervisor relied on the title of the section, and not on its content.

There are other possible justifications for the apparent inconsistencies. As I argue in this book, the Castilian king presents the figure of Mercury/Hermes Trismegistus as a model of a wise man and courtier; as such, Alfonso sought to be precise in this presentation but, unfortunately, his sources did not always help in this endeavour. Alfonso says that he read in Eusebius and Jerome that Tat, the son of Hermes Trismegistus, lived during the time of Joshua – thus, right after Moses. Since the *GE* relies on the authority of Eusebius to harmonize pagan and biblical events, Alfonso

9 Fraker, *Scope of History*, 197–8; for Hermes's "troublesome linkage to Mercury," see also Fraker, *Scope of History*, 204–5; Fraker, "Hermes Trismegistus," 90–1.

10 "Del philosopho Tat que ovo nombre Hermes, e fue fijo del otro Hermes Trimegisto, e fue Mercurio." *GE2* I, 48.

11 "E tanto vos contamos aquí de la razón del saber de Hermes, que ovo d'otra guisa nombre Tat, e fue fijo del otro Hermes Trimegisto, que fue Mercurio." *GE2* I, 55.

needs to introduce the name of Hermes and Tat at this precise historical moment. Besides, here, more than anywhere else, it is clear that Alfonso wants to identify Hermes Trismegistus with the god Mercury. We saw how Eusebius also said that *TSOI* – where the god Mercury played a significant role – took place during the time of Abraham. *GE1* follows this line of reasoning and situates *TSOI* in the age of the patriarch. This gap between Abraham and Moses, together with his difficulties in harmonizing different sources and extensively adapting pagan knowledge, might have forced Alfonso to be calculatedly ambiguous with respect to Mercury/Hermes Trismegistus and his legend.

However, there is an even larger issue with Hermes's dating in *GE2*: neither Hermes Trismegistus nor Tat are mentioned in Eusebius and Jerome's *Chronicle*, which contradicts what Alfonso says. The relevant chronological tables in the second book of the *Chronicle* contain no reference to Hermes in the twelfth year of Joshua, where Alfonso claims it should be, nor is this mentioned anywhere else in the book.[12] Why then does *GE2* introduce a reference to Hermes and erroneously claim it comes from Eusebius? Lida de Malkiel thinks that "this synchronism was gratuitously attributed to Eusebius and Jerome";[13] however, Alfonso always conveys the utmost respect for Eusebius and Jerome and quotes them accurately the majority of the time,[14] so it is difficult for me to imagine this quotation as spurious. I would like to suggest a more plausible explanation.

Francesco Patrizi (1529–97), a Venetian Neoplatonic philosopher and humanist, wrote in the third part of his *Nova de universis philosophia*, which is dedicated to Hermes Trismegistus: "It seems, however, that this Hermes Trismegistus was indeed a contemporary of Moses, but a little bit his senior; Eusebius wrote in the *Chronicle* that Cath [Tat], the son of Trismegistus, flourished in the first year of Armeus, king of Egypt, which was twenty years before the death of Moses."[15] Therefore Patrizi, a distinguished humanist who dealt with numerous ancient and medieval sources, used a version of the *Chronicle* that included a reference to Hermes and his son Tat around the time of Moses, just like in the *GE*. Patrizi places Hermes a little earlier, and Alfonso a little later, than Moses, but it looks like both of them used versions that interpolated a passage on Hermes and Tat. In fact, this kind of interpolation

12 Eusebius, *Eusebi Chronicorum canonum* 2:33. Key contemporary Hermetic tradition specialists who have tracked mentions of Hermes in ancient sources – including Christian ones – also did not spot any appearances in the *Chronicle*. However, they did find Hermes mentioned in other works by Eusebius, in *Praeparatio evangelica* in particular. See Claudio Moreschini, *Hermes Christianus* (Turnhout: Brepols, 2011), 83, 84, 153, 187, 263, and 278; Copenhaver, *Hermetica* xv, xxxi, xliii, 93, and 164; and Bull, *Tradition of Hermes*, 37, 54, 55, 75, 89, 98, 208, 237, and 387.

13 Lida de Malkiel, "La General Estoria (I)," 121–2.

14 Almeida, introduction, *GE2* I, xl.

15 "Videtur autem Hermes his Trismegistus coetaneus quidem fuisse Mosy, sed paulo senior. Scribit n. Eusebius in Chronico; Anno Armei Aegypti regis primo, Cath filium Trismegisti floruisse. Is autem annus ante Mosis obitum vigesimus circiter fuit." Patrizi, *Nova de Universis Philosophia*.III, 3r.

in chronicles, particularly in that of Eusebius, was a common practice during late antiquity and up until the Renaissance.[16]

Situating Hermes Trismegistus around the time of Moses, or even before, was also a general tradition in the pre-modern world.[17] Notably, this occurs in Augustine's *The City of God*, which provides important testimony because, as we saw earlier, Alfonso takes some references from it to characterize Mercury in *GE*1. As we will see, Augustine also identifies Mercury with Hermes Trismegistus, distinguishes between several Mercuries, and was a model for the Iberian sources on Mercury that Alfonso used. For these reasons, in the next section I want to focus on Augustine's connection to the construction of Alfonso's Hermeses.

"Elder Mercury" in Augustine's *The City of God*

The *GE* regards *The City of God* as an important historical reference, taking from it the structure of dividing the world into six ages, as well as numerous quotes. For instance, as we saw in Chapter Three, when Alfonso introduces the mythological Mercury in the allegorical/*glossae* section of *TSOI* in *GE*1,[18] he quotes *The City of God* VII verbatim, when Augustine describes Mercury as the middle courier (*medius currens*), who can be identified with the speech that runs between men and merchants – an idea that is echoed later in the *GE*2 section we are discussing here. Augustine also explains that Mercury "is called Hermes in Greek, since speech, or interpretation, which undoubtedly belongs to speech, is called *hermeneia*."[19] Therefore, the identification of the god Mercury with Hermes Trismegistus is confirmed by Augustine.

The City of God includes a chronological account of the parallel history of earthly and heavenly cities from the time of Abraham, and Augustine's layout influenced subsequent historians. Book XVIII includes a chapter on "The kings at the time when Moses was born."[20] There we find out that during Moses's time, the brother of Prometheus, Atlas, "is said to have been a great astrologer, which gave rise to the myth presenting him as carrying the sky. However, there is a mountain called by his name whose lofty height seems a more probable source for the popular belief

16 On interpolations in a translation of Eusebius's *Chronicle*, see Antonio López Fonseca and José Manuel Ruiz Vila, "Alfonso Fernández de Madrigal traductor del Génesis: una interpolación en la traducción *De las crónicas o tienpos* de Eusebio-Jerónimo," *eHumanista* 41 (2019): 360–82. See also Van Bladel, *Arabic Hermes*, 139.

17 According to a topos of Christian apologetics, Trismegistus was an ancient prophet prior to the Greeks, but he lived with Moses, after the rise of Hebraic wisdom, "from which Christianity had its origins." Moreschini, *Hermes Christianus*, 76.

18 *GE*1 I, 318.

19 "[…] ideo Ἑρμῆς Graece, quod sermo vel interpretatio, quae ad sermonem utique pertinet, ἑρμηνεία dicitur." Augustine, *Civitate Dei* VII, xiv. For my quotations from *The City of God*, I am following the Latin text in the volumes of the Loeb Classical Library. I am also checking my translation against those of the specialists in charge of the respective volumes, whom I reference in the Bibliography.

20 "Quorum regum aetate Moyses natus sit." Augustine, *Civitate Dei* XVIII, viii.

about him supporting the heavens."[21] This information is also found in Eusebius's *Chronicle*[22] – but then Augustine goes on to introduce Mercury – who is absent in Eusebius:

> Mercury is also said to have lived in these times; [he was] the grandson of Atlas by his daughter Maia, a subject familiar even in popular literature. He was noted for his skill in many arts, which he also transmitted to men, and as a result of this service, they decreed that he would become a god following his death, or even believed that he was one.[23]

This last comment about Mercury's skills and the euhemeristic interpretation of them is reminiscent of the portrait of Mercury that we saw in *TSOI* in *GE*1. Therefore, the placement of Mercury during Moses's time, or slightly after him, has a precedent in *The City of God*. Soon after, Augustine not only directly identifies Mercury with Hermes Trismegistus but also points to the existence of several Mercuries:

> For as far as philosophy is concerned [...] studies of that kind shone in those lands [i.e., Egypt] around the era of Mercury, whom they called Trismegistus, long before the wise men and philosophers of Greece, to be sure, but after Abraham and Isaac and Jacob and Joseph, and indeed after Moses. For research shows that it was at the time of Moses's birth that Atlas lived, that great astronomer, brother of Prometheus and maternal grandfather of the elder Mercury, whose grandson was the aforesaid Mercury Trismegistus.[24]

Here we find several contact points with the story of the three Hermeses in *GE*2. First, Augustine affirms that this Mercury, related to Egypt, was called Trismegistus. Augustine also identifies him with the mythological grandson of Atlas. Since Atlas

21 "Frater eius Atlans magnus fuisse astrologus dicitur; unde occasionem fabula invenit ut eum caelum portare confingeret; quamvis mons eius nomine nuncupetur, cuius altitudine potius caeli portatio in opinionem vulgi venisse videatur." Augustine, *Civitate Dei* XVIII, viii.

22 Eusebius, *Eusebi Chronicorum canonum* 2:21. Bull thinks that Augustine relies on Eusebius when he makes Atlas and Moses coeval, and that Cyril does the same. In *Against Julian*, Cyril affirms that Atlas, the maternal grandfather of Hermes, was born when Moses was seven. See Bull, "Hermes between Pagans and Christians: The Nag Hammadi Hermetica in context," *The Nag Hammadi Codices and Late Antique Egypt* (2018), *Byzantinische Bibliographie Online*, https://www.degruyter.com/database/BYZ/entry/byz.812ed353-3727-48c8-8ea8-0987979ea4db/html (last accessed May 13, 2023), 242–3. Bull refers to Cyril, *Contra Julianum*. I.11.

23 "His temporibus etiam Mercurius fuisse perhibetur, nepos Atlantis ex Maia filia, quod vulgatiores etiam litterae personant. Multarum autem artium peritus claruit quas et hominibus tradidit; quo merito eum post mortem deum esse voluerunt sive etiam crediderunt." Augustine, *Civitate Dei* XVIII, viii.

24 "Nam quod adtinet ad philosophiam [...] circa tempora Mercurii, quem Trismegistum vocaverunt, in illis terris eius modi studia claruerunt, longe quidem ante sapientes vel philosophos Graeciae, sed tamen post Abraham et Isaac et Iacob et Ioseph, nimirum etiam post ipsum Moysen. Eo quippe tempore quo Moyses natus est fuisse reperitur Atlas ille magnus astrologus, Promethei frater, maternus avus Mercurii maioris, cuius nepos fuit Trismegistus iste Mercurius." Augustine, *Civitate Dei* XVIII, xxxix. On this quotation and Hermes Trismegistus in Augustine, see Moreschini, *Hermes Christianus*, 74–9.

had been alive at the time of Moses's birth, Mercury – the grandson of Atlas – must have lived after Moses. But Augustine adds that this was "the elder Mercury" (*Mercurii maioris*), which confirms the existence of at least two Mercuries, an elder and a younger one.

A younger Mercury appeared earlier in *The City of God* VIII, in a passage where Augustine famously quotes, comments on, and criticizes the Hermetic treatise *Asclepius*, which identifies two Hermeses. Bull highlights that there is another Hermetic treatise, the *Korê kosmou*, where two Hermeses are identified; in it, Isis tells Horus "about a primordial and celestial Hermes, in addition to a Hermes who instructed herself and her husband."[25] *The City of God* VIII refers to an episode in the *Asclepius* where Hermes Trismegistus informs Asclepius about the prophecy of the future ruin of Egypt and neglecting the cult of the statues – which Augustine interprets as the arrival of Christianity.[26] As I pointed out in Chapter Two, I think the prophecy that King Samnetico of Egypt recounts to his son Vafre in *GE*4 is strongly reminiscent of this passage from the *Asclepius*, which Alfonso might have taken from *The City of God*.[27] Augustine clarifies that the character prophesying in "that same book [i.e., the *Asclepius*], about whom we are dealing with, is Hermes himself."[28] A little later he directly quotes the *Asclepius* – and allegedly one Hermes: "'Does not Hermes, my ancestor whose name I bear, have his dwelling in the city to which he has given his name, and does he not help and protect all men who come from every place?'" Augustine clarifies: "For this elder Hermes, that is to say, Mercury, whom he calls his ancestor, is said to have his dwelling in Hermopolis, that is, in the town that bears his name."[29] In this way, Augustine acknowledges that the Hermes talking in the *Asclepius* had an ancestor, the elder Hermes (*Hermes maior*), and clarifies that the city where he had sanctuary is Hermopolis. The Egyptian city of Khemenu was called Hermopolis, "The city of Hermes," by the Greeks. As we have already discussed, the Greeks identified Hermes with Thoth, whose main cult centre was in Khemenu. Hermes and Thoth were subsequently worshipped in the same temple in Hermopolis.[30] This city was also home to the cult of the Babylonian god Nabû, who Aramean immigrant workers introduced to the city.[31] Therefore, the cult of Hermes Trismegistus, who was "constructed from the complex functions and nature of the Egyptian Thoth, and drawing upon the similar roles of Hermes, Nabû, Sin and other deities whose spheres of power encompassed the revelation of hidden

25 Bull, *Tradition of Hermes*, 99.
26 Augustine, *Civitate Dei* VIII, xxvi–xxvii.
27 *GE*4 I, 46.
28 "Hermes ipse, de quo nunc agitur, in eodem ipso libro." Augustine, *Civitate Dei* VIII, xxvi.
29 "Adiungens deinde aliud: 'Hermes,' inquit, 'cuius avitum mihi nomen est, nonne in sibi cognomine patria consistens omnes mortales undique venientes adiuvat atque conservat?' Hic enim Hermes maior, id est Mercurius, quem dicit avum suum fuisse, in Hermopoli, hoc est in sui nominis civitate, esse perhibetur." Augustine, *Civitate Dei* VIII, xxvi.
30 Donald Bailey, "Classical Architecture," in Christina Riggs (ed.), *The Oxford Handbook of Roman Egypt* (Oxford: Oxford University Press, 2012), 192.
31 Bezalel Porten, *Archives from Elephantine: The Life of an Ancient Jewish Military Colony* (Oakland: University of California Press, 1968), 166.

wisdom,"[32] might have originated in Hermopolis. In this part of *The City of God* VIII Augustine is trying to demonstrate that gods like Hermes and Aesculapius, who were worshipped in Egyptian temples, had been historical men – the references in the *Asclepius* to the elder ancestors of Hermes and Asclepius is proof of this.[33]

Augustine also probably had Cicero's *De natura Deorum* in mind – a work he quotes in other parts of *The City of God*.[34] In a passage that develops a skeptical argument about the existence of gods, Cicero explains that, according to different authors, five Mercuries have existed, of whom I want to single out the last three:

> The third is purported to be the son of the third Jove and Maia, as well as the father of Pan by Penelope. The fourth has the Nile for [his] father; the Egyptians consider it is impious to pronounce his name. The fifth, worshipped by the people of Pheneus, is said to have killed Argus and consequently to have fled in exile to Egypt, where he gave the Egyptians their laws and letters. His Egyptian name is Theuth.[35]

Thus, Cicero separates Mercury, son of Maia – daughter of Atlas – from the Mercury who killed Argus. In contrast, as we saw in Chapter Three, these are features of the lone Mercury depicted in Ovid's *Metamorphoses*. Cicero also says that his fifth Mercury fled to Egypt and gave the Egyptians their letters, whereas Augustine points out that it was actually Isis who did this[36] – as occurs in the *GE* and other testimonies. It is also remarkable that the fourth and fifth Mercuries are linked to Egypt, and the last one is called Theuth, that is, Thoth, the Egyptian god associated with Hermes – who merged with Hermes and became Hermes Trismegistus, and whose name later evolves into Tat.[37] Bull thinks that Cicero's list of Mercuries is based on the Egyptian theology of Memphis, as are the two Hermeses of pseudo-Manetho, whom I will introduce below.[38] Cicero was also familiar with Plato's *Phaedrus*,[39] which includes the myth of Theuth – a clear embodiment of Thoth – who proposes teaching letters to the Egyptians to his king, Thamus, who turns down the idea because he prefers his subjects to rely on memory.[40] Therefore, Augustine gathers his ideas about Mercury from both classical authors (e.g., Cicero) and the Hermetic tradition (e.g., the *Asclepius*).

32 Green, *City of the Moon God*, 85.

33 In Augustine, *Civitate Dei* VIII, xxvi, which quotes *Asclepius*, 37 (see translation in Copenhaver, *Hermetica*, 90).

34 For instance, Augustine, *Civitate Dei* IV, xxx.

35 "[…] tertius Iove tertio natus et Maia, ex quo et Penelopa Pana natum ferunt, quartus Nilo patre, quem Aegyptii nefas habent nominare, quintus quem colunt Pheneatae, qui Argum dicitur interemisse ob eamque causam Aegyptum profugisse atque Aegyptiis leges et litteras tradidisse: hunc Aegyptii Theuth appellant, eodemque nomine anni primus mensis apud eos vocatur." Cicero, *De natura deorum*.III, xxiii. I am following the translation by H. Rackham in Loeb's edition, with minor changes.

36 Augustine, *Civitate Dei* XVIII, xxxix.

37 On Cicero's Hermeses' possible connections with Egypt, see Bull, *Tradition of Hermes*, 88.

38 Bull, *Tradition of Hermes*, 88.

39 Cicero expresses ideas from Plato's *Phaedrus* in *De Oratore*.II.310, II.325, II.359, and III.24.

40 Plato, *Phaedrus*, 274–5.

Before ending this section I want to further discuss this *Hermes maior*, who, according to Augustine, was Mercury and lived in Hermopolis – a feature that associates him with Trismegistus. This *Hermes maior* will serve as the main reference for Isidore, who talks about two Mercuries in his *Chronica maiora* and introduces the second one as *alter Mercurius* (the other Mercury). Isidore and Augustine were sources for Lucas de Tuy, who presents a *Hermes minor* as one of three Mercuries in the *Chronicon mundi*, which I consider to be a direct source for the story in *GE2*. The transition from two to three Mercuries in Lucas de Tuy can only be explained by referencing Arabic sources, where the story of the three Hermeses was diffused. However, Lucas de Tuy neither read Arabic nor used sources in that language; he used intermediary sources in Latin. Let us examine the Arabic story of the three Hermeses, how it came to appear in Latin authors, how they then incorporated it into Christian traditions – departing from Augustine – and how finally it was adopted by Lucas de Tuy, and then from him by Alfonso.

Abū Maʿshar and the Arabic Legend of the Three Hermeses

The most influential account of the history of the three Hermeses is by the Persian Abū Maʿshar (787–886), also known in the West as Albumasar. Since Alfonso talks about three Hermeses in *GE2*, Fraker suggests he was influenced by the Arabic legend of the three Hermeses and points out that one iteration was that of Abū Maʿshar – which he quotes and relates to *GE2*'s account.[41] Thus, we need to assess Abū Maʿshar's version to determine if it is indeed Alfonso's main influence, and also to consider through which channels it could have reached him. Even though Abū Maʿshar lived far away from Castile, we will see below how the Iberian Peninsula seems to have been an important centre for the transmission of his narrative – in Arabic, Latin, and then Spanish.

Abū Maʿshar traveled from the Khorasan region – in the north-eastern part of modern-day Iran – to the Abbasid court in Baghdad. His astronomical theories were influenced by Greek, Zoroastrian, Mesopotamian, and Indian astrology, as well as by Hermetic traditions from the city of Ḥarrān, where Hermes was considered a prophet.[42] His *Kitāb al-ulūf* (*Book of thousands*) is a "strange treatise of astrological history,"[43] which has only survived in fragments quoted by other authors.[44] One of these fragments is the story of the three Hermeses. In his study of the Arabic Hermes, Van Bladel focuses on five Arabic authors who transmitted Abū Maʿshar's legend: Ibn Juljul, Sāʾid al-Andalusī, Ibn al-Qifṭī (d. 1248), Ibn Abī Uṣaybiʿa (d. 1270), and Ibn Nubāta (1287–1366).[45] It is significant that Ibn Juljul and Sāʾid al-Andalusī, the two Andalusi authors, and also the earliest ones, claim to be quoting Abū Maʿshar

41 Fraker, *Scope of History*, 209–10.
42 Pingree, *The Thousands of Abū Maʿshar*, 16–18.
43 Charles S. F. Burnett, "The Legend of the Three Hermes and Abū Ma'Shar's *Kitāb Al-Ulūf* in the Latin Middle Ages," *Journal of the Warburg and Courtauld Institutes* 39, no. 1 (1976): 231.
44 See Pingree's edition of *The Thousands of Abū Maʿshar*, in which he attempts to reconstruct the book as much as possible through the various remaining fragments.
45 Van Bladel, *Arabic Hermes*, 122–35.

directly – whereas Ibn al-Qifṭī (Syrian) and Ibn Abī Uṣaybiʿa (Egyptian) refer to Ibn Juljul as an intermediary source. Therefore, the Andalusi authors were instrumental in the transmission of the legend. Furthermore, the Egyptian Ibn Nubāta included the story in a book about Andalusi historical characters.

Cottrell has convincingly questioned Van Bladel's reconstruction of the history of the three Hermeses and his assumptions that the legend originated with Abū Maʿshar and that the only significant authors to spread Abū Maʿshar's legend were those mentioned above.[46] However, I suggest that Abū Maʿshar was at least the origin of the legend of the three Hermeses that reached Alfonso. These dynamics, as well as the academic success of Van Bladel's theory, push me to explain this theory and to track its path from its origin until it reached Alfonso.

It is a well-known fact that the *Kitāb al-ulūf*, which contains the legend, was available in the Iberian Peninsula in the tenth century, because Ibn Juljul's and Sāʾid al-Andalusī's versions follow it. I am going to mainly quote the latter for his proximity – physical and intellectual – to Alfonso.[47] Sāʾid al-Andalusī was an astronomer, mathematician, and *qāḍī* (judge) in Toledo, where he died just before the city was conquered by the Christians. As we saw, Toledo would be a centre of translation from Arabic and then become part of Alfonso's kingdom. Al-Andalusī's book, *Kitāb tabaqāt al-umam* (*Book of the categories of nations*), is a genuine history of the sciences *avant la lettre*, in which information is arranged according to the different nations through which they passed. Sāʾid al-Andalusī claims that the knowledge was transmitted from eastern to western nations until it arrived in al-Andalus, whereas for Alfonso the final recipient would be his own kingdom – in this way, both authors offer versions of the *translatio studii* theory. Since the *Tabaqāt* is organized in nations, Sāʾid al-Andalusī divides Abū Maʿshar's account and refers to the Hermeses on two separate occasions: once in the chapter on Babylon and once in the chapter on Egypt. This idea is connected to the abovementioned evidence that Hermes Trismegistus, who has an Egyptian origin, absorbed features of the Babylonian god Nabû, who is astrologically linked to the planet Mercury.

Sāʾid al-Andalusī explains how the Babylonians were interested in astronomical observations and celestial secrets, and they profited from that knowledge "to build temples which drew the power of the stars [...] and to ensure that their rays [were] projected on [the temples]"; they also "made talismans and cultivated other arts related to magic."[48] We can observe how these astrological and magical concepts, such as planetary rays and astrologically designed temples, are related both to the *Picatrix* and the historical and geographical Arabic sources that the *GE* uses – for

46 See Emily Cottrell, "'L'Hermès Arabe de Kevin van Bladel' et la question du rôle de la literature Sassanide dans la presence d'écrits hermètiques et astrologiques en langue arabe," *Bibliotheca Orientalis* 72 (2015): 377–92.

47 I follow the translation of Eloísa Llavero Ruíz and Andrés Martínez Lorca but also keep in mind Van Bladel's rendering in *The Arabic Hermes*; I will complement both with Ibn Juljul's version, which is also included in Van Bladel.

48 Sā'id al-Andalusī, *Historia de la filosofía y de las ciencias o libro de las categorías de las naciones [Kitāb Ṭabaqāt al-umam]*, eds Eloísa Llavero Ruíz and Andrés Martínez Lorca (Madrid: Trotta, 2000), 77.

instance, in the story of Doluca that we discussed in Chapter Two. Sāʾid al-Andalusī also specifies that:

> The most known and illustrious of all the Chaldean sages is Hermes the Babylonian, contemporary of the Greek philosopher *Suqrāṭ* [Socrates]. Abū Maʿshar mentioned in his *Book of thousands* [*Kitāb al-ulūf*] that it was this Hermes who restored the majority of the Ancients' books about astronomy and other branches of philosophy and that he had compiled numerous books on various sciences.[49]

Later al-Andalusī comments on some of this Babylonian Hermes's astrological theories, such as the *maṭāriḥ shuʿāʿāt al-kawākib* (the projections of the astral rays),[50] which connect him with Arab astrological beliefs and Arabic works that would eventually be translated into Latin, especially *De radiis* (*On the rays*) by al-Kindī.[51] Since he has already introduced one of the Hermeses, Sāʾid al-Andalusī seizes the opportunity to quote Abū Maʿshar and introduce the other two in this chapter:

> Abū Maʿshar says: "Various Hermeses [*al-Harāmis*] existed, the first of them lived before the Flood, and, as the Hebrews claim, he is the prophet Enoch [*Khanūj*], which is to say Idrīs – peace be upon him. After the Flood, there were other Hermeses who possessed vast knowledge and discernment, yet the most remarkable of them were just two: the first of them is the Babylonian that we have just mentioned, and the other a disciple of the sage Pythagoras [*Phīthāgūras*] who lived in Egypt.[52]

Later, in the chapter on Egypt, Sāʾid al-Andalusī reasserts that the first Hermes had lived there:

> A group of sages pretended that all the known sciences before the Flood were all invented by Hermes I, who lived in the plateau of Upper Egypt. This figure is [the one] to whom the Hebrews give the name Enoch, son of Jared, son of Mahalalel, son of Enos, son of Seth, son of Adam, and is the prophet Idrīs, peace be upon him [...]. Hermes was the first to predict the Flood and announced that it was a heavenly punishment of water and fire that would reach the earth. Because of this, and fearing that the knowledge of the sciences and arts would disappear, he built the pyramids and temples that are in the plateau of Upper Egypt. In them, he represented all the arts and instruments, and he described all sciences with the goal of conserving them for generations to come, out of fear that his legacy would disappear from the planet.[53]

In his quotation of this same passage, Ibn Juljul specifies that Hermes I "built the temples [*al-barābī*] [...] and the mountain known as the *birbā* of Akhmīm, which he chiselled out, portraying in it carvings of all the arts and their uses."[54] These accounts are clearly connected to the "Hermetic Egypt" described by al-Waṣīfī and al-Masʿūdī, whom Alfonso used as a source for the story of Doluca and other parts

[49] Al-Andalusī, *Historia de la filosofía*, 77.
[50] Al-Andalusī, *Historia de la filosofía*, 78.
[51] On this treatise, see Saif, *Arabic Influences*, 30.
[52] Al-Andalusī, *Historia de la filosofía*, 77.
[53] Al-Andalusī, *Historia de la filosofía*, 105–6.
[54] Translation in Van Bladel, *Arabic Hermes*, 126.

of the *GE*. Al-Masʿūdī describes the Egyptian temples – transliterated as *berba* in Castilian. I mentioned in Chapter Two how al-Masʿūdī mentions that Dhū l-Nūn al-Miṣrī al-Ikhmīmī visited temples and pyramids in Akhmīm to study the knowledge hidden in their inscriptions. Stories about recovering the knowledge that Hermes saved are also connected to the pseudo-Aristotelian *Hermetica* and related literature on Balīnūs (Apollonius of Tyana) – as we saw earlier.[55] These traditions align with Sāʾid al-Andalusī, who, after describing how Hermes I saved wisdom for posterity, explains how some wise men lived in Egypt after the Flood, and they cultivated many knowledges, especially "talismans, charms, burning mirrors, and alchemy [*al-kīmiyā*]." Sāʾid al-Andalusī mentions Hermes II as among those sages – which seems to be a mistake, because this figure must be Hermes III, also an Egyptian, according to the list he provided in the chapter on Babylon. According to Sāʾid al-Andalusī "this wise man travelled throughout the entire country, going from one city to the other, and knew the history of their monuments and the nature of the people who lived there. He composed an excellent book on the art of alchemy and another one on poisonous animals."[56] Ibn Juljul offers a slightly longer version of the third Hermes and adds that

> he lived in the city of Egypt. He was after the Flood. He is the author of *Poisonous animals*. He was a philosopher and a physician, knowledgeable in the natures of lethal drugs and infectious animals. He travelled around in different countries, wandering in them, knowing the foundations of cities, their natures, and the natures of their peoples. He is the author of a valuable discourse on the art of alchemy; part of it is related to crafts like glass, stringing precious stones, implements of clay, and such things.[57]

Thus, the famous story of the three Hermes by Abū Maʾshar is not only connected to that of the three Hermeses in *GE2* but also with many other Arabic sources that were used in the *GE* or other works by Alfonso – such as the *Lapidario* and his astrological texts. Ibn Juljul also adds that the third Hermes had "a student who is known, whose name was Asclepius."[58] This character closely connects that account to the one in the *GE*. We therefore have to wonder where the story of the three Hermeses originated and if they really came to the *GE* through Abū Maʿshar.

In his (reconstructed) edition of the *Kitāb al-ulūf*, Pingree suggests that the legend of the three Hermeses is Abū Maʿshar's own development, and he would have been influenced by his forerunner Ibn Nawbakht (d. 923), an Iraqi astrologer of Iranian origin. According to Pingree, Ibn Nawbakht read the *Pentateuch* of Dorotheus of Sidon (first century BCE), known in the Western world as *Carmen astrologicum*. This book was written in Greek, and the Arabic translation is based on an earlier translation into Pahlavi. The *Carmen astrologicum* mentions the "praiseworthy by three natures, Hermes, the King of Egypt."[59] According to Pingree, Ibn Nawbakht, due to Ḥarrānian influences, transformed this Hermes into a Babylonian sage who

55 See Martin Plessner, "Balīnūs."
56 Al-Andalusī, *Historia de la filosofía*, 107.
57 Translation in Van Bladel, *Arabic Hermes*, 126–7.
58 Van Bladel, *Arabic Hermes*, 126–7.
59 Dorotheus of Sidon, *Carmen Astrologicum*, 20.

becomes king of Egypt in his lost – but partially preserved through quotations – *Kitāb al-nahmaṭān fi'l-mawālīd* (*Book of the nahmaṭān* [?] *concerning nativities*). Then Ibn Nawbakht inspired Abū Maʿshar who, influenced by the epithet "Trismegistus," developed the idea of the three Hermeses, one of them being the Babylonian sage.[60] In my opinion, Hermes's ancient connections with Babylon and the god Nabû cast doubts on this model. Other objections have been expressed by Cottrell[61] and Van Bladel. The last offers his own hypothesis on the origin of the three Hermeses in Abū Maʿshar, which is also based on lost or partially preserved works.

Van Bladel focuses on the influence that Greek Byzantine chronographers had on Abū Maʿshar. The chronographers made amendments to and quoted from previous chronicles, which at times creates difficulty in determining the original authors of certain writings.[62] Besides, some of the sources used by Greek chronographers were not completely reliable. Among these sources, Van Bladel singles out the *Book of Sothis*, allegedly written by the Egyptian historian Manetho (third century BCE), which actually must be "a work of Roman Egyptian chronography dating at the latest from about 400 CE, but probably written considerably earlier."[63] The *Book of Sothis* includes the story of two Hermeses, the antediluvian one and his postdiluvian successor. As Broek explains, according to pseudo-Manetho,

> Thot, the first Hermes, had engraved his wisdom on steles in the "sacred language" and in hieroglyphs. After the Flood, "the second Hermes" who was the son of Agathodaemon and the father of Tat, translated these texts from the sacred language into Greek and deposited them in books in the inner sanctuaries [*adyta*] of Egyptian temples.[64]

The reference to the Flood makes pseudo-Manetho's account the most direct precedent to Abū Maʿshar. Centuries later, the Byzantine chronicler Syncellus (d. *c.* 810 CE) quotes and comments on the story of the two Hermeses from the *Book of Sothis* and claims that he is taking it from a (now lost) work by the Egyptian monk Panodorus (*c.* 400 CE).[65] It cannot be proven that Abū Maʿshar used either Syncellus or Panodorus. However, Panodorus had a contemporary, an Alexandrian monk called Annianus (fifth century), whose chronicle, now lost, is also mentioned by Syncellus. According to Van Bladel, since the works of Annianus and Panodorus were connected, "there is every reason to assume that Annianus mentioned [...] the story of the two Hermeses in his chronicle."[66] Given that Abū Maʿshar cites Annianus by name in another book, the *Kitāb al-qirānāt* (*Book of conjunctions*), and there are

60 This is my summarized version of the complex explanation provided by Pingree, *Thousands of Abū Maʿshar*, vii–viii.

61 She even offers her own – and I think more accurate translation – of the *Kitāb al-Nahmaṭān*'s quotation in the *Fihrist* of al-Nadīm. Cottrell, "L'Hermès Arabe," 377–401.

62 He refers to the specific case of Annianus: Van Bladel, *Arabic Hermes*, 139.

63 Van Bladel, *Arabic Hermes*, 154.

64 Van den Broek, "Hermes Trismegistus I," 477. On Manetho, see also Bull, *Tradition of Hermes*, 49, 87, and 121.

65 Van Bladel, *Arabic Hermes*, 137. On Syncellus's account of the pseudo-Manetho, see also Copenhaver, *Hermetica*, xv–xvi.

66 Van Bladel, *Arabic Hermes*, 138.

"indications" that he took from him "more than a few details about ancient history," Van Bladel comes to the conclusion that "until more evidence comes to light, we must conclude that Annianus is almost certainly the mediating source for the tale given in the *Book of Sothis*," and then in Abū Maʿshar.[67] Van Bladel skilfully connects other dots to uphold this theory; however, it still seems somewhat speculative to me. At least within this theory the importance of Christian chroniclers, who transmitted the legend and followed the model of Eusebius,[68] is noteworthy, as this influence also occurs in the *GE*.

We find a similar construction in the explanation of the origin of the third Hermes. Van Bladel highlights that, in his account of the three Hermeses, just after discussing the second, Ibn Juljul states: "That is what Abū Maʿshar stated," and then continues and discusses the third one. This detail leads Van Bladel to assert that the story of the third Hermes may come from another source. He finds a hint as to what this source may be in Ibn Nubāta. This fourteenth-century Egyptian poet wrote a book that explains in detail a famous work of Andalusi satire that was full of names of significant historical figures. Among his stories, Ibn Nubāta includes what he claims Abū Maʿshar said about Hermes. Van Bladel emphasizes that "his account contains slightly different sections on Hermes" than those of Ibn Juljul, which makes him think that Ibn Nubāta is not following Ibn Juljul but rather Abū Maʿshar, or another source.[69] Ibn Nubāta includes most of the information about the first Hermes that we saw in works by previous authors, but then he adds a strange excerpt where he introduces Asclepius as a successor or disciple of Hermes and identifies him with Balīnūs (Apollonius of Tiana). This identification is justified through a bizarre etymology similar to what, supposedly, happened with Aristotle's name. According to Ibn Nubāta, Balīnūs took "the sciences and secrets" (*al-ʿulūm wa al-asrār*) from Aristotle. Of course, the reference to Balīnūs seems connected with the Arabic literature on Apollonius, especially the *Sirr al-ḫalīqa* (*The secret of creation*), whereas the mention of Aristotle and Hermes leads us to the pseudo-Aristotelian *Hermetica* – topics that I introduced earlier in this book. Despite how well he knows the *Hermetica* genre, Van Bladel "finds no reason to doubt" that these sentences could have originally appeared in Abū Maʿshar.[70] Even though Ibn Nubāta also comments that "others claim that Hermes, the master of Balīnūs, was after the Flood, and was not this [Hermes],"[71] he does not assert that a specific number of Hermeses existed.

Ibn Nubāta omits the reference to the second Hermes that we find in Ibn Juljul and Ṣāʿid al-Andalusī. However, the information that previous authors attributed to the third Hermes is introduced by Ibn Nubāta with the phrase "al-Kindī said," and Van Bladel uses this statement to justify his claim about the origin of the third Hermes. According to Van Bladel, "Abū Maʿshar's text must have originally cited

67 Van Bladel, *Arabic Hermes*, 146 and 154.
68 Van Bladel, *Arabic Hermes*, 137.
69 Van Bladel, *Arabic Hermes*, 157.
70 Van Bladel, *Arabic Hermes*, 159.
71 Van Bladel, *Arabic Hermes*, 158.

al-Kindī," but his name disappeared from the traditions that we saw earlier.[72] In his *Fihrist*, Ibn al-Nadīm famously says that Abū Maʿshar took advice or teachings from al-Kindī.[73] Ibn al-Nadīm also said that al-Kindī was familiar with a philosophical Hermetic text,[74] because one of his disciples, al-Sarakhsī (d. 899), wrote about the Sabeans of Ḥarrān, as I mentioned in Chapter One.[75] According to Van Bladel, al-Kindī developed an account of a more recent Hermes from al-Sarakhsī or a related source, and then Abū Maʿshar used that account for his third Hermes.[76] Like Pingree, Van Bladel thinks that the idea of three Hermeses is Abū Maʿshar's development, "perhaps in order to fill out an idea of a 'triplicate Hermes' [*Hirmis al-muthalath*],"[77] from the original Trismegistus nickname. In my opinion, Ibn Nubāta's evidence is too weak to support the claim about the origin of the third Hermes in al-Kindī. Ibn Nubāta wrote four centuries after Abū Maʿshar and does not specify the number of Hermeses, and it seems clear that he is attaching a number of extemporaneous sources to his account. Ibn Nubāta claims that al-Kindī wrote that Hermes "is the master of the Andalusi talismans."[78] It is extremely difficult to believe that the fame of the Andalusi talismans (and magic) reached al-Kindī, because the first known and most important Andalusi book of this kind, *Ghāyat al-ḥakīm*, was written a century after al-Kindī's death in 873. We also know that the *Ghāya* was known in fourteenth-century northern Africa through Ibn Khaldūn; thus, its fame could have reached Ibn Nubāta through other channels.

Cottrell also cast doubts on Van Bladel's theory, arguing that the legend of the three Hermeses has an ancient origin that predates Abū Maʿshar, who could have taken it from different sources. According to Cottrell, in addition to the two Hermeses found in the *Asclepius*, we have to take into account the third Hermes mentioned by the Roman emperor Julien the Apostate (331–62 CE), who said that "the Egyptians, as they reckon up the names of not a few wise men among themselves, can boast that they possess many successors of Hermes, I mean of Hermes who in his third manifestation visited Egypt."[79] Fraker, following Plessner, also thinks that "the account of Abū Maʿshar is but one variant of a widespread archetypical Hermes story."[80] In this vein, Walbridge asserts that "the notion of the three *Hermai* did not necessarily originate with the Muslims," and the Arabic version might not have originated with pseudo-Manetho but "from some other Graeco-Egyptian attempts to provide a plausible historical setting for the *Hermetica*."[81] In fact, as Fraker

72 Van Bladel, *Arabic Hermes*, 158.

73 Al-Nadim, *The Fihrist: A 10th Century AD Survey of Islamic Culture*, ed. Bayard Dodge (Chicago: Kazi Publications, 1998), 335.22–3.

74 Al-Nadim, *Fihrist*, 385.1–2, in Van Bladel, *Arabic Hermes*, 160–1.

75 On al-Sarakhsī, see Mattila, "Sabians," 98–104.

76 Van Bladel, *Arabic Hermes*, 161–2.

77 Van Bladel, *Arabic Hermes*, 161–2.

78 Van Bladel, *Arabic Hermes*, 158.

79 Julian the Apostate, *Against the Galilaeans*.176B. Cottrell points to this third Hermes from antiquity in "L'Hermès Arabe," 378 and 387.

80 Fraker, *Scope of History*, 209.

81 John Walbridge, *The Wisdom of the Mystic East: Suhrawardi and Platonic Orientalism* (New York: State University of New York Press, 2001), 21.

deduces from the account of pseudo-Manetho by Syncellus given in Copenhaver, "Tat is at once the son of Hermes Thrice Great and a Hermes in his own right."[82] A similar suggestion is provided by Bull.[83] This interpretation would mean that pseudo-Manetho talked about three Hermeses – and, as we saw, the *GE* echoes this tradition by also including Tat among the three. Abū Maʿshar does not mention Tat, but as we saw, this character appears in the *Mukhtār al-ḥikam* – *Bocados de oro* is a translation of this Arabic text – after Hermes, the third of the Ūrānī, who lived before the Flood. Mentions of Agathodaemon, Hermes, Tat, and the Flood could all connect the version of the *Mukhtār* with that of pseudo-Manetho. In fact, the *Ghāya* provides evidence that al-Qurṭubī was also aware of the existence of several Hermeses, because he affirms that in Būdashīr's time, the first Hermes made eighty-five images (talismans) at the source of the Nile in order to safeguard the continuous stream of its waters. As Pingree indicates in his edition, the page where this passage is found was omitted in the *Picatrix*, the Latin translation ordered by Alfonso; but we do not know if it was included in the intermediary and lost Spanish translation, and the Castilian king might have known about several Hermeses from that source.[84]

Despite the shaky elements in Van Bladel's theory that I've highlighted above, and Cottrell's own criticisms, Van Bladel's hypothesis about the three Arabic Hermeses appears in his entry for the *Encyclopaedia of Islam* and seems to be canonical.[85] Since earlier specialists have connected the story of the three Hermeses in the *GE* to Abū Maʿshar's account,[86] which my own inquiry also suggests, I have considered it important to closely examine the theory and its most recent developments. However, I think that the story of the three Hermeses in the *GE* is a mixture of sources from different traditions. I also believe that its main inspiration does not come directly from Abū Maʿshar but from an intermediary source very close to Alfonso: Lucas de Tuy. In order to track how the three Hermeses came down to Lucas de Tuy, we have to examine the first Latin versions of the legend, which are also found in the Iberian Peninsula.

Three Hermeses in Three Twelfth-Century Alchemical and Cosmological Treatises

Three centuries after the death of Abū Maʿshar, the legend of the three Hermeses appears in three prologues to Latin works that claim they are transmitting the antediluvian wisdom of the Hermetic tradition. They are connected to each other and included in three Arabic alchemical works: *Liber de compositione alchemiae*

82 Fraker, "Hermes Trismegistus," 90; and Copenhaver, *Hermetica*, xv–xvi.

83 Bull, *Tradition of Hermes*, 121.

84 In *Ghāya* IV.3, 311–12, and *Picatrix*, 189, note. See also David Pingree, "The Ṣābians of Ḥarrān and the Classical Tradition," *International Journal of the Classical Tradition* 9, no. 1 (2002): 25; and as he indicates, for the legends linking Hermes and Būdashīr, consult Ingolf Vereno, *Studien zum ältesten alchimistischen Schrifttum* (Islamkundliche Untersuchungen 155) (Berlin: Schwarz, 1992), 241–6.

85 Kevin van Bladel, "Hermes and Hermetica," in Fleet et al. (eds), *Encyclopaedia of Islam, THREE*.

86 See especially Fraker, *Scope of History*, 208–9.

(*The book on the composition of alchemy*) by Morienus, *Septem tractatus Hermetis sapientia triplicis* (*The seven treatises on the wisdom of the triple Hermes*),[87] and *Liber de sex rerum principiis* (*The book on the six principles of things*).[88] The exact dates and the authorship of these texts are debatable, but they probably all date from the second half of the twelfth century. Plessner connected the prologues with Abū Maʿshar's legend of the three Hermeses, for they have commonalities – such as a reference to the Flood.[89] Based on this reference in Plessner, Fraker makes a connection between these prologues and the three Hermeses of the *GE* and briefly points out their similarities and differences, but he did not take the analysis beyond that.[90] Using more recent editions and scholarly sources, I will further develop the assessment of those prologues and then suggest intermediary links – unnoticed until now – between them and the *GE*.

The *Liber de compositione alchemiae* includes a "Prologue of [Robert of] Chester" (*Praefatio Castrensis*), in which he states that he translated the book in 1144 and talks "about the three Mercuries" (*De tribus Mercuriis*). Chester was an English Arabist who worked in the Iberian Peninsula in the 1140s, when he also translated the famous algebra book by al-Khwārizmī. In his edition of this work, Ruska expressed doubts about this attribution, but Lemay has convincingly confirmed it.[91] This book is, for the most part, a translation of the Arabic *Risālat Maryānus al-rāhib al-ḥakīm li al-amīr Khālid Ibn Yazīd* (*The letter of the wise monk Maryanus to Prince Khālid Ibn Yazīd*). It consists of a dialogue in which the legendary monk Morienus Romanus (Maryanus the Byzantine) teaches the alchemical art of Hermes to the Umayyad prince Khalid Ibn Yazid (*c.* 668–704). The Arabic original does not mention the three Hermeses, thus Chester took the legend of *De tribus Mercuriis* from somewhere else. Chester's work is considered the first translation of an Arabic alchemy book available in the Latin West, which explains the wide influence it had.[92] As I mentioned in Chapter One, the Spanish Jewish convert, Petrus Alfonsi, must have read this book in Arabic before Chester's translation was available and used it as inspiration for exemplum XXV of his *Disciplina clericalis*, entitled "The philosopher Marianus."[93]

87 These first two books were published by J. Ruska in "Zwei Bücher De Compositione Alchemiae und ihre Vorreden," *Archiv für Geschichte der Mathematik, der Naturwissenschaft und der Technik* 11 (1928), 28–37. The *Liber de Compositione Alchemiae* is also edited by Lee Stavenhagen, *A Testament of Alchemy: Being the Revelations of Morienus to Khālid Ibn Yazīd* (Lebanon: Brandeis University Press, 1974).

88 I follow the Latin edition by Paolo Lucentini and Mark D. Delp (eds), *Hermetis Trismegisti de Sex Rerum Principiis* (Turnhout: Brepols, 2006).

89 See M. Plessner, "Hirmis," in *Encyclopedia of Islam*, new edn (Leiden: Brill 1971), 3: 463–5.

90 Fraker, "Hermes Trismegistus," 90–1.

91 Richard Lemay, "L'authenticité de la préface de Robert de Chester à sa traduction du Morienus," *Chrysopoeia* 4 (1990–1): 3–32.

92 On the differences between the texts, see Marion Dapsens, "De la *Risālat Maryānus* au *De Compositione alchemiae*: Quelques réflexions sur la tradition d'un traité d'alchimie," *Studia graeco-arabica* 6 (2016): 121–40 ; see also, Sébastien Moureau, "Min al-kīmiyāʾ ad alchimiam: The Transmission of Alchemy from the Arab-Muslim World to the Latin West in the Middle Ages," *Micrologus* 28 (2020): 87–141.

93 "Exemplum de Mariano." Petrus Alfonsi, *Disciplina clericalis*, 139.

The second book, the *Septem tractatus Hermetis sapientia triplicis,* seems to be another translation of an Arabic alchemy book by Hermes. We do not know when it was written, who wrote it, or who translated it. The book includes a prologue on Hermes that is extremely similar to that in *Liber de compositione alchemiae*, thus it was most probably based on it. Since this second prologue is slightly more extensive, and Burnett considers it a less adulterated version, I reproduce and translate it here:

> In the history of divine things, we read about three distinguished philosophers, each of whom was named Hermes. The first of them, Enoch, lived before the Flood and was the one who went to heaven in a fiery chariot accompanied by angels. The second was Noah, who was saved from the Flood of many waters in the ark, under God's mandate. Both of them were called either by the alternate name Hermes, or by the name Mercury, to differentiate [them] from the Hermes who reigned in Egypt after the Flood [...] this third one was a very distinguished man. He was honoured with the royal crown and governed as king of Egypt for a long time. He was said to be three times great due to triple merit. For it is said that he was king, philosopher, and prophet and excelled as the discoverer of all liberal and mechanical disciplines.[94]

Some of the information included here seems related to Abū Maʿshar. The first Hermes was Enoch and lived before the Flood, and the third Hermes was the king of Egypt. This last one, the "discoverer of all liberal and mechanical disciplines," can be interpreted as an intellectual, medieval European rendering of Abū Maʿshar's account of the first prediluvian Hermes "saving all the sciences and disciplines," which were discovered after the Flood by another Hermes – who cultivated many arts as well. The identification of the second Mercury as Noah is not in Abū Maʿshar – since it also appears in Chester's prologue, it might have been an attempt to reinforce the Hermeses' connection with both the Bible and the Flood. This text is slightly corrupt, which I mark with "<...>," but it seems to indicate that only the first two Hermeses were also known as Mercury, which is also mentioned in Chester. This appearance of Mercury might be influenced by Latin authors, such as Cicero, Augustine, Isidore, etc. or even the *Asclepius*. It aims to strengthen the relationship between the Roman god and Hermes Trismegistus, which I referred to earlier.

The third prologue is found in *Liber de sex rerum principiis*. The book is "a cosmological text written under the pseudonym of Hermes Mercurius Triplex, or Trimegistus, and was probably composed sometime in the latter half of the twelfth century."[95] Despite the text's attribution, "there is a compelling reason to doubt that

94 "In historiis divinarum rerum, tres praeclaros viros philosophos, quemlibet vocatum Hermetem, legimus. Horum primus Enoch ante diluvium fuit, qui angelis comitantibus, igneo curru in coelum abiit. Secundus autem Noe, qui in archa, Dei iussu, a diluvio multarum aquarum salvus evasit. Eorum enim alteruter alio nomine Hermes, alio nomine vocatus est Mercurius, ad differentiam Hermetis, qui post diluvium regnavit in Aegypto... hic enim tertius clarissimus vir, qui regali diademate decoratus, diu rex Aegypto imperavit, a trina virtute Ter magnus dictus est. Ipsum namque ferunt Regem, Philosophum, atque Prophetam fuisse, qui et totius liberalis mechanicaeque disciplinae inventor fertur extitisse." In Burnett, "The Legend of the Three Hermes," 231. My translation.

95 Delp, "A Twelfth Century Cosmology. The Liber de Sex Rerum Principiis," in Paolo Lucentini and Mark D. Delp (eds), *Hermetis Trismegisti de Sex Rerum Principiis* (Turnhout:

it actually belongs to the Hermetic tradition," because it quotes well-known authors from the time when it was probably written.[96] The prologue of this work includes a summarized version of the account of the first two Hermeses that we saw in the *Septem tractatus*'s prologue, but it also provides more information on the third one, who in this case seems to be a Mercury as well:

> We read in the old histories of the divine things that there have been three philosophers. The first of them was Enoch, who was also called both Hermes and by other name, Mercury; another one was Noah, who in a similar way was called Hermes and Mercury; and the third Hermes was rightly called Mercurius Triple, because he flourished as king, philosopher, and prophet. For he held the kingdom of Egypt after the Flood with extreme justice, excelled in the liberal and the mechanical arts, and was the first to reveal [the art of] astronomy. He completed the *Golden sceptre*, the *Book of longitude and latitude*, the *Book of elections*, the *Ezich* – i.e., the canons on the adequation of the planets and the astrolabe – and many other excellent works. This Triple or Trismegistus was also the first to unveil alchemy in his teachings. Morienus, truly a supreme philosopher, produced a work on his writings. He started to investigate the secret nature of alchemy, about which, writing in the most careful way, he finally composed that [work].[97]

The prologue offers a clear justification for why Hermes was called Triple (*Triplex*) by explaining that he was regarded as a king (he ruled Egypt fairly), philosopher (he mastered the mechanical and the liberal arts, which granted that title in the twelfth century),[98] and prophet (which seems to be related to the art of astronomy/astrology and its power to foresee the future).

As Fodor explains, and we observe here, in the Arabic tradition, "Hermes is not merely a prophet, but also king and philosopher."[99] Interestingly, this Arabic theory about the meaning of "Trismegistus" made its way into the Renaissance

---

Brepols, 2006), 1. Delp also affirms that "there are factors that make it unlikely that the treatise was composed much after 1150." Delp, "Twelfth Century Cosmology," 15–16.

96 Such as Bernardus Silvestris, William of Conches, Honorius Augustodunensis, and Adelarth of Bath. See Delp, *De sex rerum principiis*, 2. Silvestris's *Cosmographia*, written in 1147, is the latest authority quoted, and it points to the book's *terminus post quem*. See Delp, "Twelfth Century Cosmology," 12.

97 "Legimus in ueteribus diuinorum historiis tres fuisse philosophos, quorum primus Enoch, qui et Hermes et alio nomine Mercurius dictus fuit ; alius Noe, qui similiter Hermes et Mercurius nuncupatus fuit; tertius vero Hermes Mercurius Triplex vocatus fuit, quia et rex et philosophus et propheta floruit. Hic enim post diluvium cum summa aequitate regnum Aegypti tenuit, et in liberalibus et mechanicis artibus praevaluit et astronomiam prius elucidavit. Virgam auream, Librum longitudinis et latitudinis, Librum electionis et Ezich, id est canones super adaequationem planetarum et super astrolapsum, et alia multa opere luculento complevit. Hic etiam Triplex sive Trismegistus inter ludos suos prius alchimiam edidit. Morienus uero summus philosophus scriptis eius operam dedit, et secretam alchimiae naturam longo labore rimari coepit, de qua subtiliter scribens illam tandem composuit." *Hermetis Trismegisti De sex rerum principiis*, 147. My translation.

98 As Alfonso still thinks in the thirteenth century. See Rico, *Alfonso el Sabio*, 135–9.

99 See A. Fodor, "The Origins of the Arabic Legends of the Pyramids," *Acta Orientalia Academiae Scientiarum Hungaricae* 23, no. 3 (1970): 343. There, Fodor also reminds us that "this threefold distinction also goes back to an antique tradition."

world through Iberian intermediaries. Marsilio Ficino introduced a reference to this triple dimension in the prologue of his translation of the *Hermetica*. Campanelli thinks that it "comes straight from *De tribus Mercuriis*" (the prologue of the *Liber de compositione alchemiae*), and in this way Ficino not only "keeps alive the Hermes of the alchemic literature translated from Arabic" but also bestowed new life to this feature, which he transmitted to many other early modern authors.[100] However, Campanelli fails to mention an additional possibility: Hermes/Mercury as prophet, king, and philosopher also appears in the *Picatrix*, translated into Latin in Alfonso's court, which Ficino knew and quoted in other works, such as *De vita*.[101] In the *Picatrix* we find that "The wise men said about the aforementioned Hermes that he was the lord of three crucial things, namely king, prophet, and wise man."[102] Significantly, "wise men" (*sapientes*) is how the *Picatrix* translates *al-ṣābiʾūn* (the Sabeans) – identified with the Ḥarrānians in the *Ghāya*,[103] where we find that "among the Sabeans, Hermes was called Trismegistus [*aṭras maġīsṭus*] because he had triple wisdom [*muthalath ḥikma*], as he was king, prophet, and wise man."[104] This introduces the likelihood that Ficino took this reference to the triple dimension of Hermes as king, prophet, and wise man from the *Picatrix*, and not from the *Liber de compositione alchemiae*. Another, more interesting possibility is that Robert of Chester took this reference from the *Ghāya* – or an intermediary source – and used it to complement the account of the three Hermeses he took from Abū Maʿshar. The triple dimension comes from the Arabic world, as Fodor points out, but Robert of Chester wrote his prologue in the Iberian Peninsula – where the *Ghāya* had been written and was still available – and the *Liber de sex rerum principiis* has a prologue most probably inspired by Chester's prologue and translation.

The prologue of the *Liber de sex rerum principiis* also mentions astronomical books by Hermes that do not appear in either *De tribus Mercuriis* or the prologue to the *Septem tractatus*. Some of those books – such as the *Liber electionis* – are incorporated into the body of text, which leads Delp to consider whether this prologue was not the first of its kind.[105] It also introduces a reference to Morienus

100 Maurizio Campanelli, "Marsilio Ficino's Portrait of Hermes Trismegistus and Its Afterlife," *Intellectual History Review* 29, no. 1 (2019): 57–8.

101 On the relationship between Ficino's *De vita* and the *Picatrix*, see Denis J. J. Robichaud, "Ficino on Force, Magic, and Prayers: Neoplatonic and Hermetic Influences in Ficino's Three Books on Life," *Renaissance Quarterly* 70, no. 1 (2017): 44–87. Marsilio Ficino, *De vita libri tres* (*Three Books on Life*, 1489), trans. Carol V. Kaske and John R. Clarke (Tempe, Arizona: The Renaissance Society of America, 2002).

102 "Qui sapientes de prefato Hermete dixerunt quod erat dominus trium floridarum rerum, videlicet rex, propheta et sapiens." *Picatrix* III.vii, 35.

103 Who, as we have seen, many specialists identify with the inhabitants of Ḥarrān, and who, especially in this section on the powers of the planets (III.vii), have been interpreted as the inhabitants of this place.

104 *Ghāya* III.7, 225.

105 Delp, "Twelfth Century Cosmology," 7–9

and the work that "he finally composed," which appears to be a clear indication that it was inspired by *De tribus Mercuriis*.[106]

Thus, there is evidence that the legend of the three Hermeses in Abū Maʿshar's *Kitāb al-ulūf* was quoted in other works, first in Arabic and then in Latin. Burnett points out that there are two references to the *Kitāb al-ulūf* in a twelfth-century Latin work, *De essentiis*, written in 1143 by Hermann of Carinthia.[107] As we saw in Chapter One, Hermann was an important translator of diverse Arabic works, many of which he found in Spain while living there. *De essentiis* is an original treatise in which Hermann deals with cosmology and Aristotelian categories and quotes many other works, one of them the *Kitāb al-ulūf*. Since the Andalusi authors Sāʿid al-Andalusī and Ibn Juljul quote the legend of the three Hermeses from the *Kitāb al-ulūf* – and are in fact the main transmitters of this legend – we know that the book was available in the Iberian Peninsula before Hermann arrived there.

Abū Maʿshar's reputation among Christian translators in Spain is also demonstrated in the two translations of his most important work, the *Kitāb al-mudkhal al-kabīr* (*Book of the great introduction*): *Liber introductorius maior* by Johannes Hispaniensis (John of Seville in English) in 1133, and *Introductorium in astronomiam* by Hermann of Carinthia in 1140. Since Hermann had translated Abū Maʿshar's most important treatise, it is plausible that he also translated the *Kitāb al-ulūf*, as Burnett suggests, especially considering that Hermann quotes it in *De essentiis*.[108] Some sources even identify Robert of Chester, the author of the prologue and translator of the *Liber de compositione alchemiae*, with Robert of Ketton – who was also active in the Iberian Peninsula in the 1140s. Even though this identification is currently disputed,[109] Burnett still defends the position that they were the same person. If Robert of Chester was actually Ketton, it would be significant, because Ketton was a friend of Hermann of Carinthia, and they collaborated on numerous translation endeavours from Arabic.[110] Hermann might have shared his translation of the *Kitāb al-ulūf* with his friend Ketton, who would have found the story of the three Hermeses in it and then included it in the prologue to his translation of the *Liber de compositione alchemiae*.[111] Since this alchemy book includes many references to Hermes, the mythical creator of the art, it is not surprising that Chester decided

[106] This reflection has been also made by Angus Braid, https://theamalricianheresy.wordpress.com/a-note-on-dating-the-latin-morienus/ (last accessed February 17, 2023). See also Delp, "Twelfth Century Cosmology," 9.

[107] Burnett, "Legend of the Three Hermes," 231–2. See also Hermann of Carinthia, *De Essentiis: A Critical Edition with Translation and Commentary*, trans. Charles S. F. Burnett (E. J. Brill: Leiden, 1982).

[108] Burnett, "Legend of the Three Hermes," 231–2. See also Burnett, "The Establishment of Medieval Hermeticism," 130.

[109] Because Ketton lived in the kingdom of Navarre, and Chester in that of Castile, in the city of Segovia.

[110] Charles Burnett, "Ketton, Robert of (fl. 1141–1157)," in *Oxford Dictionary of National Biography* (Oxford: Oxford University Press, 2004).

[111] It is striking that the author of *De sex rerum principiis* does not mention the innovative *De essentiis* (1140) among its contemporary sources, but he most probably took the prologue from *De tribus mercuriis* (1144). See Delp, "Twelfth Century Cosmology," 16–17.

to clarify the identities of the Hermes(es) in the prologue of the book using the information he had available. What we can say with certainty is that there was a Latin translation of the *Kitāb al-ulūf*'s story of the three Hermeses which was circulating in Castile in the twelfth century and that this influenced the Castilian writer, Robert of Chester, in his writing of *De tribus Mercuriis*.

Now we come to the crucial question of how the legend of the three Hermeses passed from Arabic to Latin, and from there to the *GE*. It is possible that Alfonso had read the legend in one of the three prologues we have just examined. However, despite Alfonso's interest in alchemy,[112] and some scanty references in the *GE*, there is no direct evidence that he knew about any of those prologues. However, a legend about the three Mercuries does appear in one of the *GE*'s most important sources, the *Chronicon mundi* by Lucas de Tuy, which situates this work as the most likely inspiration for the passage in *GE*2. My hypothesis suggests that the derivation of the three Hermeses in Lucas de Tuy is effectively Abū Maʿshar, transmitted through one of the three Latin prologues mentioned above. However, I suggest there was another intermediary source between the Latin prologues and Lucas de Tuy: Petrus Comestor. To understand the setting of the three Hermeses in both Lucas de Tuy and Petrus Comestor we must examine an earlier Iberian source that they both used: Isidore of Seville. In his *Chronica maiora*, Isidore introduced two Mercuries, who were inspired by the two Hermeses that Augustine took from the *Asclepius*.

Two Mercuries of Isidore's *Chronica Maiora*

In Chapter One I showed how the *Etymologies* reveal not only Isidore's wide use of classical sources – many of them now lost – but also shed light on the interconnected Mediterranean world in which Isidore lived. In *Etymologies* VIII Isidore collates information on Mercury; some of this comes from *The City of God* VII, as Isidore uses the same words as Augustine to describe Mercury as a middle courier (*medius currens*) between men and merchants and explains that his name comes from the Greek term ἑρμηνεία ("interpretation").[113] Isidore also explains that "on account of his power and knowledge of many arts he is called Trismegistus, that is, thrice great [*ter maximus*]," which might also come from Augustine, but he adds that they imagined him with a dog's head – which indicates that Isidore was aware of late antiquity's hybrid deity Hermanubis, who combined features of Hermes and Anubis.[114] Isidore – like Cicero – mentions Hermes Trismegistus as an Egyptian legislator and relates Mercury with Hermetic arts such as astrology, divination, and magic.[115] Thus, the *Etymologies* record the first references to Hermes Trismegistus in Hispanic literary traditions, as well as many other traditions related to him.

112 See J. H. Nunemaker, "Noticias sobre la Alquimia en el 'Lapidario' de Alfonso X," *Revista De Filología Española* 16, (1929): 161–8.

113 *Civitate Dei* VII, xiv.

114 "Hermes autem Graece dicitur APO TES ERMENEIAS, Latine interpres; qui ob virtutem multarumque artium scientiam Trimegistus, id est ter maximus nominatus est. Cur autem eum capite canino fingunt." *Etymologies*.VIII, xi, 45–9.

115 *Etymologies*.V, i, 2 and VIII, ix, 8.

But Isidore wrote other works in which Hermetic traces can be detected, such as the *Chronica maiora* or *Chronicon*, a universal chronicle. Martín regards this work as expressing Isidore's desire to write an original chronicle and not just a continuation of the works of Eusebius, Jerome, and their followers.[116] Isidore's chronicle would be the fruit of Visigoth intellectual media, and it would establish a turning point: the cultural independence of their kingdom as the inheritor of the Western Roman Empire. One of the clear innovations of this chronicle with respect to Eusebius is the introduction of two Mercuries.

Although less than the *Etymologies*, the *Chronica maiora* also had a broad dissemination – proven by its many preserved manuscripts. From these manuscripts, we know that Isidore made two redactions, one in 616 and another in 626. In his recent scholarly edition, Martín has reliably fixed the text for both redactions.[117] Other than the two redactions, book V of the *Etymologies* includes an epitome of the *Chronica maiora* which derives from the second version. Isidore wrote the *Etymologies* from approximately 600 to 625, which makes the epitome a posterior addition that Martín does not doubt is by Isidore himself.[118] As we will see, the three versions – first redaction, second redaction, and epitome – are important for tracking the references to Hermes/Mercury in late medieval authors. The *Chronica maiora*'s main source is the *Chronicle* of Eusebius and Jerome, but it has many other sources, among which Augustine's *The City of God* stands out. Due to the influence of Augustine, the second redaction incorporates the division of the world into six ages; *The City of God* is also important for its chapters on the history and mythology of Greece and their euhemeristic interpretation.[119] Those chapters include references to two Mercuries, which I consider an Augustinian legacy in the *Chronica maiora*.

The first mention of Mercury in Isidore's *Chronica maiora* seems to be inspired by both Eusebius and Augustine. Eusebius reveals that Atlas, the brother of Prometheus, lived around the time of Moses, and that he was a great astrologer.[120] Augustine likely took this information from Eusebius but then introduces Mercury, grandson of Atlas, and affirms that "he was renowned for his skill in many arts, which he also transmitted to men, and in exchange for this service they decreed that he should be a god after his death, or even believed that he was one."[121] Regarding Mercury, the *Chronica maiora* seems to adapt Augustine to the chronological setting of Eusebius in a more precise way.

[116] See José Carlos Martín, "La 'Crónica universal' de Isidoro de Sevilla: circunstancias históricas e ideológicas de su composición y traducción de la misma," *Iberia: Revista de la Antigüedad* 4 (2001): 206–7. See also the introduction to his edition *Isidori Hispalensis Chronica* (Turnhout: Brepols, 2003).

[117] Martín, Introduction générale to *Isidori Hispalensis Chronica*, 13*–20*.

[118] Martín, Introduction générale to *Isidori Hispalensis Chronica*, 20*.

[119] Chapters 36–76 are about Greece, except 54–5, which are on Moses. On the *Chronica maiora*'s sources, see Martín, Introduction générale to *Isidori Hispalensis Chronica*, 20*–35*.

[120] Eusebius, *Eusebi Chronicorum canonum* 2:21.

[121] "Multarum autem artium peritus claruit quas et hominibus tradidit; quo merito eum post mortem deum esse voluerunt sive etiam crediderunt." *Civitate Dei* XVIII, viii.

Isidore borrows from Eusebius the claim that the servitude of the Hebrews in Egypt lasted 144 years, as well as a reference to Prometheus.[122] However, there is a difference between *Chronica maiora*'s first and second redaction: one says that Atlas "was considered a great astrologer," and the second that "he discovered astrology and first examined the movement and the arrangement of heaven."[123] This information about Atlas can be found in both Eusebius and Augustine, but then Isidore follows only Augustine and introduces Mercury: "And then Mercury the grandson of Atlas was skilled in many arts and, on account of this, after his death was carried to the gods."[124] As we can observe, the last sentence is slightly different from what we saw in Augustine. We could understand the last statement in the same figurative sense (i.e., he was considered a god), but it literally says that Mercury was "physically" transported or carried across to the gods (*in deos translatus*). This second sense opens the possibility that Isidore was not only already aware of Mercury's identification with Hermes – he read it in *The City of God* – but also with Enoch. In fact, the *Vulgate* uses the same Latin verb to express that Enoch was carried to heaven by God: *Enoch placuit Deo, et translatus est in Paradisum*.[125] Moreover, earlier in the *Chronica maiora*, when Isidore says that Enoch was carried away by God, he uses the same verb (*translatus est*) that he later uses with Mercury and implies that he is aware of the apocryphal Enochian literature, rejected by the Church, when he affirms: "It is said that [Enoch] wrote several things, but due to the antiquity of [their] suspicious faith they are rejected by the Fathers."[126] If Isidore identifies Mercury with Enoch, he does not make it clear, either because of the "suspicious" Enochian tradition, or because of the chronological problems: Mercury lived during Moses's time, but Enoch's account is in Genesis.

The second redaction of Isidore's *Chronica maiora* includes a second reference to Mercury that is particularly pertinent for our investigation as it was used by Lucas de Tuy and Petrus Comestor, with both adding the three Hermeses to it. After pointing out that the biblical judge Gideon ruled for forty years, Isidore affirms that: "At this time *the other* Mercury discovered the lyre and gave it to Orpheus"[127] (italics are mine). The *Chronica* is referring to the "baby Hermes" discovering the famous lyre

[122] *Chronica maiora* 44, 34–5; and *Chronica maiora* 45, 36–7 (in *Isidori Hispalensis Chronica*). The same information is found in Eusebius, *Eusebi Chronicorum canonum* 2:21.

[123] "[…] frater ieus Atlans magnus est astrologus habitus." *Chronica maiora* 1.46, 36; "[…] frater eius Atlans astrologiam repperit motumque caeli et rationem primus considerauit." *Chronica maiora* 2.47, 37.

[124] "Tunc fuit et Mercurius nepus Atlantis multarum artium peritus et ob hoc post mortem in deos translatus." *Chronica maiora* 47, 37.

[125] Ecclesiasticus 44:16. It makes reference to Genesis 5:24, which affirms that Enoch "walked with God, and was no more seen, because God took him" (*ambulavitque cum Deo et non apparuit quia tulit eum Deus*).

[126] "[…] translatus est a deo, quique etiam nonnulla scripsisse fertur, sed ob antiquitatem suspectae fidei a patribus refutata sunt." *Chronica maiora* 1 and 2, 9.

[127] "Gedeon annos XL. Hac aetate alter Mercurius lyram repperit et Orpheo tradidit." *Chronica maiora* 2.77–7[a], 49.

in the *Homeric Hymn to Hermes*.[128] Isidore recounts the story of Hermes's lyre in the *Etymologies*, where he also affirms that Mercury gave it to Orpheus.[129] Eusebius also states in his *Chronicle* that Gideon ruled for forty years,[130] and then he briefly mentions Orpheus: "[at this time] Orpheus the Thracian is considered important, whose pupil was Musaeus the son of Eumolpus."[131] In my view, when Isidore decided to introduce "the other" Mercury, he did so through his association to the lyre and Orpheus, whom Eusebius had mentioned at the time of Gideon.

The epitome of *Chronica maiora* that Isidore included in the *Etymologies* does not include the first mention of Hermes, but it does incorporate a shortened version of the second mention: "Gideon forty years. Mercury made the lyre."[132] Consistently, the epitome omits the description of this second Mercury as "the other" (*alter*). This "other Mercury" (*alter Mercurius*) is key, because it confirms that there was a first Mercury, grandson of Atlas, who lived at the time of (or right after) the Hebrews' servitude in Egypt, and another Mercury, who lived at the time of judge Gideon. We can assume that if Isidore placed the first Mercury around the time of Moses, it was based on Augustine's statement, but I have not found any precedent for a second Mercury who was a contemporary of Gideon. Therefore, we have to assume that this chronological setting of the two Mercuries originated with Isidore, which as we will see is also echoed in Petrus Comestor, Lucas de Tuy, and Alfonso X.

Three Hermeses in Lucas de Tuy's *Chronicon Mundi*

Lucas de Tuy (d. 1249) was probably born at the end of the twelfth century in León.[133] This city, and the entire kingdom of León, would become part of the kingdom of Castile in 1230 under the crown of Fernando III, Alfonso's father. Lucas studied and climbed the career ladder in the Church of Saint Isidore in León. Strategically situated on the pilgrimage route of Santiago de Compostela, this church would become an important cultural centre after the transfer of the mortal remains of Isidore in 1063. Lucas was appointed bishop of Tuy, in Galicia, in 1239, an office that he held until his death in 1249 – hence his appellation. As he indicates in the prologue, Lucas wrote the *Chronicon mundi* while he was still deacon in León – thus, before 1239 – and it was commissioned by Queen Berenguela – daughter of Alfonso VIII of Castile, wife of Alfonso IX of León, mother of Fernando III, and grandmother of "our" Alfonso X.[134]

[128] See Athanassios Vergados, *The "Homeric Hymn to Hermes:" Introduction, Text and Commentary* (Berlin, Boston: De Gruyter, 2013); and *The Orphic Hymns*, trans. and eds Apostolos N. Athanassakis and Benjamin M. Wolkow (Baltimore: Johns Hopkins University Press, 2013).

[129] Isidore, *Etymologies*.III, xxii.8.

[130] Eusebius, *Eusebi Chronicorum canonum* 2:45.

[131] "Orfeus Trax clarus habetur, cuius discipulis fuit Musaeus filius Eumolpi." Eusebius, *Eusebi Chronicorum canonum* 2:47.

[132] "Gedeon ann. XL. Mercurius lyram condidit." Isidore, *Etymologies*.V, xxxix.11.

[133] On Lucas de Tuy's life, see Falque, introduction to *Lucae Tudensis Chronicon mundi*, vii–xii.

[134] Lucas de Tuy, *Chronicon mundi. Praefatio*.2, 148–89 and 1, 47–51. For contextual information, see Falque, introduction to *Lucae Tudensis Chronicon mundi*, xvi–xxi.

Around this time, Berenguela was acting regent in the northern lands while her son waged his war against Muslims in the south, which would yield enormous territorial conquests. The *Chronicon mundi* is one of three great historiographical productions written in Latin during the reign of Fernando III, along with the *Chronica latina regum Castellae* (*Latin chronicle of the kings of Castille*, 1226–30/1236–9) attributed to Juan de Soria, bishop of Osma, and the *Historia de rebus Hispaniae* (*History of the events of Spain*, 1240–3/1246–7) by Rodrígo Jiménez de Rada, bishop of Toledo.[135]

It is significant that these works were written in Latin by churchmen, because the turn to Castilian that Alfonso would make soon after they were written has been interpreted as a way of promoting a more secular culture.[136] The *Chronicon Mundi* has not been regarded as a highly historically significant work due to Lucas compiling various well-known sources and subsequently weaving them together based on his own criteria; however – as Falque reminds us – his historiographical technique "has value and is worth studying."[137] The work is divided into four books, which cover the origin of the world until Fernando III's time – the same plan that Alfonso originally had for his *GE*. Lucas's source selection was influenced by the long years he spent in the Church of Saint Isidore, as well as the hagiography that he dedicated to the saint, the *Miracula sancti Isidori* or *De miraculis sancti Isidori* (*On the miracles of Saint Isidore*).[138] In fact, as Fernández-Ordóñez points out, Lucas conceives the *Chronicon mundi* from "an Isidorian perspective."[139] Accordingly, the first two books of the *Chronicon mundi* use Isidore's historiographical works as primary sources. Specifically, the *Chronica maiora* of Isidore occupies the majority of the first book – which follows the Augustinian six ages of the world, from the Creation to the Visigoth king Suintila (588–633 CE).

Isidore's *Chronica maiora* provides the *Chronicon mundi*'s first book with a universal perspective – the extant three books from this work focus on the history of Spain.[140] However, according to Sánchez Alonso, Lucas does not copy Isidore's *Chronica maiora* "at face value, but makes suppressions, changes of order, and enlargements in particular."[141] In making his additions to Isidore's *Chronica Maiora*, Lucas borrows from Petrus Comestor's *Historia scholastica*, bringing in from that source other aspects of biblical and pagan history.[142]

These facts help us understand the background to the history of the three Hermeses in the *GE*, because as we will see below, Lucas's *Chronicon mundi* includes two references to Mercury. Both references are placed according to Isidore's timeline

[135] On these three works and how they differ from the *GE*, see Inés Fernández Ordóñez, "De la historiografía fernandina a la alfonsí," *Alcanate: Revista de estudios Alfonsíes* 3 (2002–3): 93–134.

[136] See Martínez, *El humanismo medieval*, 15–16; and Falque, introduction to *Lucae Tudensis Chronicon mundi*, xxvi–xxvi.

[137] Falque, introduction to *Lucae Tudensis Chronicon mundi*, xxi.

[138] Falque, introduction to *Lucae Tudensis Chronicon mundi*, xiii.

[139] Fernández Ordóñez, "De la historiografía," 10.

[140] Falque, introduction to *Lucae Tudensis Chronicon mundi*, xxxv.

[141] Benito Sánchez Alonso, *Historia de la historiografía española*, 2 vols (Madrid: CSIC, 1947), 1:105.

[142] Falque, introduction to *Lucae Tudensis Chronicon mundi*, xxxviii.

in the *Chronica maiora*; the first is complemented with classical sources and the second with Comestor's *Historia scholastica*. I suggest that Lucas took the story of the three Hermeses from Comestor because Comestor had also borrowed a reference to Mercury in the time of Gideon from Isidore – Lucas's main source. Both Lucas de Tuy and Petrus Comestor are major sources in the *GE*. I argue that Alfonso was inspired by Lucas de Tuy and took the history of the three Hermeses and situated it after Moses due to this, but then he expanded on the story by using other sources.

Turning to the first reference to Mercury, Lucas quotes the section on Mercury and Atlas from Isidore's *Chronica maiora* verbatim and situates it in the time of Joseph, during the Israelites' Egyptian captivity. In most manuscripts the *Chronicon mundi* only differs slightly from the *Chronica maiora*:

> Then Atlas discovered many things related to astrology and examined the movement and arrangement of heaven in a more subtle way than others that came before him. Then Mercury, grandson of Atlas, was wise in many arts and because of that after his death he was carried across into the gods.[143]

We notice that Lucas preserved Isidore's wording about Mercury being wise in many arts and being carried up to the heavens. As Falque notes in her edition, one of the preserved manuscripts of the *Chronicon mundi* includes a large and significant addition about Mercury; it says:

> [...] and this was the first <...> [he] says under judge Gideon, and it is said that he was the son of Jupiter and, according to Fulgentius, was partly in charge of commerce, partly supervised businesses, whence it is thought that he was the god of merchants. It is also said that this [Mercury] was Hermes, who also spoke in a prudent way, and according to Fulgentius for this reason he was thought to be the god of speech and eloquence.[144]

There is a lacuna in the text that I indicate with "<...>." I interpret it as "this [Mercury] was the first <...> [Isidore] says under judge Gideon." "The first" would indicate that Lucas is now talking about the first Mercury that appears in the *Chronica maiora*, at the time of the Egyptian captivity, because the second one, "the other Mercury" (*alter Mercurius*), according to Isidore, will appear during the time of Gideon and is also in the *Chronicon mundi*. The rest of the information that the interpolation provides corresponds to Fulgentius (late fifth–early sixth century) – as Lucas affirms and as we saw in Chapter Three. There I pointed out that Alfonso took information for the description of Mercury and his identification with Hermes from this section

[143] "Tunc etiam Atlas in astrologia multa reperit motumque celi et rationem pre ceteris, que precesserat, subtilius considerauit.Tunc fuit et Mercurius nepos Atlantis multarum artium peritus et propter hoc post mortem in deos translatus." Lucas de Tuy, *Chronicon Mundi*.I, 26, 29.

[144] "[...] et iste fuit primus <...> dicet sub iudice Gedeone et dicitur fuisse filius Iouis et secundum Fulgentium dicitur Mercurius quasi mercium curator quasi negotiationibus indendebat unde fungitur fuisse deus mercatorum. Iste etiam dicut est Hermes qui idem sonat quod discretus secundum Fulgentium unde fingitur fuisse Deus sermonis et eloquentie." Lucas de Tuy, *Chronicon Mundi*.I, 26, 29, footnote.

of the *Chronicon mundi*.[145] Alfonso affirms that "[Mercury] was wise in many arts, and lived until Moses's time, according to what Lucas says."[146] Indeed, Lucas affirms that Mercury was "multarum artium peritus," and a few lines below, on the same page, narrates Moses's birth.[147]

Just a few pages later, Lucas presents the second mention of Mercury that derives from Isidore – that of Gideon's times. The reference is enlarged to include the story of the three Hermeses. In the *Chronicon mundi*, the first mention of Mercury, during the time of Joseph (Egyptian captivity) – which Alfonso quotes in *GE*1 – appears just six pages prior to the second mention of Mercury, during the time of Gideon. In fact, the *Chronicon mundi*'s brief first book only dedicates one paragraph to Joseph's time, one to Joshua's time, and another to that of Gideon – which includes the three Mercuries, including Trismegistus.[148] It is intriguing that Alfonso decides to situate the three Hermeses and Trismegistus in Joshua's time and not that of Gideon, as in the *Chronicon mundi*, even though Alfonso certainly read those few pages of the *Chronicon* containing the three Mercuries. Indeed, *GE*2 reports that "Bishop Lucas also says in the chronicle of the time of this Joshua [...] that this king, Busiris, was much crueller than the other kings and princes of that land"; and it also says that "Bishop Lucas narrates it in this way: that at the time of Joshua's reign, when Cadmus and Phoenix came out of Thebes in Egypt, then Jupiter came together with Europa."[149] These quotations are faithful renderings of the *Chronicon mundi*, which are cited alongside other passages from the same pages in Lucas's book.[150] One possible explanation for the reference to Hermes Trismegistus in Joshua's time, and not in Gideon's, is what I suggested at the beginning of the chapter: Alfonso found a version with interpolations of Eusebius and Jerome's *Chronicle* that mentioned Hermes Trismegistus and Tat living during the time of Joshua. In view of the chronological disparity between Eusebius/Jerome and Lucas, he decided to stick with the more authoritative source. Furthermore, if Tat lived during the time of Joshua, it is possible that his father, Hermes Trismegistus, lived a few years earlier (i.e., in Moses's time), which is what Augustine says in *The City of God* – Alfonso's

145 See Wilbur Devereux Jones, *Fulgentius the Mythographer* (Columbus: Ohio State University Press, 1972), 59–60.

146 "[...] fue sabio de muchas artes, e alcançó fasta'l tiempo de Moisén, segund cuenta Lucas." *GE*1 I, 318.

147 Lucas de Tuy, *Chronicon Mundi*.I, 28, 29.

148 In Lucas de Tuy, *Chronicon Mundi*.I: Joseph 26, 27–9; Joshua 30, 34–5; and Gedeon 34, 37 (pages in modern edition).

149 "Otrossi cuenta ell obispo Lucas en la crónica del tiempo d'este Josué [...] que este rey Busiris mucho era más cruel que los otros reyes nin los otros príncipes de toda essa tierra." *GE*2 I, 34. "Ell obispo Lucas lo cuenta assí: Diz que en el tiempo del reinado de Josué, cuando Cadmo e Fénix salieron de Tebas de Egipto, que estonces se ayuntó Júpiter a Europa." *GE*2 I, 34.

150 "Rexit Iosue populum annis uiginti septem [...] Busiris rex ualde crudelis fuit is ospites, ita ut eorum multos decapitaret et tormentis afficeret multis." Lucas de Tuy, *Chronicon Mundi*.I, 30, 34–5. "Cathmo in Greciam recedente, terra a Phenice Phenicea dicta est. Tunc Europe, filie Phenicis, fabulose Iupiter mixtus est." Lucas de Tuy, *Chronicon Mundi*.I, 31, 35. Lucas is also mentioned, for instance, in *GE*2 I, 110 and 111.

other important reference. The question that remains concerns where Lucas found the three Mercuries.

Lucas places the second Mercury in Gideon's time because he is following Isidore; it can be reasonably assumed that he adds the reference to the three Mercuries – which he took from Petrus Comestor – to it. I will now present Comestor's version of Isidore's second Mercury and then that of Lucas, so we will be able to appreciate the similarities and differences between them – and also between them and the *GE*. I argue that Comestor took Mercury living in Gideon's time from Isidore but the addition of the three Mercuries from one of the Latin alchemical and hermetic treatises I examined above.

Petrus Comestor and the Three Hermeses in the *Historia Scholastica*

Petrus Comestor was born around 1100 in Troyes. There, he was educated in the Church of Saint-Loup, where he would eventually hold diverse ecclesiastical offices. Later in his life, around 1150, Comestor studied under Petrus Lombardus (1100–60) at the Cathedral School of Paris, where he would become professor of theology (1164–8) and then chancellor of all Parisian schools (1168–78). Comestor's books are based on what he taught in Paris,[151] with his most important work being the *Historia scholastica*, a historical Bible and a universal chronicle. It presents historical events from the Creation to the birth of Jesus Christ. Following previous chroniclers, it includes summarized chronological concordances of the Bible alongside Greek, Roman, and pagan events (the *incidentia*). As we saw, the *Historia scholastica* influenced the *GE*. Both cover the same historical period, are divided into Augustine's six ages, and follow the biblical books; but the main differences are that Alfonso wrote in a vernacular language, included more extensive information about pagan events, and incorporated Arabic and more diverse Judaic and classical sources. Petrus was an avid reader who "devoured" books, hence his nickname "eater" (*comestor*). The sources for the *Historia scholastica* include the Bible, Flavius Josephus, the Patristic, Carolingian authors, classical and late antiquity works, and authors from the twelfth century in particular.[152] Among these latter sources are Isidore's *Chronica maiora* and *Etymologies*, from which I think Comestor gained insight for the placement of his Hermeses' account.

Comestor does not incorporate the first mention of Mercury found in Isidore's *Chronica maiora*, but he does include an expanded version of the second. As we saw above, in that second mention the *Chronica maiora* says that the biblical judge Gideon ruled for forty years and then adds that "At this time the other Mercury discovered the lyre and gave it to Orpheus."[153] Comestor extensively elaborates the reference to Mercury – who becomes triplicated – and the musical instrument's discovery:

151 On Petrus Comestors's life, see Sylwan, introduction to *Petri Comestoris Scolastica historia*, x–xiii.

152 On the *Historia scholastica*'s sources, see Sylwan, introduction to *Petri Comestoris Scolastica historia*, xix–xxix.

153 "Hac aetate alter Mercurius lyram repperit et Orpheo tradidit." *Chronica maiora* 2.77[a], 49.

> At the time of Gideon, Mercury discovered the syrinxs by taking this name from Syrinx, the wife of Cadmus, who by reason of [her] zeal for harmony had departed from her husband. [Mercury] discovered the lyre in this way: he found the shell of a dead and rotten turtle, whose tendons were drying in the mouth of the shell and giving off a slender hissing [sound] when moved by a breeze. It is uncertain which of the Mercuries this one was: either Hermes, or the philosopher Trismegistus, or the younger Mercury. For it is said that there were three of them, according to Josephus.[154]

There are many remarkable things in this excerpt. Clearly, this was not Comestor's most accurate and consistent rendering of classical events (*incidentia*). First, he is confusing the syrinx – a wind instrument – with the lyre – a string one. As we saw, the syrinx is associated with Mercury in the *Metamorphoses*, where he uses it to put Argus to sleep. The lyre is discovered by "baby Hermes" in the *Homeric Hymn to Hermes*: Hermes finds a turtle and kills it to make the instrument. I think Comestor is taking this "watered-down" version from Isidore's *Etymologies*, where we find a similar account:

> They say that the lyre was first invented by Mercury in this way: when the Nile was retreating into its channels, it left behind various animals in the fields, and a tortoise was one that was marooned. When it was rotting, and its tendons were still extended inside the shell, it gave a sound when Mercury struck it. Mercury made the lyre out of this form and gave it to Orpheus, who was especially keen of this [musical] matter.[155]

Comestor offers a summarized version of this story, in which he omits the references to the Nile and Orpheus, whom as we saw Isidore mentions in the *Chronica maiora* as the recipient of the lyre. Actually, in the *Homeric Hymn* Hermes gives the lyre to Apollo, not to Orpheus,[156] and it is Apollo who traditionally bestows the lyre on Orpheus.[157]

[154] "Temporibus Gedeonis Mercurius invenit syringas, trahens hoc nomen a Syringa uxore Cadmi, quae propter zelum harmoniae a viro suo recesserat. Invenit etiam lyram hoc modo: Reperit etiam concham testudinis mortuae, et putrefactae, cujus nervuli arentes, et extensi in ore conchae, ad auram tenuem sibilum reddebant. Incertum est autem quis fuerit iste Mercurius utrum Hermes, an Trismegistus philosophus, an Mercurius minor. Tres enim leguntur fuisse secundum Josephum." Petrus Comestor, *Historia scholastica*, 274–5. I am using and translating the 1699 Madrid edition (which would later be used for the edition of the *Patrologia latine* 198, 1053–644), see Sylwan, introduction to *Petri Comestoris Scolastica historia*; Sylwan's modern edition only includes the book of Genesis.

[155] "Lyram primum a Mercurio inventam fuisse dicunt, hoc modo. Cum regrediens Nilus in suos meatus varia in campis reliquisset animalia, relicta etiam testudo est. Quae cum putrefacta esset, et nervi eius remansissent extenti intra corium, percussa a Mercurio sonitum dedit; ad cuius speciem Mercurius lyram fecit et Orpheo tradidit, qui eius rei maxime erat studiosus." Isidore, *Etymologies*.III, xxii, 8.

[156] See Athanassios, "*Homeric Hymn*"; and Athanassios, *The Orphic Hymns*.

[157] Hygini, *De Astronomica*.2.7, cited in Theony Condos, *Star Myths of the Greeks and Romans: A Sourcebook, Containing The Constellations of Pseudo-Eratosthenes and the Poetic Astronomy of Hyginus* (Grand Rapids: Phanes Press, 1997), 134.

I have not been able to find any classical reference to Syrinx as Cadmus's wife, but it seems that there is another confused element here. Classical literature offers a wide range of references to the wedding between Cadmus and Harmonia.[158] We also have myths in which Cadmus plays the lyre – not the syrinx – and Harmony is involved. In the *Dionysiaca* of Nonnus, Typhon threatens the harmony (ἁρμονία) of the universe; to defeat him, Zeus asks Cadmus to distract the giant with a melody (ἁρμονία) on his lyre, and as a reward for completing this task, he offers him as wife the young lady Harmonia (also ἁρμονία), daughter of Aphrodite and Ares.[159] Thus, Comestor's version has some "disruptions" to the ancient story that came to us (e.g., Cadmus's wife is Syrinx and she abandons him to study "harmony"). It is difficult to know if these confusions are Comestor's fault or if he founded them in other authors or *glossae*. The last obvious mistake is that Comestor says Josephus mentions that there were three Mercuries, and Trismegistus was among them. Josephus does not talk about Hermes or Mercury at all in his works. It is, however, possible that Comestor remembered a story from Josephus in which Seth was said to have preserved the vast sum of astrological lore that was revealed to him from annihilation by flood or fire. In fact, Bull hypothesizes that Josephus's inspiration for this story might have come from the story of the two Hermeses in pseudo-Manetho.[160] As Sylwan points out, Josephus is Comestor's most important source after the Bible, but sometimes he attributes quotes to him that come from an intermediary source, such as the *Glossae* (*ordinaria* and *interlinearis*, collections of biblical commentaries).[161] Besides, even though Comestor uses a vast number of sources from the twelfth century, he usually hides their authors.[162] Therefore, Comestor could have accurately drawn the story of the three Hermeses from a contemporary source – that I will suggest below – and then falsely attributed it to Josephus.

For his *incidentia* on Gideon, Comestor undoubtedly took the information that Mercury lived at that time and invented the lyre from Isidore – this information is not in Eusebius. Since Comestor talks about several Mercuries here, why did he not include the previous reference to the first Mercury who lived at the time of the captivity in Egypt that is in Isidore's *Chronica maiora*? Furthermore, if Comestor inventively elaborates on the references to Mercury and the lyre, why does he not mention that Mercury gave it to Orpheus – as the *Chronica maiora* does? I think the answer to these questions is that Comestor was not using the *Chronica maiora* for this part of the *Historia scholastica*, but the *Etymologies*, where, as we saw, Isidore included an epitome of his *Chronica maiora*. As I mentioned earlier, the epitome does not include the first mention of Hermes, and it does incorporate a shortened version of the second mention without Orpheus and the designation

158 Matia Rocchi, *Kadmos e Harmonia: un matrimonio problemmatico* (Rome: Bretschneider, 1989).

159 See Marta Otlewska-Jung, "Chapter 10 Ἁρμονίη κόσμου and ἁρμονίη ἀνδρῶν: On the Different Concepts of Harmony in the Dionysiaca of Nonnus," in *Nonnus of Panopolis in Context III* (Leiden: Brill, 2021), 207.

160 Bull, *Tradition of Hermes*, 54. Josephus, *Jewish Antiquities*, 1.67.1–71.5.

161 Sylwan, introduction to *Petri Comestoris Scolastica historia*, xxiv.

162 Sylwan, introduction to *Petri Comestoris Scolastica historia*, xxvi–xxvii.

of this Hermes as "the other" (*alter*). The *Etymologies* just say: "Gideon forty years. Mercury made the lyre."[163] Comestor used and elaborated on the information in his own way. Besides, the (uncredited) quotation of the passage from the *Etymologies* where Hermes invents the lyre that Comestor places here reinforces my thesis that Comestor was using this work.

Since he was talking about Mercury, in all probability Comestor "the book-eater" remembered that he had recently read about the existence of three Mercuries in the prologue of a work that was diffused around Europe at the time he was writing his *Scholastic History*: either the *Liber de compositione alchemiae* (or *Liber morienus*), the *Septem tractatus Hermetis sapientia triplicis*, or the *Liber de sex rerum principiis*. The first prologue is from 1144, and the other two were inspired by it and also written around the middle of the twelfth century, or soon after.[164] The *Historia scholastica* was finished around 1170.[165] Comestor uses a vast number of twelfth-century books as sources, which he had access to due to his prominent positions in Paris's schools, the intellectual centre of Europe at the time. We can imagine that the first translation of a book of alchemy into Latin, or a new book on Hermetic-cosmological sciences – which included the prologues on the three Mercuries – reached Paris at this time and aroused great curiosity. Comestor might have had privileged access to one of those prologues, but he might have been reluctant to acknowledge his source, because they were treatises related to alchemy and astrology – arts the Church viewed with suspicion. His cautiousness could justify the false attribution to Josephus, whom Comestor quotes innumerable times, often in a "colourful way." At any rate, the only known mentions of the three Hermeses in Latin prior to the *Historia scholastica* are in those three prologues. The puzzled way in which he also deals with the sources on the lyre and the syrinx here justifies the addition of the vague reference to the three Mercuries. Comestor affirms that he does not know which of the three Mercuries is the one from Gideon's time, but he could be "Hermes, or the philosopher Trismegistus, or the younger Mercury." Comestor also decided to omit identifying the first two Mercuries with Enoch and Noah, because it would have distorted the chronological calculations of his "historical Bible," where biblical and pagan facts had to coincide in the same chronology. However, his brief summary could have been taken from one of the three prologues, because a Hermes, a Trismegistus the philosopher, and a Mercury are indeed mentioned in them. The soubriquet of the last one, the "younger Mercury" (*Mercurius minor*), could come from *The City of God* – another important source for Comestor. As we saw, inspired by the Hermetic treatise *Asclepius*, Augustine mentions an "elder Mercury" (*Mercurius maior*); therefore, it is logical to assume that a younger Mercury also existed.

163 "Gedeon ann. XL. Mercurius lyram condidit." Isidore, *Etymologies*.V, xxxix, 11.

164 As we saw, concerning the *Liber de sex rerum principiis*, Delp affirms that "there are factors that make it unlikely that the treatise was composed much after 1150." Delp , "*Twelfth Century Cosmology*," 15–16.

165 Sylwan, introduction to *Petri Comestoris Scolastica historia*, xi.

Three Hermeses: From Petrus Comestor to Lucas de Tuy

Lucas de Tuy certainly took his section on the three Hermeses from Petrus Comestor. Lucas quotes some sentences word for word, but he also introduces subtle yet relevant changes in other places. Lucas presents the information in a clearer and more certain way than Petrus Comestor. I highlight Lucas's changes in italics in both my translation and the original Latin in the footnote. I will indicate the interpolation present in one of the manuscripts with < … >:

> *Gideon judged the people [of Israel] for forty years. The other* Mercury discovered the syrinxs by taking this name from Syrinx, the wife of Cadmus, who by reason of the study of harmony *departed* from her husband. [Mercury] *discovered* the lyre in this way: he *found* the shell of a dead and rotten turtle, whose tendons were drying and extended and, *struck by a blow of the air*, were giving off a slender hissing, [and] *to imitate this [Mercury] invented the lyre and gave it to Orpheus. It is said that he came to Spain and founded the city of Flowers. There were three Mercuries: the first was* Hermes <*… the son of Jupiter and grandson of Atlas, who it is said was deified*>; *the second one was* the philosopher Trismegistus; *and the third was* the younger Mercury, brilliant by *[his] many studies.*[166]

As we saw, the first book of the *Chronicon mundi* is based on Isidore's *Chronica maiora*, which Lucas complements with information from Comestor. I assume Lucas realized that in this passage Comestor was using his main source, Isidore – who inspired him to place the second Mercury in Gideon's times – so Lucas decided to combine and clarify his two primary references. We observe this at the beginning of the above quote. Lucas does not include the previous lengthy account of Gideon's rule that we see in Comestor – as his book is briefer and much different in scope – and he summarizes it with the succinct phrase, "Gideon judged the people [of Israel] for forty years." This is the exact wording Isidore used. The next sentence in Isidore is: "At this time the other Mercury discovered the lyre and gave it to Orpheus."[167] According to my hypothesis, Comestor used the epitome of the *Etymologies*, but Lucas referenced the original passage from the *Chronica maiora*, so he decided to restore Isidore's specification that this Mercury, from Gideon's time, was "the other" Mercury, as well as the reference to Orpheus – neither the first Mercury nor Orpheus were included in the epitome.

Lucas chose to follow Comestor's expanded version of the second mention of Mercury and its erroneous reference to the syrinx instead of the lyre, but Lucas also introduces some small grammatical and stylistic amendments. Lucas adds a clarification, letting us know that the turtle's tendons were "stricken by a blow of air."

166 "*Gedeon iudicauit populum quadraginta annis. Aliter* Mercurius inuenit siringas trahens hoc nomen a Siringa uxore Cadmi, que propter *studium* armonie a uiro suo *recessit. Reperit* etiam liram hoc modo: *inuenit* concam testudinis mortue, cuius nerui arentes et extensi *flatu aure percussi* tenuem sibilum reddebant *ad quorum imitationem liram reperit et Orfeo tradidit. Hic fertur in Yspaniam uenisse et ciuitatem Florem condidisse. Tres fuerunt Mercurii. Primus fuit Hermes [… filius Iouis et nepos Athlantis qui dicitur fuisse deificatus]. Secundus iste, qui et* Tremegistus philosophus. *Tercius* Mercurius minor *in multis studiis clarus*." *Chronicon mundi*.1.34, 37.

167 "Hac aetate alter Mercurius lyram repperit et Orpheo tradidit." *Chronica maiora* 2.77[d], 49.

Next, in a substantial addition Lucas explains that "to imitate" the sound of the air vibrating the tendons, Mercury "invented the lyre and gave it to Orpheus." By adding Orpheus back into the discussion here, and especially the addition of the lyre, Lucas makes the confusion even greater. Furthermore, I cannot determine about whom Lucas is thinking when he then states that "he came to Spain and founded the city of Flowers" – was this Orpheus or Mercury?

Finally, we get to our three Mercuries, the crucial part of the piece, which Lucas presents in a more succinct and organized form than Comestor. From the beginning, Lucas affirms that there were three Mercuries, whereas Comestor only summarizes it at the end and attributes this declaration to an "apocryphal" Josephus. This declaration reminds us of the *GE*, which says: "we find that there were three Hermeses."[168] Perhaps because he knows that it was inaccurate, Lucas omits Comestor's mention of Josephus – whose work he knew well. Besides, even though Comestor expresses doubts as to which Mercury he is talking about, Lucas numbers them and imposes an order of their sequence in history. Thus, we know that "the first was Hermes." As I indicated above, in one of the manuscripts of the *Chronicon mundi* there is an interpolation clarifying that this first Mercury was "the son of Jupiter and grandson of Atlas, who it is said was deified."[169] The clarification makes sense, because it lets us know that this Hermes was the one taken from Isidore that Lucas mentioned earlier, to whom he already attributed these features. Then Lucas says that "the second was this one, who was the philosopher Trismegistus" (i.e., the Mercury who lived at the time of Gideon and gave the lyre to Orpheus). Comestor expresses doubts about which one was Gideon's Hermes, but Lucas is certain that he was the second one. Finally, Lucas reveals that "the younger Mercury" was the third – but he also adds that he was "shining due to [his] many studies" (*in multis studiis clarus*). This phrasing in reminiscent of Augustine's in *The City of God*. When describing Egypt during the time of Mercury, Augustine writes, "called Trismegistus," when "studies of that kind [i.e., philosophy] shone" (*eius modi studia claruerunt*).[170] As we saw above, Augustine is referring to the grandson of the elder Mercury – who in turn, was Atlas's grandson. If the grandfather was "the elder Mercury," it is logical to think that the grandson was "the other" Mercury mentioned by Isidore, and also the "younger Mercury" Comestor introduced. By trying to match the three Mercuries with his sources, Lucas affirms that Trismegistus was the second one and the young Mercury – related to words derived from *clarus* and *studiis* – was the third, while if he followed Augustine they would have been identified as the same figure.

Even though he was not completely successful, Lucas tried to close the circle not only by clarifying who the two original Hermeses were – implied in the *Asclepius*, mentioned by Augustine, and collected by Isidore – but also by including them in the enhanced list of three Hermeses from Comestor, which have an Arabic origin. In this way, he paved the way for the section on Hermes in the *GE*, where the Arabic

168 "[...] fallamos que fueron tres los Hermes."

169 This is the manuscript that Falque calls B, from Barcelona, and the one I think Lucas was using in relation to his first mention of Mercury, in which I pointed out earlier that there is another interpolation on Mercury.

170 Augustine, *Civitate Dei* XVIII, xxxix.

The story of the Three Hermeses in the *General Estoria*, Genealogy of sources and references

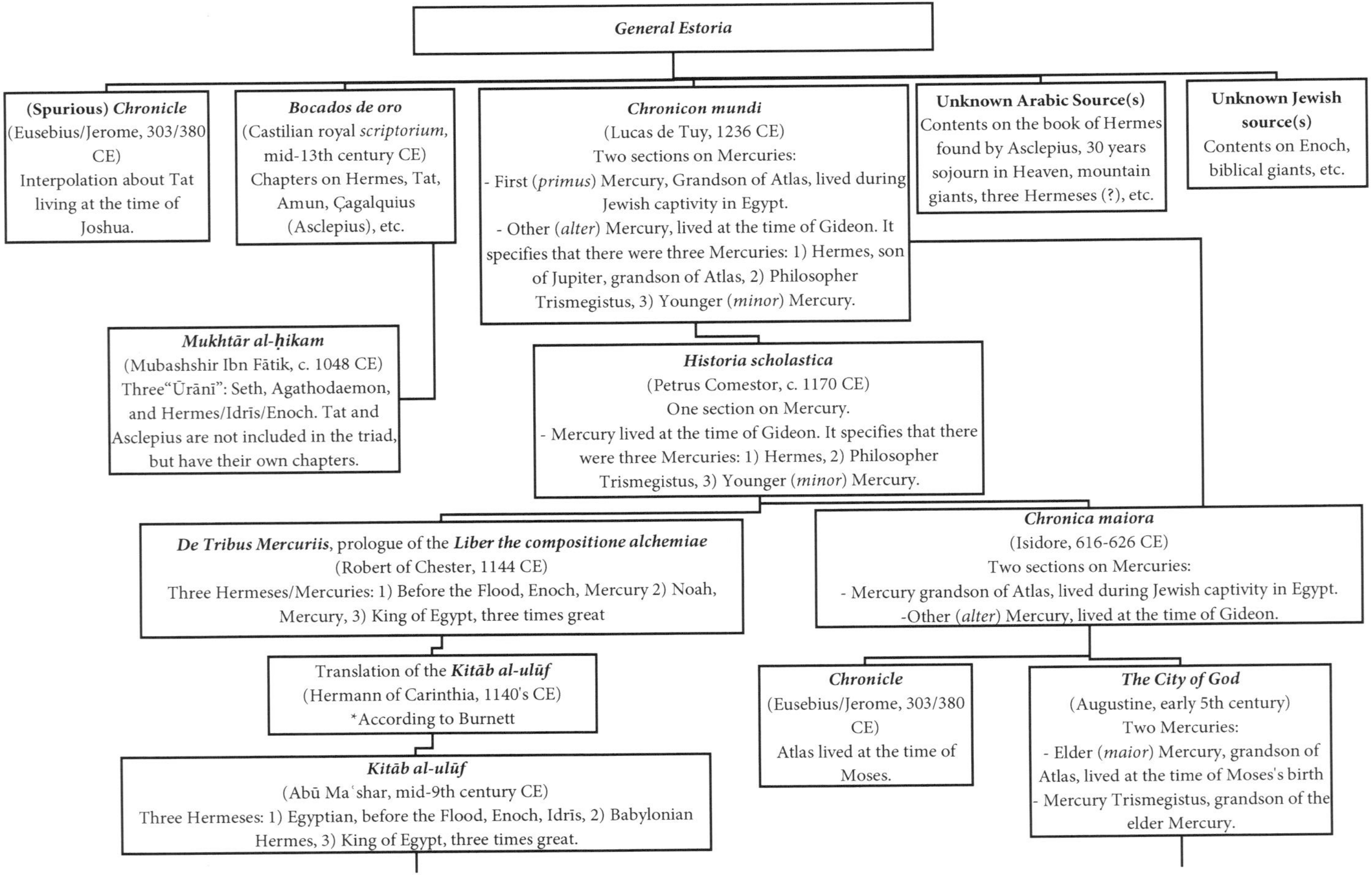

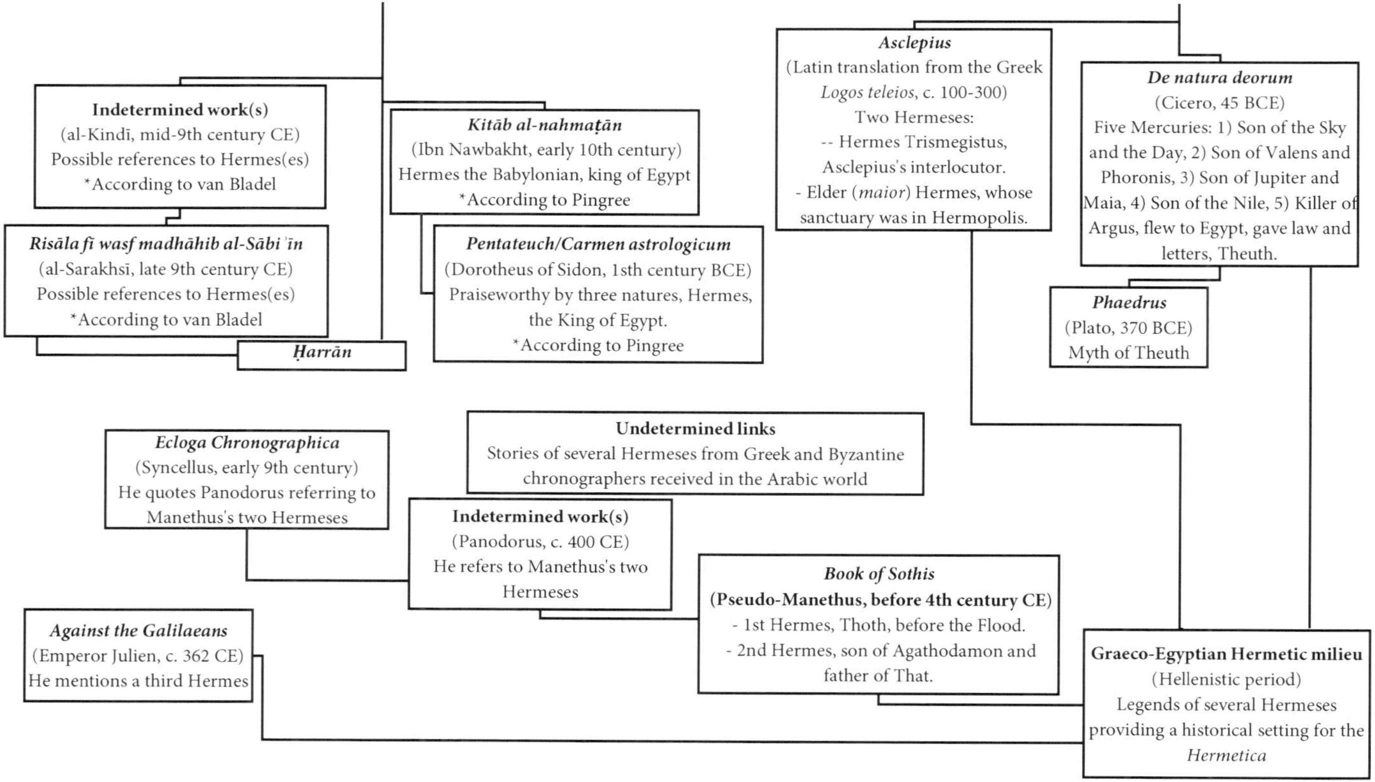
Indetermined work(s)
(al-Kindī, mid-9th century CE)
Possible references to Hermes(es)
*According to van Bladel
Risāla fī wasf madhāhib al-Sābi ʾīn
(al-Sarakhsī, late 9th century CE)
Possible references to Hermes(es)
*According to van Bladel
Ḥarrān
Kitāb al-nahmaṭān
(Ibn Nawbakht, early 10th century)
Hermes the Babylonian, king of Egypt
*According to Pingree
Pentateuch/Carmen astrologicum
(Dorotheus of Sidon, 1sth century BCE)
Praiseworthy by three natures, Hermes, the King of Egypt.
*According to Pingree
Asclepius
(Latin translation from the Greek Logos teleios, c. 100-300)
Two Hermeses:
-- Hermes Trismegistus, Asclepius's interlocutor.
- Elder (maior) Hermes, whose sanctuary was in Hermopolis.
De natura deorum
(Cicero, 45 BCE)
Five Mercuries: 1) Son of the Sky and the Day, 2) Son of Valens and Phoronis, 3) Son of Jupiter and Maia, 4) Son of the Nile, 5) Killer of Argus, flew to Egypt, gave law and letters, Theuth.
Phaedrus
(Plato, 370 BCE)
Myth of Theuth
Undetermined links
Stories of several Hermeses from Greek and Byzantine chronographers received in the Arabic world
Ecloga Chronographica
(Syncellus, early 9th century)
He quotes Panodorus referring to Manethus's two Hermeses
Indetermined work(s)
(Panodorus, c. 400 CE)
He refers to Manethus's two Hermeses
Book of Sothis
(Pseudo-Manethus, before 4th century CE)
- 1st Hermes, Thoth, before the Flood.
- 2nd Hermes, son of Agathodamon and father of That.
Against the Galilaeans
(Emperor Julien, c. 362 CE)
He mentions a third Hermes
Graeco-Egyptian Hermetic milieu
(Hellenistic period)
Legends of several Hermeses providing a historical setting for the Hermetica

components are increased. Not surprisingly, the chronological difficulties would increase when Alfonso had to match the sources we have seen so far with some new, and unknown ones, both of Arabic and Latin backgrounds.

Conclusion

Previous researchers have presented various hypotheses about the origins of the legend of the three Hermeses in *GE2*. Driven by the legend's context in the work – in the lengthy section on the book of Hermes – and its Eastern flavor, Lida de Malkiel suggested an Arabic origin.[171] In the decades that followed, Pingree popularized the Arabic version of the legend by Abū Maʿshar in his edition of the *Kitāb al-ulūf*, and Plessner connected that legend with the prologues of the three twelfth-century Latin treatises, which are reminiscent of the Arabic version. With this new information in hand, Fraker suggested Abū Maʿshar as a possible source of the legend in *GE2*, and he also pointed to those Latin prologues as possible intermediaries. Throughout this chapter I have outlined a much more complex and richer picture of the origins of the legend, its transmitters, and its whereabouts in the Iberian Peninsula from late antiquity onwards. I have also proposed two possible direct sources for the legend that are difficult to dismiss because they are among Alfonso's most important historical references and are also connected to each other: Petrus Comestor and Lucas de Tuy. Therefore, we are in a better position to outline the historical and intellectual lineage of the legend of the three Hermeses and the journey it took to reach Alfonso.

I agree with Cottrell about the legend's origin in the Hellenistic world and it arising from the same lore that gave birth to the syncretic figure of Hermes Trismegistus. As Bull suggests, it is likely that lists of three or more Hermeses were created within the philosophical and theological speculations that developed in Egypt's intellectual centres, such as Memphis, and from there it reached the Greek/Hellenistic and Latin cultures. The two Hermeses – plus Tat in pseudo-Manetho – and the third Hermes mentioned by Emperor Julian are evidence of these Egyptian origins in Greek, while Cicero's five Mercuries are Latin evidence. The existence of more than one Hermes is also suggested by Hermetic treatises such as the *Korê kosmou* (in Greek) and the *Asclepius*, which is actually the Latin rendering of a Greek work. The two Hermeses of the *Asclepius* were noticed by Augustine, and by mentioning them in *The City of God* – where he also relates them to the mythological Mercury – he made them accessible to Latin Christendom. Since Hermes Trismegistus and his incarnations were considered historical figures, he was soon included in the works of Christian chroniclers. Hermes is absent from the most influential chronicle, Eusebius's, which was translated into Latin by Jerome; however, some subsequent chroniclers added two Hermeses as part of the Christian chronologies. In the eastern Mediterranean, the Alexandrian Panodorus (*c.* 400 CE) – and perhaps his contemporary Annianus, according to Van Bladel – inserted pseudo-Manetho's two Hermeses (antediluvian and postdiluvian) in their chronicles; centuries later, the Byzantine Syncellus (ninth century) talked about the two Hermeses and quoted Panodorus. In the western

[171] For the sake of space, I will not repeat the references found earlier in the chapter.

Mediterranean, Isidore included two Mercuries in the second book of his *Chronica maiora*. This cannot come as a surprise due to the exchange of thought that occurred throughout the ancient Mediterranean, and also due to Isidore's curiosity about Hermes Trismegistus, as he shows in his *Etymologies*. In fact, I regard the two Hermeses in Isidore's *Chronica maiora* as an attempt to integrate Augustine's two Hermeses within Eusebius's chronology, since they are Isidore's most important chronicle authorities.

Islamic civilization's development and reception of Greek and Near Eastern cultures led to works on Hermetic sciences and catalogues of Hermeses appearing in Arabic. The most influential list is that of the three Hermeses in Abū Maʿshar's *Kitāb al-ulūf*. Van Bladel suggests that this author was influenced by the epithet Trismegistus and the works of Greek chroniclers who mentioned an antediluvian and a postdiluvian Hermes. Even though we cannot dismiss those influences, I agree with Cottrell's criticism of the theory and believe that the inspiration might have come from the city of Ḥarrān or from earlier Arabic versions from the Hermetic lore. Specialists such as Plessner, Fraker, Walbridge, and Fodor claimed that Abū Maʿshar's three Hermeses are only one version of the legend. However, this version was prominent in the Iberian Peninsula. During the heyday of Andalusi culture, the historians of sciences Ibn Juljul and Sāʾid al-Andalusī quoted Abū Maʿshar's legend and contributed to its diffusion in the Arabic-speaking world.

After Andalusi territories fell into Christian hands and precious Arabic books became part of the spoils of victory, learned men from Europe flocked to Spain to translate them. The *Liber de compositione alchemiae* – the first book on alchemy in Latin – was translated in 1144 by Robert of Chester, who inserted a prologue on the three Hermeses in the Arabic original: *De tribus Mercuriis*. Since this prologue mentions the antediluvian and postdiluvian Mercuries, it is probable that the list was taken from Abū Maʿshar. Furthermore, there is evidence that the *Kitāb al-ulūf* was also translated into Latin in the twelfth century, because Hermann of Carinthia quotes it in his *De essentiis*. Hermann of Carinthia worked in Spain, where he translated other works by Abū Maʿshar. Therefore, Hermann could have made the legend of the three Hermeses accessible to Chester, as Burnett suggests. *De tribus Mercuriis* is echoed in the prologues of the other two Latin books on Hermetic sciences, which is an indication of the diffusion of Hermann's text.

According to my hypothesis, *De tribus Mercuriis*, or one of the other two prologues containing the three Hermeses, reached Paris a few decades later, where it fell into the hands of Petrus Comestor. Comestor took the reference that one Mercury had lived at the time of the biblical Gideon from Isidore – who probably established that date, as we saw – and decided to also include the reference to the three Mercuries that he had recently read in one of the Latin prologues. In fact, Comestor did not take the reference to Mercury in Gideon's time from the *Chronica maiora* but from the epitome of this work that Isidore included in his *Etymologies* – and this explains why, for instance, Comestor does not mention an earlier Mercury during the time of Joseph.

A few decades later the three Hermeses "came back" to Spain. The first book of Lucas de Tuy's *Chronicon mundi* is mostly based on Isidore's *Chronica maiora*, which is complemented with some other sources, especially Comestor's *Historia scholastica*.

Lucas mentions Isidore's two Mercuries, one in Joseph's time and another in Gideon's time, and supplements the second with Comestor's additions – including the three Mercuries. Lucas takes verbatim quotes from Comestor but also elaborates and presents his data in a more ordered fashion.

The journey ends with the three Hermeses in *GE2*. Eusebius and Jerome's *Chronicle* represents the ultimate chronological authority in the *GE*, followed by Petrus Comestor and Lucas de Tuy. However, Isidore and Augustine are also important references for Alfonso. This suggests that references to Mercury and his different embodiments could be found among some of the main sources Alfonso used for the *GE*. It is possible that Alfonso did have – as he affirms – a version of Eusebius and Jerome's *Chronicle* with an interpolation that stated that Tat, son of Hermes Trismegistus, had lived around the time of Joshua, right after Moses. Isidore and Lucas situate one Mercury during the time of the Egyptian captivity, at the end of which Moses was born, and this means that his son could have lived a little later. The second Mercury in Isidore, Lucas, and Comestor is in Gideon's time, many years after Moses. Because of these contradictions, Alfonso might have privileged his main source, Eusebius – which also provides a convenient chronology, midway between Moses and Gideon – and situated his section on Hermes Trismegistus and the three Hermeses in Joshua's time.

Both Comestor and Lucas de Tuy mention the story of the three Mercuries along with Gideon's Mercury. Looking for consistency – as always – Alfonso might have also decided to concentrate everything in his section on Joshua. Even though the two possibilities remain open, I am inclined to think that Alfonso took inspiration from Lucas, rather than from Comestor, to talk about the three Mercuries. Alfonso had undoubtedly read the brief sections of Lucas's *Chronicon mundi* where Hermes Trismegistus and the other two Mercuries are mentioned – because he directly quotes him from those pages. To introduce his list, Lucas also categorically affirms that there were three Mercuries ("Tres fuerunt Mercurii"), which the *GE* also states in Castilian ("fueron tres los Hermes"). At the beginning of Gideon's section, Lucas talks about "the other Mercury" ("alter Mercurius"), because he had introduced a first Mercury in Joseph's section – and these are the two Mercuries that he takes from Isidore. Reminiscent of this, the *GE* talks about "The other Hermes" ("el otro Hermes") in the title and the end of this section.

Alfonso had other works at his disposal to supplement the *Chronicle* of Eusebius – which included Hermes and Tat– and the three Mercuries from Lucas. At least some of the Castilian king's collaborators were familiar with the *Bocados*. In that work, Hermes Trismegistus, Tat, and Asclepius are mentioned, the same characters who appear in this section of the *GE*. In Augustine and Isidore, Alfonso might have found not only several Mercuries and evidence that one of them was Hermes Trismegistus but also information from classical sources about the mythological Mercury as the god of merchants, which *GE2* also mentions. Alfonso added some unknown Arabic sources, especially the book of Hermes found by Asclepius that the passage develops later – as we will see in Chapter Five. Some Jewish sources might have been added to the mix, because Hermes's relationship with Enoch is emphasized, and biblical and apocryphal giants appear in the story. These sources align with the other magical and astrological books translated or composed by Alfonso in which Hermes Trismegistus has a significant role.

This might be one of those cases in which the *GE* uses numerous and varied sources, which many times confronted Alfonso and his team with strange, improbable, and inconsistent data, as Almeida reflects. In these instances Alfonso's talent and the originality of his work is truly evident, as he persistently attempted "to match the sources and understand their meaning using all available resources."[172] I also think that in this section on Hermes Trismegistus Alfonso presents one of his *estorias unadas* (joined histories), explained by Fernández-Ordóñez as the will to transcend the strictly chronological layout of events and to collect essential information on a main character or event,[173] as happens here. Even though Mercury had appeared earlier in the *GE*, Alfonso decided not to dwell on an explanation of Mercury as Hermes Trismegistus – an important figure connected to his astrological and magical interests. Justified by previous chroniclers, this figure is going to be deeply scrutinized in *GE2*. Undoubtedly, Hermes was the perfect topic for one of these Alfonsine *historias unadas*, cross-cutting examinations on specific topics and characters that appeared throughout different sources, and even in different embodiments. It would be similar to the case of Hercules later in *GE2*, which "is the result of combining many different sources in a *estoria unada* that enhances the importance of that character so admired by Alfonso."[174] Hercules's case has even more similarities with that of Hermes, as in his *estoria* "we find that there were four Hercules."[175] Furthermore, in slight contradiction with the *GE*, the other great historical work by Alfonso, the *Estoria de España* (*History of Spain*), presents a chapter "On the three Hercules that existed in the world and why they were called like that";[176] according to Fernández-Ordóñez, this section is the result of combining another earlier Castilian chronicler writing in Latin, Rodrigo Jiménez de Rada, with some unknown Arabic sources.

The analysis of the section on Hermes in *GE2* reveals the deep interconnection of all the intellectual traditions that existed in the Iberian Peninsula and materialized in the sources used by Alfonso. To summarize my explanation of how the legend of the three Hermeses spread through various intellectual paths and intercultural influences, a diagram will conclude this chapter. Stories about Hermes and the origins of wisdom sprang from Egyptian-Hellenistic and classical, and then Patristic, Byzantine, Arabic, Jewish, Latin, and Castilian sources, all of which are echoed in the narrative on Hermes Trismegistus in the *GE*. Thus, the Castilian Hermes comes to represent the cultural transactions that occurred throughout the Mediterranean Sea for more than one thousand years, and also some of the agents in those transactions.

172 Almeida, introduction to *GE2* I, xli.

173 Fernández-Ordóñez, *Las Estorias de Alfonso*, 55. See also Almeida, introduction to *GE2* I, lvi.

174 Fernández-Ordóñez, *Las Estorias de Alfonso*, 76. The length "History of Hercules" is in *GE2* II, 42–118.

175 "Mas fallamos que fueron cuatro Ércules." *GE2* II, 43.

176 "De los tres Hércules que ouo en el mundo, e porque se pusieron assi nombre." *Primera Crónica General*, chapter 4, in Fernández-Ordóñez, *Las Estorias de Alfonso*, 76–80.

Hermes's many faces represent the Mercury of Ovidian mythology, the hybrid Greco-Egyptian god of knowledge, the biblical Enoch, the erudite inventor of occult arts, and the legendary sage whose fame came to the Western lands from the Levant, among other roles. Ultimately, this figure is an embodiment of most wisdom traditions, the archetypical model of the learned man and subject that Alfonso sought to reshape for his kingdom, and the Spanish Hermes that my book seeks to portray.

5

Hermes's Wisdom and the Liberal Arts in the *General Estoria*

Introduction

The key aspect of Hermes Trismegistus in ancient times was his association with various forms of knowledge; nothing better characterizes him than as a master of ancient wisdom. *GE2* reveals the existence of not just one, but three wise men named Hermes, one of whom was Hermes Trismegistus, identified with the god Mercury. Even though Hermes Trismegistus was well known to Alfonso, who had mentioned him in previous astrological and magical works, this is his first appearance in the *GE*. Alfonso reminds readers of the recurrence of Mercury, identified with one of the Hermeses: "One of them was he whom they called Mercury, whose case we have already talked about in this history."[1] Then Alfonso refers back to three fundamental features of the god Mercury whom he mentioned earlier in the *GE*. The first two (he was the god of the merchants and the son of Jupiter) were well-known, but the third is a somewhat unique characteristic among ancient and medieval sources: Mercury was the god of the *trivium*. Moreover, Alfonso affirms that the surname "Trismegistus" derives from *trivium*, an assertion that is not explicitly found in any other Hermetic or historical work.

> [Mercury] was a consummate master of the three knowledges of the *trivium* – which are grammar, dialectics, and rhetoric – as we have already told you in this history. On account of this, they called him Trismegistus, that is, master of these three knowledges in a more accomplished way than any other wise men at that time; and they also called him god of the *trivium*, because those who wanted to learn something about some of these arts or all of them entrusted themselves to him. Now we are going to talk to you about other things that happened on account of the knowledge of this Hermes Trismegistus.[2]

1 "Et el uno d'ellos fue al que dixieron Mercurio, sobre cuya razón avemos ya dicho ante d'esto en esta estoria." *GE2* I, 48.

2 "[Mercurio] fue complidamientre maestro de los tres saberes del trivio, que son la gramática, la dialética e la rectoria, assí cuemo vos lo avemos departido en esta estoria ante d'esto. Et dixiéronle por ende este nombre Trimagisto, fascas maestro de tres saberes más complidamientre que todos los otros sabios d'aquella sazón, e llamáronle otrossí dios del trivio, e los que en alguna d'estas tres artes o en todas querién aprender algo a Mercurio se acomendauan. Agora dezir vos emos d'otras cosas que acaecieron sobre razón del saber d'este Hermes Trimegisto" *GE2* I, 48.

This association of Hermes with the liberal arts reframes his Hellenistic role as master of all knowledge. The liberal arts – *trivium* and *quadrivium* – are extremely important to Alfonso's scientific and educational goals. He considered them as both the essence of wisdom and the only path towards it. Many specialists have focused on Alfonso's relationship with the liberal arts and the medieval background connected to it.[3] In the *GE*, most exemplary characters from antiquity are associated with the liberal arts, but none more so than Mercury/Hermes. In the Latin Middle Ages, wisdom was often represented by the liberal arts, so it is not surprising that Alfonso associates Hermes with them. What is truly intriguing is how the *GE* explains the origins of Hermes's vast knowledge, which occurs in two different sections that are related to the Eastern and Western traditions that converged at Alfonso's court. Previous scholars have focused on each one separately, but I am going to analyze them as a pair.

The first section is located immediately after the abovementioned quotation, in a chapter called "On the reasons for the knowledge of Hermes." Alfonso mentions that the knowledge of the liberal arts elevated Hermes to the status of a god, and then explains the divine origins of this knowledge. Although the section does not mention the *trivium* again, its placement in the *GE* helps to clarify the extent of Mercury's knowledge of it. As I mentioned in Chapter Four, specialists have connected this first section to Arabic Hermetic sources. In this section, the knowledge of Hermes is explained from a Hermetic point of view and has an undeniably Arab and Jewish esoteric flavour.

The second section, which focuses on the liberal arts from a Western perspective, starts just twenty-two pages after the first one and is called "On the knowledge Mercury possessed," and offers a completely different explanation of the origins of that knowledge. First, I will focus on the Hermetic section, then the Mercurial one, which I connect to Mercury's other appearances in the *GE* that reference the liberal arts. Finally, I will investigate the Western and Eastern origins of these traditions that link Hermes/Mercury to the *trivium* and *quadrivium*. As we will see, the merging of wisdom traditions from diverse backgrounds in the figure of Hermes had begun many centuries earlier, but was re-elaborated by Alfonso in a unique way that connects the genealogy of Hermes's wisdom to his own intellectual and political claims during his time.

How Hermes Gained His Knowledge

After revealing that Hermes/Mercury's knowledge of the *trivium* was so extensive that he was considered its god, Alfonso elaborates on this statement through a section with a distinctly Hermetic narrative. Despite its Arabic flavour, the tale starts with an Ovidian quotation about Mount Parnassus, which Alfonso classifies as one of the seven largest mountains on earth – according to a book by Asclepius.[4] Asclepius (*Esculapio*) is a figure deeply attached to the Hermetic tradition and frequently identified as Hermes's disciple, as we have seen earlier. Asclepius describes how "he found a book of Hermes, the great philosopher about whom we have talked, and he did not understand anything in it."[5] We must remember that for Alfonso: 1) a philosopher is a specialist

3 See Martínez, *El humanismo medieval*, 257–73; and Rico, *Alfonso el Sabio*, 142–66.

4 *GE2* I, 48–9. The quotation is from *Met.*I, 313–17.

5 "Dize que falló un libro de Hermes, el grant filosofo que vos avemos dicho, e non entendié en él ninguna cosa." *GE2* II, 49.

in the liberal arts; 2) "finding stories," especially finding lost books, is a characteristic of Hermetic and alchemical literature.[6] Asclepius was unable to understand the book until he found an old Chaldean woman and told her: "I found a book of Hermes which had many figures [who were] so different from each other that they did not look alike."[7] It seems that Asclepius is referring to hieroglyphics or cuneiform script, which are also the presumed inspiration for some astrological and magical signs that appear in the *Picatrix*.[8] The old woman's Chaldean background reinforces this section's connection to the Arabic legend of the three Hermeses, which included a Babylonian Hermes. We also discover that the woman "was of the same nature of the giants, called Goghgobón, and the niece of Nimrod – the giant who made the Tower of Babel due to fear of the Flood."[9] Nimrod (*Nemprot*) appeared earlier in the *GE*, as did the biblical giants, whom Alfonso identified with the Titans who attacked the Olympian gods – a likeness that he might have taken from Josephus.[10] Genesis 6:4 states: "The *Nephilim* were on the earth in those days – and also afterward – when the sons of God went in to the daughters of humans, who bore children to them. These were the heroes that were of old, warriors of renown." The Hebrew word *Nephilim* probably means "the fallen ones" – which would indicate their connection to the fallen angels, usually identified with the "sons of God." The Hebrew Bible qualifies the *Nephilim* as *Gibborim*, "the mightiest," an intensive form of *gabar* (mighty), which can also be translated as "great warrior," "of great stature," or "giant." For this reason, the Greek Septuagint and the Latin *Vulgate* both translated *Nephilim* as "giants."

The mysterious passage in Genesis is reminiscent of the ancient Near Eastern myth about rebellion in the pantheon, and it generated a substantial number of narratives.[11] The most prominent is the Jewish apocryphal Enochian literature, starting in the last two centuries BCE, which did not enter into the Christian biblical canon but resonates with it – as well as with many other religious traditions. Alexander explains how certain Jewish intellectuals in the Second Temple period came to regard Enoch as a major figure of sacred history and started a tradition which continued developing "with surprising vitality down to the Middle Ages, and which constantly challenged the dominant Mosaic paradigm of Judaism. They created a figure who, transcending humanism, was assimilated into Christianity, Gnosticism, and Islam."[12]

Among this literature of Enoch – in which he reveals secrets acquired during his heavenly encounters with God and angels – the *Book of Watchers* stands out, the first of five or more separate works that together make up 1 Enoch (6–36). The only complete copy of 1 Enoch is in Ethiopic; 2 Enoch is preserved in Old Church Slavonic, and 3 Enoch in Hebrew. Aramaic fragments of 1 Enoch and other related literature, such

6 See, for instance, Fodor, "The Origins of the Arabic Legends of the Pyramids," 337–8.

7 "Falle un libro de Hermes en que avié muchas figuras departidas las unas de las otras, de guisa que non se semejaban." *GE2* I, 49.

8 See the signs for the planets in *Picatrix* IV.ii.19–26.

9 "[...] era de la natura de los gigantes, e quel dizién Goghgobon por so nombre proprio. E fuera sobrina de Nemprot, el gigant que fiziera la grant torre de Babel por miedo del diluvio." *GE2* I, 50.

10 Josephus, *Antiquitates*, 4.35.

11 See Patricia Crone, *The Qur'ānic Pagans and Related Matters* (Leiden: Brill, 2016), 17.

12 Alexander, "From Son of Adam," 87.

as the *Book of the Giants*, were found among the Dead Sea Scrolls.[13] The Enochian watchers (*iyrin*, in Aramaic) are a category of angels sent to earth to watch over humans, but they illicitly instructed men in arts such as metallurgy, ornamentation, goldsmithery, make-up, magic, and astrology. The watchers lusted after women and procreated with them. Their offspring are the *Nephilim* (giants), who pillaged the earth and wreaked havoc. This turmoil and the corruption of humanity led to the Flood. In the Greek version of 1 Enoch the watchers are called *Egrēgoroi*.

Goghgobón, the giant woman with whom Asclepius consults, also appears in different *GE2* manuscripts as Godgobon, Yothbon, Yocbon, Yoglibon, Zogbon, Goachgobon, Gochbongobon, Eggobon, Hochgobon, Oghgobon, Othgobon, and Agotgobon.[14] I suggest that some of these variants could be related to the Hebrew word *Gibborim* or the Greek *Egrēgoroi*, perhaps through some intermediary transliteration into other languages. Van Bladel connects the Arabic versions of the "watchers" and their Persian intermediaries, where the Flood is an important element, with Abū Maʿshar's story of the three Hermeses – also closely connected with this section of *GE2*, as we saw in Chapter Four. Van Bladel also suggests that Abū Maʿshar took the Enochian tradition's stories about giants and "watchers" from Greek chronographers and then spread them throughout the Arabic-speaking world.[15]

When Asclepius shows the book of Hermes to Goghgobón in *GE2*, she observes that "these letters/figures are from my relatives the giants, from whose lineage I come, and these figures are such that from a single one many works can be made and many words can be kept on it, that is why we say that it is a figure of knowledge, power, and great virtue."[16] The story is connected to the Enochian tradition, but the language – power, virtue – hints at Arabic magic. The lineage of giants she comes from helped establish civilization by changing the course of rivers and building roads, castles, towers, and mountains using their great strength.[17] These giants had a more productive impact than those in 1 Enoch. According to Goghgobón, the giants also imprisoned Gog and Magog beyond the Riphean Mountains (*montes Rifeos*) – probably the Ural Mountains. Even though these characters come from the Bible, the legend of the monsters Gog and Magog being caged behind the Ural or Caspian Mountains – associated with the Gates of Alexander – developed in Syriac in the seventh century, is alluded to in the Quran (18:83–102), and was transmitted through various other works, such as the Arabic book of Alexander and the works of Arab geographers, who often refer to Gog and Magog as giants.[18]

The Church Fathers embraced this story of the fallen angels, their gigantic offspring, and their illicit teachings, particularly those on magic. Justin the Martyr (d. 165), Clement

13 Crone, *Qurʾānic Pagans*, 17–18.

14 See variants in the critical apparatus, *GE2* I, 632 and 634. See also Solalinde's edition, *General estoria: segunda parte*, 1:36 and 39.

15 Van Bladel, *Arabic Hermes*, 145–6.

16 "Estas figuras letras fueron de los gigantes mios parientes de cuyo linage yo vengo, e estas figuras son tales que por una que yo veo sola en ella se fazen muchas obras, e enciérranse en ella munchas palabras; e dezímosle nós que es figura de saber e de poder e de muy grand vertud." *GE2* I, 50.

17 *GE2* 1, 50–1.

18 See Miquel, *Géographie humaine*, 2: 497–511; and John Andrew Boyle, "Alexander and the Mongols," *Central Asiatic Journal* 24, no. 1/2 (1980): 23–5.

of Alexandria (d. 215), Tertullian (d. 220), and Lactantius (d. 320, all CE) emphasized that "angels taught humans astrology, magic, metallurgy, cosmetics, and idolatry."[19] This tradition is echoed in Quran 2:102, which affirms that two Babylonian angels, Hārūt and Mārūt, taught people magic.[20] We find allusions to this magical education in the section of *GE2* that we are discussing here. According to Alfonso, the giants' power was related to astrology and magic because "they were the first men who measured the course of the stars and knew about everything, including the power and natures of the four elements."[21] In fact, the letters of the giants in which the book of Hermes was written are also linked to astrological knowledge, because they "were taken from the highest heavens where there are many stars, and from many figures, hence there are great differences between them."[22] The old woman describes the astrological techniques through which the giants developed their figures, including meticulous observations and tracing lines between the seven planets, the seven heavens, the dragon's head and tail, the twelve zodiac signs, etc., and asserts that they composed these figures "in order that a man could understand what is coming and what has already happened according to the provision of the heavens" – a clear reference to divination.[23] As Tester has studied, the dragon's head and tail (*la cabeça e la cola del dragon*) are the ascending and descending nodes of the moon, related to the Babylonian legend of Marduk and the dragon Tiamat, where they were given specific astrological signs.[24] The astrological information provided by the Babylonian woman also resembles details found in books of astrology that were translated and produced by Alfonso's *scriptorium*. For instance, in order to "raise the horoscope" (*levantar el horóscopo*), the *Libro de las cruces* (*Book of crosses*, 1259) includes methods for making figures (*hacer figuras*) or graphical representations of the related positions of the astral bodies at a given time; among them, those described by *GE2*: the tail and head of the dragon, the zodiac signs, etc.[25]

Yet, as we have come to expect in the *GE*, Alfonso incorporates other sources in this passage. For instance, he includes Greek mythological figures who were considered giants not found in his Arabic sources, such as Vulcan, who allegedly was the first metallurgist.[26] Interestingly, according to Enochian literature, watchers taught metallurgy to humans. Other giants were masters of trades and crafts such as goldsmithery, carpentry, and pottery. Thus, this version portrays the giants in a more sympathetic light compared to 1 Enoch. After the reference to Vulcan, Alfonso mentions that seven giants searched for the largest mountains on earth, lived there, and gave them their names. Counting, measurement, and logical classification of

19 Crone, *Qur'ānic Pagans*, 20.

20 Crone, *Qur'ānic Pagans*, 27.

21 "E ellos fueron los primeros omnes que mesuraron los cursos de las estrellas e los movimientos de los cielos e lo sopieron todo, e conocieron el poder e las naturas de los cuatro elementos." *GE2* I, 51.

22 "Las nuestras letras fueron sacadas de los más altos cielos en que están las munchas estrellas e de munchas figuras, e en que á gran departimiento de las unas a las otras." *GE2* I, 54.

23 "[...] por que podié omne entender e saber lo que avié de venir e lo que fuera segunt que lo dava la gracia de los cielos." *GE2* I, 54–5.

24 Jim Tester, *A History of Western Astrology* (Woodbridge: Boydell & Brewer, 1987), 121–2.

25 José A. Sánchez Pérez, "El Libro de las Cruces," *Isis* 14, no. 1 (1930): 77–9.

26 *GE2* I, 52.

geographical accidents, such as rivers and mountains, is characteristic of Arabic geographers, as we saw in Chapter Two.[27] Among the giants' many accomplishments, Fraker highlights "their roads [...], their topographical science, and skill at finding sites for their cities,"[28] which are also features related to Arabic geographical genres.

I cannot expand on the possible provenance of these mountains' names here, but it is significant that the sixth giant "was Giblem, his mountain is in Cilicia, and they call it mount *Gibel*,"[29] because *jabal* is the Arabic word for mountain. Then we learn that "the seventh giant is called Doobio, and his mountain Doma," but this giant "was also called Deucalión, and his mountain Parnassus."[30] Parnassus, as well as other mythological characters mentioned here, comes from the *Metamorphoses* and other works by Western authors. Alfonso does mention a specific source: some information is "according to the Book of the lineages of the giants and the other gentiles."[31] The *Libro de las generaciones de los dioses de los gentiles* (*Book of the generations of the gentiles' gods*) – whose specific reference is uncertain – is a recurring source in the *GE*.[32] It is difficult to know if *GE2*'s source is a convenient adaptation of that title or a real "book of giants."

The *Book of the Giants* is actually an Enochian book found among the Dead Sea Scrolls. Mani (216–74 CE) – the founder of Manichaeism – reworked 1 Enoch and the *Book of Giants* into his own *Book of Giants* in Syriac, which was widely diffused throughout the Middle East in different versions and languages – including Arabic – and was even translated into Latin as *Liber de Ogia*.[33] Ogia – *Ohya* in Syriac – is a giant who survived the Flood. This name could also be the inspiration for Alfonso's Goghgobón or Oghgobon – although we do not know if the *Liber de Ogia* reached Castile. It is significant that some versions of Mani's *Book of Giants* mention that the *divs* or *devs* (giants) "taught people the use of clay to make bricks and build houses," because *GE2* emphasizes that construction was among the skills the giants taught.[34] Skjaervo points out that Iranian traditions added "the motif of fettering the giants to a mountain."[35] As we saw above, subsequent Syriac and Arabic traditions linked the giants Gog and Magog to mountains, but apparently this tradition could date back to Mani, or even earlier.

27 See Miquel, *Géographie humaine*, 1: 4–24.

28 Fraker, *Scope of History*, 206.

29 "El vi fue Giblem, el el so monte es en Cecilia e llámanle el mont Gibel." *GE2* II, 53.

30 "Al seteno gigant llamaron Doobio, e al so mont dízenle Doma." [...] los llamaron por estos otros nombres a Doobién Deucalión e al so mont el mont Parnaso." *GE2* II, 53.

31 "[...] segunt se falla en el Libro de los linages de los gigantes e los otros gentiles." *GE2* II, 53.

32 On this work, see Pilar Saquero Suárez-Somonte and Tomás Gonzalez Rolán, "Aproximación a la fuente latina del 'Libro de las generaciones de los dioses de los gentiles' utilizada en la *General Estoria* de Alfonso X el Sabio," *Cuadernos de Filología Clásica. Estudios Latinos* 4 (1993): 93–111.

33 Apparently, with influences from Iranian literature. See Prods Oktor Skjaervo, "Iranian Epic and the Manichean 'Book of Giants.' Irano-Manichaica III," *Acta Orientalia Academiae Scientiarum Hungaricae* 48, nos 1/2 (1995): 191. See also W. B. Henning, "The Book of the Giants," *Bulletin of the School of Oriental and African Studies* 11, no. 1 (1943): 52–74.

34 See Skjaervo, "Iranian Epic," 205. *GE2* I, 52.

35 See Skjaervo, "Iranian Epic," 205.

In this regard, I would like to point out the similarities of some motifs of this section in *GE2* with preserved excerpts from the *Phoenician History* by Philon of Biblos, a scholar and antiquarian who lived during the early Roman Empire. Despite writing in Greek, Philon "claimed to be transmitting a Phoenician theogony originally written by one Sanchouniathon."[36] The *Phoenician History* is now lost, but it was quoted by the third-century CE Neoplatonic scholar Porphyry of Tyre, who was in turn quoted by Eusebius in his *Praeparatio evangelica* (*Preparation for the Gospel*, early fourth century CE). López-Ruiz points out that the fragments of the *Phoenician History* recorded by Eusebius include cosmogonic traditions associated with the Egyptian Hermopolis and the Hermetic tradition, and they even quote the cosmogonic writings and commentaries by Taautos/Thoth, Hermes's alter ego.[37] Significantly, one of the preserved sections of *Phoenician History* is on "History of culture-first inventors," and it includes giants who invented things for the original humans and were related to mountains; we find out that the first beings on earth "gave birth to sons who were great in size and stature, whose names were given to the mountains over which they ruled." One of the descendants of these giants or Titans is "Taautos, who invented the first script for writing, whom the Egyptians call Thoyth, the Alexandrians Thoth, and the Greeks Hermes." In a similar way to our section of *GE2*, these fragments continue mixing Middle Eastern traditions with Greek ones, for instance, we find out that "when Kronos became a man, he relied on Hermes Trismegistus as a counsellor and aid, for he was his secretary."[38] Therefore, stories about giants who taught skills to the first humans and were associated with mountains appear to have been connected at an early stage to both the Hermetic and Enochian traditions. This section of *GE2* echoes all of them and also identifies Hermes Trismegistus with Enoch:

> No one must doubt that Enoch – who was called Hermes and was father of all the philosophers – was from the lineage of the giants, from both [his] father and mother, even though he did not have a big body like them. This Hermes was the one who had more will, more delight, and more power to look in this world for all the knowledges above in the sky and below in the earth; and this is why some said that he lived above more than forty years, and there he learned all the knowledges of heaven.[39]

Alexander assumes that the inhabitants of Ḥarrān, who were star-worshipper and had Hermes as their prophet, identified Hermes Trismegistus with Enoch.[40] But there was earlier contact between the Hermetic and Enochian traditions. Echoes of 1 Enoch

36 Carolina López-Ruiz, *Gods, Heroes, and Monsters. A Sourcebook of Greek, Roman, and Near Eastern Myths in Translation* (Oxford: Oxford University Press, 2017), 57–8.

37 Eusebius, *Praeparatio evangelica* 1.10.1–5, in López-Ruiz, *Gods, Heroes, and Monsters*, 59.

38 Eusebius, *Praeparatio evangelica* 1.10.6–17, in López-Ruiz, *Gods, Heroes, and Monsters*, 59–61.

39 "E ninguno non deve dubdar que Enoch, el que fue dicho Hermes e fue padre de todos los filósofos, que non fue del linage de los gigantes de padre e de madre, maguer que non fue de grant cuerpo como ellos. E este Hermes fue aquel que mayor voluntad ovo e mayor sabor e mayor poder de vuscar en este mundo todos los saberes de las cosas de suso del cielo e de las cosas de yuso de la tierra, e por end dixieron algunos d'éll que morara de suso más de cuarenta años e que allá aprendió todos los saberes del cielo." *GE2* I, 52.

40 See primary and secondary sources in Alexander, "From Son of Adam," 115–18.

appear in the Hermetic writings, and the famous Hermetic alchemist Zosimus (*c.* 300 CE) paraphrases the story of the watchers in his *Physica*, where he affirms that Hermes also mentioned it.[41] Orlov points out that fragments of the *Book of Giants* label Enoch as a distinguished scribe and astrologer, and that in the *Book of Jubilees* 4:17 he is attested as the one who "learned (the art of) writing, instruction, and wisdom and who wrote down in a book the signs of the sky"[42] – features that could identify him as Hermes. The subsequent identification of Hermes with the Quranic Idrīs also points to Ḥarrān, from where Muslim scholars would have taken it.[43] According to Quran 19:56–7: "And recite in the Book the account of Idrīs. Indeed, he was a man of truth and a prophet. And we raised him to a lofty place." Many Arabic sources discuss this connection in depth.[44] As we saw earlier in this book, both Abū Maʿshar and al-Mubashshir mentioned that Hermes was also known as Idrīs and Enoch. The *Rasāʾil Ikhwān al-Ṣafāʾ* – the cosmological encyclopedia with Ismaʿili, Sufi, and Hermetic influences written by an esoteric group of sages in Basra around the ninth century – includes a quotation on Hermes/Idrīs that is closely related to this passage of *GE2*:

> And so it is related about Hermes the thrice-endowed with wisdom – and who is the prophet Idrīs, peace be upon him – that he ascended to the sphere of Saturn and revolved with it for thirty years until he witnessed all the states of the celestial sphere. Then he descended back to earth and instructed people about star-lore. God Most High said [of him]: "and We raised him up to a lofty place" (Q 19:57).[45]

Van Bladel observes that according to ancient astrology, Saturn was in the seventh celestial sphere and had an orbital period of thirty years; thus, "Hermes could learn all the states of the heavenly sphere by abiding with the outermost planet through one of its cycles."[46] Even though the most recent edition of *GE2* affirms that Hermes "lived above more than forty years," several manuscripts maintain that it was thirty years, which was the number Solalinde chose to reference in his edition.[47] It appears that this information comes from some intermediary source or the *Rasāʾil Ikhwān al-Ṣafāʾ* itself, which was well known in al-Andalus – probably after al-Qurṭubī brought it to Córdoba.[48]

41 See Jack Lindsay, *The Origins of Alchemy in Graeco-Roman Egypt* (London: Muller, 1970), 179; and Crone, *Qurʾānic Pagans*, 24.

42 Andrei A. Orlov, "Overshadowed by Enoch's Greatness: 'Two Tablets' Traditions from the Book of Giants to Palaea Historica," *Journal for the Study of Judaism in the Persian, Hellenistic, and Roman Period* 32, nos 1–4 (2001): 141–2.

43 Alexander, "From Son of Adam," 115–18.

44 See, especially, Van Bladel, *Arabic Hermes*, 164–232; and John C. Reeves and Annette Yoshiko Reed, *Enoch from Antiquity, Volume I* (Oxford: Oxford University Press, 2018), 284–96.

45 Translation from F. Jamil Ragep and Taro Mimura (eds and trans.), *Epistles of the Brethren of Purity, On Astronomia: An Arabic Critical Edition and English Translation of Epistle 3* (Oxford: Oxford University Press, 2015), 62–3.

46 Van Bladel, *Arabic Hermes*, 181.

47 *GE2* I, 633; and Solalinde's *General estoria: Segunda parte*, I, 37.

48 See Callataÿ, "Magia en al-Andalus," 333–7

Fraker has proposed a late-antique collection of writing on astrological medicine in Greek, the *Kyranides*, as the main source for this passage in *GE*2.[49] The text's prologue relates a story about the narrator's visit with an old Syrian man who deciphers the symbols on a number of towers and steles, including information about ancient giants who built towers and were punished by God. This text was translated from Greek into Latin by one of the Castilian kings named Alfonso, most likely Alfonso VIII (1158–1214) – the great-grandfather of our Alfonso – who reigned in the second half of the twelfth century.[50] Fraker sees some parallels between Asclepius's visit to the old Babylonian woman who can translate a book of Hermes and the *Kyranides*'s narrator's visit to an old Syrian man who can translate the hieroglyphs on an old antediluvian stele, which also discusses the past and future. However, there are several differences between the narrative in the *Kyranides* and the *GE*. For instance, in the *Kyranides* the giants follow the traditions about evil giants or Nephilim who run amok on earth, but as Fraker acknowledges, *GE*2 "leaves out everything that might put the giants in a bad light."[51] Besides, as we have seen, although this passage incorporates traditions from many different ancestries, they all have a common origin: the literature of Enoch, which is eventually associated with Hermes.

My analysis of this section has focused on why Alfonso elaborates on such a mélange of ancient sources to explain "the knowledge of Hermes," which he had only just summarized in its introductory chapter as the *trivium*. It is significant that Alfonso emphasizes that "Enoch – who was called Hermes and was father of all the philosophers – was from the lineage of the giants."

As we have seen previously, the meaning of "philosopher" has evolved over time. By late antiquity, "Hermes the Egyptian was viewed as the supreme philosopher, or rather the one who stood at the head of the Greek philosophical tradition."[52] In the Latin alchemical works that we discussed in Chapter Four, prologues on the three Hermeses define Hermes as a philosopher – as well as a prophet and king – and affirm that he discovered the liberal and mechanical arts. For Alfonso, philosophers were masters of the liberal arts, and it happens that the "father" of all of them, Hermes, spent thirty years in heaven acquiring his knowledge of both the sky and the earth. Since magic is part of astrology, astrology is part of astronomy, and astronomy is one of the liberal arts, Alfonso provides a lineage of wisdom related to Hermes that could appeal not only to Christians but also to Jews and Muslims because it is based on Hermes's incarnations as Enoch and Idris. But let us not forget that for Alfonso, Hermes was also Mercury, and he reminds readers of this in the summary at the end of the section: "And this is all we told you about the knowledge of Hermes, who had the name Tat, and was son of the other Hermes Trismegistus, who was Mercury."[53] It is also significant that the next sentence quotes the *History of the Arabs* (*Estoria*

49 Fraker, "Hermes Trismegistus," 94–5.

50 See Fraker, "Hermes Trismegistus," 97.

51 See Fraker, "Hermes Trismegistus," 94.

52 Litwa, *Hermetica II*, 8.

53 "E tanto vos contamos aquí de la razón del saber de Hermes, que ovo d'otra guisa nombre Tat, e fue fijo del otro Hermes Trimegisto, que fue Mercurio." *GE*2 I, 55.

de los aláraves),[54] an undetermined Arabic source. This is further evidence of the sources' Arabic provenance, and the general Arabic influence in this section of *GE*2.

By tracing these interconnected stories, not only are we able to offer specific information about Alfonso and his sources, but we can also emphasize the importance – indeed the centrality – of non-Romance sources for properly understanding the background to Mercury/Hermes and the depiction of his wisdom in the *GE*. Alfonso's genealogy of knowledge is related to a genealogy of power – *translatio studii* and *translatio imperii* respectively. As Martínez points out, Goghbobón – the giant who reveals the secrets of Hermes's book to Asclepius – is the niece of Nimrod, first human king after the Flood. In *GE*4 Alfonso affirms that he is a descendant of Nimrod through his mother, the German princess Elisabeth of Swabia.[55] And the *GE* also identifies Nimrod with Saturn, the father of Jupiter – with whom Alfonso constantly identifies himself. In *GE*1 Alfonso claims he also descends from Jupiter through his relative Frederick I.[56] Therefore, following Martínez, the lineage is: Saturn (Nimrod) > Jupiter > Mercury (Hermes Trismegistus) > German dynasty > Alfonso. This makes Alfonso a descendant not only of Hermes but also of the good giants, humanity's benefactors. Consistent with this double lineage, just twenty-two pages after "On the knowledge of Hermes," *GE*2 presents another section titled "On the knowledge Mercury possessed," on which I will focus below. In the Arabic-Hermetic story we have just examined, Alfonso employs Ovidian undertones to explain "the knowledge of Hermes." In contrast, "On the knowledge Mercury possessed" is included in a story from the *Metamorphoses* that incorporates Arabic Hermetic elements. "On the knowledge of Hermes" connects him with the divine origin of knowledge, a topic developed throughout the *GE* and is connected to Seth and his descendants in particular – passages not examined here because they are not directly associated with Hermes.[57] For its part, "On the knowledge Mercury possessed" connects him to other appearances in the *GE* that are related to Ovid and that consistently introduce Hermetic elements. In order to contextualize "On the knowledge Mercury possessed," I will provide an overview of Mercury's appearances in the *GE* – especially those I have not yet touched upon – and emphasize the liberal arts and Hermetic elements.

On the Knowledge Mercury Possessed

The first mention of Mercury in the *GE* occurs during the description of a Persian temple that is decorated with depictions of the planetary gods as animals. These gods do not look very Persian. Their description is inspired by a passage from the *Metamorphoses*: the Olympian gods fled to Egypt in the guise of animals to escape from the Titans, identified with the biblical giants. Alfonso then presents this section

54 *GE*2 I, 55–6.

55 *GE*4 II, 505.

56 *GE*1 I, 392. Martínez, *El humanismo medieval*, 279. On these lineages, see also Erik Ekman, "Cuenta la estoria: Narrative and Exegesis in Alfonso X's 'General Estoria,'" *Hispanic Journal* 27, no. 1 (2006): 31–2; and Erik Ekman, "Translation and Translatio: 'Nuestro Latín' in Alfonso El Sabio's General Estoria," *Bulletin of Spanish Studies* (2002) 93, no. 5 (2016): 767–9.

57 I recommend the analysis of Fraker, *Scope of History*, 206; and Martínez, *El humanismo medieval*, 304–5.

from the *Metamorphoses* and reproduces its verses in Latin.[58] We find out that in the Persian temple there was an image "of a stork, in which [form] they worshipped the planet Mercury, whom they called god of the *trivium*, that is, the three liberal knowledges."[59] Although the *GE* had already referred to the planet Mercury, this is the first time the god Mercury appears; not surprisingly – since astrological components are so important in this work – the god is identified with the planet, as well as with the liberal arts. While the other gods in the temple are each described in one short sentence, Alfonso provides a long explanation about the relationship between Mercury's image and the arts of the *trivium*. According to the philosophers (i.e., specialists in liberal arts),

> this figure [of the stork] has a long neck, in which he tastes what he eats, and in it he ponders which is healthy and which unhealthy, and what is healthy passes to the body, and what he understands to have no goodness he holds in his long neck and spits out [...] hence philosophers say that the wise man has a long neck, because he needs to assess, weigh, and polish the word before pronouncing it.[60]

The *Metamorphoses* mentions that Mercury transformed himself into an ibis, not a stork. I have not found a similar comparison between the body of a stork and the practical use of the *trivium*, but there is an analogous comparison with an ibis in the rhetorician Aelian (*c.*175–235 CE). In *De natura animalium* he states that the ibis "is said to be beloved of Hermes the father of speech because its appearance resembles the nature of speech: thus, the black wing-feathers might be compared to speech suppressed and turned inwards, the white to speech brought out, now audible."[61] These stories about the stork and ibis teach the same lesson: the rhetorician has to discriminate between his words and ideas and pick those worth saying. In Castile – where it can still be found nesting in belltowers – the stork was more common than the Nile's ibis. The resemblance of the two birds – white and stylized – could justify the change, but there might be more to it. As Schiesaro explains, in the *Metamorphoses*, "the specific choice of an ibis was promoted by the established identification between the Greek god Hermes and the Egyptian Thoth, whose sacred bird was the ibis."[62] But the connection between the stork, ibis, and Hermes seems to go beyond this. We have already explored the ways in which Hermes/Mercury was the mythical creator of alchemy in Hellenistic Egypt, but further to this, Carl Jung, in his studies

58 *Met.*V.327–31, reproduced in *GE*1 I, 169.

59 [...] e otra imagen de cigüeña, e en ésta aoravan a la planeta de Mercurio, a quien llamavan ellos dios del trivio, fascas de los primeros tres saberes liberales." *GE*1 I, 169.

60 "E en esta figura porque dizen que assí como aquella ave á luengo el cuello, en que prueva las cosas que come e siente allí cual será sana e cual enferma, e lo sano passa al cuerpo e lo ál con que se non falla bien e entiende quel nuzrá retiénelo en el cuello, que á luengo [...]. Onde tal dizen los filósofos que deve seer el sabio de luengo cuello, fascas que antes mesure e pese e esmere la palabra que á a dezir que la diga." *GE*1 I, 169.

61 In Philip A. Harland, "Egyptians: Aelian on Egyptian Views and Customs about Animals and Animal-Worship (Late Second Century CE)," *Ethnic Relations and Migration in the Ancient World*, http://philipharland.com/Blog/?p=13870 (last accessed April 18, 2023).

62 Alessandro Schiesaro, *Ibis redibis Materiali e Discussioni Per l'Analisi Dei Testi Classici*, no. 67 (2011): 105.

of alchemical imagery in old treatises, pointed out that the stork is an *avis Hermetis* (a bird of Hermes).[63]

A few pages later, *GE*1 insists on Mercury's assimilation with a stork during the Ovidian story of the gods' transfiguration into animals, which is explained through magic: "Since all of them were very wise due to their knowledge of the stars and the magical art – which is the knowledge of charms, which they all mastered – they transfigured into those figures that we mentioned in order to hide themselves from the giants."[64] Alfonso expands on the individual characteristics of the gods, particularly those of Mercury.

> Mercury transformed himself and hid in the shape of a stork. According to what the gentile authors and other masters say, Mercury means god of the merchants. He was also the god of the *trivium* among gentiles, because he was the most accomplished master of these three knowledges: grammar, dialectics, and rhetoric. Mercury is also the name of the planet that goes close to the sun, not leaving him night and day. It is a small star, which can be seen on a clear day by whoever looks at it.[65]

Here we find the basic information that Mercury is the god of the merchants, as well as a more elaborate claim: he was also the god of the *trivium*, and a description of the arts that comprise it follows. Finally, his identification with the planet is expanded upon through astronomical references.

The portrait of Mercury/Hermes continues to be developed and specific details are further elaborated upon when he next appears in the *GE*, during *TSOI*. As we saw in Chapter Three, Mercury appears when Jupiter summons him to rescue Io from Argus. *GE*2 immediately connects Mercury's deeds with magic and the liberal arts, when he "assembled in front of him a herd of goats, which it is said that he made with his spell, because Mercury was very wise in the *trivium*, and even in the *quadrivium*."[66] To further the connection with one art in particular, astronomy, Alfonso reminds readers that "now his name is that of one of the planets, the one

63 C. G. Jung, *Psychology and Alchemy*, eds and trans. Gerhard Adler and R. F. C. Hull (Princeton: Princeton University Press, 1980), 524–7.

64 "[…] ellos como eran muy sabios por el saber que avién de las estrellas e por el arte mágica, que es el saber de los encantamentes, yl sabién ellos muy bien todos, trasfiguraron en aquellas figuras que diximos por encobrirse de los gigantes." *GE*1 I, 171.

65 "Mercurio se trasformó e se ascondió en figura de cigüeña; e segund lo esponen los auctores de los gentiles e los otros maestros Mercurio quier dezir como dios de los mercaderos; e otrossí era dios del trivio entre los gentiles, e son el trivio la gramática e la dialética e la rectórica, porque era el más complido maestro d'estos tres saberes que otro entre sos gentiles. E es otrossí Mercurio nombre d'aquella planeta que anda cerca'l sol, que se nuncua e d'él nin de noche nin de día. E es una estrella pequeña, e verla puede allí qui bien la catare con el día claro." *GE*1 I, 171.

66 "[…] acogió ante sí una manada de cabras que dizen que fizo él por su encantamiento, ca era Mercurio muy sabio en el trivio e aun en el cuadruvio." *GE*1 I, 311.

called Mercury, which always follows the sun, night and day, and never separates from him."[67]

In the *Metamorphoses* Mercury uses three objects to kill Argus – a syrinx, a magic wand, and a curved sword. As we saw, Alfonso took from medieval commentators on Ovid the idea that the syrinx was composed of seven reeds representing the liberal arts. But the Castilian king furthers this allegorical interpretation and explains that – while playing the syrinx – Mercury defeated Argus with his rhetorical and dialectical/logical arts "by reasoning with him about the questions that Argus presented and talking covertly about issues related to the seven liberal arts. And telling him that Pan loved Syrinx, who had been transformed into reeds."[68] Arnulf of Orléans connected the story of Syrinx and her seven reeds to the seven liberal arts and the *translatio studii* that took place between Greece and Rome.[69]Alfonso expands upon this interpretation, directly connects the seven liberal arts with Mercury, and elaborates on this theory of the transmission of knowledge between nations – of which he is a part.[70]

The second device is Mercury's wand, the caduceus, conventionally associated with the healing god Asclepius and Hermes Trismegistus. Ovid describes it as a *medicata virga* (healing wand),[71] but according to Alfonso it

> had such a nature that when he touched with it anything alive, one of its ends made it sleep, and the other woke it up. Mercury touched Argus with the end that made him sleep in such a way that he could not wake up even if he wanted to, because that was the nature and power of the staff.[72]

As we saw, these specific terms, nature (*ṭabīʿa*) and power (*quwwa*), are related to Arabic theories of magic. Finally, when Argus falls asleep Ovid narrates how Mercury cuts his head off with a curved sword (*falcato ense*),[73] referring to his famous *harpe*. Significantly, Alfonso calls this sword *alfange*, the Andalusi sabre: "He drew the *alfange* that he had brought, since that was the name of Mercury's sword; in Latin it is called *arpe*, and it has a curved shape, as the edge has the form of an arc."[74] Alfonso

67 "E es agora el su nombre d'una de las planetas, e es a la que dizen Mercurio, e es aquella que anda siempre con el sol de noche e de día, que nunca d'él se parte." *GE*1 I, 311.

68 "E venció Mercurio a Argo, fascas al mundo razonándose con él sobre las preguntas quel fazié Argo fablandol él encubiertamientre de las razones de las siete artes liberales, e diziendol que amara Pan a Siringa tornada en cañaveras en las riberas del río Ladón." *GE*1 I, 320.

69 Arnulf of Orléans. *Arnulphi Aurelianensis Allegoriae*, I.12, 203.

70 *GE*1 I, 320.

71 *Met.*I.715.

72 "[...] avié natura que a la cosa viva que tañié con el un cabo que la adormié, e con el otro la espertava. E tanxo a Argo con la parte que adormié, e firmó en éll el sueño, de guisa que maguer que Argo quisiesse espertar non pudiesse, ca tal era la natura e el poder de la verga." *GE*1 I, 311.

73 *Met.*I.716.

74 "Sacó el su alfange que trayé, ca assí avié nombre la espada de Mercurio; en el latín le dize arpe, e era d'una fechura corva como que querié venir en arco d'aquella parte de lo agudo." *GE*1 I, 313.

only uses the word *alfange* one other time in the *GE*, also in relation to Mercury's weapon and the *trivium* – as we will see below.

After *TSOI*, Mercury next appears in the section about the three Hermeses and "the knowledge of Hermes." The section following *TSOI* is the story of the Rape of Europa, which includes its own subsection "On the knowledge that Mercury possessed." To understand this subsection, we must delve into Mercury's kinship with Jupiter, because it can explain how he acquired his knowledge. As we saw earlier, scholars such as Maravall and Martínez have seen the influence of *adab*, the complex ideal of education in Arabic culture, in Alfonso's oeuvre, particularly in his didactic and historical works. According to Alfonso, the great men of antiquity – mythical and biblical – learned the liberal arts and polished their customs in a way that is reminiscent of how the sons of caliphs and viziers received an *adab* education grounded in urbane politeness and all disciplines of knowledge. Throughout the *GE*, Mercury's connection to the liberal arts is justified through his lineage and education. In line with this logic: Saturn taught Jupiter, then Jupiter taught his sons Mercury and Minerva, and Mercury instructed Io, Europa, and Perseus.

Jupiter is briefly introduced at the beginning of *GE*1 in the description of the Persian temple and escape to Egypt. *GE*1 then presents Jupiter's upbringing twice more. The first occurs in *TSOI*, where he is introduced as "the wisest, and highest, and most powerful king that ever existed among the gentiles."[75] As we saw in Chapter Three, Jupiter's lineage started in Crete with Celio (Caelus), father of Saturn and grandfather of Jupiter.[76] We are also told that Jupiter's wisdom sprung from the education he received from his father Saturn, "who took care of the customs of that son […] since he saw that he worked on higher and nobler things […] and the knowledges of the stars, and the *quadrivium*."[77] Then Jupiter is presented in the guise of one of the *adab*-inspired courtiers that I claim the *GE* is describing: from a noble lineage, given an upright education – including falconry – and possessing knowledge of the liberal arts, comprising astrology and magic.

However, a few chapters after this introduction we are given an "alternative" background for Jupiter, according to which he was born in Athens, where he "studied and learned so much that he knew very well the *trivium* and the *quadrivium*, which are the seven arts called liberal."[78] According to this account, at the time, Athens was the best place to study the liberal arts. For instance, their inhabitants "wrote in each of the seven gates of the city the name of one of the knowledges of the so-called

75 "[…] fue Júpiter el más sabio e más alto e más poderoso rey que en los gentiles." *GE*1 I, 374.

76 *GE*1 I, 302–5.

77 "E Saturno su padre paró mientes en las costumbres d'aquel fijo. E pues que vío que se trabajava de cosas más altas e más nobles […] e con los saberes de las estrellas, e del cuadruvio, que son más altas cosas que tod esto ál, asmó cómol diesse el poder del aire e del cielo." *GE*1 I, 304.

78 "[…] allí estudió, e aprendió ý tanto que sopo muy bien todo el trivio e tod el cuadruvio, que son las siete artes a quel llaman liberales." *GE*1 I, 378.

liberal arts."[79] Whoever crossed through one of those doors and followed its path could find masters to teach him the respective art, and even lodging for the duration of his education there. Wise men from all over the world flocked to Athens to study, because "there stood the first schools of the knowledges of Greece, from where the Latins later gained their knowledge."[80] Therefore, Athens was a milestone in the *translatio studii* theory. We also learn that

> They called those seven arts liberal, and not other arts – according to Remigius, and before him Donatus and others – for these two reasons: first, because they could only be studied by the free man, who was not a servant/slave or who made a living from a trade; second, because those who studied them had to be free from any care or concern for others, because that is what one who is learning needs in order to do it well.[81]

This definition dates back to classical sources, as we will see in the next section. Then Alfonso discusses "On King Jupiter and the explanations of the knowledges of the *trivium* and the *quadrivium*."[82] In addition to a description of the specific arts, Alfonso introduces several important reflections. For instance, even though "previous wise men" thought the *trivium* must be learned first, Alfonso believes the opposite. Several specialists consider this opinion to have been influenced by Arabic thought.[83] Alfonso rationalizes that while the arts "of the so-called *trivium* show man how to express convenient, true, and correct reason, whatever the topic [reason] he is talking about," the four arts of the *quadrivium* "are all about understanding and demonstration by evidence," and "they talk about things according to their quantities."[84] Martínez observes that under the influence of Aristotle – recovered through translations from Arabic – Alfonso assumes that there is a methodological requirement for the observation and scientific analysis of reality, whose weight and measurement is quantifiable.[85] This quote also reveals that Alfonso passed from the *qualitas* – typical of the traditional *quadrivium* as exposed, for instance, by Isidore – to the *quantitas*. This is why Alfonso says that the *quadrivium* – which talks about quantifiable things – must precede the

79 "[...] o fizieron escrivir en cadaúna d'aquellas siete puertas de la cibdad el nombre d'uno de los saberes de las siete artes a que llaman liberales." GE1 I, 376.

80 "[...] allí fueron primeramientre las escuelas de los saberes de Grecia, dond vino a los latinos después el saber que ovieron." *GE*1 I, 377.

81 "E llamavan liberales a aquellas siete artes e non a los otros saberes, segund departe Ramiro sobr'el Donat e otros con él, por estas dos razones: la una porque non las avié a oír si non ombre libre que non fuesse siervo nin omne que visquiesse por mester, la otra porque aquellos que las oyén que avién a seer libres de todo cuidado e de toda premia que les otre fiziesse, ca tod esto á mester qui aprende pora bien aprender." *GE*1 I, 378.

82 "Del rey Júpiter e de los departimientos de los saberes del trivio e del cuadruvio." *GE*1 I, 378; the section on liberal arts runs from 378 to 385.

83 See Martínez, *El humanismo medieval*, 281–5; and Rico, *Alfonso el Sabio*, 152–3.

84 "Onde estas tres artes que dixiemos a que llaman trivio muestran all omne dezir razón conveniente, verdadera e apuesta cualquier que sea la razón [...] E las cuatro son todas de entendimiento e de demostramiento fecho por prueva [...] fablan de las cosas por las cuantías d'ellas." *GE*1 I, 379.

85 In Martínez, *El humanismo medieval*, 281. See also Rico, *Alfonso el Sabio*, 146.

trivium – which talks about the names and terms for things – because "naturally, the things existed before their names and terms."[86] The division between "arts of speech" and "arts of things" can also be traced back to the *Eptateuchon* of Thierry of Chartres – whom I will introduce below – and his discussion of "artes sermocinales" and "artes reales."[87] Alfonso concludes that "the arts of the *trivium* express the names of things and make man well-reasoned [whereas] the arts of the *quadrivium* show the nature of things and make man wise."[88]

After organizing the arts into a hierarchy and describing them, Alfonso adds a final brief chapter: "On the knowledges beyond the seven liberal arts."[89] These are metaphysics, physics, and ethics. In thirteenth-century Europe, these disciplines increased in importance due to the influence of recently discovered Aristotelian works. By sticking to the liberal arts Alfonso remained entrenched in the intellectual world of the twelfth century, although he also attempts to adjust the new trends to the old seven arts programme, as happens in this chapter.[90] While the definitions of metaphysics, physics, and ethics have an Aristotelian flavour, they also emphasize elements that aided Arabic magic theory; thus, physics

> is the knowledge of natures, [which serves] to understand all things that have bodies, as well as the heavens, and the stars, and the other things that are in the skies above, and also [serves to] understand how their natures are made, born, and die. [Whoever studies physics] must understand the nature of elements and how each of them operates in these things.[91]

This summary emphasizes knowledge of the stars' influence on earthly things, as well as knowledge of their natures and the elements they are composed of, and how sublunar bodies are subjected to processes of generation and corruption. Saif explains how these components of Aristotelian philosophy were reinterpreted by Arabic thought and became requirements for the practice of magic.[92] In Alfonso's scheme of knowledge, the liberal arts must be learned first, because only then can the wise scholar understand the natures of and mutual influence between heavenly and earthly things, which gives him access to the practice of magic.

86 "[...] las cosas fueron ante que las vozes e que los nombres dellas naturalmientre." *GE*1 I, 379.

87 Edouard Jeauneau, "Le Prologus in *Eptatheucon* de Thierry de Chartres," *Medieval Studies*, 16, no. 1 (1954): 171–5.

88 "[...] muestran all omne dezir razón conveniente, verdadera e apuesta cualquier que sea la razón [...] son todas de entendimiento e de demostramiento fecho por prueva [...] fablan de las cosas por las cuantías dellas [...] por las tres del trivio se dizen los nombres a las cosas, e éstas fazen al omne bien razonado, e por las cuatro del cuadruvio se muestran las naturas de las cosas, e estas cuatro fazen sabio ell omne." *GE*1 I, 379.

89 "De los saberes que son sobre las VII artes liberales." *GE*1 I, 384.

90 See Rico, *Alfonso el Sabio*, 144–9.

91 "El segundo saber es el de las naturas pora coñocer todas las cosas que an cuerpos, assí como los cielos e las estrellas e las otras cosas que son de los cielos a ayuso, e entender sus naturas de cómo se fazen, naciendo e muriendo, e se deve coñocer la natura de los elementos, e de cómo obra cadaúno d'ellos en estas cosas." *GE*1 I, 384.

92 Saif, "From *Ġāyat al-Ḥakīm*," 299–306.

The next significant step in Alfonso's scheme of knowledge leads from Jupiter to Mercury in the subsection "On the knowledge Mercury possessed," barely twenty pages after the section on the three Hermeses and Asclepius. As in *TSOI*, in *GE2*'s section on the Rape of Europa Mercury appears as an accomplished courtier and the obedient offspring of Jupiter.[93] The legendary king requests his son's help in order to satisfy his lust for the maid Europa. Jupiter addresses him: "Son, you are my faithful servant and faithfully accomplish all orders I give you. Thus, do not delay now, because I need you, and go down as fast as you can."[94] As in the Ovidian original, Mercury follows Jupiter's command and leads a herd of splendid bulls and cows within proximity of Europa's palace. In Ovid, Jupiter transforms himself into a beautiful and gentle bull. Europa approaches, pets, and even rides Jupiter, who seizes the opportunity to snatch her away across the sea. Alfonso interprets this to mean that Jupiter

> through his magical charms, first made it so that Europa could not see any [of the other bulls] and according to the author [Ovid], [Jupiter] then transfigured himself with his knowledge (i.e., charmed the eyes of whoever saw him so he appeared as he wanted) and showed himself in the figure of a bull.[95]

But after relating – and condemning – the outcome of Jupiter's conquest, Alfonso decides to extol Mercury's role in the story – which is very brief in Ovid – and announces: "Now we are going to tell you about the great knowledge that Mercury, his son, had of the *trivium*, so much that the gentiles called him god of it."[96] By doing this, Alfonso not only reiterates that Mercury is god of the *trivium*, but also repeats the explanation we saw above that the liberal arts are related to his father Jupiter, the king of Athens.

The subsection "On the knowledge Mercury possessed"[97] contains a thorough explanation of the relationship between Mercury and the three arts of the *trivium*, and also implicitly his relationship with the *quadrivium*. We learn that "Mercury was so wise in the three sciences of the *trivium* that the wise men called them 'mercurial ministers.'"[98] Alfonso refers to an unidentified *Summa of rhetoric* – probably by Remigius of Auxerre – which he even quotes in Latin: "gramatica

93 *Met.*II.831–75.

94 "Fijo tu eres mio fiel servient e cúmplesme fielmientre todos los mandados que te yo mando. Pues non te tardes agora ca te he mester." *GE2* I, 74. This is a close translation of *Met.*II. 837–8: "fide minister ait iussorum, nate, meorum, pelle moram solitoque celer delabere cursu."

95 "Fízosse primero por sos encantamientos mágicos quel non pudiesse ver ninguno, e segunt cuenta el autor transfiguróse allí por so saber (e esto es que encantó los ojos de cuantos lo viessen que les semejasse que era aquello que él queríe) e mostróse en figura de toro." *GE2* I, 74–5.

96 "Agora contar vos emos del grand saber que mercurio so fijo ovo en el trivio, tanto quel llamaron los gentiles dios del." *GE2* I, 77.

97 "Del saber que Mercurio ovo." *GE2* I, 77.

98 "E en tod el trivio fue tan sabio este Mercurio que fallamos que a aquellas tres ciencias que vos decimos del trivio que las llamaron los sabios ministras mercuriales." *GE2* 1, 77.

prima omnium mercurialum ministrarum" (grammar is the first of all the mercurial ministers).[99] This *Summa* could have helped inspire Alfonso to associate Mercury with the *trivium*, although he interprets this association in his own way. The quote affirms that "ex coniugio sermonis et sapiencie opus insolubile prodeatur" (from the marriage of speech and wisdom came forth an indissoluble work) – a clear reference to Martianus Capella, as I will explain in the next section – but Alfonso changes "speech" (*sermon*) to "reason" and affirms that

> this is what this Latin word means in our language of Castile: that reason and wisdom joined together in one, and that reason is the *trivium* and wisdom the *quadrivium*, and from this merger came forth a work that cannot ever be unmade or lost. Reason always needs wisdom, and wisdom reason; therefore, the *trivium* always needs the *quadrivium* and vice versa. It seems that it is very necessary for the wise person, in order to be and be seen as wise, to be well reasoned, and for the well-reasoned person to be wise, in order to look as though he puts together his reason with wisdom.[100]

Then the chapter develops the *Summa*'s explanation of the arts of the *trivium* more faithfully, but it concludes with the relationship between reason and wisdom, which seems particularly suitable for the wise Mercury. Alfonso insists that the three arts of the *trivium* are called "mercurial ministers, that is, 'servants of Mercury,'" because the three of them serve him, and this means that he knew all of them very well, and better than any other wise man of his time. And that is why the wise men named those arts on account of the name of Mercury."[101]

The next chapter interprets the story of Europa and introduces some of Mercury's merits. This interpretation is loosely based on John of Garland's commentary, who only dedicated two verses to the myth: "Jupiter kidnapped Europa with a vessel, there was a bull depicted on it, and the name of the ship was Bull."[102] *GE2* expands on this information and increases the importance of Mercury. First, Alfonso follows up from the previous section: "Mercury was as wise as [he was] well-reasoned,"[103] which, consistent with the previous explanation, means that he mastered both the *quadrivium* and the *trivium*. To prove that these skills did indeed help Mercury serve Jupiter, Alfonso refers to "master John" (of Garland), whom he then interprets for his own purposes:

99 *GE2* I, 78. See Rico, *Alfonso el Sabio*, 151; and Lida de Malkiel, "La General Estoria (I)," 116.

100 "E estos latines quieren assí dezir en el nuestro lenguaje de Castiella: que se ayuntaron la razón e la sapiencia en uno, e es la razón el trivio e la sapiencia el cuadrivio, e d'este ayuntamiento diz que salió obra que se non puede desfazer nin perder nuncua, e que á siempre mester la razón a la sapiencia e la sapiencia a la razón, fascas el trivio al quadrivio e el cuadruvio al trivio. E parece que muy mester es que el sabio para parecer e ser sabio que sea muy bien razonado, e el bien razonado mester á otrossí de ser sabio e que paresca que pone su razón con sapiencia." GE2 I, 78.

101 "[…] ministros mercuriales fascas siruientes de mercurio, ca todos tres le seruien, e esto es que los sabie él todos muy bien e mejor que otro sabio que a la su sazon fuesse. Et por esso les dixieron los sabios nombre de Mercurio mercuriales." *GE2* I, 79.

102 "Iupiter Europam rapuit rate, taurus in illa/ pictus erat, taurus nomine navis erat." John of Garland, *Integumenta Ovidii*, 151–2: 47.

103 "Assí cuemo era Mercurio muy sabio assí era muy bien razonado." GE2 I, 79.

> [...] the interpreter of Ovid clarifies that when he says Jupiter sent Mercury for the cows, it means that Jupiter had a wise and very reasonable herald who he sent to Europa, and the herald was so wise and well-reasoned in front of the princess that he convinced her to go out to the harbour to see many valuables that he had in the ship. Jupiter was in that ship, which had a bull painted on the sail.[104]

Garland does not mention Mercury. Misquoting his source, Alfonso suggests that, since Mercury was well-reasoned and wise (i.e., skilled in the *trivium* and *quadrivium*), he would have used his acumen and persuasive skills with the princess to convince her to approach the ship with a painted bull on it, and then Jupiter would have seized the opportunity to kidnap her. Thus, Mercury uses his skills acquired through his mastery of the liberal arts to persuade Europa, just as he had used them to entice Argos and then educate Io.

According to the narrative logic of the *GE*, Mercury derives his mastery of the liberal arts from his father Jupiter; this is also the case with his sister Minerva. *GE1* says that Pallax, or Pallas – the surname of Athena/Minerva – was "very wise and a master of the *trivium* and *quadrivium*, which are the seven liberal arts, and especially of the *quadrivium*," but also that she was "daughter of King Jupiter."[105] Later in *GE1*, Alfonso elaborates on this and insists that Minerva "knew the liberal arts" and that they "also called her goddess of the *trivium* and *quadrivium*."[106] She is, indeed, the only other divinity to whom the liberal arts are repeatedly ascribed that I have found in the *GE*. But Alfonso highlights that her education came from her father, an interpretation of the myth of Minerva emerging from Jupiter's head: "We can interpret that this lady was born from King Jupiter's brain in this way: the knowledges this lady knew came from his great knowledge, or that such a wise lady was taught by the brain of Jupiter."[107]

This logic of family-transmitted knowledge of the liberal arts continues later in *GE2*. Jupiter transmitted the liberal arts to his children Minerva and Mercury, and then they both teach them to their younger half-brother, Perseus.[108] This is also the last Ovidian tale included in the *GE* in which Mercury appears. Perseus is another example of the educated courtier. As the son of Jupiter, he is from an aristocratic lineage, and Io/Isis and Europa are in his mother Danae's lineage.[109] Like Abraham, Jupiter, and many other heroes in the *GE*, he was "well parented" (*bien*

104 "Onde dize el esponedor del Ovidio que aquello que el Ovidio dize que envió Júpiter a Mercurio por las vacas; que se entiende que ovo Júpiter sabio e bien razonado mandadero que envió a Europa; e el mandadero tanto fue sabio e bien razonado ante la Infante; que la movió que salliese e fuesse al puerto a veer muchas noblezas que tenié él ý en su nave. E estava Júpiter en essa nave, e toro pintado en el blanque della." *GE2* I, 79.

105 "[...] muy sabia e muy maestra en el trivio e en el cuadrivio, que son las siete artes liberales, e sobre todo en el cuadrivio [...] E fue Pallas fija del rey Júpiter." *GE1* I, 129.

106 "[...] sopo los saberes liberales [...] E llamáronla otrossí deessa del trivio e del cuadruvio." *GE1* I, 363.

107 "Mas esto se puede entender d'esta dueña nacer del meollo del rey Júpiter enesta guisa: que del grand saber d'él que salieron los saberes que esta dueña sabié, o que tal dueña e tan sabia del meollo de Júpiter serié enseñada." *GE1* I, 364.

108 *GE2* I, 374–417.

109 *GE2* I, 374.

criado) and interested in reading from an early age. His other qualities include an amalgam of learning, good behaviour, and martial talents: "[Perseus] grew very ingenious, with a great understanding, very wise in all the knowledges of the eight arts, very accomplished in goodness and natural intelligence, with a brave heart, very resourceful, and a good knight who skilfully used weapons."[110] It is remarkable that the reference is to eight and not seven arts. Alfonso quickly clarifies that magic is the additional art that a talented noble man should pursue.

> We even find that after [Perseus] fought and performed those great deeds, he studied and learned things that made him very wise in the seven knowledges and magic, which was the knowledge that all great people used at that time – because through [magic] they did all they wanted. And he knew the secrets of the four knowledges that make the *quadrivium*.[111]

Perseus's famous deeds include flying and using magical weapons, which can only be logically explained – at least in Alfonso's mind – through the use of magic. Yet Perseus also counts on his household. Alfonso explains that Mercury, Pallas, and Perseus were brothers, the sons of King Jupiter.[112] His brothers are instrumental when Perseus must fight the fearsome Medusa, because "it is said that he asked for help from his siblings Mercury and Pallas for it. Mercury gave him an *alfange*, which was a sword in the shape of a sickle to cut grain, and Pallas a crystal shield [...]."[113] This is the second and final section of the *GE* where Alfonso mentions the Arabic word *alfange*. The first is in *TSOI*. He uses an allegorical explanation to relate these gifts to the liberal arts:

> Master Juan says that Perseus should be understood as virtue, or man full of virtues; and the *alfange* of Mercury as the three knowledges that are called the *trivium*, part of the so-called seven liberal arts: grammar, dialectics, and rhetoric, from which originates the well-shaped reasoning that grants man understanding, which Perseus held in a very accomplished way. The crystal shield of Pallas should be understood as the four knowledges of the *quadrivium* that give man the reason from whence he learns how to break down things to distinguish between them. Because it is worth knowing that the *trivium* makes man well-reasoned, and the *quadrivium* makes him wise, just as we find in Aristotle's writings. Thus, Perseus was very wise in these knowledges, and with them he defeated Medusa and her sisters.[114]

110 "[...] salio muy engeñoso e de grant entendimiento e fue muy sabio en todos los saberes de las ocho artes e muy cumplido de bondat e de seso natural, e muy esforçado de coraçon e muy fardit e buen cavallero en armas." *GE2* I, 381.

111 "E aun fallamos que después que lidió e fizo grandes fechos que estudió e aprendió aquello por que fue muy sabio en los siete saberes e en la mágica que era el saber de que todos los grandes usauan en aquel tiempo, por que fazien por ella lo que querién, e sopo las poridades de los cuatro saberes, que son el cuadruvio." *GE2* I, 381.

112 "[...] un su dios a que llamavan Mercurio e una deessa a que dizién Pallas e este Perseo que fueron hermanos fijos del rey Júpiter." *GE2* I, 386.

113 "Et dizen que pedió a aquellos sus hermanos Mercurio e Pallas ayuda pora ello. E diol Mercurio un alhange, que era una espada fecha como a manera de foz de segar mies, e Pallas un escudo de cristal segunt cuentan las glosas del libro Juvenal." *GE2* I, 386.

114 "De Perseo dize Maestre Johan que se entiende por éll vertud o omne lleno de vertudes. Por el alhange de Mercurio; los tres saberes que an nombre Triuio, que son en las siete artes a que

The first thing to notice is another free interpretation by Alfonso. Garland merely says: "The spear of Pallas is the objection that repels, the helmet/ is the reason, the shield is the strength in reason./ Perseus is the virtue, the *harpe* means eloquence."[115] The arts of the *trivium* are only indirectly suggested: Pallas's "reason" and "objection" could be related to dialectic, whereas Mercury's *harpe* is eloquence (rhetoric). Garland's lines do not fit with *GE2*'s previous arguments, so Alfonso initially affirms that the shield (*quadrivium*) "gives man the reason," but then reverts to his own position and gives reason back to the *trivium*, which makes man "well-reasoned." To reinforce his claims, Alfonso says that he is following Aristotle, the alleged origin of the liberal arts. Garland states that "after the war Perseus studied and fed on the secret of Minerva/ and drank the sweet waters of Pallas."[116] Yet according to *GE2*, Perseus seems to learn from both Minerva and Mercury.

We can appreciate the same pattern in another episode relaying Perseus's deeds: the rescue of Andromeda from the sea beast.[117] Garland says that Perseus is virtue (*est Perseus virtus*), but Alfonso embellishes this: "Perseus is the man full of virtues and knowledge."[118] By adding knowledge to virtue, the wise king rounds off a moral concept rooted in Christian as well as Arabic traditions – *adab* in particular – which is consistent with the hero wielding a Muslim weapon. In Alfonso's subjective interpretation of Garland, both the *alfange/trivium* and the shield/*quadrivium* have educational and behavioural merits. The gods providing the weapons are now metonymically identified with the *trivium* and *quadrivium*:

> The wise men indicate that Mercury should be understood as the *trivium*, the three knowledges, because his *alfange* is well-shaped reasoning and the understanding of things [...] master John [of Garland] says that the bowing of the *alfange*, which is a curved sword that bends over itself, means that, through the understanding reached through these three knowledges, the man full of virtues bends the inclinations of pride in himself by bowing it like the curved sword. And [the virtuous man] instructs [the inclinations to pride] not to come out of his limbs, nor to materialize or affect his will.[119]

---

dizen liberales: la gramática, la dialética, e la Rectórica, don viene ell apuesto razonamiento que da a omne buen entendimiento. Et esto ovo Persseo muy complidamientre. Por el escudo del cristal de pallas entiéndese los quatro saberes del cuadrivio, que enseñan all omne la razón por ó aprende departir las cosas cuál es cada una. Ca assí es de saber que el trivio faze al omne seer bien razonado e el cuadrivio le faze sabio, assí como fallamos por escriptos de Aristótil. Et destos saberes fue Perseo muy sabio e con estos vencio éll a Medusa e a sus hermanas." *GE2* I, 390.

115 "Palladis est hasta pellens obiectio, cassis/ est ratio, clipeus in ratione vigor./ Est Perseus virtus, harpe facundia fertur." *Integumenta*, V, 245–7.

116 "Post bellum Perseus studuit vivitque Minerve/ Secretum, dulces Palladis hausit aquas. " *Integumenta*, V, 237–8.

117 *GE2* I, 399–400

118 "Persseo otrossí es tanto como ombre lienno de vertudes e de saber." *GE2* I, 406.

119 "[...] por Mercurio nos dan los sabios a entender el trivio, que son los tres saberes cuyo alhange es el apuesto razonamiento e ell entendimiento de las cosas [...] e por aquel recorvamiento dell alfange que es espada fecha como corva e ques torna en sí, diz maestre Johan que se entiende que el omne lleno de uertudes e que estos tres saberes á por el entendimiento que alcança con ellos retorna en si los mouimientos de la sovervia cuando

As we saw, the search for a "moralized," Christian Ovid was a popular European trend at that time, but the insistence on education as relating to behaviour – close to Arab parameters pertaining to *adab* – and the spotlight on Mercury are unique to Alfonso. Besides, it is remarkable that morals and knowledge are portrayed as a recognizable Arab weapon. Alfonso adds Minerva's shield to Mercury's *alfange*, which fights for the same causes, and adds interesting nuances:

> Pallas should be understood as the *quadrivium*, which are the four knowledges. Pallas's shield is the reason to know the quantities and natures of things well, through which man apprehends these four knowledges. With this knowledge of the *quadrivium* as a shield, man roots out the vices in himself and fights against them.[120]

Thus, there is also a relationship between restraint from vices and the *quadrivium*, between morals and knowledge. This allegorical interpretation suggests a bond between the *quadrivium* and quantity. Beaujouan reminds us that Boethius "equated the *quadrivium* with the division of mathematics into four parts, according to whether quantity is or is not discontinuous and immobile," a criterion followed by subsequent medieval authorities – whom Alfonso used.[121] But here the *quadrivium* is not only about mathematical quantity but also about "the natures of things," knowledge often related to magic in the *GE*. Consequently, Alfonso elaborates on Garland and suggests that science, the liberal arts, astrology, and magic are what make Perseus a virtuous and accomplished hero. Perseus's magical skills reappear just after he kills the gorgons:

> With the *alfange* of Mercury [Perseus] beheaded Medusa, who was the oldest one, and took away the head. After he had gained the head, it turned out to be of such power and virtue, that he immediately took off and started to walk in the air. He was flying with the help of the head, along with the magical knowledge that he had.[122]

Because of his magical knowledge, Perseus knows how to take advantage of the head's power and virtue, corresponding to the Arabic *quwwa* and *khāṣṣa* – as we have seen. Hence, Perseus adds magic to his knowledge of the liberal arts, which is unmistakably defined using Arabic-related terms. In the second part of this chapter I

la quiere fazer como es aquella espada recorvada, e castígalos que los non dexa salir fuera de los mienbros nin de uenir al fecho nin aun a la su uoluntat." *GE*2 I, 406.

120 "Por Pallas diz que se entiende el quadruvio que son los quatro saberes. Ell escudo de Pallas es la razon de las quantias e de las naturas de las cosas de saberlas bien, a que viene omne por aquellos quatro saberes. E por el saber d'éstos derrayga omne los malos uicios de sí e se defiende d'ellos con el saber del cuadruvio como con escudo." *GE*2 I, 406.

121 Guy Beaujouan, "The Transformation of the Quadrivium," in Robert L. Benson and Giles Constable (eds), *Renaissance and Renewal in the Twelfth Century* (Cambridge: Harvard University Press, 1982), 463; and Martínez, *El humanismo medieval*, 281–2.

122 "[…] descabesçó con el alhange de mercurio a Medusa, que era la mayor, e tomo la cabeça e fuesse con ella. E luego que la ovo ganada de tal poder e de tal vertut era la cabeça que essa ora se alçó suso alto e començo a andar por el aer volando con ella, otrossi con el saber de la mágica que sabie ell." *GE*2 I, 387–8.

will explore the two traditions that link Mercury with the liberal arts in the *GE*. One is derived from Western classical and medieval traditions in Latin, the other from Eastern traditions linked to Arabic Hermetic sources.

Mercury and the Development of the Liberal Arts in the West

In the aforementioned sections on Hermes/Mercury and the liberal arts, Alfonso respects the well-known division into the three verbal arts of the *trivium* (grammar, rhetoric, and dialectic/logic) and the four mathematical arts of the *quadrivium* (geometry, arithmetic, music, and astronomy). According to Hicks, this simple outline "belies the complexities and tensions within the long-standing tradition of the *artes liberales*," which "established itself as a dynamic discursive apparatus and pedagogical paradigm that shifted continuously to accommodate different cultural contexts and philosophical viewpoints."[123] This is precisely what the study of the liberal arts in the *GE* demonstrates; it incorporates Alfonso's stances on education and knowledge rather than simply reflecting the cultural background of medieval Europe. In this sense, the choice of Mercury as the god and representative of the liberal arts – particularly of the *trivium* – reflects both a stance and a process of translation, interpretation, and elaboration of distinct traditions associated with him. The primary and secondary sources on the liberal arts are countless. Here I can only offer a partial picture of them; nevertheless, the widespread connection with Mercury/Hermes will become clear.

The liberal arts arose from the *paidea*, or education, among Greeks. Scholars have debated the existence of an institutionalized educational curriculum in antiquity and have attempted to trace it in philosophical works.[124] For instance, in the *Posterior Analytics*, Aristotle suggests that the Pythagorean-inspired programme for educating the guardians of Plato's *Republic* was also the programme used in his Academy: arithmetic, geometry, astronomy, and music – the future *quadrivium*; however, as Engress points out, later in the *Posterior Analytics*, Aristotle extended the *μαθήματα* (mathematical disciplines) to include the entire universe of knowledge.[125] In *Politics*, Aristotle defined the "liberal sciences" as fitting subjects of instruction for free men who seek intellectual excellence[126] – this definition is reminiscent of the *GE*'s own programme. The Sophists were probably the first to establish a systematic education in the liberal arts, particularly Hippias of Elis (late fifth century BCE), who was reputed to have learned mathematics, astronomy, and rhetoric – achievements that Plato mocks in his dialogue on the Sophist. The Romans acknowledged the reputation of Greek instructors when they adopted their ideals of education – evidence of the *translatio*

[123] Andrew Hicks, "Martianus Capella and the Liberal Arts," in Ralph Hexter and David Townsend (eds), *The Oxford Handbook of Medieval Latin Literature* (Oxford: Oxford University Press, 2012), 307.

[124] For a summary of these discussions, see Alain Bernard, Christine Proust, and Micah Ross, "Mathematics Education in Antiquity," in *Handbook on the History of Mathematics Education* (New York: Springer New York, 2013; 2014), 44–6.

[125] Gerhard Endress, "Mathematics and Philosophy in Medieval Islam," in Jan P. Hogendijk and Abdelhamid I. Sabra (eds), *The Enterprise of Science in Islam: New Perspectives* (Cambridge: The MIT Press, 2003), 124.

[126] Aristotle, *Politics*, VIII.1.

studii supported by Alfonso. In *De oratore* Cicero affirms that Hipias mastered the *liberales doctrinae atque ingenuae* (the liberal doctrines related to free men), which he expands to include geometry, music, *literarum cognitionem et poetarum* (literature), *de naturis rerum* (physics), *de hominum moribus* (ethics) and *de rebus publicis* (politics) for the orator.[127] Quintilian (35–95 CE) also included several disciplines within a complete programme of instruction for the rhetor.[128] Seneca (4–65 CE) discussed the liberal arts numerous times, particularly in *On Liberal and Vocational Studies*, where he describes five of the disciplines: grammar, music, geometry, arithmetic, and astronomy.[129]

But the oldest and most highly influential Roman account of the liberal arts is the lost work, *Libri novem disciplinarum*, by Varro (116–27 CE), who described the nine educational disciplines that the Romans adopted from the Greeks. It is likely that these disciplines were the future seven customary ones, plus medicine and architecture.[130] Despite their opposition towards anything associated with pagan culture, the Church Fathers eventually adopted the Roman system of education. Augustine – who had been a rhetoric teacher – addressed the liberal arts in several works, such as *De ordine* and the lost *Disciplinarum libri* – for which Varro was likely the main source.[131] Varro's *Libri novem disciplinarum* most probably included an allegorical personification of the liberal arts as muses, and a "journey upwards" (ἄνοδος), which can be interpreted as a Platonic influence – this was difficult for Augustine to accept.[132] These features, however, would be enhanced by the most influential account on the liberal arts in the Middle Ages, *De nuptiis Philologiae et Mercurii* (*On the marriage of Philology and Mercury*) by Martianus Capella, who consolidated the seven customary disciplines and Mercury/Hermes's relationship with them.

The dates and many details of Capella's life are unknown, but he was probably not a Christian, used Greek sources, lived in Carthage, and wrote *De nuptiis c.* 470–80.[133] It is unclassifiable and a difficult work to interpret, as it is a mixture of prose, verse, allegory, the humourous Menippean satires of Varro, Middle-Platonism – such as the *Chaldean oracles* – Neoplatonism, theurgy, and *Hermetica*.[134] Mercury is introduced as "the god

[127] Cicero, *De oratore*, III. 32.

[128] Quintilian, *Institutio oratoria*, I.10,1.

[129] Seneca, *Moral letters to Lucilius*, 88.

[130] See the classical reconstruction of the work from quotes in other authors by F. Ritschl, *Opuscula Philologica, iii* (Leipzig: Teubner, 1877), 352–402.

[131] See Danuta R. Shanzer, "Augustine's Disciplines: *Silent diutius Musae Varronis?*," in Karla Pollmann and Mark Vessey (eds), *Augustine and the Disciplines: From Cassiciacum to Confessions* (Oxford: Oxford Academic, 2011), 73–4.

[132] See Shanzer, "Augustine's Disciplines," 75.

[133] Danuta Shanzer, *A Philosophical and Literary Commentary on Martianus Capella's "De nuptiis Philologiae et Mercurii," Book 1* (Berkeley: University of California Press, 1986), 1–28.

[134] See Shanzer, *Philosophical and Literary Commentary*; Stephen Gersh, *Middle Platonism and Neoplatonism*, The Latin Tradition vol. 1 (Notre Dame: University of Notre Dame Press, 1986); and Julieta Cardigni, "Presencias herméticas en *De nuptiis Mercurii et Philologiae* de Marciano Capela," *Anales De Historia Antigua, Medieval y Moderna* 50 (2016): 37–53.

of wit and fluent speech but lacking the gravitas of real learning."[135] For this reason he tries to marry Wisdom, Divination, and the Soul, who reject him; finally, he finds the perfect bride: Philology – learning, literally the love of letters and study. As a result of this marriage, Philology is granted immortality and a cosmic journey through the spheres. Mercury's wedding gifts are seven maids embodying the liberal arts – whose description occupies the last seven of the work's nine books. In *De nuptiis*, Mercury is sometimes a young god, the messenger of the gods, but on other occasions he is assimilated to Thoth/Hermes Trismegistus, to *nous*/reason – Neoplatonic intellect – and to the planet Mercury.[136] This Mercury in *De nuptiis* shares many features with the Mercury in the *GE*, where he is also associated with Hermes, reason, a planet, and the liberal arts. Alfonso might have known about this description of Hermes through later medieval interpreters, as Capella was a pivotal influence on writers of the Carolingian period, and then in the twelfth century.

In *De nuptiis* Mercury is identified with the planet several times within astrological references. For instance, when Jupiter says that Mercury "often flies before the sun";[137] or later when Mercury is also warned "not to decide anything without the counsel of Apollo [the sun], because it was illicit to go astray from his close union with him, because he [Mercury] travelled through the houses of the zodiac, and Apollo did not allow him to go astray for more than one month."[138] This characterization is reminiscent of when Alfonso affirms that "Mercury is also the name of that planet which goes close to the sun, not leaving him night and day."[139] – as we saw above.

Moreover, at the beginning of *De nuptiis* book 2 Mercury is associated with Thoth and Hermes Trismegistus. To foresee the success of their marriage, Philology plays an arithmological game with Pythagorean references, in which she associates numbers with the letters of her and Mercury's name. Philology remarks that she is not going to use the usual name of the god but a "starry appellation" (*siderea nuncupatione*) that Jupiter gave him when he was born and that was only known through "the ingenuities of the Egyptians."[140] As Stahl points out, Hugo Grotius discovered that according to the calculations described in *De nuptiis*, this name had to be Thoth, which in this Neopythagorean context relates to Hermes Trismegistus.[141] Philology also discovers that Mercury's name is connected with the number three, and her

135 Michael Herren, *The Anatomy of Myth: The Art of Interpretation from the Presocratics to the Church Fathers* (Oxford and New York: Oxford University Press, 2017), 142.

136 *De nuptiis*, 2.101; 1.92; and 1.8, 25, 29. See Julieta Cardigni, "Los personajes principales en *De nuptiis Mercurii et Philologiae* de Marciano Capela: Una propuesta de análisis," *Revista Chilena De Estudios Medievales* no. 16 (2019): 28.

137 "[...] Phoebi antevolans saepe." *De nuptiis*, 1.92.

138 "[...] neque eum sine Apollinis consilio quicquam debere decernere aut fas ab eius congressibus aberrare, cum zodiaca eum hospitia praemetatem numquam abesse menstrua praecursione permitteret." *De nuptiis* 1.8. Similar thoughts are expressed in 1.25 and 1.29. See Cardigni, "Presencias herméticas," 47.

139 "E es otrossí Mercurio nombre d'aquella planeta que anda cerca'l sol, que se nuncua e d'él nin de noche nin de día." *GE*1 I, 171.

140 *De nuptiis* 2.101–4.

141 William Harris Stahl, Richard Johnson, and E. L. Burge, *Martianus Capella and the Seven Liberal Arts*, 2 vols (New York: Columbia University Press, 1971), 2: 35.

own name with the number four. These numbers are associated with the *trivium* and *quadrivium*. Even though those terms did not yet exist, it seems that Capella was aware of the concepts – consequently, this could be the origin of the idea of Mercury as god of the *trivium* that is found in the *GE*.

Early medieval scholars continued to develop the liberal arts. The term *quadrivium* ("four ways") was coined by Boethius (*c.* 480–524 CE), who wrote works on arithmetic, music, and possibly geometry.[142] Boethius also equated the *quadrivium* "with the division of mathematics into four parts, according to whether quantity is or is not discontinuous and immobile."[143] Then, Cassiodorus (*c.* 490–583), in *De artibus ac disciplinis liberalium litterarum* (*On the arts and disciplines of the liberal letters*), and Isidore, in the *Etymologies*, described the seven liberal arts in an encyclopedic manner. In contrast to Boethius, Isidore tried to link the arts of the *quadrivium* to physics.[144]

The next important breakthrough took place in the ninth century when, as Hicks explains, "both the allegorical and the encyclopedic components of the *De nuptiis* fuelled and shaped the pedagogical programmes of the Carolingian Renaissance."[145] Even though the term *trivium* was coined by then, it was apparently not used by the most relevant of Capella's commentators: Remigius of Auxerre and Scotus Erigena – and *quadrivium* was only used by the former.[146] Remigius highlighted that Mercury is *sermo*, rhetorically constructed discourse,[147] because in *De nuptiis* Jupiter affirms that Mercury is "our trust, discourse [*sermo*], benignity, true genius, and faithful messenger, interpreter of my mind, and sacred honour [*honos sacer*]."[148] As we have seen, Alfonso quotes Remigius several times in sections related to Mercury – for instance, in his description during *TSOI* and through his alleged *Summa* on the "mercurial ministers" that associate *trivium* with *sermo* and *quadrivium* with *sapientia* (wisdom). Another Carolingian author, Scotus Erigena (800–77) interpreted *honos sacer* (sacred honour) as *ho nous sacer*, "sacred intellect (or reason)," in keeping with the Neoplatonic tones of Capella.[149] Alfonso relates Mercury to reason many times, for instance, in *TSOI*, where Jupiter "sent Mercury his son, that is, good and wise reason, since that means Mercury,"[150] and Mercury represents "the word or reason that runs among men."[151]

[142] Henri-Irénée Marrou, "Les arts libéraux dans l'Antiquité classique," in *Arts libéraux et philosophie au Moyen Âge* (Paris ; Vrin; Montréal: Institut d'études médiévales, 1969), 18–19.

[143] Beaujouan, "Transformation," 463.

[144] Beaujouan, "Transformation," 463.

[145] Hicks, "Martianus Capella," 314.

[146] Hicks, "Martianus Capella," 317.

[147] See Cardigni, "Los personajes principales," 28

[148] "[...] nostra ille fides, sermo, benignitas/ Ac verus genius, fida recursio/ interpretesque meae mentis, honos sacer." *De nuptiis* 1.92.

[149] See Gersh, *Middle Platonism*, 598; and Cardigni, "Presencias herméticas," 47.

[150] "[...] Envió a Mercurio su fijo, esto es, buena razón e sabia, ca esso quiere dezir Mercurio." *GE*1 I, 320.

[151] "Mercurio [...] tanto quiere mostrar como palabra o razón que corre medianera entre los hombres." *GE*1 I, 318.

Interest in *De nuptiis* was renewed in the twelfth century, especially by authors linked to the Platonic cathedral school of Chartres, whose influence, as we have seen, extended to Alfonso's works.[152] In turn, these authors – such as Thierry of Chartres, William of Conches, and Bernard Silvestris – owe a profound debt to Remigius of Auxerre for their own interpretations of Capella.[153] This hierarchy of authorities helps us understand Alfonso's sources. Thierry of Chartres authored the *Heptateuch* or *Eptateuchon*, a massive compendium of texts related to the seven arts, which became the foundation of the School of Chartres's curriculum and uses *De nuptiis*'s allegory to express the Chartrian ideal.[154] Its prologue states:

> Since the two principal instruments of the philosopher are the understanding [*intellectum*] and its interpretation [*interpretation*]; and since the *quadrivium* illumines the understanding, while the *trivium* provides an elegant, rational, and adorned interpretation of it, it is manifest that the *Eptateuchon* is a unique and single instrument of all philosophy. Philosophy, moreover, is the love of wisdom.[155]

This is the epitome of the twelfth-century definition of the philosopher as master of the liberal arts – which Alfonso embraced in the thirteenth century. We also find a theorization of the relationship between the *trivium* and *quadrivium* that is analogous to that found in the *GE*. As we saw above, according to Alfonso, "reason is the *trivium* and wisdom the *quadrivium*," and later he associates them with Mercury and Minerva – something that he elaborates on using the Latin commentaries of Ovid.[156]

Jeauneau highlights how Thierry and other Chartres-linked thinkers maintained that the seven liberal arts are embodied in the marriage of Mercury/*trivium* and Philology/*quadrivium*, which represent *eloquentia* and *sapientia* (wisdom).[157] All of them quoted a famous sentence in Cicero's *De inventione* (1.1.1): "eloquentiam sine sapientia multum obesse, sapientiam vero sine eloquentia parum prodesse" (eloquence without wisdom is greatly harmful, but wisdom without eloquence is hardly useful.)[158] Again, we can wonder why Alfonso identified the *trivium* with reason, and not just eloquence or speech (*sermo*).

Finally, I want to highlight the Hermetic influences in Chartres. Since this school was mainly inspired by Platonic thought, its members valued *De nuptiis*,

152 See Martínez, *El humanismo medieval*, 57–63. On Chartres, see Wetherbee, *Platonism and Poetry*.

153 Hicks, "Martianus Capella," 317.

154 Wetherbee, *Platonism and Poetry*, 26.

155 "Nam, cum sint duo precipua phylosophandi instruments, intellectus eiusque interpretatio, intellectum autem quadruvium illuminet, eius vera interpretationem elegantem, rationabilem, ornatam trivium subministret, manifestum est Eptatheucon totius phylosophye unicum ac singulare esse instrumentum. Phylosophya autem est amor sapientie." *Incipit prologus Theoderici in Eptatheucon*, in Édouard Jeauneau, "Note sur l'École," *Studi medievali* ser. 3, vol. 5 (1964): 854.

156 *GE2* I, 78; and *GE2* I, 406.

157 Édouard Jeauneau, *Lectio philosophorum: Recherches sur l'École de Chartres* (Amsterdam: Hakkert, 1973), 90.

158 As cited in Hicks, "Martianus Capella," 320.

Macrobius's commentary on *De somnium scipionis*, and the Hermetic *Asclepius* as their main references and "for the insights they provided into the meaning of Plato's cosmology"; they founded the study of ancient literature, including the *integumenta*, or hidden meaning of texts, in these works.[159] Due to Chartres's influence, among the *magistri* – urban twelfth-century teacher-scholars – "the practical value assigned to arithmetic, astrology, and even magic, had a significant effect in encouraging the revival of scientific study, as well as enhancing the prestige of learning in general."[160] Undoubtedly, Alfonso reflected on this in the next century. As Burnett indicates, twelfth-century authors combined classical texts, the inspiration of the *Asclepius*, and Arabic cosmological writings – which began to spread in Europe mostly thanks to the work of translators in the Iberian Peninsula.[161]

We have ascertained that the intellectual history of the liberal arts in the Western world is enmeshed not only with the god Mercury but also with his Hermetic aspects. Yet Alfonso's access to Hermetic Arabic sources was substantially greater than that of most erudite men in northern Europe, and Egyptian and Hellenistic Hermetic traditions came to Alfonso mainly through Arabic channels. Let us now explore how ancient sources connected Hermes Trismegistus to the disciplines of the liberal arts and how the Arabic-speaking world interpreted and translated these sources, placing Hermes in them before they reached Castile.

Hermes Trismegistus's Patronage of the Liberal Arts and its Arabic Accommodations

Hermes Trismegistus's relationship to the liberal arts dates back to his Greek and Egyptian counterparts, Hermes and Thoth. Hermes was the god of eloquent speech and rhetoric, both relevant to the *trivium*. As Van den Broek suggests, Thoth's most characteristic feature, "which in some way determined most of his other qualities, was that he was considered the inventor of counting and writing"; as god of the moon, he also became the chief measurer of time, "who distinguished seasons, months, and years and also determined the regnal years of the pharaohs"; moreover, he also divided the lands of Egypt into *nomes*.[162] These skills made him a patron of the mathematical arts of the *quadrivium*, as we will see below. With the merging of these two gods into Hermes Trismegistus, this figure came to be identified as the inventor of Egyptian philosophy, arts, and sciences. Since prominent Greek thinkers – such as Pythagoras and Plato – had allegedly studied in Egypt, Hermes came to be associated with the origin of civilization's knowledge. In this sense, it is significant that a quote by the Neoplatonic philosopher Iamblichus (*c.* 245–325 CE) in *De mysteriis Aegyptiorum* (*On the mysteries of the Egyptians*) begins by mentioning "Hermes, the god who presides over rational discourse [*logos*]," and affirms that in ancient times Egyptian priests dedicated the "discoveries of their wisdom [to him],

159 Wetherbee, *Platonism and Poetry*, 30 and 48.
160 Wetherbee, "Philosophy, Cosmology," 23.
161 See Burnett, "The Establishment of Medieval Hermeticism," 69.
162 Van den Broek, "Hermes Trismegistus, I: Antiquity," 474–5.

attributing all their own writings to Hermes."[163] This attribution corresponds with "Thoth's role as 'lord of divine words' and inventor of script, language, and literature in Egyptian theologies."[164] In his study of the Hermetic tradition, Bull argues that Egyptian priests, knowledgeable in Hellenistic philosophy, created the *Hermetica* by adapting and translating their traditions into Greek.[165] Since Hermes was the creator of all wisdom, Hermetic traditions translated into Greek attributed the prestigious disciplines of the Greek *paideia*, which would become part of the liberal arts, to him.

There is a remarkable statement in *On Arithmetic* by Aristoxenus (*c.* 375–335 BCE), a lost work preserved in the anthology of Stobaeus (fifth century CE): "For number contains all else, and there is a ratio between all the numbers to each other. The Egyptians, moreover, say that it [sc. the ratio] is an invention of Hermes, whom they call Thoth, and they say that it was discovered from the orbit of the divine luminaries."[166] The Stoic Chaeremon (first century CE) indicates that the Hermetic tradition created astronomy/astrology, and from it the mathematical arts. Astronomy and astrology, in their Western form, originated in Babylon, and then Egypt contributed the solar year of 365 days, with twenty-four-hour days, and the teaching of the decans. By the time the Greeks began to engage with astronomy, the Egyptians had already made their own advancements and asserted themselves as the originators of the science, and claimed that their god of learning, Thoth, had discovered it.[167]

The relationship between astrology and Hermetism becomes clearer when we remember that this word can be traced back to the Greek word *hermaïkos*, which means "pertaining to Hermes"; and this adjective is most often used in astrology "regarding the motions and influences of the planet Mercury, the Latin name for Hermes," while authors such as Iamblichus used it in reference to Hermeticism.[168] The Roman astrologer Firmicus Maternus (fourth century CE) – well versed in Egyptian sources – acknowledged the relationship between the disciplines attributed to Hermes and the professions practised by those born under the influence of the planet Mercury. In this way Mercury creates, among other things,

> philosophers, teachers of the art of grammar, or geometers: often he makes those who measure heavenly phenomena or study them so that they can contemplate the presence of the gods, or men skilled in sacred writings. Often he makes orators […] makes philologists skilled in difficult writings […] magicians […], astrologers […] scribes […] astronomers, astrologers […] learned men of letters, orators, geometers.[169]

163 Iamblichus, *De Mysteriis* 1.1.
164 Bull, *Tradition of Hermes*, 13.
165 Bull, *Tradition of Hermes*, 13–15.
166 Bull, *Tradition of Hermes*, 45.
167 Bull, *Tradition of Hermes*, 384.
168 Bull, *Tradition of Hermes*, 20.
169 *Matheseos* III. VII. 1–28, see Firmicus Maternus, *Ancient Astrology*, 99–103. This is the translation by Rhys Bram, whose edition I follow. The Latin original is: "Mercurius […] facit philosophos grammaticae artis magistros aut geometras aut caelestia saepe tractantes aut qui ad hoc spectent, ut deorum possint praesentiam intueri, aut sacrarum litterarum peritos; facit etiam frequenter oratores […] facit philologos aut laboriosarum litterarum peritos […] magos […] mathematicos […] scribas […] mathematicos, astrologos […]

We can observe the close relationship between these trades and the liberal arts. Besides, Bull observes that some of these occupations in Firmicus only make sense in the context of Egyptian temples – and, implicitly, to priests related to a Hermetic cult.[170]

This relationship with astrology, mathematical arts, and Egyptian priesthood was mentioned by Diodorus (first century BCE), who described Hermes as the sacred scribe of Osiris, advisor of Isis, and inventor, among other things, of language, letters, astronomy, and music.[171] Diodorus also affirms that the education of Egyptian priests consisted of "two systems of letters – sacred and demotic – as well as geometry and arithmetic, which serve as the foundation for astrology, the most important art."[172] This testimony correlates with that of Chaeremon, who described the Egyptian priests' way of life as ascesis, ritual purity, singing hymns, and contemplation, but also the practice of astrology, arithmetic, and geometry. As Bull remarks, Chaeremon portrayed the Egyptian priests as experts in the *quadrivium*[173] – although this term did not yet exist. This picture corroborates what we find in the Hermetic *Asclepius*.

In the *Asclepius*, Hermes Trismegistus complains that the Sophists do not understand the disciplines of arithmetic, music, and geometry (*ἀριθμητικὴν et musicen et geometriam*), which are part of the pure philosophy he intuits; the practitioner of his philosophy must only "wonder at the recurrence of the stars, how their measure stays constant in prescribed stations and in the orbit of their turning; he should learn the dimensions, qualities, and quantities of the land [...] in order to commend, worship and wonder at the skill and mind of God."[174] Thus, the measurement of God's creation, which depends on mathematical and astronomical skills, is performed solely in order to admire the skill of the creator and worship him. This cannot come as a surprise, because arithmetic, music, and geometry "are often grouped together and attributed to the Egyptians, and sometimes to the Egyptian Hermes, by both Christian and Pagan authors."[175] Yet Hermes's connection with knowledge also reached the Arabic world.

As we saw above, the Hermes-worshipping inhabitants of Ḥarrān probably identified Hermes Trismegistus with the Quranic Idrīs, and Muslim scholars might have taken the assimilation of Hermes with Enoch and Idrīs from Ḥarrān.[176] Muslim sages also associated Idrīs with Enoch, although it is possible that his name is derived from the biblical Ezra via its Greek spelling.[177] Lory points out that some Quran commentators derived Idrīs's name from the Arabic root D-R-S, which means to examine, deepen,

doctos grammaticos oratores geometras." Found at: https://penelope.uchicago.edu/Thayer/E/Roman/Texts/Firmicus_Maternus/home.html

170 Bull, *Tradition of Hermes* 183–4.

171 Diodorus, *Bibliotheca* 1.16.

172 Bull, *Tradition of Hermes*, 394.

173 Bull, *Tradition of Hermes*, 396.

174 "[...] ut apocatastasis astrorum, stationes praefinitas cursumque commutationis numeris constare miretur; terrae uero dimensiones, qualitates, quantitates [...] miretur, adoret atque conlaudet artem mentemque diuinam." *Asclepius* 13. Translation by Copenhaver.

175 Bull, *Tradition of Hermes*, 384.

176 See primary and secondary sources in Alexander, "From Son of Adam," 115–18.

177 Quran 19:57 and 21:85. Alexander, "From Son of Adam," 118.

study, etc., and emphasized his role as a transmitter of knowledge and techniques, which he obtained through divine revelation. Once identified with Hermes, and as a "civilizing hero," Idrīs was acknowledged, among many other things, as the "founder of astronomy and mathematics, who gives access to all the messages from the sky and all the temporal references."[178]

We saw that the Greek system of education or *paideia* aimed to construct a rational organization of disciplines; I have also mentioned the Abbasid Caliphate's translation movement, focused on the Greek sciences in particular, that reached its peak in the ninth century.[179] Not surprisingly, Rosenthal noticed a very perceptible preference in Muslim civilization for the classification of the science, and this tendency is due to the classical heritage, "which [...] exercised perhaps its most pervasive influence upon intellectual life in Islam."[180] Robinson explains that Muslim scholars agreed on a fundamental division between *ʿulūm naqliyya* (the transmitted or traditional sciences), "all of which owed their existence to God's revelation," and the *ʿulūm ʿaqliyya* (the rational sciences), "all of which were derived from man's capacity to think" and "might equally be referred to as Greek, foreign, or ancient sciences."[181] Rosenthal provided several examples that allow us to appreciate how Muslims assimilated Greek knowledge into their own patterns of thought, and how their own developments paralleled the European *trivium* and *quadrivium*. For instance, al-Khwārizmī divided his brief encyclopedia of the sciences (*Mafātīḥ al-ʿulūm*) into two books: one devoted to the Islamic sciences – including jurisprudence, *al-kalām* (speculative theology), grammar, *adab*, poetry, prosody, and history – and the second devoted "to the sciences originating from foreigners such as the Greeks" – including philosophy, logic, medicine, arithmetic, geometry, astronomy, music, mechanics, and alchemy.[182] In *Iḥṣāʾ al-ʿulūm* (*Enumeration of the sciences*), al-Fārābī classified the sciences into five groups: 1) linguistics; 2) logic; 3) the mathematical sciences: arithmetic, geometry, optics, mathematical astronomy, music, technology, and mechanics; 4) the natural sciences, including magic, talismans, alchemy, and metaphysics; and 5) politics, jurisprudence, and speculative theology (*kalām*).[183] *Iḥṣāʾ al-ʿulūm* was influential in Castile because it was translated twice in Toledo during the second half of the twelfth century – once by Dominicus Gundissalinus, and then by Gerard of Cremona.[184]

Another work known in Iberia, the *Rasāʾil Ikhwān al-Ṣafāʾ* – mentioned above – included complex classifications of the sciences. The *Rasāʾil* distinguishes between three large groups of sciences: propaedeutic, religious, and philosophical. The philosophical sciences are divided into four kinds: propaedeutic-mathematical, logical, natural, and metaphysical. Interestingly, the propaedeutic-mathematical sciences correspond to the four sciences of the Western *quadrivium*, given here with

178 Pierre Lory, "Hermès/Idris, prophète et sage dans la tradition islamique," in Antoine Faivre (ed.), *Présence d'Hermès Trismegiste*. Recueil d'articles de P. Lory, no. 7 (Paris: Cahiers de l'hermétisme, 1988), 102.

179 See especially Gutas, *Greek Thought, Arabic Culture*.

180 Franz Rosenthal, *The Classical Heritage in Islam* (London: Routledge, 1975), 52.

181 Robinson, "Education," 453.

182 Rosenthal, *Classical Heritage*, 54.

183 Rosenthal, *Classical Heritage*, 54.

184 See Burnett, "Translating Activity," 1049.

their Arabic transliterations: arithmetic (*arithmāṭīqī*), geometry (*jūmaṭriyā* or, also in Arabic with a word derived from Persian, *handasah*), astronomy (*asṭurnūmiyā*) or knowledge of the stars, and music (*mūsīqī*).[185] As we observe in the above passages, the mathematical sciences of the *quadrivium* are consistently bundled together.

Even more interesting for us is al-Qurṭubī's classification of the sciences in the *Ghāya*. According to al-Qurṭubī, this book of magic and its companion, *Rutbat al-ḥakīm* (*The rank of the sage*) – dedicated to alchemy – were destined to form the two final steps of a philosophical ladder. Al-Qurṭubī himself chose to call these two treatises "the two conclusions [of philosophy]" and in both works underlines "how deficient and imperfect 'the Sage' would remain until he mastered these twin-sciences."[186] De Callataÿ points out how the prologues of both works make it clear that "alchemy and magic should be considered the last two sciences of the *curriculum scientiarum* of 'the Sage,' that is, in other words, the truly accomplished philosopher."[187] At the end of the *Ghāya*, al-Qurṭubī outlines the sage's curriculum and divides it into ten categories that he should master before undertaking the last two, and most important, sciences. These categories include the following sciences: 1) agriculture, grazing, and navigation; 2) command of the armies, war strategies, taming of animals, veterinary medicine, medicine, and falconry; 3) the civilized sciences, in charge of urban matters such as grammar, language, *adab*, writing, and chancellery matters; 4) political science; 5) ethics; 6) mathematical sciences, including arithmetic (*al-ʿadad*), geometry (*al-handasa*), the science of the stars (*al-nujūm*), and music (al-*mūsīqī*); 7) logic; 8) medicine; 9) the science of nature; and 10) metaphysics.[188] Thus, the four sciences of the *quadrivium* are once more collected together – the *Picatrix* translated them using their medieval Latin names: *arismetrica, geometria, astronomia,* and *musica.*[189]

The *Picatrix* translated the *Ghāya*'s organization of the disciplines and the way to acquire them for a thirteenth-century Castilian audience. The book narrates how the wise Hermes (*Hermes sapientem*) was asked "what do science and philosophy have in common," and he answered, "[a] perfect nature."[190] As Attrell and Porreca observe, the Hermetic concept of a perfect nature "is a recurring theme throughout the *Picatrix*, and it refers to a kind of *telos* built into the seven liberal arts. It constitutes a state of mystical fulfillment that the magician achieves by aligning himself with the planets governing his own nativity and closely

185 Rosenthal, *Classical Heritage*, 54–8. See also Godefroid de Callataÿ, "Encyclopaedism on the Fringe of Islamic Orthodoxy: The *Rasāʾil Ikhwān al-Ṣafāʾ*, the *Rutbat al-Ḥakīm* and the *Ghāyat al-Ḥakīm* on the Division of Science," *Asiatische Studien/Études Asiatiques: Zeitschrift Der Schweizerischen Asiengesellschaft/Revue de la Société Suisse-Asie* 71 (2017): 858–65.

186 de Callataÿ and Moureau, "Towards the Critical Edition," 386.

187 de Callataÿ, "Encyclopaedism," 866.

188 *Ghāya* IV.5, 334. I am summarizing the translation and classification of de Callataÿ, "Encyclopaedism," 868–9.

189 *Picatrix* I.ii.1.

190 "Et quidam Hermetem sapientem interrogaverunt, rogantes: Cum quibus sciencia et philosophia iungebantur? Respondit: Cum natura completa." *Picatrix* III.vi.5.

adhering to ceremonial scruples."[191] Many spells in the *Picatrix* provide "shortcuts for becoming knowledgeable and/or skilled at performing certain tasks," including, of course, those related to the liberal arts; but if we look at these spells, we can appreciate the paradox that the *Picatrix* "repeatedly recommends a thorough knowledge of nature as a prerequisite for the practice of magic, while knowledge of nature – via the seven liberal arts, inter alia – is one of the more frequently seen objectives of the rituals that fall under this category."[192] Even though some liberal arts are occasionally ascribed to other planets, the *Picatrix* consistently attributes them to Mercury, ambiguously associated with Hermes Trismegistus throughout the treatise. Since the *Picatrix* was most probably read by compilers of the *GE*, its stance on Mercury deeply interests us here.

To ascertain how Arabic depictions of Mercury/Hermes and the liberal arts were adapted into Latin, I am going to compare some sections of the *Ghāya* with their translations in the *Picatrix*. The translation occasionally adds or omits some arts, which could be due to mistakes or are deliberate amendments. Another possibility is that the Castilian translator was using a different manuscript of the *Ghāya* than that used by Ritter and Plessner – whose Arabic edition I follow.[193] For instance, a passage in *Ghāya* III states that: "Mercury is the source of intellectual strength and has insight into the development of the sciences of *al-jadal* (dialectic, debate), philosophy, *al-ḥisāb* (arithmetic), *al-misāḥa* (surveying, related to geometry), *al-hay'a w-al-qaḍā'* (judiciary astrology), *al-ʿiyāfa wa al-zajara* (augury, prognostication through the flight of birds), *al-fa'l* (omen), *al-kitāba*, *al-balāgha* (rhetoric)."[194] The *Picatrix* translates it as: "Mercury is the source of intellective strength, and he oversees the learning of sciences, wisdoms, dialectic, *grammar*, philosophy, geometry, judicial astrology, geomancy, the art of the scribes, and auguries with birds."[195] The translation omits arithmetic – which might be a mistake, because arithmetic is associated with Mercury in other passages – yet keeps geometry and astronomy. It also omits rhetoric, but adds grammar to dialectic, which boosts Mercury's connection to the *trivium*. Since the *Ghāya* ascribes philosophy to Mercury, it might already encompass all the liberal arts in the mind of the Alfonsine translator; moreover, Mercury aids all learning, including that obtained through astrology and other divinatory arts. The *Ghāya* continues a couple of lines below:

> Among the trades, [Mercury] has *khaṭāba* [rhetoric, homiletics), poetry, commerce, calculation, knowledge of the composition of *alḥān* [melodies, music],

[191] Attrell and Porreca, "Introduction," 8–9.

[192] Astrell and Porreca, "Introduction," 18; see also the useful classification of spells by their goals on page 24.

[193] The scholarly edition that Saif is preparing, which is based on several manuscripts, will provide us with a more accurate picture.

[194] *Ghāya* III.1, 154.

[195] "Mercurius est minera virtutis intellective. Et habet aspectum ad sciencias addiscendum et sapiencias et dialecticam. grammaticam. philosophiam, geometriam, astronomiam cum suis iudiciis, geomanciam, notariam et augurium avium secundum sermocinacionem." *Picatrix* III.i.8.

> painting, dyeing, and the nice and extraordinary trades, which are produced by the *riyāḍiyyāt* [mathematics], [...] among the places, he has the *majālis* [councils, assemblies] of *kalām* [speech, speculative theology], and the places of *munāẓarāt* [debates] of *ʿulamāʾ* [scholars, wise men].[196]

The *Picatrix* translates it: "from the trades, [Mercury has] preaching/oratory, versification, commerce (trading with carts), geometry, interpretation of dreams, drawing, fashioning, all professions that are discovered through subtle thought [...] and among the places [he has] the house of preaching."[197] Even though the translation skips music, it keeps versification; in the Middle Ages, poetry was frequently associated with music – especially for Alfonso, who composed the *Cantigas de Santa María* (*Songs of Saint Mary*). The Arabic consistently relates Mercury with all kinds of speech and eloquence, but also commerce – a feature of the ancient god. The *Picatrix* keeps these references but changes mathematics to geometry. Thus, between the Arabic and Latin versions all the liberal arts are associated with Mercury, who is also the patron of astrology and other divinatory arts.

There is an even closer bond in *Ghāya* III.7 where, according to Plessner, "the reader is now considered sufficiently prepared in the theory of magic to be initiated into its practice."[198] Among other things, it specifies which requests, related to certain professions, are suitable for each planet: "Ask Mercury concerning matters related to scribes, people of arithmetic, *al-muhandisīn* [geometricians], astrologers, *al-khuṭabāʾ* [orators], *al-fuṣaḥāʾ* [eloquent men], *al-bulaġāʾ* [rhetoricians], scholars, philosophers, *al-ḥukamāʾ* [wise men], owners of speech, *al-udabāʾ* [possessors of *adab*], poets."[199] In another work, I pointed out how this list of professions is reminiscent of Mercury's trades in *Firmicus maternus*. I suggested that Firmicus adapted his Egyptian Hermetic materials to the realities of fourth-century Rome, and in a similar fashion, al-Qurṭubī adapted his sources to the Caliphate of Córdoba.[200] The *Picatrix* translates the above passage as: "Seek from Mercury petitions appropriate to clerks [*notariis*], scribes, arithmeticians, geometricians, astrologers, grammarians, public speakers, philosophers, rhetoricians, poets."[201] This translation adds grammarians and astrologers; thus, if we consider poetry to be part of music, all the liberal arts, with the exception of dialectics, are again represented here. I would like to briefly address the reference to the arts of the scribes and clerks in the *Picatrix*. Attrell and Porreca suggest that they were its most plausible addressees, as evinced by the nature of most spells described in the work.[202] Taking up this idea, elsewhere I suggested that in the Caliphate of Córdoba, the *kuttāb* were figures equivalent to clerks and scribes – also in need of spells to please

196 *Ghāya* III.1, 154.

197 "Ex magisteris predicare (oratoria), versificare, carpentariam, geometriam et exposiciones somniorum, debuxandi et figurandi, et omnia magisteria que subtili ingenio sunt reperta [...] et ex locis domum predicandi." *Picatrix* III.i.8.

198 Plessner, "Introduction," lxx.

199 *Ghāya* III.7, 197.

200 Udaondo Alegre, "If You Want to Pray to Mercury," 222–3.

201 "Petas a Mercurio peticiones appropriatas notariis, scribis, arismetricis, geometricis, astrologis, grammaticis, sermocinantibus, philosophis, rethoricis, poetis." *Picatrix* III.vii.7.

202 Attrell and Porreca, "Introduction," 16–18 and 23.

their superiors, neutralize their rivals, and enhance the knowledge and skills related to their profession.[203] The *kuttāb*'s knowledge was epitomized by *adab*, a perfunctory familiarity with all the disciplines necessary for an educated man.[204]

In medieval Castile, the disciplines equivalent to those of *adab* were those included in the *trivium* and *quadrivium*, which encompassed everything a learned courtier would need – including magic, according to Alfonso. In my previous work I defended the position that the *Ghāya* conceived of Mercury/Hermes as the patron and exemplar of the *kuttāb*, its intended audience. Once translated into Castilian and Latin, Hermes played the same role for courtiers, clerks, and those able to read and learn. As happens in modern languages, Latin did not find an accurate word to translate *adab* or *udabā'* (possessors of *adab*) – in the passage I just quoted it is omitted. According to my interpretation, the concept was absorbed to characterize the ideal courtier under the patronage of Mercury, and it filtered into the *GE*. We can observe these features a litle later, when the *Ghāya* says that Mercury

> shows *al-ʿaql* (reason), *al-nuṭq* (enunciation, speech), *al-kalām*, *al-ghawr* (deepness in thought), *al-dhakā* (intelligence), *al-fiṭna* (discernment, intelligence), *ḥusn* (refinement, goodness) of *al-taʿallum* (learning), *al-munāẓara* (debate), *al-adab*, philosophy, advance of knowledge, arithmetic, surveying, *al-handasa* (geometry), astrology, *al-kihāna* (divination), augury, omen, writing (*al-kitāba*), rhetoric, *al-faṣuḥa* (eloquence), *ḥalāwa* (sweetness) and swiftness of speech, knowledge of sciences, memory, praise on account [of memory], initiative [with memory] to recollect things and compose poetry, knowledge of books and *al-dawāwīn* (diwans, collections of poetry) [...].[205]

According to the *Picatrix*, Mercury

> signifies sense perception and the rational intellect, good eloquence, and a strong and deep intelligence concerning matters, good intellect, good memory, good apprehension and an agile mind competent to learn sciences, those who labour in the sciences and philosophy; understanding of how things will happen, arithmetic, geometry, astrology, geomancy, magic [*nigromanciam*], auguries, scribes, grammar, smooth talkers [rhetoricians]; easy understanding of the questions of wise men, he who labours in the sciences, and the desire to be exalted through the knowledge of these sciences, he who desires to make books, verses, and rhythms, he who writes books, calculations [charts], and the sciences, he who wants to know the secrets of the wise men, he who explains philosophy [...].[206]

203 Udaondo Alegre, "If You Want to Pray to Mercury," 201–11.

204 After the publication of my work, I found that Coulon had briefly suggested that certain passages of the *Ghāya* "remind [us of] the codes and references of court literature (*adab*), suggesting that it could have been written in the court of a sovereign or destined for courtiers, or in any case for readers familiarized with that literature." Coulon, *La Magie*, 159. I hope my article confirmed Coulon's hypothesis.

205 *Ghāya* III.7, 201.

206 "[...] significat sensum et intellectum racionabile,, bonam eloquenciam et intelligenciam rerum forcium et profundarum, bonum intellectum, bonam memoriam, bonam apprehensivam, agilitatem aptam ad sciencias docendas, in scienciis et philosophia laborantes, intelligenciam rerum eventarum, arismetricam, geometriam, astrologiam, geomanciam, nigromanciam, augurios, scribas, grammaticam, blande sermocinantes,

First, I want to address the reference to *al-ʿaql* (reason) that the *Picatrix* highlights and emphasizes using many variations of *intellectum racionabile*: it opens the possibility that in the *GE*, the insistence that Mercury (and the *trivium*) represent reason might come from the *Picatrix*, since the relationship between Mercury and reason is clearer than in the Western thinkers mentioned above. As Jolivet indicates, most illustrious Arabic philosophers – such as al-Kindī, al-Fārābī, and Ibn Sina – used *al-ʿaql* to translate the Greek *nous* used by Aristotelian and Neoplatonic philosophers.[207] But *nous* is also an important concept in the *Hermetica*, where it is granted by Hermes's teachings. Kahane and Pietrangeli have studied the echoes of the Hermetic *nous* in Castilian, translated as *seso*[208] – for instance, in the sapiential *Bocados de Oro*, as we saw in Chapter One – but also as reason. I would like to add this Latin rendering of the mercurial *al-ʿaql* as reason in the *Picatrix*, because this feature characterizes Mercury in the *GE*.

The Latin word *scientia* – repeated three times in this quote – is more accurately translated as "knowledge" than "science." Thus, it might justify the *GE*'s insistence about the "knowledges" (*saberes*) of Mercury that we saw above. In this quotation – translated from Arabic – we once again find references to all the liberal arts, including *al-munāẓara* (debate, dialectics), which is not translated into Latin, but it could be subsumed by some of the categories related to intellect and logic. I also wish to draw attention to the Arabic *adab*, which is added alongside philosophy, which the *Picatrix* seems to translate as "those who labour in knowledges" (*scientia laborantes*), an expression that is repeated twice. There are also significant references to several divinatory arts, to which the *Picatrix* adds magic (*nigromancia*).[209] My last quotation is from the invocation to Mercury in *Ghāya* III.7, which contains numerous Hermetic associations:

> Peace be with you, oh Mercury, virtuous sir, sincere, *al-ʿāqil* (reasonable), *al-nāṭiq* (eloquent), *al-fahm* (understanding), *al-munāẓir* (insightful), learned in all the arts of the arithmetician and the scribe, good-natured, learned in *akhbār* (reports, history) of heaven and earth, noble sir, frugal, content, beneficial to wealth and commerce […] lord of the inspiration of the prophets, *al-ʿaql* (reason), *al-kalām* (speech), *al-ʾakhbār*, fineness of learning, of all sciences, intelligence, discernment, *adab*, philosophy, the advance of knowledge, the geometry of lofty and earthly things, of surveying, astrology, augury, omen, rhetoric, the composition of poetry, books and diwans (collections of poetry), eloquence […].[210]

The *Picatrix* translates it as:

> May God save you, good sir Mercury, you who are sincere, perceptive, intelligent, wise, and an instructor [*infusor*] of every kind of writing, arithmetic, computation,

levem apprehensionem erga peticiones sapientum, in scienciis laborantem ipsisque scienciis cupientem exaltari, libros, versus, ritmos facere cupientem, librorum, computacionis, scienciarum scriptorem, secreta sapientum scire desiderantem, philosophiarum explanatorem." *Picatrix* III.vii.14.

207 Jolivet, "The Arabic Inheritance," 130.

208 Kahane and Pietrangeli, "Hermetism," 446–7.

209 On the translation of *nigromancia* – originally divination through dead beings – as magic, see Attrell and Porreca, "Introduction," 10–12.

210 *Ghāya* III.7, 221–2.

> and knowledge of heaven and earth! You are a noble lord and temperate in your joys. Lord, sustainer, and subtle interpreter of riches, commerce, profits, and deep perception. You are the disposer and [astrological] ruler of prophecy and prophets and their perceptions, reason, instruction, learning of diverse sciences, of subtlety, intellect, philosophy, geometry, the sciences of heaven and earth, divination, geomancy, poetry, writing, [and] eloquence [...].[211]

This illustration of the disciplines related to Mercury is a summary of all the attributes we discussed in this chapter. The *Ghāya* continuously connects him to *adab* and the scribal art, as well as to *al-ʿaql* (reason). Alongside this we also find references to all the arts of the *trivium* and *quadrivium*. It is obvious that many of the *Ghāya*'s Arabic sources had a Hellenistic origin, since Mercury is also consistently associated with the attributes of the god, not only relating him to rhetoric/eloquence but also to commerce and all kinds of teachings and learnings. The above passage implies that the knowledge of all conventional disciplines, including both *ʿulūm naqliyya* and *ʿulūm ʿaqliyya*, has learning magic as its final step. As we saw in the first part of the chapter, the *GE* reserves the same privilege to those who mastered the *trivium* and the *quadrivium*. In both cases, Mercury/Hermes is the patron of this instruction. Therefore, the association of the liberal arts with Mercury in the *GE* could have also been influenced by the *Picatrix*.

Conclusion

The liberal arts were Alfonso's main reference concerning knowledge and education, as he was deeply influenced by the great French twelfth-century schools of thought. Even though this intellectual framework was relatively outdated by Alfonso's time, he managed to enhance the knowledge of the liberal arts in his kingdom through his privileged access to Arabic sources, especially concerning the *quadrivium*. Not surprisingly, most great kings and characters of antiquity found in the *GE* are described as wise in the liberal arts, yet no one as much as Mercury, "very wise in the *trivium*, and even in the *quadrivium*." I have shown how the association between Hermes Trismegistus and the arts related to both the *trivium* and *quadrivium* dates back to the Near Eastern and Hellenistic setting where this syncretic character was born, how this link filtered into both the medieval Latin and Arabic-speaking worlds, and how these two worlds merged together once more in the multicultural court of Alfonso. We have also seen how the connection between Mercury/Hermes and the sciences of the liberal arts can be found in both Eastern and Western authorities. The Castilian king relies on sources from these two origins, which makes his Hermes Trismegistus the paradigm of Eastern-Western education and its wisdom traditions that Alfonso

211 "Mercuri bone domine, tu qui es veridicus, sensatus, intelligens et in omni manerie scribarum, arismetrice, computacionis, sciencie celorum et terre sapiens et infusor! Dominus nobilis es et modice leticie, diviciarum, mercacionum, lucrorum, sensuum profundoruni dominus et sustentator ac subtilis intellector. Tu es propheciarum prophetarum eorumque sensus, racionis, doctrine, sciencias divers as apprehendendi, subtilitatis, intellectus, philosophie, geometrie, celorum et terre scienciarum, divinacionum, geomancie, poetice, scribendi, bene loquendi." *Picatrix* III.vii.32.

promoted. Furthermore, this portrayal of a Castilian Hermes exemplifies the ideal of a knowledgeable courtier that the wise king aimed to foster within his realm, and also legitimizes Alfonso's own intellectual and political ambitions in his era through the *translatio studii* and *translatio imperii* theories.

The knowledge of Hermes/Mercury is explained in two significant passages in *GE2*, one about "the knowledge of Hermes" – where a divine provenance is justified through stories containing Hermetic, Arabic, and Jewish echoes – and another on "the knowledge of Mercury" – where Mercury's education, lineage, and effective use of the liberal arts are emphasized. I have connected this second section to all of Mercury's appearances in the *GE*, which are deeply interrelated. However, these two significant passages are connected as well, because Ovid is used to illustrate the story of the book of Hermes and Asclepius, and the episodes from the *Metamorphoses* are explained through the use of Arabic magic. This interconnectedness reflects the history of the liberal arts and their bond with Hermes – in both the East and West. Since he was born in the Hellenistic world, Hermes Trismegistus was attached to the rhetorical and mathematical arts – an inheritance of the Greek Hermes and the Egyptian Thoth, whose devotees were educated in these disciplines. These Hermetic associations were adopted by the Western world when Martianus Capella linked Mercury with philology and associated him with all the liberal arts, but they were also adopted by the Muslim world when Arabic scholars adapted Greek sciences and disciplines, including Hermetic ones. Alfonso drew from these different worlds: he read the European interpreters of Capella, who mixed reflections on Mercury, the *trivium*, and the *quadrivium* with the Hermetic *Asclepius*; he translated Arabic books of astronomy and magic, where Hermes played a predominant role. When Alfonso interprets the Ovidian stories he uses both European commentators and Arabic books of magic, especially the *Picatrix*. As we have seen, the *Picatrix* consistently associates Mercury not only with the liberal arts but also with reason, and this insistence is reflected in the *GE*. The *Picatrix* also identifies Hermes/Mercury as a planet and does not forget his Greek and Roman attributes, such as being the patron of commerce. Moreover, the *Picatrix* also associates Mercury with *adab*, the comprehensive education of the Arab princes and courtiers – an education I believe Alfonso saw as embodied in Mercury as well. Consequently, Alfonso translated and interpreted the legendary, all-encompassing wisdom of Hermes Trismegistus with unique Western and Eastern parameters – including liberal arts, *adab*, and Arabic magic – that came together in thirteenth-century Castile. In this way, Alfonso helped legitimize both his kingdom and himself as the epitome of intellectual and political prestige among both Muslim and Christian realms.

Conclusion

Throughout this book we have observed the progressive development and transformation of Hermetic traditions related to the genesis, translation, and interpretation of knowledge. We have examined their assimilation into the cultural heritages that became part of Alfonso's intellectual endeavours. And we have ascertained the crucial role that Hermes Trismegistus played in each of these distinct periods and cultural traditions. The study of Hermes's profound impact on scholars in the Iberian Peninsula across the centuries and how Alfonso integrated him into numerous works, especially the *GE*, has helped us understand the concept of a distinct *Hermes Hispanus* that flourished in medieval Spain's diverse society.

We have also determined that this Spanish Hermes is a product of translation and interpretation – even more so than his previous versions. The first Hermetic writings claimed themselves to be Greek translations of ancient Egyptian wisdom associated with the teachings of Hermes. From late antiquity through the Middle Ages these traditions were translated into numerous Eastern and Western languages. Arabic culture reached its zenith during the medieval period and extended its brilliance to the Iberian Peninsula; thus, it is not surprising that the "Arabic Hermes" emerged as the predominant embodiment of the ancient sage during that time, and that it did not take him long to travel to al-Andalus. When European scholars in eleventh-century Iberia were able to access and translate the Arabic sciences, the legend of Hermes underwent another transformation, this time to suit Latin expressions of knowledge. Eventually, Alfonso the Wise combined and developed Arabic and Latin genres influenced by the Hermetic tradition in Castilian.

In order to follow all these threads, I analyzed Castilian translations of specific Arabic genres, such as sapiential literature and *adab*-influenced books of geography and history; I have shown how the Alfonsine reception of the classical tradition was exceptional due to the incorporation of Hermetic sciences, such as astrology and magic; I have examined how Alfonso combined the knowledge of Church Fathers and Christian historians to explain the Arabic legend of the three Hermeses; and finally, I have outlined how the Castilian king explained the transmission of the liberal arts through Arabic and Latin legends related to Hermes. Thus, in thirteenth-century Castile a cohesive narrative on the origins of wisdom and its association with Hermes was created by using various traditions and having them interpret each other.

Across Alfonso's oeuvre, Hermes is quoted as one of the greatest authorities, especially in astrological and magical books translated or composed from Arabic sources. And, in the historical narratives of the *GE* the ancient sage assumes the role of a historical figure. For a king who was nicknamed "the Wise," no historical figure could be more appealing than Hermes, who is deeply connected with the origins of all knowledge. Nonetheless, Hermes's knowledge in the *GE* does not derive from a single source; he consolidates the essence of education across disciplines and sciences from both Eastern and Western traditions. His significant presence in Castilian sapiential books translated from Arabic, such as the *Bocados de oro* or *Poridat de las poridades*, reveals how Hermes embodies the synthesis of knowledge and morals advocated by *adab*. Ancient and medieval Latin authorities associated Hermes with the *trivium* and the *quadrivium*, which served as the quintessential educational framework during the Middle Ages. Since Alfonso approaches history as a didactic enterprise, the ancient characters and kings in the *GE* are presented as exemplary. Therefore, it is not surprising that Hermes/Mercury is staged as a significant role model; he behaves as a perfect vassal, son, and educator and exhibits exceptional command of all the disciplines with which his traditions have connected him – from dialectics to magic.

Therefore, it is worth considering to whom Alfonso is offering Hermes as a role model. As we saw, the overall purpose of the *GE* was to educate his subjects; however, I have suggested that Alfonso presents Hermes/Mercury as an exemplary figure specifically targeted towards his educated courtiers and clerks, who form a distinct group within this European setting. As a conclusion to this study, I would like to establish a link between this theory and previous scholars' findings.[1] This will also allow me to confirm how Hermes uniquely represents the connection between Alfonso's scientific and historical narratives. Specialists have found evidence of a knowledgeable Castilian intellectual elite who may have been influenced by Hermetic doctrines. Montero has constructed a credible intellectual portrait of this group in the studies she has dedicated to the first treatise of Alfonso's *Libro* (*or libros*) *del saber de astrología* (*Book of the knowledge of astrology*; composed around 1276–7), which specialists usually call *Libro de las estrellas de la ochava esfera* (*Book of the stars of the eighth sphere*). This treatise, subdivided into four parts, provides the theoretical and background information necessary for understanding the other ten extant treatises, which explain how to make and use astronomical instruments. The treatise's main source is the *Kitāb ṣuwar al-kawākib al-thābita* (*Book of the images of the fixed stars*, 964) by the Persian al-Ṣūfī (903–86). Alfonso ordered the translation of this Arabic work in 1256, along with other books of magic and astrology that we saw earlier, such as the *Picatrix*, the *Libro de las cruces* (*Book of the crosses*), and the *Libro cumplido de los judicios de las estrellas de Alí Aben Ragel* (*The complete book of the judgements of the stars*) – translated from the *Kitāb al-bāriʾ fi akhām al-nujūm* by ʿAlī Ibn al-Rijāl (d. 1037). The main translator of these books was the Jew Yehudah ben Mosheh, whose prominent role, as Montero points out, "makes him responsible for a significant portion of the scientific and Hermetic ideology of Alfonso's court."[2] Yehudah ben Mosheh and Guillén Arremón d'Aspa first compiled the *Libro del saber*

[1] For a thorough study on the preserved manuscripts of Alfonso's scientific works, see Laura Fernández Fernández, *Arte y ciencia en el scriptorium de Alfonso X el Sabio* (Seville: Editorial Universidad de Sevilla, 2013), especially 39–42 and 73–344.

[2] Ana M. Montero, "Reconstrucción de un ideal de espiritualidad en los hombres del saber de la corte de Alfonso X," in Emilio González Ferrín (ed.), *Encrucijada de culturas. Alfonso X y su tiempo: homenaje a Francisco Márquez Villanueva* (Seville: Fundación Tres Culturas del Mediterráneo, 2014): 512.

de astrología in 1256, and then in 1276 it was revised by Yehudah ben Mosheh, Juan de Mesina, Juan de Cremona, and Samuel ha-Levi.[3] According to the book's prologue, Alfonso authored the final revisions of its language and arguments. During this period (1276–9), Alfonso ordered two compilations of magical-astrological treatises, the *Astromagia* and the *Libro de las formas e las imágenes*.[4] The truly interesting thing is that work on the *GE* began around 1272; therefore, its composition coincides with the compilation of all these magical and astrological works in the same Alfonsine *scriptorium*.

Although the *Libro de las estrellas de la ochava esfera* was derived from an earlier translation of an Arabic book, it has insertions, comments, and amendments which necessarily come from Alfonso, Yehudah ben Mosheh, or other members of the *scriptorium* – just like in many parts of the *GE*, translation is conceived of as a methodical interpretation. Montero suggests that these additions offer an intellectual and spiritual proposal that aligns with Alfonso's non-scientific books of Alfonso, such as the *Setenario* or the *GE*; thus, all these works and genres from the second half of the thirteenth century take part in a "coherent ideological conglomerate,"[5] an idea I have been defending throughout this book. Thus, the *Libro de las estrellas*'s digressions allow us to reconstruct the prototype of a wise man, who was not only interested in scientific matters, such as astrology, but also sought spiritual encounters. According to Montero, this man would now be referred to as a magician, and he emerges in numerous passages and illustrations in the manuscripts of Alfonso's oeuvre.[6] We have discussed many of these texts, and the illustration printing on this book's cover – from the *Astromagia* – depicts a magician invoking Mercury. By extension the example of Mercury/Hermes presented in the *GE* would appeal to these courtiers, clerks, and magicians, or to those who aspired to become one.

The main identifying feature of the prototypical Alfonsine wise man was "a limitless interest for all fields of knowledge."[7] In thirteenth-century Castile, knowledge included both the Western *trivium* and *quadrivium* and the Eastern influences of Arabic *adab*, history, geography, wisdom literature, and astronomy; and astrological magic was the pinnacle of all this knowledge. In the *Libro del saber de astrología*, Castilian readers could find examples of those who "talked about nature" in the past, "such as astrologers, wise men who made the laws, particularly prophets, and also those who knew about divinity and theology, who agreed that in the heavens there were noble spirits in knowledge and virtue."[8] Hermes Trismegistus seems to fulfill

3 See *Libros del saber*, 7. For a complete enumeration and description of the members of Alfonso's scientific atelier, their chronology, and the books in which they collaborated, see Fernández Fernández, *Arte y ciencia*, 59–72, and for their method of production, 50–9.

4 See Alejandro García Avilés, "Two Astrological Manuscripts of Alfonso X," *Journal of the Warburg and Courtauld Institutes* 59 (1996): 15–16.

5 Montero, "Reconstrucción de un ideal," 517.

6 Montero, "Reconstrucción de un ideal," 517.

7 Montero, "Reconstrucción de un ideal," 519.

8 "Los que fablaron en naturas, cuemo los estrelleros, cuemo los sabios que fizieron las leyes, et sennaladamente los profetas, et dessi los que sopieron divinidad et theología. Todos se acordaron que en los cielos avía spíritos muy nobles de entendimiento e de virtud." *Libros del saber*, 10.

all these requirements: he was not only an astrologer, legislator, and prophet but also conspicuously informed about divinity – as someone who spent time in heaven. The *Libro del saber* then explains how the wise men controlled these heavenly and noble spirits, and through them performed good deeds. I interpret these spirits as the *rūḥāniyyāt*, "the spiritual agents who determine the qualities (virtues) of natural things, including human beings, and transmit astral influences." As Saif explains, the *rūḥāniyyāt* are depicted in the *Ghāya/Picatrix*, and in particular in sections taken from works of the pseudo-Aristotelian *Hermetica*, which, as we saw, rely on the authority of Hermes.[9]

The *Libro del saber* specifies that these wonders could only be performed "by men who possessed good understanding, subtle wit, and spirit, and who conducted their lives and deeds in an orderly and tidy manner, in such a way that they aligned their spirits with those of the heavenly spirits; and that is why saints and philosophers truly knew about all things."[10] Thus, there is a correlation between knowledge and behaviour, which is an essential aspect of Arabic *adab* and also present in the *Picatrix* – a work that was influenced by *adab*.[11] As Montero observes, there is nothing in the *Libro del saber* that associates this behaviour with Christian, Muslim, or Jewish dogmas, which makes it applicable to and comprehendible by all of them. Moreover, the exemplary wise men of the past are described as philosophers several times.[12] As we saw, for Alfonso a philosopher is an expert in the liberal arts, an essential requirement for the practice of magic, and in the *GE* the most distinguished expert in the *trivium* and the *quadrivium* is Hermes/Mercury. These wise men embodied a particular spirituality, which led them to privilege disciplines that connected the terrestrial with the celestial world. For them, the natural world, especially the stars, bore a divine imprint; thus, the sky is conceived as a new Bible, allowing knowledge of God to be obtained through his creations. These ideas are reminiscent of the most recent and accurate interpretations of the ancient *Hermetica*, which highlight its portrayal of a spiritual way of life.[13] As Montero deduces, in the Alfonsine court this kind of wisdom and spirituality was reserved for a close circle of elite wise men who possessed the necessary expertise.[14]

Fernández Fernández points out that both the *Libro del saber* and the *Lapidario* enumerate the qualities sought by those who read the manuscript, including a vast array of knowledges and "good judgement" (*buen seso*).[15] In a similar sense, Fraker points out that in the *GE* the "master science" of astrology is edifying and inspires faith in God, but also that this kind of "astrological piety is a rare species," and

9 See Saif, "A Preliminary Study," 60–3.

10 "Pero esto non lo fazian otros omes sinon aquellos que eran de buenos entendimientos et de sotiles ingenios et spíritos, et que fazian sus vidas et sus fechos ordenadamientre et limpia, assi que se acordaron los spíritos con los otros spíritos celestiales. et por esto sopieron los sanctos. et los sabios philósophos todas las cosas ciertamientre." *Libros del saber*, 10.

11 Coulon, *La Magie*, 159

12 Montero, "Recontrucción de un ideal," 523.

13 See Hanegraaff, *Hermetic Spirituality*, 11–22.

14 Montero, "Reconstrucción de un ideal," 520.

15 Fernández Fernández, *Arte y ciencia*, 45.

"it is a mistake to suppose that everywhere in medieval Christendom there were men and women who found God by contemplating the stars." Fraker suggests that Alfonso obtained the belief that astrology was edifying from sources that could be categorized as Hermetic and had an Islamic origin.[16] Throughout this book I have examined many of the Hermetic sources that Fraker speculates about, including some from Christian authors. Fraker concludes that the *Picatrix* was the main source on Hermetic sciences for the *GE*'s compilers, as it was translated in their circle and was accessible to them.[17] I have traced these influences not only through more recent bibliography on both the *Picatrix* and the *Ghāya* but also by extending my research to include other original books that Alfonso ordered to be compiled concurrently with the *GE*.

In his study on the tradition of Hermes, Bull examines passages of the *Hermetica* that I believe illustrate very similar beliefs to Alfonso's abovementioned wise men. The *Hermetica* "share the interest of contemporary philosophical schools in astronomical observations, but sees the main purpose of such observation to be reverence for the cosmic deity";[18] this is strikingly similar to the Alfonsine "astrological piety." The *Hermetica* was interested "in horoscopes, astral amulets, and medicine," and the term *mageia* (magic) is mentioned, together with philosophy and medicine, "as one of the arts given by Isis and Osiris to the prophets of Egyptian temples."[19] Bull argues that the *Hermetica*'s authors were priests in Egyptian temples. Many Hermetic sources, including the *Asclepius*, describe these priests as "the true philosophers," who – in addition to astronomy – practise arithmetic, music, and geometry in a more thoughtful way than contemporary "false" philosophers or sophists, who do not really understand them. Moreover, the *Asclepius* affirms that when such a man practises astrology, he "wonders at the recurrence of the stars, how their measure stays constant in prescribed stations and in the orbit of their turning; he should learn the dimensions, qualities, and quantities of the land [...] in order to commend, worship, and wonder at the skill and mind of God."[20] Therefore, the act of measuring God's creation, which relies on mathematical and astronomical abilities, is undertaken solely to appreciate the creator's mastery and worship him. This essential Hermetic virtue of *eusebeia* (εὐσέβεια) has been thoroughly analyzed by Hanegraaf, who defines it as "an attitude of profoundly felt respect or awe that may be captured, along an ascending scale of intensity, by such terms as reverence, admiration, and veneration."[21]

Despite the presence of a similar reverence for God's cosmic creation in the *GE* and other Alfonsine works, I do not believe our Castilian scholars practised any form of Hermetism – a term I have avoided throughout this book. I understand

16 Fraker, *Scope of History*, 172.

17 Fraker, *Scope of History*, 173

18 Bull, *Tradition of Hermes*, 458.

19 Bull, *Tradition of Hermes*, 458

20 "[...] ut apocatastasis astrorum, stationes praefinitas cursumque commutationis numeris constare miretur; terrae uero dimensiones, qualitates, quantitates [...] miretur, adoret atque conlaudet artem mentemque diuinam." *Asclepius*, 13. Translation by Copenhaver.

21 See Hanegraaff, *Hermetic Spirituality*, 194–5. For a more detailed explanation, I refer to the entire section in the book on the Hermetic *eusebeia*, 186–219.

Hermetism to mean a coherent corpus of dogmas and rituals – those of a religion or a cult – which may have existed in antiquity.[22] In this sense, I agree with Van Bladel, who does not conceive a specific form of Arabic Hermetism or Hermeticism, terms that he thinks many specialists use inconsistently.[23] Since Arabic Hermetism did not exist in a coherent manner, it is not possible for Castilian scholars to have inherited or imitated it, especially considering that their main sources of Hermetic knowledge – considered restrictively as those attributed to Hermes – mainly originated from that language.

Nevertheless, ancient priests – who, as per Bull, interpreted and translated Egyptian wisdom in the *Hermetica* – cultivated disciplines and professed beliefs that are reminiscent of those of the Alfonsine court's wise men. It is possible that certain beliefs held by these ancient priests were stirred in Castile through a lengthy process of successive translations. Castilian scholars translated Arabic scientific *Hermetica* and interpreted it through a suitable intellectual framework, which fulfilled an analogous function to the theoretical *Hermetica* in Hellenistic times. The ancient *Hermetica* is believed to have been compiled by Egyptian priests and contains wisdom passed down by ancient sages associated with Hermes Trismegistus, as well as his disciples, including Agathodaemon, Tat, Ammon, and others. It also includes figures considered to be gods, such as Isis and Osiris. In turn, the wise Castilian men who compiled the *Libro del saber de astrología* and many other works continuously allude to ancient wise men who were considered philosophers, prophets, or astrologers. The *GE* gives these allusions concrete shape by referencing specific historical characters, such as Doluca, Abraham, Jupiter, Minerva, and of course Mercury/Hermes. Furthermore, Alfonso "humanized" gods through the use of euhemerism. Other common threads found in ancient *Hermetica* and scientific Alfonsine books, as well as in the three monotheistic religions, are the conception of knowledge as revelation and the mystical ascent to heaven in search of divinity. This ascent is presented as the culmination of studying the astronomical wonders of the skies.[24] As we saw, the most characteristic celestial anabasis narrated in the *GE* is that of Hermes, which explains how knowledge was revealed to him.

Examining a wide range of prologues in thirteenth-century Castilian scientific books, González-Casanovas emphasizes Alfonso's agency in building a "wise court" composed of the abovementioned erudite men. In all these prologues, we find the king's authority as a "reader, interpreter, and transmitter of knowledge," associated with both "moral wisdom and secular sapience." González-Casanovas identifies the product of the king's efforts as an "intellectual aristocracy" which, through the utilization of reason, becomes part of the privileged community of the educated. Thus, the translation of classical and oriental culture that Alfonso sponsored involved a profound change within the Castilian court.[25] In this way, the translations required

22 On the term Hermetism and scholarly discussions about it, see Bull, *Tradition of Hermes*, 27–30.

23 Van Bladel, *Arabic Hermes*, 17–22.

24 Montero, "Reconstrucción de un ideal," 530–1.

25 Roberto J. González-Casanovas, "Alfonso X's Scientific Prologues: Scholarship as Enlightenment," *Medieval Perspectives* 6 (1991): 114.

and contributed to the creation of a specific kind of elite translators from different religions. As we saw, the prologues present proof of Christian, Muslim, and Jewish scholarly cooperation on these projects. Montero indicates that natural philosophy "provided an area of intellectual encounter, a safe harbour where Jews, Arabs and Christians could interact and work together."[26] The prologues also emphasize how these intellectuals became part of the court; they established their professional position within the royal administration and linked the advancement of knowledge with a secular humanist heritage.[27] I read these courtiers/scholars, who were recruited and instructed by Alfonso, as those with whom the character of Mercury/Hermes in the *GE* resonated.

We find further evidence of Hermetic influences in the court of Alfonso in the pictures and miniatures that illustrate many of his productions. This topic has been thoroughly analyzed by a prominent expert in the field, Domínguez Rodríguez, who concludes that Alfonso's entire body of work – including written and painted testimonies – appears to be grounded in a Hermetic worldview, in which elements such as astrology, religion, philosophy, magic, and other scientific aspects are significant. The *Lapidario* is one of the most richly illustrated books commissioned by Alfonso. Domínguez Rodriguez connects the illustrations in this work to its prologue, which betrays a Hermetic background when it refers to the influences of the "virtues" of the stars on terrestrial things.[28] In the prologue of the *Lapidario*, as well as in different illustrations, Alfonso presents himself as an inspired wise man who, according to Hermetic ideals, is responsible for discovering the hidden science and transmitting it.[29] This emphasis on the king's agency in recovering long-lost ancient knowledge – which so closely resembles Hermetic narratives – is particularly prominent in prologues redacted by courtly Jews.[30] In fact, Yehudah ben Mosheh was the main compiler and translator of the *Lapidario*.

In this manner, Alfonso became Hermes's successor, carrying forth the same lineage of knowledge and transmitting it to his followers/subjects. As we saw, Martínez points out that Alfonso connects his own lineage with that of Hermes in the *GE*.[31] By including Hermes as a historical figure, Alfonso validates his own lineage for both political and intellectual purposes. Hermes becomes a principal asset in Alfonso's strategy to legitimate himself through the *translatio imperii* and *translatio studii* notions we saw earlier. Alfonso presents himself not only as the inheritor of the *imperium* held by illustrious rulers of antiquity but also as the one who retrieves wisdom traditions that no one but Hermes Trismegistus represented.

Alfonso, the king of Castile and León, who also claimed authority over the rest of *Espanna* (Spain) – geographically understood as the Roman *Hispania* – and temporarily over the medieval European Holy Roman Empire, appropriated and assimilated the figure of Hermes Trismegistus and presented him as an example

26 Montero, "A Possible Connection," 16.
27 González-Casanovas, "Alfonso X's Scientific Prologues," 116
28 Domínguez Rodríguez, *Astrología y arte*, 19.
29 Domínguez Rodríguez, *Astrología y arte*, 27
30 Fernández Fernández, *Arte y ciencia*, 45.
31 Martínez, *El humanismo medieval*, 279.

for his subjects. He profited from Hermes's long sojourn in the Iberian Peninsula, the many traditions that furnished his teachings, and the talents of his vassals who professed different religions. Therefore, the presence of the medieval *Book of secrets of the Spanish Hermes* in the list of books Johannes Trithemius included in his *Antipalus maleficiorum* – mentioned in the Introduction – becomes much more understandable. Even though this book is still lost, I hope my study has offered insight into what a Spanish Hermes and his secrets could have meant for pre-modern Castilian, Spanish, and European learned men.

Bibliography

Primary Sources

A Testament of Alchemy: Being the Revelations of Morienus to Khālid Ibn Yazīd. Edited by Lee Stavenhagen. Lebanon: Brandeis University Press, 1974.

Abraham Ibn Ezra on Elections, Interrogations, and Medical Astrology. Edited and Translated by Shlomo Sela. Leiden: Brill, 2010.

Abū Maʿshar. *The Abbreviation of The Introduction to Astrology: Together with the Medieval Latin Translation of Adelard of Bath.* Translated by Charles Burnett, Keiji Yamamoto, and Michio Yano. Leiden: Brill, 1994.

Alfonso X el Sabio. *Astromagia: Ms. Reg. lat. 1283a.* Edited by Alfonso D'Agostino. Naples: Liguori, 1992.

Alfonso X el Sabio. *General estoria: Segunda parte.* Edited by Antonio G. Solalinde, Lloyd A. Kasten, and Victor R. B. Oelschläger. 2 vols. Madrid: Consejo Superior de Investigaciones Cientificas, 1957–61.

Alfonso X el Sabio. *General estoria.* Edited by Pedro Sánchez-Prieto Borja et al. 5 parts in 10 vols. Madrid: Biblioteca Castro, 2009.

Alfonso X el Sabio. *Lapidario. Libro de las formas e imágenes que son en los cielos.* Edited by Pedro Sánchez-Prieto Borja. Madrid: Biblioteca Castro, 2009.

Alfonso X el Sabio. *Las siete partidas del Rey Don Alfonso el Sabio, cotejadas con varios códices antiguos por la Real Academia de la Historia.* 3 vols. Madrid: Imprenta real, 1807.

Alfonso X el Sabio. *Setenario.* Edited by Kenneth H. Vanderford. Buenos Aires: Instituto de Filología, 1945.

al-Andalusī, Sāʾid. *Historia de la filosofía y de las ciencias o libro de las categorías de las naciones [Kitāb Ṭabaqāt al-umam].* Edited by Eloísa Llavero Ruíz and Andrés Martínez Lorca. Madrid: Trotta, 2000.

Arnulf of Orléans. *Arnulphi Aurelianensis Allegoriae super Ovidii Metamorphosin.* In Fausto Ghisalberti, "Arnolfo d'Orléans, un cultore di Ovidio nel secolo XII," *Memorie del Reale Istituto Lombardo di Scienze e Lettere* 24 (1932): 157–234.

Augustine. *De haeresibus ad Quodvultdeus.* Available online at https://www.tertullian.org/tertullianistae/de_haeresibus.htm. Last accessed August 13, 2023.

Augustine. *The City of God Against the Pagans.* Edited and translated by George E. McCracken et al. Loeb Classical Library vols 411–17. Cambridge, MA: Harvard University Press, 1957–72.

al-Bakrī, Abū ʿUbayd. *Kitāb al-masālik wa-l-mamālik.* Edited by Adrien van Leeuwen and André Ferre. 2 vols. Qarṭāj: Dār al-ʿArabīya li-l-Kitāb, 1992.

Bocados de Oro: kritische Ausgabe des altspanischen Textes. Edited by Mechthild Crombach. Romanistische Versuche und Vorarbeiten 37. Bonn: Romanisches Seminar der Universität Bonn, 1971.

Capella, Martianus. *De nuptiis Philologiae et Mercurii. Vol. 1, Libri I – II.* Edited and translated by Lucio-Luciano Lenaz Cristante. Hildesheim: Weidmann, 2011.

Cicero. *On the Nature of the Gods. Academics.* Translated by H. Rackham. Loeb Classical Library 268. Cambridge, MA: Harvard University Press, 1933.

Cicero. *On the Orator: Books 1–2*. Translated by E. W. Sutton and H. Rackham. Loeb Classical Library 348. Cambridge, MA: Harvard University Press, 1942.

Dorotheus of Sidon. *Carmen Astrologicum*. Edited by David Pingree. Leipzig: B. G. Teubner, 1976.

Epistles of the Brethren of Purity, On Astronomia: An Arabic Critical Edition and English Translation of Epistle 3. Edited and translated by F. Jamil Ragep and Taro Mimura. Oxford: Oxford University Press, 2015.

Eusebius of Caesarea. *Eusebi Chronicorum canonum*. 2 vols. Edited by Alfred Schöne. Dublin: Weidmannos, 1967.

Eusebius of Caesarea. *Praeparatio Evangélica/Evangelica (Preparation for the Gospel)*. Translated by E. H. Gifford. Available online at: https://www.tertullian.org/fathers/eusebius_pe_00_eintro.htm (last accessed February 17, 2023).

Firmicus Maternus, Julius. *Ancient Astrology: Theory and Practice. Matheseos Libri VIII*. Translated by Jean Rhys Bram. Park Ridge: Noyes Press, 1975.

al-Garnāṭī, Abū Ḥāmid. *Tuḥfat al-albāb (El regalo de los espíritus)*. Edited by Ana Ramos. Madrid: CSIC, 1990.

Gotefridi Viterbiensis. *Pantheon. In Germanicorum Scriptorum qui rerum a Germanis per multas aetates gestarum historias vel annales posteris reliunquerunt*. Edited by Burcardo Gotthelffi o Struvio. Foreword by Joannis Pistori Nidani. Vol. 4. 3rd edn. Ratisbonae: Joannis Conradi Peezii, 1726.

Hermann of Carinthia. *De Essentiis: A Critical Edition with Translation and Commentary*. Translated by Charles S. F. Burnett. E. J. Leiden: Brill, 1982.

Hermes. *Hermetica: The Greek Corpus Hermeticum and the Latin Asclepius in a New English Translation, with Notes and Introduction*. Translated by Brian P. Copenhaver. Cambridge, UK and New York: Cambridge University Press, 1992.

Hermes. *Hermetica II. The Excerpts of Stobaeus, Papyrus Fragments, and Ancient Testimonies in an English Translation with Notes and Introductions*. Translated by M. David Litwa. Cambridge, UK and New York: Cambridge University Press, 2018.

Hermetis Trismegisti de Sex Rerum Principiis. Edited by Paolo Lucentini and Mark D. Delp. Turnhout: Brepols, 2006.

Iamblichus. *On the Mysteries (De Mysteriis)*. Edited by Emma C. Clarke, Atlanta: Society of Biblical Literature, 2003.

Isidore of Seville. *De viris ilustribus*. Biblioteca Digital Hispánica. Available online at: http://bdh.bne.es/bnesearch/detalle/bdh0000042217 (last accessed January 15, 2023).

Isidore of Seville. *Isidori Hispalensis episcopi: Etymologiarum sive originum libri xx*. Edited by Wallace Martin Lindsay. Oxford: Oxford University Press, 1911.

Isidore. *Isidori Hispalensis Chronica*. Edited by José Carlos Martín. Turnhout: Brepols, 2003.

al-Jāḥiẓ (Ǧāḥiẓ). *Le Kitāb at-tarbīʿ wa-t-tadwīr de Ǧāḥiẓ*. Edited by Ch. Pellat. Damas: Institut français de Damas, 1955.

John of Garland. *Integumenta Ovidii*. Edited by Fausto Ghisalberti. Messina and Milan: Principato, 1933.

Josephus, Flavius. *Judean Antiquities*. Edited by Louis H. Feldman. Books 1–4. Leiden: Brill, 2004.

Julian. *Letters. Epigrams. Against the Galilaeans. Fragments*. Translated by Wilmer C. Wright. Loeb Classical Library 157. Cambridge, MA: Harvard University Press, 1923.

L'Abrégé des merveilles. Translated by Carra de Vaux. Paris: Librairie C. Klincksieck, 1898.

Lelli, Fabrizio. "Hermes among the Jews: Hermetica as Hebraica from Antiquity to the Renaissance," *Magic, Ritual, and Witchcraft* 2, no. 2 (2007): 111–35.

Leonis Magni Epistolae XV. In *Migne Patrologiae Cursus Completus – Latin vol.* 54, 677–80. Paris: Venit Apud Editorem, 1846.

Libros del Saber de Astronomía del Rey Alfonso X El Sabio. Facsimile (ms. 56). Edited by Ana Domínguez et al. 2 vols. Barcelona: Ebrisa; Planeta DeAgostini, 1999.

Lucas de Tuy. *Lucae Tudensis Chronicon mundi*. Edited by Emma Falque. Turnhout: Brepols, 2003.

Marsilio Ficino. *De vita libri tres* (*Three Books on Life*, 1489). Translated by Carol V. Kaske and John R. Clarke. Tempe, AZ: The Renaissance Society of America, 2002.

al-Masʿūdī. *Les prairies d'or*. Edited and translated by Charles Barbier de Meynard and Abel Pavet de Courteille. 9 vols. Paris: Imprimerie impériale, 1861–1917.

Medieval French Ovide Moralisé, The, An English Translation. Edited and translated by K. Sarah-Jane Murray and Matthieu Boyd. 3 vols. Cambridge: D. S. Brewer, 2023.

al-Mubaššir Ibn Fātik, Abū l-Wafā'. *Muḫtar al-ḥikam wa-maḥāsin al-kalim / Los Bocados de Oro (Mujtār al-ḥikam)*. Edited by ʿAbdarraḥmān Badawī. Madrid: Publicaciones del Instituto Egipcio de Estudios Islámicos, 1958.

Ibn al-Nadim. *The Fihrist: A 10th Century AD Survey of Islamic Culture*. Edited by Bayard Dodge. Chicago: Kazi Publications, 1998.

Orphic Hymns, The. Translated and edited by Apostolos N. Athanassakis and Benjamin M. Wolkow. Baltimore: Johns Hopkins University Press, 2013.

Ovid. *Metamorphoses*. Edited by Hugo Magnus. Gotha: Friedr. Andr. Perthes, 1892. Latin text available at the Perseus Digital Library: http://www.perseus.tufts.edu/hopper/text?doc=Perseus%3Atext%3A1999.02.0029%3Abook%3D1%3Acard%3D1 (last accessed September 28, 2022).

Patrizi Francesco, *Nova de universis philosophia in qua Aristotelica methodo non per motum, sed per lucem, & lumina, ad primam causam ascenditur*. Ferrara: Benedetto Mammarelli, 1591.

Petrus Alfonsi. *Disciplina Clericalis*. Edited by Esperanza Ducay and María Jesús Lacarra. Zaragoza: Guara Editorial, 1980.

Petrus Comestor. *Historia Scholastica*. Madrid: Antonio González de Reyes, 1699.

Picatrix: A Medieval Treatise on Astral Magic. Translated by David Porreca and Dan Attrell. University Park: The Pennsylvania State University Press, 2019.

Pierre le Mangeur (Petrus Comestor). *Petri Comestoris Scholastica Historia. Liber Genesis*. Edited by A. Sylwan. Turnhout: Brepols, 2005.

Pingree, David (ed.). *Picatrix. The Latin Version of the Ghāyat al-ḥakīm*. London: The Warburg Institute, 1986.

Plato. *Lysis. Symposium. Phaedrus*. Edited and translated by Christopher Emlyn-Jones and William Preddy. Loeb Classical Library 166. Cambridge, MA: Harvard University Press, 2022.

Plato. *Platonis Opera. Phaedus*. Edited by John Burnet. Oxford: Oxford University Press, 1953.

Pseudo-al-Mas'ūdī. *Akhbār al-zamān*. Edited by 'Abd Allāh al-Ṣāwī. Cairo: Maṭba'at 'Abd al-Ḥamīd Aḥmad Ḥanafī, 1938.

Pseudo-Majrīṭī. *Picatrix: Das Ziel des Weisen*. Edited by Hellmut Ritter. Leipzig: B. G. Teubner, 1933.

al-Qurṭubī, Maslama b. Qāsim. *Picatrix: Das Ziel des Weisen*. Edited by Hellmut Ritter. Leipzig: B. G. Teubner, 1933.

Ritter, Hellmut (ed.). *Ghāyat al-Ḥakīm: An Edition of the Text in Arabic*. London: The Warburg Institute, 1962.

Secreto de los secretos. Poridat de las poridades. Edited by Hugo Bizarri. Valencia: Universidad de Valencia, 2010.

Trithemius, Johannes. *Antipalus maleficiorum*. In *Paralipomena opusculorum Petri Blesensi et Joannis Trithemii*. Edited by Johannes Busaeus, 292–311. Mainz: E. Balthasaris Lippi Typographeo, 1605.

Secondary Sources

Alexander, Philip S. "From Son of Adam to Second God: Transformations of the Biblical Enoch." In by Michael E. Stone and Theodore A. Bergen (eds), *Biblical Figures Outside the Bible*, 87–122. Harrisburg: Trinity Press International, 1998.

Alvar Ezquerra, Carlos. "*La Grande e General Estoria*." In Patrizia Botta et al (eds), *Rumbos del hispanismo en el umbral del Cincuentenario de la AIH*, 2: 19–23. Roma: Bagatto, 2012.

Alvar, Carlos. *Traducciones y traductores. Materiales para una historia de la traducción en Castilla durante la Edad Media*. Madrid: Centro de Estudios Cervantinos, 2010.

Asl, Mohammad Karimi Zanjani. "*Sirr al-Khaliqa* and Its Influence in the Arabic and Persianate World: ʿAwn b. al-Mundhir's Commentary and Its Unknown Persian Translation." *Al-Qantara* 37, no. 2 (2016): 435–73.

Attrell, Dan, and David Porreca. Introduction to *Picatrix: A Medieval Treatise on Astral Magic*, 1–33. Translated by David Porreca and Dan Attrell. University Park: The Pennsylvania State University Press, 2019.

Auerbach, Erich. *Mimesis: The Representation of Reality in Western Literature*. Princeton: Princeton University Press, 1968.

Bailey, Donald. "Classical Architecture." In Christina Riggs (ed.), *The Oxford Handbook of Roman Egypt*, 189–204. Oxford: Oxford University Press, 2012.

Beaujouan, Guy. "The Transformation of the Quadrivium." In Robert L. Benson and Giles Constable (eds), *Renaissance and Renewal in the Twelfth Century*, 463–87. Cambridge: Harvard University Press, 1982.

Beck, Roger. *A Brief History of Ancient Astrology*. Hoboken: John Wiley & Sons, 2007.

Bellido Morillas, José María. "Dos visiones Hispano-medievales de un cuento del Egipto faraónico: Variaciones de Abū Ḥāmid Al-Garnāṭī y Juan Ruiz De Alcalá, Arcipreste de Hita, sobre El príncipe predestinado." *Revista de literatura* 71, no. 141 (2009): 195–206.

Beltrán Fortes, José. "Greco-orientales en la Hispania Republicana e Imperial a través de las menciones epigráficas." In María Paz de Hoz and Gloria Mora (eds), *El oriente griego en la Península Ibérica. Epigrafía e historia*, 185–204. Madrid: Real Academia de la Historia, 2013.

Benaisa, Amin. "The Onomastic Evidence for the God Hermanubis." In *Proceedings of the Twenty-Fifth International Congress of Papyrology*, edited by T. Gagos, 67–76. Ann Arbor: University of Michigan Press, 2010.

Bernard, Alain, Christine Proust, and Micah Ross. "Mathematics Education in Antiquity." In *Handbook on the History of Mathematics Education*, 27–53. New York: Springer New York, 2013–14.

Bizzarri, Hugo O. "Libro de los buenos proverbios." In José Manuel Lucía Megías and Carlos Alvar Ezquerra (eds), *Diccionario filológico de literatura medieval española. Textos y transmisión*, 796–800. Madrid: Castalia, 2002.

Bizzarri, Hugo O. "Poridat de las poridades. Secreto de los secretos." In José Manuel Lucía Megías and Carlos Alvar Ezquerra (eds), *Diccionario filológico de literatura medieval española. Textos y transmisión*, 926–30. Madrid: Castalia, 2002.

Bolton, Diane K. "Remigian Commentaries on the 'Consolation of Philosophy' and Their Sources." *Traditio* 33 (1977): 381–94.

Bonebakker, Seger Adrianus. "Adab and the Concept of Belles-Lettres." In Julia Ashtiany et al. (eds), *'Abbasid Belles-Lettres*, 16–30. Cambridge: Cambridge University Press, 1990.

Boyle, John Andrew. "Alexander and the Mongols." *Central Asiatic Journal* 24, no. 1/2 (1980): 18–35.

Brancaforte, Benito. *Las "Metamorfosis" y las "Heroidas" de Ovidio en la "General Estoria" de Alfonso el Sabio*. Madison: The Hispanic Seminary of Medieval Studies, 1990.

Brown, Norman O. *Hermes the Thief: The Evolution of a Myth*. Lindisfarne Books, 1990.

Bull, Christian H. *The Tradition of Hermes Trismegistus*. Leiden: Brill, 2018.

Bull, Christian H.. "Hermes between Pagans and Christians: The Nag Hammadi Hermetica in Context." *The Nag Hammadi Codices and Late Antique Egypt.* (2018): 207–60. Also available online at: *Byzantinische Bibliographie Online*, https://www.degruyter.com/database/BYZ/entry/byz.812ed353-3727-48c8-8ea8-0987979ea4db/html (last accessed May 13, 2023).

Burnett, Charles S. F. "The Legend of the Three Hermes and Abū Ma'Shar's Kitāb Al-Ulūf in the Latin Middle Ages." *Journal of the Warburg and Courtauld Institutes* 39, no. 1 (1976): 231–4.

Burnett, Charles. "A Hermetic Programme of Astrology and Divination in mid-Twelfth-Century Aragon: The Hidden Preface in the *Liber novem iudicum*." In Charles Burnett and W.F. Ryan (eds), *Magic and the Classical Tradition*, 99–118. London: Warburg Institute, 2006.

Burnett, Charles. "Gerard of Cremona." In Kate Fleet et al. (eds), *Encyclopaedia of Islam, THREE*. https://referenceworks.brill.com/display/entries/EI3O/COM-27411.xml?rskey=8uwZLa&result=1 (last accessed June 23, 2021).

Burnett, Charles. "Hermann of Carinthia and the *Kitāb al-Isṭamāṭīs*: Further Evidence for the Transmission of Hermetic Magic." *Journal of the Warburg and Courtauld Institutes* 44 (1981): 167–9.

Burnett, Charles. "Ketton, Robert of (fl. 1141–1157)." In *Oxford Dictionary of National Biography.* Oxford: Oxford University Press, 2004. Available online at: https://www.oxforddnb.com/display/10.1093/ref:odnb/9780198614128.001.0001/odnb-9780198614128-e-23723 (last accessed October 8, 2023).

Burnett, Charles. "*Nīranj*: A Category of Magic (Almost) Forgotten in the Latin West." In C. Leonardi and F. Santi (eds), *Natura, scienze, e società medievali: Studi in onore di Agostino Paravicini Bagliani*, 37–66. Florence: SISMEL, 2008.

Burnett, Charles. "Ṯābit Ibn Qurra the Ḥarrānian on Talismans and the Spirits of the Planets." *La corónica: A Journal of Medieval Hispanic Languages, Literatures, and Cultures* 36, no. 1 (2007): 13–40.

Burnett, Charles. "The Coherence of the Arabic-Latin Translation Program in Toledo in the Twelfth Century." *Science in Context* 14, nos 1–2 (2001): 249–88.

Burnett, Charles. "The Establishment of Medieval Hermeticism." In Peter Linehan and Janet L. Nelson (eds), *The Medieval World*, 126–45. Abingdon: Routledge, 2001.

Burnett, Charles. "The Translating Activity in Medieval Spain." In S. K. Jayyusi (ed.), *The Legacy of Muslim Spain*, 1036–58. Leiden: Brill, 1992.

Burrus, Virginia. *The Making of a Heretic: Gender, Authority, and the Priscillianist Controversy*. Oakland: University of California Press, 1995.

Calasso, Giovanna. "Les remparts et la loi, les talismans et les saints: la protection de la ville dans les sources musulmanes médiévales." *Bulletin d'études orientals* 44 (1992): 83–104.

Callataÿ, Godefroid de, and Sébastien Moureau. "A Milestone in the History of Andalusī Bāṭinism: Maslama b. Qāsim al-Qurṭubī's Riḥla in the East." *Intellectual History of the Islamicate World* 5 (2017): 86–117.

Callataÿ, Godefroid de, and Sébastien Moureau. "Towards the Critical Edition of the *Rutbat Al-Ḥakīm*: A Few Preliminary Observations." *Arabica* 62 (2015): 385–94.

Callataÿ, Godefroid de. "Encyclopaedism on the Fringe of Islamic Orthodoxy: The *Rasāʾil Ikhwān al-Ṣafāʾ*, the *Rutbat al-Ḥakīm* and the *Ghāyat al-Ḥakīm* on the Division of Science." *Asiatische Studien/Études Asiatiques: Zeitschrift Der Schweizerischen Asiengesellschaft/Revue de la Société Suisse-Asie* 71 (2017): 857–77.

Callataÿ, Godefroid de. "Magia en al-Andalus. Rasā'il ijwān al-Ṣafā', Rutbat al-ḥakīm y Ghāyat al-ḥakīm (Picatrix)." *Al-Qanṭara* 34 (2013): 297–344.

Callataÿ, Godefroid, de. "Magia en al-Andalus: *Rasā'il ijwān al-Ṣafā', Rutbat al-ḥakīm y Gāyat al-ḥakīm (Picatrix)*." *Al-Qanṭara* 34, no. 2 (2013): 297–344.

Campanelli, Maurizio. "Marsilio Ficino's Portrait of Hermes Trismegistus and Its Afterlife." *Intellectual History Review* 29, no. 1 (2019): 53–71.

Cardigni, Julieta. "Los personajes principales en *De nuptiis Mercurii et Philologiae* de Marciano Capela: Una propuesta de análisis." *Revista Chilena De Estudios Medievales*, no. 16 (2019): 26–38.

Cardigni, Julieta. "Presencias herméticas en *De nuptiis Mercurii et Philologiae* de Marciano Capela." *Anales De Historia Antigua, Medieval y Moderna* 50 (2016): 37–53.

Carlos Villamarín, Helena de. "Achegamento á Poesía De Epoca Visigoda: A Poesía De Tema Científico." In Eva María Díaz Martínez and Juan Casas Rigall (eds), *Iberia Cantat: Estudios Sobre Poesía Hispánica Medieval*, 9–30. Santiago: Universidade de Santiago de Compostela, 2002.

Catalán, Diego. "El taller historiográfico Alfonsí. Métodos y problemas en el trabajo compilatorio." *Romania* 84, no. 335 (3) (1963): 354–75.

Chadwick, Henry. *Priscillian of Avila: The Occult and the Charismatic in the Early Church*. Oxford: Clarendon Press, 1976.

Chico, María Victoria. "La vida como un viaje: viaje y peregrinación en la composición pictórica de las Cantigas De Santa María de Alfonso X El Sabio." *Revista de filología románica* 4 (2006): 129–33.

Condos, Theony. *Star Myths of the Greeks and Romans: A Sourcebook, Containing The Constellations of Pseudo-Eratosthenes and the Poetic Astronomy of Hyginus*. Grand Rapids: Phanes Press, 1997.

Cook, Michael. "Pharaonic History in Medieval Egypt." *Studia Islamica*, no. 57 (1983): 67–103.

Cornell, Vincent. "The Way of the Axial Intellect: The Islamic Hermetism of Ibn Sab'īn." *Journal of the Muhyiddin Ibn 'Arabi Society* 22 (1997): 41–79.

Cottrell, E. "'L'Hermès Arabe de Kevin van Bladel' et la question du rôle de la littérature Sassanide dans la presence d'écrits hermètiques et astrologiques en langue arabe." *Bibliotheca Orientalis* 72 (2015): 336–401.

Cottrell, Emily. "Adam and Seth in Arabic Medieval Literature." *Aram* 22 (2010): 509–47.

Cottrell, Emily. "Al-Mubashshir Ibn Fatik." In H. Lagerlund (ed.), *Encyclopedia of Medieval Philosophy*, 1: 815–18. Dordrecht: Springer, 2011.

Cottrell, Emily. "Al-Mubaššir Ibn Fātik and the α Version of the Alexander Romance." In Richard Stoneman, Kyle Erickson, and Ian Richard Netton (eds), *The Alexander Romance in Persia and the East*, e234–53. Eelde: Barkhuis, 2012.

Coulon, Jean-Charles. *La magie en terre d'Islam au Moyen Age*. Paris: Comité des travaux historiques et scientifiques, 2017.

Crombach, Mechthild, (ed.). *Bocados de Oro: kritische Ausgabe des altspanischen Textes*. Romanistische Versuche und Vorarbeiten 37. Bonn: Romanisches Seminar der Universität Bonn, 1971.

Crone, Patricia. *The Qur'ānic Pagans and Related Matters*. Leiden: Brill, 2016.

Cuesta Torre, María Luzdivina. "Los comentaristas de Ovidio en la General Estoria II, Caps. 74–115." *Revista de literatura medieval* 19 (2007): 137–69.

Dangler, Jean. *Edging Toward Iberia*. Toronto: University of Toronto Press, 2017.

Dapsens, Marion. "De la *Risālat Maryānus* au *De Compositione alchemiae*: Quelques réflexions sur la tradition d'un traité d'alchimie." *Studia graeco-arabica* 6 (2016): 121–40.

De Lauretis, Teresa. *Alice Doesn't: Feminism, Semiotics, Cinema*. Bloomington: Indiana University Press, 1984.

Delp, Mark D. "A Twelfth Century Cosmology. The *Liber de Sex Rerum Principiis*." In Paolo Lucentini and Mark D. Delp (eds), *Hermetis Trismegisti de Sex Rerum Principiis*, 1–120. Turnhout: Brepols, 2006.

Devereux Jones, Wilbur. *Fulgentius the Mythographer*. Columbus: Ohio State University Press, 1972.

Dodge, Bayard. *The Fihrist of al-Nadim, A 10th Century Survey of Muslim Culture*. Translated Bayard Dodge. New York and London: Columbia University Press, 1970.

Domínguez Rodríguez, Ana. *Astrología y arte en el "Lapidario" de Alfonso X el Sabio*. Murcia: Real Academia Alfonso X el Sabio, 2006.

Don Juan Manuel. "Libro de la caza." In Jose M. Blecua (ed.), *Obras completas*, 1:549–60. Gredos: Madrid, 1981.

Ducène, Jean-Charles. "La description géographique de la Palestine dans le Kitāb Al-Masālik Wa-l-Mamālik D'abū ʿUbayd Al-Bakarī (m. 487/1094)." *Journal of Near Eastern Studies* 62, no. 3 (2003): 181–91.

Ekman, Erik. "Translation and Translatio: 'Nuestro Latín' in Alfonso El Sabio's General Estoria." *Bulletin of Spanish Studies* 93, no. 5 (2016): 767–82.

Ekman, Erik. "Cuenta la Estoria: Narrative and Exegesis in Alfonso X's 'General Estoria.'" *Hispanic Journal* 27, no. 1 (2006): 23–35.

Ekman, Erik. "Ovid Historicized: Magic and Metamorphosis in Alfonso X's *General Estoria*." *La corónica: A Journal of Medieval Hispanic Languages, Literatures, and Cultures* 42, no. 1 (2013): 23–46.

El-Daly, Okasha. *Egyptology: The Missing Millenium. Ancient Egypt in Medieval Arabic Writings*. London: Routledge, 2005.

Endress, Gerhard. "Mathematics and Philosophy in Medieval Islam." In Jan P. Hogendijk and Abdelhamid I. Sabra (eds), *The Enterprise of Science in Islam: New*

Perspectives, 121–76. Cambridge: The MIT Press, 2003.

Ephal, Israel. "Nebuchadnezzar the Warrior: Remarks on His Military Achievements." *Israel Exploration Journal* 53, no. 2 (2003): 178–91.

Fernández Fernández, Laura. *Arte y ciencia en el scriptorium de Alfonso X el Sabio*. Seville: Editorial Universidad de Sevilla, 2013.

Fernández-Ordóñez, Inés. "De la historiografía fernandina a la alfonsí." *Alcanate: Revista de estudios Alfonsíes* 3 (2002–3), 93–134.

Fernández-Ordóñez, Inés. *Las estorias de Alfonso el Sabio*. Madrid: Istmo, 1992.

Fernando Gasco la Calle. "El Viaje De Apolonio De Tiana a La Bética (Siglo d.C.)." *Revista De Estudios Andaluces* 4, no. 1 (1985): 13–22.

Festugière, André-Jean. *La révélation d'Hermés Trismégiste*. 4 vols. 3rd edn. Paris: Gabalda, 1950.

Fidora, Alexander. "Dominicus Gundissalinus and the Introduction of Metaphysics into the Latin West." *The Review of Metaphysics* 66, no. 4 (2013): 691–712.

Fierro, Maribel. "Alfonso X 'the Wise': The Last Almohad Caliph?" *Medieval Encounters: Jewish, Christian, and Muslim Culture in Confluence and Dialogue* 15, nos 2–4 (2009): 175–98.

Fierro, Maribel. "*Bāṭinism* in al-Andalus. Maslama b. Qāsim al-Qurṭubī (d. 353/964), author of the *Rutbat al-Ḥakīm* and the *Ghāyat al-Ḥakīm* (*Picatrix*)." *Studia Islamica* 84 (1996): 87–112.

Fierro, Maribel. "*Mawālī* and *Muwalladūn* in al-Andalus." In Monique Bernards and John Nawas (eds), *Patronate and Patronage in Early and Classical Islam*, 194–245. Leiden: Brill, 2005.

Fierro, Maribel. "Plants, Mary the Copt, Abraham, Donkeys and Knowledge: Again on Bāṭinism during the Umayyad Caliphate in al-Andalus." In Hinrich Biesterfeldt and Verena Klemm (eds), *Differenz und Dynamik im Islam, Festschrift für Heinz Halm zum 70*, 125–44. Geburtstag, Würzburg: Ergon Verlag, 2012.

Finamore, John. *Iamblichus and the Theory of the Vehicle of the Soul*. Oxford: Oxford University Press, 1985.

Fodor, A. "The Origins of the Arabic Legends of the Pyramids." *Acta Orientalia Academiae Scientiarum Hungaricae* 23, no. 3 (1970): 335–63.

Fontaine, Jacques. "Isidore de Séville et l'astrologie." *Revue des études latines* 31 (1953): 271–300.

Forcada, Miquel. "Astronomy, Astrology and the Sciences of the Ancients in Early al-Andalus (2nd/8th–3rd/9th Centuries)." *Zeitschrift für Geschichte der Arabisch-Islamischen Wissenschaften* 16 (2007): 1–74.

Foster, Regula. *Das Geheimnis der Geheimnisse: Die arabischen und deutschen Fassungen des pseudo-aristotelischen "Sirr al-asrār / Secretum secretorum."* Wiesbaden: Ludwig Reichert Verlag, 2006.

Fowden, Garth. *Empire to Commonwealth: Consequences of Monotheism in Late Antiquity*. Princeton: Princeton University Press, 1993.

Fowden, Garth. *The Egyptian Hermes: A Historical Approach to the Late Pagan Mind*. Princeton: Princeton University Press, 1993.

Fraker, Charles F. "Hermes Trismegistus in General Estoria II." In Ivy A. Corfis and Ray Harris-Northall (eds), *Medieval Iberia: Changing Societies and Cultures in Contact and Transition*, 87–98. Woodbridge: Tamesis Books-Boydell & Brewer, 2007.

Fraker, Charles F. *The Scope of History: Studies in the Historiography of Alfonso el Sabio*. Ann Arbor: University of Michigan Press, 1996.

Franco-Sánchez, Francisco. "*Al-masālik wa-l-mamālik*: Precisiones acerca del título de estas obras de la literatura geográfica árabe medieval y conclusiones acerca de su origen y estructura." *Philologia Hispalensis* 2, no. 31 (2017): 37–66.

Friedlander, Walter J. *The Golden Wand of Medicine: A History of the Caduceus Symbol in Medicine*. Westport: Greenwood, 1992.

Gabrieli, Francesco. "Frederick II and Moslem Culture." *East and West* 9, no. 1/2 (1958): 53–61.

García Avilés, Alejandro. "Alfonso X y el *Liber Razielis*: Imágenes de la magia astral judía en el scriptorium alfonsí." *Bulletin of Hispanic Studies* 74, no. 1 (1997): 21–39.

García Avilés, Alejandro. "Two Astrological Manuscripts of Alfonso X." *Journal of the Warburg and Courtauld Institutes* 59 (1996): 14–23.

García Bazán, Francisco. "Los aportes neoplatónicos de Moderato de Cádiz." *Anales del Seminario de Historia de la Filosofía* 15 (1998): 15–36.

García Sanjuán, Antonio. "Al-Bakri." *Real Academia de la Historia: DB-e*. Available online at: https://dbe.rah.es/biografias/24083/al-bakri (last accessed September 28, 2022).

Gaullier-Bougassas, Catherine. "Révélation hermetique et savoir occulte de l'Orient dans le Secretum secretorum et les Secrets des secrets français." In Catherine Gaullier-Bougassas, Margaret Bridges, and Jean-Yves Tilliette (eds), *Trajectoires européens du Secretum secretorum du pseudo-Aristote (XIIIe-XVIe siècle)*, 58–106. Turnhout: Brepols, 2015.

Genequand, C. "Platonism and Hermetism in al-Kindī's Fi al-Nafs." *Zeitschrift für Geschichte der arabisch-islamischen Wissenschaften* 4 (1987): 1–18.

Gersh, Stephen, *Middle Platonism and Neoplatonism*. Volume 1 of *The Latin Tradition*. Notre Dame: University of Notre Dame Press, 1986.

González-Casanovas, Roberto J. "Alfonso X's Scientific Prologues: Scholarship as Enlightenment." *Medieval Perspectives* 6, (1991): 113–21.

Green, Tamara M. *The City of the Moon God: Religious Traditions of Ḥarrān*. Leiden: Brill, 1992.

von Grunebaum, Gustave E. *Medieval Islam: A Study in Cultural Orientation*. 2nd edn. Chicago: University of Chicago Press, 1953.

Guo, Li. "History Writing." In Robert Irwin (ed.), *The New Cambridge History of Islam*, 4:444–94. Cambridge: Cambridge University Press, 2010.

Gutas, Dimitri. *Greek Thought, Arabic Culture*. New York: Routledge, 1998.

Hämeen-Anttila, Jaakko. *The Last Pagans of Iraq. Ibn Waḥshiyyah and the Nabatean Agriculture*. Leiden: Brill, 2006.

Hadot, Ilsetraut, "Dans quel lieu le néplatonicien Simplicius a-t-il fondé son école de mathémathiques , et où apu avoir lieu son entretien avec un manichéen?" *The International Journal of the Platonic Tradition* 1 (2007): 42–107.

Hanegraaff, Wouter. *Hermetic Spirituality and the Historical Imagination: Altered States of Knowledge in Late Antiquity*. Cambridge: Cambridge University Press, 2022.

Harlan, Sturm. *The Libro de los buenos proverbios: A Critical Edition (Studies in Romance Languages)*. Lexington: The University Press of Kentucky, 2014.

Haro Cortés, Marta. "Bocados de Oro." In José Manuel Lucía Megías and Carlos Alvar Ezquerra (eds), *Diccionario filológico de literatura medieval española. Textos y transmisión*, 224–30. Madrid: Castalia, 2002.

Haro Cortés, Marta. "*Dichos y castigos de sabios*: Compilación de sentencias en el manuscrito 39 de la colección San Román (RAH) I Edición." *Revista de Literatura Medieval* 25 (2013): 11–38.

Haro Cortés, Marta. *Los compendios de castigos del siglo XIII: Técnicas narrativas y contenido ético*. Valencia: Universitat de València, 1995.

Haskins, Charles. *Studies in the History of Mediaeval Science*. Cambridge: Harvard University Press, 1924.

Haskins, Charles. *The Renaissance of the Twelfth Century*. Cambridge: Harvard University Press, 1927.

Hegedus, Tim. *Early Christianity and Ancient Astrology*. New York: Peter Lang, 2007.

Henning, W. B. "The Book of the Giants." *Bulletin of the School of Oriental and African Studies* 11, no. 1 (1943): 52–74.

Herren, Michael. *The Anatomy of Myth: The Art of Interpretation from the Presocratics to the Church Fathers*. Oxford and New York: Oxford University Press, 2017.

Hicks, Andrew. "Martianus Capella and the Liberal Arts." In Ralph Hexter and David Townsend (eds), *The Oxford Handbook of Medieval Latin Literature*, 307–33. Oxford: Oxford University Press, 2012.

Hodgson, Marshall G. S. *The Classical Age of Islam*. Vol. 1 of *The Venture of Islam*. Chicago: The University of Chicago Press, 1974.

Hoz, María Paz de. "Cultos griegos, cultos sincréticos y la inmigración griega y greco-oriental." In María Paz de Hoz and Gloria Mora (eds), *El oriente griego en la Península Ibérica. Epigrafía e historia*, 205–54. Madrid: Real Academia de la Historia, 2013.

Jeauneau, Edouard. "Le 'Prologus in *Eptatheucon*' de Thierry de Chartres." *Medieval Studies* 16, no. 1 (1954): 171–5.

Jeauneau, Édouard. "Note sur l'École de Chartres." *Studi medievali* Ser. 3, vol. 5 (1964): 821–65.

Jeauneau, Edouard. *Lectio philosophorum: Recherches sur l'École de Chartres*. Amsterdam: Hakkert, 1973.

Jolivet, Jean. "The Arabic Inheritance." In Peter Dronke (ed.), *A History of Twelfth-Century Western Philosophy*, 113–48. Cambridge: Cambridge University Press, 1988.

Juarros, Francisco Juez. "La cetrería en la iconografía Andalusí." *Anales de historia del arte* 7 (1997): 67–86.

Jung, C. G. *Psychology and Alchemy*. Edited and Translated by Gerhard Adler and R. F. C. Hull. Princeton: Princeton University Press, 1980.

Kahane, Henry, Renée Kahane, and Angelina Pietrangeli. "Hermeticism in the Alfonsine Tradition." In David Ross (ed.), *Mélanges Offerts À Rita Lejeune*, 443–57. Gembloux: Éditions J. Duculot, 1969.

Kahn, Didier. *La table d'émeraude et sa tradition alchimique*. Paris: Les Belles Lettres, 1994.

Kasten, Lloyd A. "*Poridat de las poridades*: A Spanish Form of the Western Text of the Secretum Secretorum." *Romance Philology* 5 (1951–2): 180–90.

Khalidi, Tarif. "Masʿūdī's Lost Works: A Reconstruction of Their Content." *Journal of the American Oriental Society* 94, no. 1 (1974): 35–41.

Kingsley, Peter. "An Introduction to the Hermetica: Approaching Ancient Esoteric Tradition." In Roelof van den Broek and Cis van Heertum (eds), *From Poimandres to Jacob Böhme: Gnosis, Hermetism and the Christian Tradition*, 17–40. Leiden: Brill, 2000.

Kingsley, Peter. "*Poimandres*: The Etymology of the Name and the Origins of the Hermetica." *Journal of the Warburg and Courtauld Institutes* 56, no. 1 (1993): 1–24.

Klingshirn, William E. "Isidore of Seville's Taxonomy of Magicians and Diviners." *Traditio* 58 (2003): 59–90.

Knysh, Alexander. *Islamic Mysticism: A Short History*. Leiden: Brill, 2000.

Kraemer, Joel L. "Humanism in the Renaissance of Islam: A Preliminary Study." *Journal of the American Oriental Society* 104, no. 1 (1984): 135–64.

Labarta Gómez, Ana María. *Anillos de la península ibérica: 711–1611*. In collaboration with Carmen Barceló. Valencia: Ángeles Carrillo Baeza, 2017.

Lammer, Andreas. *The Elements of Avicenna's Physics*. Berlin: De Gruyter, 2018.

Lemay, Richard. "L'authenticité de la préface de Robert de Chester à sa traduction du Morienus." *Chrysopoeia* 4 (1990–1): 3–32.

Lida de Malkiel, M. Rosa. "La 'General estoria:' Notas literarias y filológicas (I)." *Romance Philology* 12 (1958): 111–42.

Lindsay, Jack. *The Origins of Alchemy in Graeco-Roman Egypt*. London: Muller, 1970.

López Fonseca, Antonio and José Manuel Ruiz Vila. "Alfonso Fernández de Madrigal traductor del Génesis: una interpolación en la traducción *De las crónicas o tienpos* de Eusebio-Jerónimo." *eHumanista* 41 (2019): 360–82.

López-Ruiz, Carolina. *Heroes, and Monsters. A Sourcebook of Greek, Roman, and Near Eastern Myths in Translation*. Oxford: Oxford University Press, 2017.

Lory, Pierre. "Hermès/Idris, prophète et sage dans la tradition islamique." In Antoine Faivre (ed.), *Présence d'Hermès Trismegiste*. Recueil d'articles de P. Lory, no. 7, 100–9. Paris: Cahiers de l'hermétisme, 1988.

Lucentini, Paolo, and Vittoria Perrone Compagni. *I testi e I codici di Ermete nel Medioevo*. Firenze: Polistampa, 2001.

Mahé, Jean-Pierre, and Joseph Paramelle. "Extraits hermétiques inédits d'un manuscrit d'Oxford." *REG* 104 (1991): 108–39.

Mahé, Jean-Pierre. *Hermès en Haute-Égypte*. Québec: Presses de l'Université Laval, 1978.

Makkī, Mahmūd ʿAlī. *Ensayo sobre las aportaciones orientales en la España musulmana y su influencia en la formación de la cultura hispano-árabe*. Madrid: Instituto de Estudios Islámicos, 1968.

Manzano Moreno, Eduardo. *Conquistadores, emires y califas: Los omeyas y la formación de al-Andalus*. Barcelona: Crítica, 2006.

Maravall, Jose Antonio. "La cortesia como saber en la Edad Media." *Cuadernos Hispanoamericanos* 62 (1965): 528–38.

Marenbon, John. *Medieval Philosophy: An Historical and Philosophical Introduction*. New York: Routledge, 2006.

Marenbon, John. *Pagans and Philosophers. The Problem of Paganism from Augustine to Leibniz*. Princeton: Princeton University Press, 2015.

Márquez Villanueva, Francisco. *El concepto cultural alfonsí*. Barcelona: Bellaterra, 2004.

Marrou, Henri-Irénée. "Les arts libéraux dans l'Antiquité classique." In *Arts libéraux et philosophie au Moyen Âge*, 18–19. Paris: Vrin; Montréal: Institut d'études médiévales, 1969.

Martin, Georges. "El modelo historiográfico Alfonsí y sus antecedentes." In Georges Martin (ed.), *La historia alfonsí: El modelo y sus destinos (siglos xiii–xv)*, 9–40. Madrid: Casa de Velázquez, 2000.

Martín, José Carlos. "La 'Crónica Universal' de Isidoro de Sevilla: circunstancias históricas e ideológicas de su composición y traducción de la misma." *Iberia: Revista de la Antigüedad* 4 (2001): 199–239.

Martínez, Salvador H. *Alfonso X el Sabio: una biografía*. Madrid: Polifemo, 2003.

Martínez, Salvador H. *El humanismo medieval y Alfonso X el Sabio: Ensayo sobre los orígenes del humanismo vernáculo*. Madrid: Polifemo, 2016.

Mattila, Janne. "Sabians, the School of al-Kindī, and the Brethren of Purity." In Ilkka Lindstedt, Nina Nikki, and Riikka Tuori (eds), *Religious Identities in Antiquity and the Early Middle Ages*, 92–114. Leiden: Brill, 2021.

McKenna, Stephen. *Paganism and Pagan Survivals in Spain Up to the Fall of the Visigothic Kingdom*. Washington: Catholic University of America, 1938.

Menéndez Pidal, Gonzalo. "Cómo trabajaron las escuelas alfonsíes." *NRFH* 5 (1951): 363–80.

Menéndez y Pelayo, Marcelino. *Historia de los heterodoxos españoles*. 4 vols. Madrid: La Editorial Católica, 1978.

Miquel, A. *La géographie humaine du monde musulman jusqu'au milieu du XXe siècle*. 4 vols. Paris: Mouton & Co., 1973–80.

Mojaddedi, Jawid. "Dhū l-Nūn al-Miṣrī." In Kate Fleet el al. (eds), *Encyclopaedia of Islam, THREE*, http://dx.doi.org/10.1163/1573-3912_ei3_COM_26009 (last accessed September 19, 2022).

Molina Martínez, Luis. "Ibn Ḥayyān." *Real Academia de la Historia: DB-e*, available online at: https://dbe.rah.es/biografias/16692/ibn-hayyan (last accessed September 19, 2022).

Molina, Luis. "Las dos versiones de la geografía de al-ʿUḏrī." *Al-Qantara* 3 (1982): 249–60.

Montero, Ana M. "A Possible Connection between the Philosophy of the Castilian King Alfonso X and the *Risālat Ḥayy ibn Yaqẓān* by Ibn Ṭufayl." *Al-Masāq: Islam and the Medieval Mediterranean* 18, no. 1 (2006): 1–26.

Montero, Ana M. "Reconstrucción de un ideal de espiritualidad en los hombres del saber de la corte de Alfonso X." In Emilio González Ferrín (ed.), *Encrucijada de culturas. Alfonso X y su tiempo: homenaje a Francisco Márquez Villanueva*, 509–34. Seville: Fundación Tres Culturas del Mediterráneo, 2014.

Moreschini, Claudio. *Hermes Christianus*. Turnhout: Brepols, 2011.

Moureau, Sébastien. "Min al-kīmiyāʾ ad alchimiam. The Transmission of Alchemy from the Arab-Muslim World to the Latin West in the Middle Ages." *Micrologus* 28 (2020): 87–141.

Nallino, Carlo Alfonso. *La littérature arabe des origines à l'époque de la dynastie umayyade: Leçons professées en arabe à l'Université du Caire*. Paris: G. P. Maisonneuve, 1950.

Noacco, Cristina. "Lire Ovide au xiie siècle: Arnoul d'Orléans, commentateur des Metamorphoses." *Troianalexandrina* 6 (2006): 131–49.

Nunemaker, J. H. "Noticias Sobre La Alquimia En El 'Lapidario' De Alfonso X." *Revista De Filología Española* 16 (1929): 161–8.

Orlov, Andrei A. "Overshadowed by Enoch's Greatness: 'Two Tablets' Traditions from the Book of Giants to Palaea Historica." *Journal for the Study of Judaism in the Persian, Hellenistic, and Roman Period* 32, nos 1–4 (2001): 137–58.

Otlewska-Jung, Marta. "Chapter 10 Ἁρμονίη κόσμου and ἁρμονίη ἀνδρῶν: On the Different Concepts of Harmony in the Dionysiaca of Nonnus." In *Nonnus of Panopolis in Context III*, 206–25. Leiden: Brill, 2021.

Pavón Torrejón, Pilar, and Inmaculada Pérez Martín. "La presencia de la cultura griega en Cádiz: la figura de Moderato de Gades." In Amado Miguel Zabala, Francisco Álvarez Solano, and Jesús San Bernardino (eds), *Arqueólogos, historiadores y filólogos: homenaje a Fernando Gascó*, 203–40. Seville: Kolaios, 1995.

Pellat, Ch. "Al-Masʿūdī." In P. Bearman et al. (eds), *Encyclopaedia of Islam, Second Edition*. http://dx.doi.org/10.1163/1573-3912_islam_COM_0704 (last accessed September 19, 2022).

Pellat, Charles. "ADAB ii. Adab in Arabic Literature." In *Encyclopædia Iranica*. Available online at: http://www.iranicaonline.org/articles/adab-ii-arabic-lit (last accessed September 28, 2022).

Philip A. Harland. "Egyptians: Aelian on Egyptian Views and Customs about Animals and Animal-Worship (Late Second Century CE)." *Ethnic Relations and Migration in the Ancient World*. http://philipharland.com/Blog/?p=13870 (last modified April 18, 2023).

Pingree, David. "Al-Ṭabarī on the Prayers to the Planets." *Bulletin d'études orientales* 44 (1992): 105–17.

Pingree, David. "Between the *Ghāya* and *Picatrix*. I: The Spanish Version." *Journal of the Warburg and Courtauld Institutes* 44 (1981): 27–56.

Pingree, David. "Some of the Sources of the *Ghāyat al-Hakīm*." *Journal of the Warburg and Courtauld Institutes* 43 (1980): 1–15.

Pingree, David. "The Ṣābians of Ḥarrān and the Classical Tradition." *International Journal of the Classical Tradition* 9, no. 1 (2002): 8–35.

Pingree, David. *The Thousands of Abū Ma'shar*. London: Warburg Institute, 1968.

Piperakis, Spyros. "Decanal Iconography and Natural Materials in the Sacred Book of Hermes to Asclepius." *Greek, Roman and Byzantine Studies* 57, no. 1 (2017): 136–61.

Plessner, M. "Hirmis." In *Encyclopedia of Islam*, new edn, 3: 463–5. Leiden: Brill 1971.

Plessner, Martin. "Balīnūs." In P. Bearman et al. (eds), *Encyclopaedia of Islam, Second Edition*. http://dx.doi.org/10.1163/1573-3912_islam_SIM_1146 (last accessed September 19, 2022).

Plessner, Martin. "Summary." In *Picatrix: Das Ziel des Weisen von Pseudo-Magriti*, translated by Hellmut Ritter and Martin Plessner, lvix–lxxv. London: Warburg Institute, 1962.

Porreca, David. "Hermes Mercurio Trismegisto en el 1300." In Valeria Buffon and Claudia D'Amico (eds), *Hermes Platonicus. Hermetismo y platonismo en el Medioevo y la Modernidad temprana*, 11–52. Santa Fe: Universidad Nacional del Litoral, 2016.

Porten, Bezalel. *Archives from Elephantine: The Life of an Ancient Jewish Military Colony*. Oakland: University of California Press, 1968.

Raggetti, Lucia. "Apollonius of Tyana's *Great Book of Talismans*." *Nuncius* 34, no. 1 (2019): 155–82.

Reed, Annette Yoshiko. "Abraham as Chaldean Scientist and Father of the Jew: Josephus, 'Ant.' 1.154–168, and the Greco-Roman Discourse about Astronomy/Astrology." *Journal for the Study of Judaism in the Persian, Hellenistic, and Roman Period* 35, no. 2 (2004): 119–58.

Reeves, John C., and Annette Yoshiko Reed. *Enoch from Antiquity to the Middle Ages, Volume I*. Oxford: Oxford University Press, 2018.

Rico, Francisco. *Alfonso el Sabio y la General Estoria*: *Tres Lecciones*. Barcelona: Ariel, 1972.

Ritschl, F. *Opuscula Philologica, iii*. Leipzig: Teubner, 1877.

Robichaud, Denis J. J. "Ficino on Force, Magic, and Prayers: Neoplatonic and Hermetic Influences in Ficino's Three Books on Life." *Renaissance Quarterly* 70, no. 1 (2017): 44–87.

Robinson, Francis. "Education." In Robert Irwin (ed.), *The New Cambridge History of Islam*, 4: 497–531. Cambridge: Cambridge University Press, 2010.

Rocchi, Matia. *Kadmos e Harmonia: un matrimonio problemmatico*. Rome: Bretschneider, 1989.

Rodríguez de la Peña, Manuel Alejandro. "*Imago sapientiae*: los orígenes del ideal sapiencial medieval." *Medievalismo* 7 (1997): 11–40.

Rodríguez López, Ana. *La consolidación territorial de la monarquía feudal castellana: expansión y fronteras durante el reinado de Fernando III*. Madrid: Consejo Superior de Investigaciones Científicas, 1994.

Rosenthal, Franz. "Al-Mubashshir ibn Fātik. Prolegomena to an Abortive Edition." *Oriens* 13–14 (1960–1): 132–58.

Rosenthal, Franz. *The Classical Heritage in Islam*. London: Routledge, 1975.

Ruska, J. "Zwei Bücher De Compositione Alchemiae und ihre Vorreden." *Archiv für Geschichte der Mathematik, der Naturwissenschaft und der Technik* 11 (1928): 28–37.

Saif, Liana. "A Preliminary Study of the Pseudo-Aristotelian Hermetica: Texts, Context, and Doctrines." *Al-ʿUṣūr al-Wusṭā* 29 (2021): 20–80.

Saif, Liana. "From *Ġāyat al-Ḥakīm* to *Šams al-maʿārif*: Ways of Knowing and Paths of Power in Medieval Islam." *Arabica* 64, nos 3–4 (2017): 297–345.

Saif, Liana. "The Cows and the Bees: Arabic Sources and Parallels for Pseudo-Plato's Liber Vaccae (Kitab Al-Nawamis)." *Journal of the Warburg and Courtauld Institutes* 79, no. 1 (2016): 1–47.

Saif, Liana. *The Arabic Influences on Early Modern Occult Philosophy*. New York: Palgrave Macmillan, 2015.

Salvo García, Irene. "'E es de saber que son en este traslado todas las estorias.' La traducción en el taller de la *General Estoria* De Alfonso X." *Cahiers d'Études Hispaniques Médiévales* 41, no. 1 (2019): 139–54.

Salvo García, Irene. "Autor frente a auctoritas: La recreación de Júpiter por Alfonso X en la General estoria I parte." *Cahiers d'Études Hispaniques Médiévales* no. 33 (2010): 63–77.

Salvo García, Irene. "L'Ovide connu par Alphonse X (1221–84)." *Interfaces (Milano)* 3, (2016): 200–20.

Salvo García, Irene. "Les sources de *l'Ovide moralisé*, livre I. Types et traitement." *Moyen-Âge* 124, no. 2 (2018): 307–36.

Salvo García, Irene. "Ovidio y la compilación de la General estoria." *Cahiers d'Études Hispaniques Médiévales* 37, no. 1 (2014): 45–61.

Salvo García, Irene. "The Latin Commentary Tradition and Medieval Mythography: The Example of the Myth of Perseus (Met. IV) in Vernacular Languages." In G. Pellissa Prades and M. Balzi (eds), *Ovid in the Vernacular: Translations of the Metamorphoses in The Middle Ages & Renaissance*, 67–86. Oxford: Medium Ævum, 2021.

Sánchez Alonso, Benito. *Historia de la historiografía española*. 2 vols. Madrid: CSIC, 1947.

Sánchez Pérez, José A. "El Libro De Las Cruces." *Isis* 14, no. 1 (1930): 77–132.

Sánchez-Prieto Borja, Pedro. "Las maravillas del mundo en la General Estoria de Alfonso X." In Constance Carta, Sarah Finci, and Dora Mancheva (eds), *Edad Media*, vol. 1 of *Antes se agotan la mano y la pluma que su historia = Magis déficit manus et calamus quam eius historia: Homenaje a Carlos Alvar*, 323–40. San Millán de la Cogolla: Cilengua, 2016.

Sánchez, Sylvaine. *Priscillien, un chrétien non conformiste*. Leiden: Beauchesne, 2009.

Saquero Suárez-Somonte, Pilar, and Tomás Gonzalez Rolán. "Aproximación a la fuente latina del 'Libro de las generaciones de los dioses de los gentiles' utilizada en la *General Estoria* de Alfonso X el Sabio." *Cuadernos de Filología Clásica. Estudios Latinos* 4 (1993): 93–111.

Schiesaro, Alessandro. "Ibis Redibis." *Materiali e Discussioni Per l'Analisi Dei Testi Classici* no. 67 (2011): 79–150.

Schipper, Hendrik. "Melothesia: A Chapter of Manichaean Astrology in the West." In Johannes van Oort, Otto Wermelinger, and Gregor Wurst (eds), *Augustine and Manichaeism in the Latin West*, 195–204. Leiden: Brill, 2001.

Schröder, Stephan. "El Asclepio de Ampurias: ¿una estatua de Agathodaimon del último cuarto del siglo II a.C.?" In Jaume Massó and Pilar Sada (eds), *Actas, II Reunión sobre escultura romana en Hispania*, 223–37. Tarragona: Museu Nacional Arqueològic de Tarragona, 1996.

Sezgin, Ursula, "al-Waṣīfī." In P. Bearman et al. (eds), *Encyclopaedia of Islam, Second Edition*. http://dx.doi.org/10.1163/1573-3912_islam_SIM_7885 (last accessed September 19, 2022).

Shanzer, Danuta R.. "*Augustine's Disciplines: Silent diutius Musae Varronis?*" In Karla Pollmann and Mark Vessey (eds), *Augustine and the Disciplines: From Cassiciacum to Confessions*, 69–112, Oxford: Oxford Academic, 2011.

Shanzer, Danuta. *A Philosophical and Literary Commentary on Martianus Capella's "De nuptiis Philologiae et Mercurii," Book 1*. Berkeley: University of California Press, 1986.

Shboul, Ahmad M. H. *Al-Mas'ūdī & His World. A Muslim Humanist and His Interest in Non-Muslims*. London: Ithaca Press, 1979.

Skjaervo, Prods Oktor. "Iranian Epic and the Manichean 'Book of Giants.' Irano-Manichaica III." *Acta Orientalia Academiae Scientiarum Hungaricae* 48, no. 1/2 (1995): 187–223.

Smith, William. *A Dictionary of Roman and Greek Antiquities*. New York: D Appleton & Co., 1874.

Solalinde, A. G. Introducción to *General estoria*, part I, vii–lxxxi. Madrid: Junta para la ampliación de estudios e investigaciones científicas/Centro de estudios históricos, 1930.

Soravia, Bruna. "Entre bureaucratie et litterature: La kitāba et les kuttāb dans l'administration de l'Espagne Umayyade." *Al-Masāq* 7 (1994): 165–200.

Soravia, Bruna. "Une histoire de la 'fitna.' Autorité et légitimité dans le 'Muqtabis' d'Ibn Hayyan." *Cuadernos de Madinat al-Zahra* 5 (2004): 81–90.

Southern, R. W. *Medieval Humanism and Other Studies*. New York: Harper and Row, 1970.

Stahl, William Harris, Richard Johnson, and E. L. Burge. *Martianus Capella and the Seven Liberal Arts*. 2 vols. New York: Columbia University Press, 1971.

Szpiech, Ryan. "The Convivencia Wars: Decoding Historiography's Polemic with Philology." In Suzanne Conklin Akbari and Karla Mallette (eds), *A Sea of Languages: Rethinking the Arabic Role in Medieval Literary History*, 135–61. Toronto: University of Toronto Press, 2013.

Tardieu, Michel. "Ṣābiens coraniques et 'Ṣābiens' de Ḥarrān." *Journal Asiatique* 274 (1986): 1–44.

Tester, Jim. *A History of Western Astrology*. Woodbridge: Boydell & Brewer, 1987.

Thorndike, Lynn. *A History of Magic and Experimental Science: During the First Thirteen Centuries of our Era*. 2 vols. New York: Columbia University Press, 1923.

Tyldesley, Joyce. *Daughters of Isis: Women of Ancient Egypt*. London: Penguin, 1995.

Udaondo Alegre, Juan. "'Et esto dixo el grant Hermes en uno de sos castigos': desvelando al Hermes árabe en la literatura sapiencial castellana." In Jason Busic and Antonio Yasmine Beale-Rivaya (eds), *eHumanista*, Special Issue, *Places of Encounter: Language, Culture, and Religious Identity in Medieval Iberia* 41 (2019): 105–41.

Udaondo Alegre, Juan. "'If You Want to Pray to Mercury, Wear the Garments of a Scribe': Kuttāb, Udabāʾ, and Readers of the Ghāyat Al-Ḥakīm in the Court of ʿAbd Al-Raḥmān III." *Journal of Medieval Iberian Studies* 14, no. 2 (2022): 201–33.

van Bladel, Kevin. "Hermes and Hermetica." In Kate Fleet et al. (eds), *Encyclopaedia of Islam, THREE*. http://dx.doi.org/10.1163/1573-3912_ei3_COM_23130 (last accessed 13 November, 2021).

van Bladel, Kevin. "The Alexander Legend in the Qurʾān 18:83–102." In Gabriel Said Reynolds (ed.), *The Quran in Its Historical Context*, 175–203. Abingdon: Routledge, 2008.

van Bladel, Kevin. *The Arabic Hermes: From Pagan Sage to Prophet of Science*. Oxford: Oxford University Press, 2009.

van den Broek, Roelof. "Hermes Trismegistus I: Antiquity." In Wouter J. Hanegraaff (ed.), *Dictionary of Gnosis and Western Esotericism*, 474–8. Leiden: Brill, 2005.

van den Broek, Roelof. "Hermetic Literature I: Antiquity." In Wouter J. Hanegraaff (ed.), *Dictionary of Gnosis and Western Esotericism*, 487–99. Leiden: Brill, 2005.

Vereno, Ingolf. *Studien zum ältesten alchimistischen Schrifttum* (Islamkundliche Untersuchungen 155). Berlin: Schwarz, 1992.

Vergados, Athanassios. *The "Homeric Hymn to Hermes": Introduction, Text and Commentary*. Berlin, Boston: De Gruyter, 2013.

Vernet Ginés, Juan. "El valle del Ebro como nexo entre Oriente y Occidente." *Butlletí de la Reial Acadèmia de Bones Lletres de Barcelona* 23 (1950): 249–86.

Vernet, Juan, and Julio Samsó. "The Development of Arabic Science in Andalucia." In Roshdi Rashed (ed.), *Encyclopedia of the History of Arabic Science*, 243–75. Abingdon: Routledge, 1996.

Walbridge, John. *The Wisdom of the Mystic East: Suhrawardi and Platonic Orientalism*. New York: State University of New York Press, 2001.

Walsh, John K. "Versiones peninsulares del '*Kitāb Ādab al-falāsifa*' de Ḥunayn ibn Isḥāq. Hacia una reconstrucción del 'Libro de los buenos proverbios.'" *Al-Andalus* 41, no. 2 (1976): 355–84.

Wasserstrom, Steven. "Jewish-Muslim Relations in the Context of Andalusian Emigration." In Mark D. Meyerson and Edward D. English (eds), *Christians, Muslims, and Jews in Medieval and Early Modern Spain: Interaction and Cultural Exchange*, 69–87. Notre Dame: University of Notre Dame Press, 1999.

Wetherbee, Winthrop. "Philosophy, Cosmology, and the Twelfth-Century Renaissance." In Peter Dronke (ed.), *A History of Twelfth-Century Western Philosophy*, 21–53. Cambridge: Cambridge University Press, 1988.

Wetherbee, Winthrop. *Platonism and Poetry in the Twelfth Century: The Literary Influence of the School of Chartres*. Princeton: Princeton University Press, 2015.

Wiet, G. "Akhmīm." In P. Bearman et al. (eds), *Encyclopaedia of Islam, Second Edition*. http://dx.doi.org/10.1163/1573-3912_islam_SIM_0471 (accessed September 19, 2022).

Williams, Steven J. *The Secret of Secrets. The Scholarly Career of a Pseudo-Aristotelian Text in the Latin Middle Ages*. Ann Arbor: The University of Michigan Press, 2003.

Zakeri, Mohsen. "*Ādab al-falāsifa*: The Persian Content of an Arabic Collection of Aphorisms." *Mélanges de l'Université Saint-Joseph* 57 (2004): 173–90.

Zeilabi, Negar. "Talismans and Figural Representation in Islam: A Cultural History of Images and Magic." *British Journal of Middle Eastern Studies* 46, no. 3 (2019): 425–39.

Index